Approaches to Teaching Scott's Waverley Novels

Approaches to Teaching Scott's Waverley Novels

Edited by

Evan Gottlieb

and

Ian Duncan

The Modern Language Association of America
New York 2009

85 Broad Street, New York, New York 10004
www.mla.org

To order MLA publications, visit www.mla.org/books. For wholesale and international orders, see www.mla.org/bookstore-orders. The EU-based Responsible Person for MLA products is the Mare Nostrum Group, which can be reached at gpsr@mare-nostrum.co.uk or the Mare Nostrum Group BV, Doelen 72, 4831 GR Breda, Netherlands. For a copy of the MLA's risk assessment document, write to scholcomm@mla.org.

Cover illustration of the paperback edition: *Fast Castle from Above*. By the Reverend John Thomson. National Gallery of Scotland.

Approaches to Teaching World Literature 110
ISSN 1059-1133

POD 2026 (first printing)

Library of Congress Cataloging-in-Publication Data

Approaches to teaching Scott's Waverley novels / edited by Evan Gottlieb and Ian Duncan.
p. cm. — (Approaches to teaching world literature ; 110)
Includes bibliographical references and index.
ISBN 978-1-60329-035-7 (cloth : alk. paper)
ISBN 978-1-60329-036-4 (pbk. : alk. paper)
1. Scott, Walter, Sir, 1771–1832. Waverley novels. 2. Scott, Walter, Sir, 1771–1832—Study and teaching. 3. Scotland—In literature.
I. Gottlieb, Evan, 1975– II. Duncan, Ian.
PR5322.W43A77 2009
823'.7—dc22 2009015674

CONTENTS

PREFACE

During the heyday of his novel-writing career in the dozen years after 1814, Walter Scott was referred to as the Author of *Waverley* and the Great Unknown because, despite rampant public speculation, he refused to forfeit his anonymity. (Financial troubles forced him officially to reveal his identity in 1827.) If Scott remains the Great Unknown to most of today's undergraduate readers, the nickname now carries a very different meaning. Although Scott was once regularly compared with Shakespeare—a comparison he actively courted—his reputation slipped dramatically as Victorian esteem gave way to modernist disdain. By the early decades of the twentieth century, the Waverley novels (as his fictions are collectively known) were no longer considered canonical or fit for serious adult consumption.

Fortunately, although Scott has yet to recover his popular readership, the critical standing of the Waverley novels (if not Scott's poetry) is on the rise again. Moreover, teaching Scott in the university or college classroom provides instructors with unique rewards. As the variety of essays in part 2 of this volume attests, the Waverley novels lend themselves to an array of university courses, such as those on Romanticism, Scottish literature and culture, eighteenth- and nineteenth-century British literature, nationalism and empire, the history of the novel, and narrative theory and those on more specialized topics such as historical, regional, and Regency fiction. The novels can be fruitfully taught in relation to the study of modern categories of gender, class, race, nation, and religion, since the novels play an influential role in the historical formation of these categories. Given their unprecedented popularity, Scott's novels also shed light on modern literary phenomena such as the rise of mass publishing, the best seller, and the cult of the author.

As this volume also recognizes, however, Scott's fictions present special challenges to prospective instructors. A turn-of-the-century schoolroom edition of Scott, which tellingly assumes that students will already be familiar with Scott's poetry, encourages instructors to devote their energies to bringing alive the atmosphere of Scott's work in the classroom: "Bits of heather and foxglove are a help, as are samples of the various Scottish plaids" (Packard xxxvii). Regardless of whether this approach worked in the past, the guiding assumption of this volume is that today's instructors are likely to need more substantive advice about how best to teach Scott's fictions to undergraduate students who are encountering Scott's prose for the first time. Indeed, many of the features that made the Waverley novels so popular and influential in his own time now often render them less accessible to undergraduate readers than the novels of Austen, Dickens, or the Brontës. As many of our survey respondents noted, the Waverley novels' linguistic variety—especially Scott's use of vernacular Scots and pastiche-antique styles—is often hard for students to decipher. Equally daunting for students and teachers alike is the density of Scott's historical and geographical references, his zest for narrative experimentation, including his frequent blending of narrative and generic conventions, as well as his invention of multiple authorial personas. All these characteristics create pedagogical complications that this volume is designed to help teachers negotiate.

The structure of this book follows that of other volumes in the Approaches to Teaching series. Part 1, "Materials," gives an overview of Scott's critical reception and summarizes the responses to the survey sent to MLA members and others who teach Scott's Waverley novels. It also reviews the recommended teaching editions of the novels, background and critical texts recommended for instructors and students, and other aids to teaching (including a much-requested map of Scotland, available at the end of the "Materials" section). Part 2 contains essays on teaching Scott's novels from a group of distinguished and experienced scholars. In every case, the utmost care has been taken to ensure that this volume will be as useful as possible, not only to practicing teachers of Scott but also to those seeking to teach one or more of the Waverley novels for the first time.

EG

Part One

MATERIALS

Critical Backgrounds

The current renaissance of Scott criticism began in the early 1960s with the English publication of Georg Lukács's *The Historical Novel*. (Two articles from the early 1950s also deserve notice: David Daiches's two-part "Scott's Achievement as a Novelist," which located that achievement—anticipating Lukács—within an aesthetic of historical realism, and Duncan Forbes's "The Rationalism of Walter Scott," which dismissed the myth of Scott's romantic immaturity by demonstrating his debt to the philosophical history of the Scottish Enlightenment.) Whereas Scott's novels had been disparaged by earlier writers like Leslie Stephen and E. M. Forster for being little more than boys' adventure stories, Lukács recovered their vital importance as representations of historical conflict and change. Several succeeding studies of the 1960s—including Alexander Welsh's *The Hero of the Waverley Novels*, A. O. J. Cockshut's *The Achievement of Walter Scott*, and Francis Hart's *Scott's Novels: The Plotting of Historical Survival*—took up the challenge of revaluing Scott's contribution to literary history. Welsh's study of Scott's passive hero as the personification of a new, middle-class "romance of property" proved especially influential, anticipating the new historicism of the 1980s in some of its methods and insights. It was in that decade that Scott scholarship truly began to take off again (a development also signaled by the quadrennial series of international Scott conferences, founded in 1979 by J. H. Alexander and David Hewitt). Graham Tulloch analyzed Scott's use of regional and antique styles in *The Language of Walter Scott*; Graham McMaster studied the Waverley novels' philosophical and political underpinnings (derived from Scottish Enlightenment social thought) in *Scott and Society*; Harry E. Shaw revisited Lukács's thesis in *The Forms of Historical Fiction*; Jane Millgate traced Scott's authorial evolution through the five-year series of Scottish novels inaugurated with *Waverley* in *Walter Scott: The Making of the Novelist*; Judith Wilt charted the mythopoeic range of all of Scott's novels (not just the Scottish ones) in *Secret Leaves*; and James Kerr, in *Fiction against History*, saw the novels invoking historical "emplotment" only to subvert it.

It is noteworthy that this phase of criticism, in the wake of Lukács, reasserted Scott's importance within the field of novel studies. That importance had always been more evident in European or North Atlantic than in British accounts of the genre, fixated (at least since F. R. Leavis's *Great Tradition* and Ian Watt's *Rise of the Novel*) on canons of moral, formal, and domestic realism ill suited to Scott's experimental mixing of different aesthetic and historical registers. Several critical studies published in the 1990s challenged the received history of the British novel by attending to the literary contexts of Scott's achievement. Ian Duncan's *Modern Romance* found the revival and recombination of prenovelistic forms in Scott crucial to the nineteenth-century ascendancy of the novel as the genre of modern life, while Fiona Robertson's *Legitimate Histories* explored the complex affinities between the Waverley novels and gothic fiction. More recent studies of the Gothic (e.g., J. Watt, *Contesting*; Gamer) have enlarged our understanding of Scott's transformation of one of the dominant literary modes of British Romanticism. The Waverley novels now figure robustly in studies of the novel, as in recent books on fiction and historicism (H. Brown; Zimmerman; Rigney); fiction and political economy (Kaufmann; Burgess); the epistolary novel, bildungsroman, travel writing, ethnography, and other genres and discourses (Watson; Moretti, *Way*; Price; Dekker, *Fictions*; Buzard, *Disorienting Fiction*); realism and romance (Shaw, *Narrating*; Bruzelius, *Romancing*); gender (Irvine) and individualism (Armstrong, *How Novels Think*).

The two most influential books on Scott and the novel published in the 1990s, however, were also contributions to the other scholarly fields in which Scott is a consequential figure: British Romanticism and Scottish studies. Ina Ferris's *The Achievement of Literary Authority* situated the impact of *Waverley* and its successors in the professional, militantly masculine reviewing culture of early-nineteenth-century Edinburgh, while Katie Trumpener's *Bardic Nationalism* set Scott's historical fiction among the immense and variegated array of literary works that engaged questions of national identity and history during the rise of the modern, multinational, and imperial British state. Trumpener develops Ferris's examination of Scott's debt to, and revision of, the Anglo-Irish "national tale" to recover a range of competing, in many cases alternative or dissident projects overshadowed by Scott's critical and commercial success. Both books speak to the work in Scottish literary and cultural studies that was invigorated by the resurgence of nationalism theory in the decade following the breakup of the Soviet Union as well as the contemporaneous renewal of debates about Scotland's destiny in the United Kingdom culminating in the reestablishment of a Scottish parliament in 1999. The early-twentieth-century nationalist account of Scott's influence, as the unionist corruption and commodification of an "organic" Scottish tradition, became the topic of lively debate, first in Tom Nairn's *The Break-up of Britain*, and then in a series of books throughout the 1990s: Murray Pittock's *The Invention of Scotland*, Robert Crawford's *Devolving English Literature*, and Cairns Craig's *Out of History*. Less overtly polemical studies of Scott's Scottish contexts include Penny Fielding's *Writing and Orality*, Susan Manning's books on Scottish and North American cultural affinities (*The Puritan-Provincial Vision*; *Fragments of Union*), and Catherine Jones's *Literary Memory*. Although Leith Davis's *Acts of Union* and Janet Sorensen's *The Grammar of Empire* do not explicitly consider Scott's novels, they do supply vital contexts for considering them. "Scott, Scotland and Romantic Nationalism" was the title of a special issue of *Studies in Romanticism* in 2001 (Duncan, Rowland, and Snodgrass). Discussions of Scott's role in the historical formations of Scottish and British national culture remain lively, if not contentious, in recent books such as Julian D'Arcy's *Subversive Scott*, Douglas Mack's *Scottish Fiction and the British Empire*, Caroline McCracken-Flesher's *Possible Scotlands*, Matthew Wickman's *The Ruins of Experience*, Kenneth

McNeil's *Scotland, Britain, Empire*, Evan Gottlieb's *Feeling British*, and Ian Duncan's *Scott's Shadow*.

The third field of literary scholarship, studies in Romanticism, has been the slowest to recognize Scott as a central rather than peripheral figure. If several of the works already mentioned (notably Trumpener's) reassessed Scott's contribution to the history of the novel in the Romantic period, James Chandler's *England in 1819* undertook the first serious reckoning of the Waverley novels alongside the canonical projects of English poetry in a full-scale reconsideration of British Romanticism as a conceptual and disciplinary field. Other important recent works—Saree Makdisi's *Romantic Imperialism*, Jerome Christensen's *Romanticism at the End of History*, Paul Hamilton's *Metaromanticism*—have confined their consideration of Scott to a single novel, *Waverley*; however Yoon Sun Lee's *Nationalism and Irony*, casting its net wider, sets Scott alongside Edmund Burke and Thomas Carlyle as founders of a modern conservative Romantic nationalism. Scott plays a central part in the conjunction of Romanticism with Scottish studies in the recent essay collection edited by Davis, Duncan and Sorensen, *Scotland and the Borders of Romanticism*.

Crucial to the flourishing of recent scholarship on Scott has been the appearance of an authoritative critical edition of the Waverley novels from Edinburgh University Press. As well as providing up-to-date scholarly texts, the Edinburgh edition has made available a wealth of information about the conditions of literary production, marketing, and reception in early-nineteenth-century Britain and beyond. Recent works in bibliography and book history such as William B. Todd and Anne Bowden's *Sir Walter Scott: A Bibliographical History*, volume 2 of Peter Garside and Rainer Schöwerling's *The English Novel, 1770–1829*, and William St. Clair's *The Reading Nation in the Romantic Period* owe a great deal to the ongoing edition, even as they furnish information vital to future scholarship.

Some Results of the Survey

Our survey confirmed that the Waverley novels are currently being taught in a wide variety of courses, from lower-level undergraduate literature surveys to mid-level genre and period courses to specialized upper-division seminars such as Enlightenment and Romance: Scotland in the Eighteenth Century, Engendering the Romantic Novel, and The Modern Celtic Fringe. Many respondents also reported teaching Waverley novels frequently at the graduate level. Whatever the course context, the specific novel cited as most frequently taught to undergraduates was *Waverley* itself; other frequently taught novels included (in descending order of popularity) *The Heart of Mid-Lothian*, *Rob Roy*, *The Bride of Lammermoor*, *Ivanhoe*, and *Redgauntlet*. Interestingly, although respondents overwhelmingly cited *Waverley* as their favorite novel to teach, many noted that undergraduate students find it particularly difficult. When respondents were asked which novels seemed most enjoyable for students, however, they most commonly answered *Rob Roy*, followed by *Ivanhoe* and *The Bride of Lammermoor*.

When asked what they consider to be the more important features of the Waverley novels for students to understand, respondents stressed a variety of factors, including (but not limited to) grasping Scottish and British history, politics, and nationalisms; understanding the generic workings of the historical novel; appreciating Scott's narrative, rhetorical, and linguistic skills; and understanding the centrality of Scott's oeuvre to the Enlightenment, Romanticism, and Victorianism. One respondent said emphatically that he always strives to impress on students "that they are great *novels*—not novelized histories—and as such among the supreme masterworks of the form in world literary history," while another said he consistently stresses that "Scott is always making readers aware of the artificiality of his narratives, and consistently forcing a recognition that 'truth' is contingent upon the medium in which it is expressed." In this vein, another added, "I also think it is essential that Scott is taught in critical contexts which emphasize the ways in which he is relevant for a modern readership." On the importance of teaching *Waverley* in particular, one respondent stated:

> As a department we insist that all our students read *Waverley* as a key cultural document. Its main importance is its contribution to the invention of culture as a totalizing social form in the early nineteenth century, with subsidiary interest in the history of nationalisms, importance of landscape, [and] general course of the historical novel.

Respondents also generally recognized that students find Scott's novels difficult—with *Waverley* often presenting the greatest number of problems—because of their copious prefatory materials, density of historical references, loquacious narrative voice, and use of Scottish forms of speech. Indeed, as one respondent put it, "The very things I think are important—the complexity around cultural translation in particular—[are] also the hardest [to teach]." Instead of shying away from these difficulties, however, the consensus was that they should be welcomed and negotiated. On the issue of cultural translation, for example, the same respondent continued, "I invite students to reflect on the experience of reading cultural difference that is not immediately assimilable and to think about the work this might be doing in troubling easy cultural assimilation." To deal with Scott's prefatory materials, one respondent counseled "encourag[ing] [students] to think about the games that are being played," while another reported that "the metafictionality of the Prefaces generally makes them a very easy sell," at least to graduate students. On the difficulties presented by Scott's use of historical materials, one respondent summed up the problem best when she wrote, "I think American undergraduates have a hard time connecting to issues connected with the Act of Union and the Jacobite uprisings. It is simply not a 'live' topic for them." The solution to this common problem, according to most respondents, is to assign or integrate into classroom lectures enough background materials—maps, historical summaries, chronologies, debates about the Stuarts—"to help them feel familiar with what matters to the text." To familiarize students with the cadences and dynamics of Scott's narrative voices, several respondents said they frequently encourage students to read passages aloud. Choosing specific passages on which to focus, moreover, was also recommended as an effective strategy for countering the typical undergraduate complaint that Scott's novels are long and "boring"; regarding *Waverley* specifically, one respondent reported:

> I find *Waverley* works best if it's broken down into important concepts which can be keyed to individual sections. . . . I tell the students to read all of it but to read it quickly, reminding them that this is how original readers would have got through it.

Respondents also frequently suggested encouraging students to find and appreciate the wit and humor in Scott's narrative asides and "digressions." On the specific difficulties presented by Scott's use of Scottish dialect, many respondents said they routinely assign Scots poetry and ballads (often by Robert Burns) before Scott in order to familiarize students with the language; having students (attempt to) read passages of Scots dialect aloud was also a popular suggestion. One respondent also noted that "there's a cumulative effect: the more Scott they've read, the more they like him because they begin to 'get' it."

Recognizing that most teachers do not often have the opportunity to teach courses devoted entirely to Scott, we asked respondents to identify which authors they commonly teach in conjunction with teaching one or more of Scott's novels. The most frequent responses (in alphabetical order) were Jane Austen, Robert Burns, Lord Byron, James Fenimore Cooper, Maria Edgeworth, William Godwin, James Hogg, John Keats, Sydney Owenson (Lady Morgan), Mary Shelley, Robert Louis Stevenson, and William Wordsworth. Common assignments for teaching the Waverley novels included reading responses (often prompted by specific questions), pop quizzes ("particularly useful to encourage students to stay on top of the reading"), group oral presentations (especially on relevant historical issues), essays, and exams.

Editions

Scott's novels were reprinted many times even during his lifetime, in both official and unofficial printings, but the most important reissue was the Magnum

Opus edition of the Waverley novels, which began to appear in 1829 and eventually ran to forty-eight volumes. Designed to help pay his heavy debts after the 1826 crash of the printing firm of which Scott was a partner, the Magnum edition gave Scott an opportunity to provide new introductions and notes to his novels. He also carried out many textual revisions, ranging from verbal corrections to more substantial changes. (The best-known example of the latter is Scott's shifting the historical setting of *The Bride of Lammermoor* from before to after the 1707 union).

Given the existence of multiple versions of the Waverley novels, then, teachers have some serious decisions to make when choosing modern editions. Because of the density of historical detail and local idiom in Scott's novels, all survey respondents agreed on the importance of choosing editions that contain extensive explanatory and historical notes as well as a glossary of Scots terms. Accordingly, Penguin Classics and Oxford World's Classics were the paperback choices of all respondents. Although both imprints offer many of the same texts, there are significant differences between them. In general, Penguin reproduces the new Edinburgh edition of the Waverley novels, based on first edition copy-texts, whereas Oxford draws its texts from the Magnum Opus edition. (For teaching purposes, this volume's list of works cited includes the paperback Penguin Classics editions instead of their hardcover Edinburgh edition counterparts whenever the former have been published.) Instructors should be aware, however, that this division is not entirely stable; the Oxford *Waverley* reprints the Clarendon edition of the original 1814 text, while also including Scott's 1829 preface to the novel and the general preface to the Magnum edition. The 1985 Penguin *Waverley*, although it carries a useful introduction and notes by Andrew Hook, unreliably reprints the Magnum edition, while the Penguin *Rob Roy* omits Scott's apparatus as well as any modern notes or commentary. Both will presumably be replaced by Edinburgh-based texts within the next few years. The Penguin *Heart of Mid-Lothian*, by contrast, is a composite edition based on early states of the text, with detailed and illuminating notes by the editor, Tony Inglis. While some survey respondents said that they used either Penguin or Oxford editions indiscriminately, others varied in their choices on a case-by-case basis, taking into account such factors as print size and quality and accessibility of the editorial introductions, as well as the specific editions on which each text was based.

Because Scott's novels are not (yet) taught as frequently as those of other canonical nineteenth-century novelists, some titles go in and out of print. At the time of this volume's preparation, the following were available in paperback: *The Antiquary* (Oxford); *The Bride of Lammermoor* (Penguin, Oxford); *Chronicles of the Canongate* (Penguin); *Guy Mannering* (Penguin); *The Heart of Mid-Lothian* (Penguin, Oxford); *Ivanhoe* (Penguin, Oxford); *Kenilworth* (Penguin); *The Tale of Old Mortality* (Oxford—UK only); *Redgauntlet* (Penguin, Oxford); *Rob Roy* (Oxford); *Waverley* (Penguin, Oxford).

The Instructor's Library

The secondary literature on Scott's Waverley novels is immense. For the "beginning teacher," the following studies were recommended by respondents:

Biographies and letters Edgar Johnson, *Sir Walter Scott: The Great Unknown*, 2 vols.; J. G. Lockhart, *Memoirs of the Life of Sir Walter Scott*; John Sutherland, *The Life of Walter Scott;* Scott, *Letters* (ed. Grierson et al.), and *Journal*

On Scott, the history of the novel, and historical fiction David Brown, *Walter Scott and the Historical Imagination*; Homer O. Brown, *Institutions of the English Novel: From Defoe to Scott*; James Buzard, "Translation and Tourism: Scott's *Waverley* and the Rendering of Culture"; Ian Duncan, *Modern Romance and Transformations of the Novel: The Gothic, Scott, Dickens*; Ina Ferris, *The Achievement of Literary Authority: Gender, History, and the Waverley Novels*; James Kerr, *Fiction against History: Scott as Storyteller*; Georg Lukács, *The Historical Novel*; Richard Maxwell, "Inundations of Time: A Definition of Scott's Originality"; Graham McMaster, *Scott and Society*; Franco Moretti, *Atlas of the European Novel, 1800–1900*; Harry E. Shaw, *The Forms of Historical Fiction: Sir Walter Scott and His Successors*; Everett Zimmerman, *The Boundaries of Fiction: History and the Eighteenth-Century British Novel*

On Scott, Scottish literature, and culture Cairns Craig, *Out of History: Narrative Paradigms in Scottish and English Culture*; Robert Crawford, *Devolving English Literature*; Leith Davis, *Acts of Union: Scotland and the Literary Negotiation of the British Nation, 1707–1830*; Ian Duncan, *Scott's Shadow: The Novel in Romantic Edinburgh*; Penny Fielding, *Writing and Orality: Nationality, Culture, and Nineteenth-Century Scottish Fiction*; Evan Gottlieb, *Feeling British: Sympathy and National Identity in Scottish and English Writing, 1707–1832*; Douglas Mack, *Scottish Fiction and the British Empire*; Susan Manning, *Fragments of Union: Making Connections in Scottish and American Writing* and *The Puritan-Provincial Vision: Scottish and American Literature in the Nineteenth Century*; Kenneth McNeil, *Scotland, Britain, Empire: Writing the Highlands, 1760–1860*; Tom Nairn, *The Break-up of Britain: Crisis and Neo-nationalism*; Murray G. H. Pittock, *The Invention of Scotland: The Stuart Myth and Scottish Identity, 1638 to the Present*; Janet Sorensen, *The Grammar of Empire in Eighteenth-Century British Writing*; Katie Trumpener, *Bardic Nationalism: The Romantic Novel and the British Empire*; Matthew Wickman, *The Ruins of Experience: Scotland's "Romantick" Highlands and the Birth of the Modern Witness*; Peter Womack, *Improvement and Romance: Constructing the Myth of the Highlands*

On Scott and Romanticism James Chandler, *England in 1819*; Jerome Christensen, *Romanticism at the End of History*; Daniel Cottom, *The Civilized Imagination*; Leith Davis, Ian Duncan, Janet Sorensen, eds., *Scotland and the Borders of Romanticism*; Paul Hamilton, *Metaromanticism: Aesthetics, Literature, Theory*; David Kaufmann, *The Business of Common Life: Novels and Classical Economics between Revolution and Reform*; Gary Kelly, *English Fiction of the Romantic Period, 1789–1830*; Yoon Sun Lee, *Nationalism and Irony: Burke, Scott, Carlyle*; Saree Makdisi, *Romantic Imperialism: Universal Empire and the Culture of Modernity*

Critical studies of Scott A. O. J. Cockshut, *The Achievement of Sir Walter Scott*; Thomas Crawford, *Scott*; David Daiches, "Scott's Achievement as a Novelist" (parts 1 and 2); Ian Duncan, "Primitive Inventions: *Rob Roy*, Nation and World System" and "Authenticity Effects: The Work of Fiction in Romantic Scotland"; Peter Garside, "Scott and the 'Philosophical Historians'"; Francis R. Hart, *Scott's Novels: The Plotting of Historical Survival*; Catherine Jones, *Literary Memory: Scott's Waverley Novels and the Psychology of Narrative*; James Kerr, *Fiction against History: Scott as Storyteller*; Andrew Lincoln, *Walter Scott and Modernity*; Caroline McCracken-Flesher, *Possible Scotlands: Walter Scott and the Story of Tomorrow*; Jane Millgate, *Walter Scott: The Making of the Novelist*; Fiona Robertson, *Legitimate Histories: Scott, Gothic, and the Authorities of Fiction*; Alexander Welsh, *The Hero of the Waverley Novels*; Judith Wilt, *Secret Leaves: The Novels of Sir Walter Scott*

Collections of essays on or by Scott J. H. Alexander and David Hewitt, eds., *Scott in Carnival*; Bruce Beiderwell, ed., *Romantic Enlightenment: Sir Walter Scott and the Politics of History* (a special issue of the *European Romantic Review*); Ian Duncan, Ann Rowland, and Charles Snodgrass, eds., *Scott, Scotland, and Romantic Nationalism* (a special issue of *Studies in Romanticism*); John O. Hayden, ed., *Scott: The Critical Heritage*; Harry Shaw, ed., *Critical Essays on Sir Walter Scott*; Ioan Williams, ed., *Sir Walter Scott on Novelists and Fiction*

Readings for Students

Many of the texts mentioned above were also recommended for students. Recognizing that undergraduate students need particularly straightforward and accessible secondary sources, however, the following additional texts were frequently suggested to introduce students to the historical, political, and cultural contexts of Scott's fiction: Marilyn Butler, *Romantics, Rebels, and Reactionaries: English Literature and Its Background, 1760–1830*; Linda Colley, *Britons: Forging the Nation, 1707–1837*; T. M. Devine, *The Scottish Nation, 1700–2000*;

Christopher Harvie, *A Short History of Scotland*; J. D. Mackie, *A History of Scotland*. Noting that undergraduates and first-time readers of Scott can often feel overwhelmed by the experience of the Waverley novels, several respondents counseled working historical materials into lectures and classroom presentations (including timelines, synopses, maps, and genealogies), instead of assigning more reading.

Aids to Teaching

Art and illustrations Despite Scott's friendship with many of the prominent artists of his day, none of the Waverley novels before 1829 was originally illustrated (although several collections contained frontispieces and occasional illustrations). Technological limitations made it difficult to illustrate books with large print runs until the advent of steel engraving, which Scott's publishers were able to use in the Magnum Opus edition. Thereafter art inspired by the Waverley novels was a lucrative business throughout the Victorian period (Allingham). Collections of the illustrations, alone or accompanied with descriptive prose or excerpts from the novels, appeared rapidly at the end of Scott's career and afterward, bearing titles such as *The Waverley Album: Containing Fifty-One Line Engravings to Illustrate the Novels and Tales of Sir Walter Scott*, *Landscape Illustrations of the Waverley Novels, with Descriptions of the Views*, and *Portraits of the Principal Female Characters in the Waverley Novels*. Many such illustrations can now be found online at the *Walter Scott Digital Archive*. Respondents also reported using art by Caspar David Friedrich and Salvator Rosa to establish the Romantic pictorial context of Scott's work.

Film and audio Several respondents reported supporting their teaching of *Waverley* with the documentary-style BBC film *Culloden*, to convey to students the violent reality of the end of the 1745 Jacobite rebellion. Based on John Prebble's 1962 book of the same name, the film is currently available only on videocassette. Even more respondents said they had accompanied their teaching of *Rob Roy* by showing part or all of the 1995 movie of the same name, starring Liam Neeson, Jessica Lange, and Tim Roth. Instructors should be aware, however, that the film is based on W. H. Murray's 1982 biography of Rob Roy rather than Scott's novel; Janet Sorensen's essay "*Rob Roy*: The Other Eighteenth Century?" helpfully elucidates the movie's agenda. Also from 1995 is Mel Gibson's bloody and bombastic *Braveheart*, loosely based on William Wallace's thirteenth-century campaign to liberate Scotland from English occupation; while unrelated to the Waverley novels, it has proved instrumental in shaping modern North American perceptions of Scottish identity and may be worth screening for that reason alone. Several on-screen versions of *Ivanhoe* also exist, including the classic 1952 movie starring Robert Taylor, Elizabeth Taylor, and Joan Fontaine, and a six-part BBC miniseries from 1997.

Music and recordings Several respondents reported using versions of Gaetano Donizetti's opera *Lucia di Lammermoor* alongside *The Bride of Lammermoor*. Many audio recordings exist; the best DVD version currently available, on the Opus Arte La Scala collection, records a 1994 production from the Teatro alla Scala, Milan, starring Mariella Devia, Vincenzo La Scola, and Renato Bruson (dir. Pier'Alli). As with many Scott adaptations for the screen and stage, instructors should be aware that *Lucia*'s plot differs significantly from the novel's. Although no audio recordings of Scott's books currently exist, instructors who wish to familiarize students with the sound of Lowland Scots may wish to play selections of Robert Burns's poetry as recited (frequently accompanied by music) by the experienced Burns impersonator John Cairney on *The Poems and Songs of Robert Burns*.

Web resources A major Internet resource on Scott's Waverley novels is *The Walter Scott Digital Archive.* Run by the Department of Special Collections at the Edinburgh University Library, the site is designed around its extensive Corson Collection of Scott holdings. As well as featuring biographical information and publication notices, the site has links to a large number of online Waverley novels (as well as poetry and prose, including Scott's letters), in addition to many portraits and engravings of Scott. Perhaps most valuable for classroom teaching purposes is the extensive image collection, featuring downloadable images of portraits, illustrations, and a variety of Scott-related memorabilia and realia, as well as the very thorough bibliography. Other useful Web sites relating to Scott include Andrew Monnickendam's *Waverley Hypertext*, a well-stocked hypertext site containing summaries, criticism, correspondence, and more; Michael Peverett's *Scott's Novels: A Brief Guide*, which consists of summaries (and some criticism) for all of Scott's novels; *British Fiction, 1800–1829: A Database of Production, Circulation, and Reception*, produced by Cardiff University's Centre for Editorial and Intertextual Research, an extraordinary archive of information on all fiction titles known to have been published in Britain in the first three decades of the nineteenth century (including records of composition and publication, newspaper advertisements, reviews, and other contemporary commentaries); the Web site of the University of Aberdeen's *Walter Scott Research Centre*, which features information about the ongoing production and publication of the Edinburgh Edition of the Waverley novels. There are also many popular Scott-related Web sites that may be of interest to students, including the home page for the Abbotsford house, which features several pages of photos of Scott's most famous residence, and *The Sir Walter Scott Way*, a Web site devoted to the ninety-two-mile cross-country walk between Moffat in south-central Scotland and Cockburnspath on the southeast Scottish coastline.

Map of Scotland, circa 1900

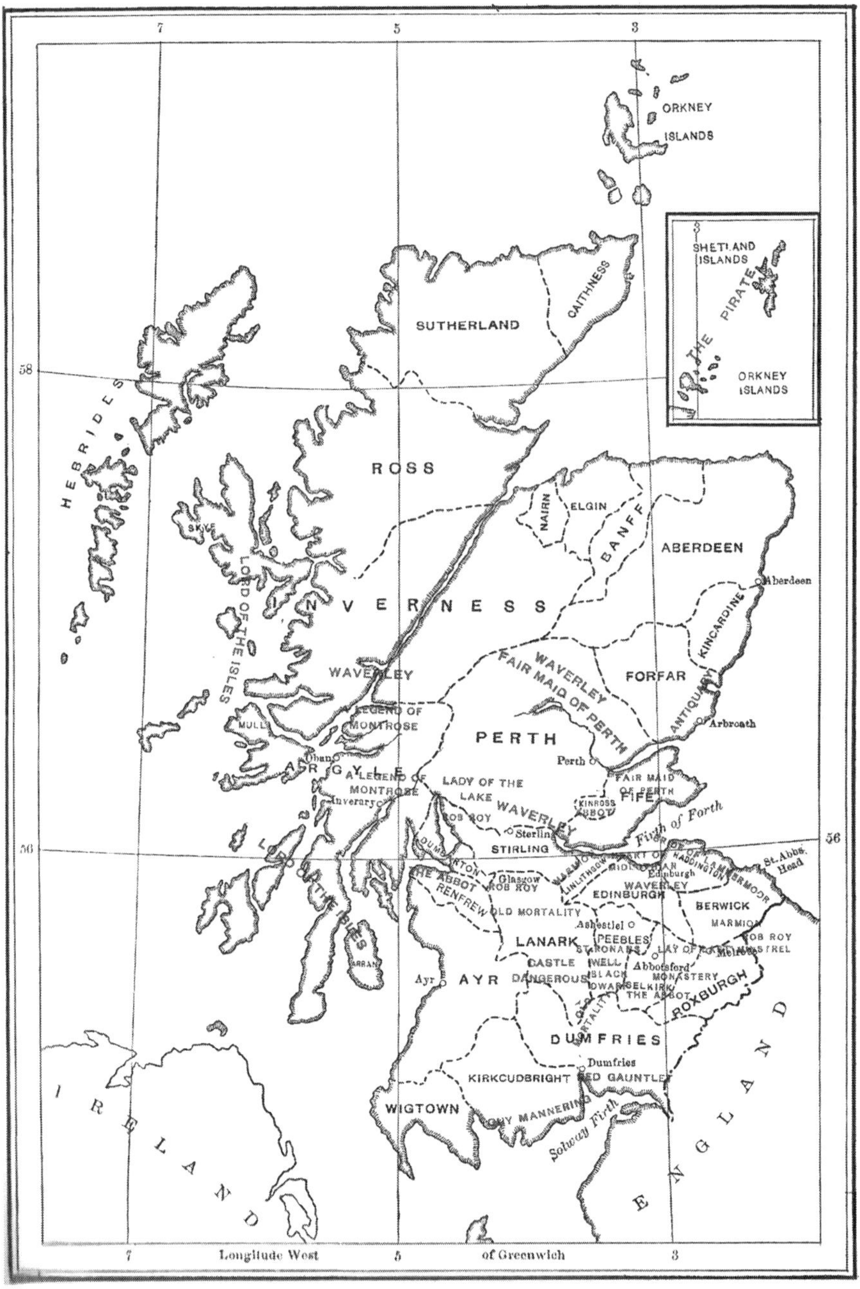

Approximate locations of Waverly novels' settings.

Part Two

APPROACHES

Introduction

Ian Duncan

It's easy to love Jane Austen, I tell my students: everybody loves Jane Austen. The real challenge is to say you love Walter Scott. Several of the contributors to this volume begin their chapters by apologizing for the difficulties most students (and many teachers) will encounter when they open a Scott novel for the first time. It is the wager of *Approaches to Teaching Scott's Waverley Novels* that a modest amount of attention and guidance can reconnect twenty-first-century readers with the imaginative energies that made these the most popular and influential works of fiction of the Romantic era. "To read Scott today is not simply to engage with the most finely documented version of the prehistory of our own political landscape," writes Simon Edwards in his essay in this volume, "but to engage with it at a level of human sympathy and understanding that is more commonly attributed to Scott's heirs among the nineteenth-century novelists."

The difficulties begin with history and language. A thorny density of reference to episodes of dynastic, religious, regional, and class conflict in the early modern history of a minor northern nation (topics even most British students now find obscure), a bewildering heterogeneity of styles and languages (especially regional and archaic languages) within a prolix, elaborately literary narrative that declines to settle into a storytelling "voice"—these raise formidable barriers in the path of an approach to the Waverley novels. Accordingly, the first two chapters of this book provide teachers and students with basic information about Scottish history and the historical conditions of Scott's linguistic practice and suggest some of the ways in which these things can be made to matter again in the classroom.

First, Douglas Mack and Suzanne Gilbert offer a concise, comprehensive, and indispensable guide to the turbulent history channeled through the great series of Scottish Waverley novels, from *Waverley* itself to *The Bride of Lammermoor* and *A Legend of Montrose* and *Redgauntlet*. Mack and Gilbert discuss the ideological origins of Scott's historical theme, the making of modern Scotland, in the polite culture of the Scottish Enlightenment. They read this Scottish history—from the religious civil wars of the late seventeenth century to the recent worldwide conflict with revolutionary and Napoleonic France—as an imperial history of the suppression and absorption of insular national differences in the fashioning of the new Great Britain, the process that Michael Hechter has called "internal colonialism." Scott was in a position to intuit that Scotland's history, the century-long emergence of a small nation into the global arena of commercial empire, would sooner or later be everyone's history. His novels, famously, weigh the human costs and benefits of modernization as they test the conjunction, or collision, of a Whig faith in progress with a Tory regret for lost worlds of tradition and allegiance. Mack and Gilbert show how Scott's liberal-conservative moderatism holds a precarious rather than self-assured place in the dialectic of history, menaced on both sides (from left and right) by fanatical challenges to the political order of modernity. If many readers associate Scott's historical theme with Jacobite counterrevolution, the series of doomed attempts to reinstate the old regime (in *Waverley*, *Rob Roy*, and *Redgauntlet*), Mack and Gilbert suggest that the Covenanter novels (*Old Mortality* and *The Heart of Mid-Lothian*), which engage the radical Presbyterian vision of a democratic millennium, were the ones that put Scott's sense of history to its severest test.

Janet Sorensen attends to the unprecedented linguistic diversity mobilized in the Waverley novels: local and social dialects of vernacular Lowland Scots; legal and administrative registers of official Scots and English; the cant of clerks, soldiers, players, beggars, and thieves; literary styles from Chaucer, Spenser, and Shakespeare to Defoe, Burns, and the Lowland ballads; snatches of Latin and Gaelic (and pidgin-English renditions of the latter); variously wild or baroque or pedantic idiolectal flourishes. Here as so often in Scott, Sorensen suggests, canny instruction may convert an apparent or initial obstacle into a source of enjoyment, even of celebration—in this case, for students increasingly aware of the polyglot makeup of their own national culture. Scott's prose resists the dynamics of transparency and identification we have come to associate with nineteenth-century realism, and Sorensen guides us along the paths of that resistance. Elaborating the general argument made by Mack and Gilbert, she explains the historical context of Scott's writing in the attempts made by eighteenth-century Scottish intellectuals to purify linguistic usage to an abstract British standard. In doing so, they made that standard their own, until "English" no longer belonged exclusively or even mainly to the English, as *Ivanhoe* makes so wonderfully clear. Meanwhile the logic of homogenization and abstraction produced its antithesis in a proliferation of regional, demotic, subcultural, and antique languages and dialects across the genres of literary Romanticism. Scott's writing invokes the set of binary oppositions that frame an Enlightenment conception of linguistic practice—universal and local, abstract and particular, oral and literary, ancient and modern, verse and prose—in order to scramble them. Students are ready to accept that Scott, after a century of being outmoded, is once again our contemporary. Certainly they are readier to accept this today than I was when I was an undergraduate thirty years ago, under the spell of an earlier aesthetic regime.

With paths mapped through the thickets of language and history, the approaches to Scott lie open. The essays that follow set forth a variety of contexts and themes for classroom discussion. Before we enter the novels themselves, James Carson's essay bids us pause on that threshold on which many students find themselves stalled—if they don't jump over it altogether. "Who shall tell us a story?" E. M. Forster asked (he meant this as a putdown) in *Aspects of the Novel*: "Sir Walter Scott, of course." In order to get to the story, though, readers of Scott first have to traverse hedges and ditches of preliminary matter, much of which is devoted to metafictional game playing with the figure of the author and the apparatus of literary production. (In one of the most elaborate of these, the 1825 preface to *Tales of the Crusaders*, the Author of *Waverley* threatens to unmake his characters when they mutiny against his proposal to convert the production of Waverley novels to a joint-stock corporation and steam-powered industrial technology.) Carson argues that Scott can play a critical role in introducing students to concepts of the author and literary production in courses on Romanticism. The case of Scott, he writes,

> provides privileged access to a variety of constructions of the Romantic author—including the high Romantic genius, the world-weary wanderer, the oral minstrel, the peasant-poet, the woman writer, the gothic novelist, and the historical romancer who figured as the Great Unknown.

Carson shows Scott struggling to maintain the role of gentleman-author between the obsolescence of the patronage system and the ascendancy of an industrializing literary market in which his novels outsold all other novels by all other authors of the age put together. He proposes pairing Scott with Samuel Taylor Coleridge, another author who reflected obsessively on his cultural status, although to very different effect.

Next, Samuel Baker refreshes the concept of intertextuality by suggesting ways in which teachers and students might gain access to Scott's novels by exploring their immense, multifarious, and continuous—if now largely subterranean—presence in popular traditions of historical and fantasy fiction, from *Gone with the Wind* to *The Lord of the Rings*. Baker sketches a more dynamic understanding of the currency of literary classics in popular media forms than through the usual route of adaptation. So, for an authentic film treatment of *Waverley*—authentic in the sense of reactivating a contemporary equivalent of the novel's "anti-conquest" fantasy of "transculturation" (to use Pratt's useful terms)—we might go to *Dances with Wolves* or *The Last Samurai*, say, rather than to the movie "Sir Walter Scott's *Waverley*," meticulously plaided and periwigged against a backdrop of the New Zealand alps that has yet to be made by Peter Weir or Peter Jackson. This approach, Baker suggests, yields its dividend once students enter the Scott novel and become aware of its dazzling internal spectrum of intertextual play:

> The seemingly careless fluency with which Scott weaves ballad, folklore, legend, and history together with romance, novel, and biography makes his works as allusive as they are alluded to—and as we move between the extensive and the intensive dimensions of Scott's intertextual reference, my students come to feel not only a new level of competence in literary study but also a new intimacy with the creative process.

(For other examples of this internal intertextual craft, see, esp., Hewitt's essay on *The Heart of Mid-Lothian*, in this volume.)

Celeste Langan's essay on teaching *Waverley* in courses on British Romanticism also attends to Scott's internal interweaving of literary forms. The combination of prose and poetry, in which poetic fragments are embedded in a narrative frame, characterizes the "new, 'hybrid' form of novelistic discourse" that Scott established, Langan argues, in an experiment that was no less radical than William Wordsworth and Samuel Taylor Coleridge's *Lyrical Ballads* sixteen years earlier. Scott makes explicit the connection between two of the great concerns of Romantic writing: the nature of the historical period, or "spirit of the age," and the status of speech and associated oral genres such as poetry and song within the modern industrializing marketplace of "literature." Langan's wonderful close reading of the famous pivotal moment in *Waverley*, in which the hero appears to turn from "the romance of his life" to "its real history" (283) demonstrates how a careful attention to the texture as well as matter of Scott's writing can instantiate, for students, "what it means to read in the Romantic period."

Next, Simon Edwards frames Scott's achievement within the field—even vaster, in his erudite view, than we had thought—of European and North American Romantic fiction and the historical novel. Edwards reminds us that Scott's impact was greater abroad than it was in Great Britain: the Waverley novels furnished readers in other regions and nations—peripheral and semiperipheral, metropolitan, provincial and colonized—with a model narrative of the emergence of national history and psychology under the stresses of modernization. Scott's American impact, the extent and complexity of which is explored in the work of Andrew Hook, Susan Manning (*Puritan-Provincial Vision*, *Fragments*), George Dekker, and Catherine Jones, among others, will be of particular interest to students in the United States and Canada. While few of us may be able to enjoy the curricular luxury of a year-long seminar on Romantic fiction, Edwards suggests a host of international and comparatist contexts for the study of Scott. If the Marquis de Sade, Johann Wolfgang von Goethe, James Fenimore Cooper, Alessandro Manzoni, and Aleksandr Pushkin represent the broad highway of a Western canon (stretching from the Adirondacks to the Caucasus), Edwards also points to intriguing byways that, although unlikely to be traveled by many of us, may nevertheless get us thinking about ways in which Scott's presence might illuminate, say, a postcolonial history of the novel: thus, *Midnight's Children* brazenly synchronizes the symbolic equivalence between individual and national destinies sketched in *Waverley*. Edwards also keeps faith with Georg Lukács, perhaps still Scott's greatest interpreter, whose argument in *The Historical Novel* (like Scott's fiction) has gained rather than lost its cutting edge with the resurgence of "archaic" national, ethnic, religious, and cultural antagonisms in the dialectic of post–Cold War globalization.

The essays by Ian Duncan and Evan Gottlieb also situate Scott within courses on the novel. Duncan explores the other term of Scott's great invention, historical fiction, by looking at how his novels produce fiction itself as the category that secures the novel as the genre of modern life. To help students forge their own imaginative link with Scott's novels as novels, rather than as novelized histories, he introduces them to the historical and philosophical matrix of their fictionality in Humean empiricism. In eighteenth-century Scotland David Hume founded a normative and socializing model of the imagination, transmitted to the nineteenth-century novel through Scott, which may be set in fruitful contrast to the Kantian-Coleridgean idea of a transcendental imagination conventionally associated with English Romantic poetry. Hume's "moderate skepticism" illuminates Scott's use of literary devices that may resemble those of a Romantic irony or postmodernist metafiction to generate a realism grounded in custom and consensus. That realism is at once liberal, produced by the play of the imagination rather than by authoritarian decree, and conservative, bound by a social consensus that always remains, however, historically contingent, provisional, and open-ended.

These days, of course, it is Austen rather than Scott that tends to close the long eighteenth century or open the nineteenth century in historical surveys of the English novel. One hundred years ago, in his *History of the English Novel*, George Saintsbury canonized twin founders of nineteenth-century realism in the chapter "Scott and Miss Austen": the great Victorian novelists, he argued, merely settled the terrain staked out for them by these peerless practitioners, respectively, of historical and domestic fiction. Gottlieb suggests ways of teaching novels by Scott and Austen alongside one another, not so much to redress a lost balance as to illuminate their surprising affinities and contrasts. Scott's narrative techniques of "Romantic postmodernity" (in McGann's phrase) can be shown to be no less foundational to the future of the novel than Austen's celebrated use of free indirect style, while both authors can be read through shared legacies of Enlightenment ideology and gothic fiction.

Diane Long Hoeveler, opening her essay with a different set of Scott-Austen pairings, outlines strategies for teaching Scott in courses on Romanticism and gender or (for that matter) on the novel and gender more broadly. A growing body of commentary (pioneered by Wilt in *Secret Leaves*) recognizes the ways in which figurations of sexuality and gender in the Waverley novels exceed, often to startling effect, the Victorian norms that they also helped establish (see also Irvine). Hoeveler takes her cue from earlier observations, by Northrop Frye and Alexander Welsh (*Hero* [1963]), of Scott's use of an archetypal binary pairing of fair and dark heroines, to examine the complex function of the "split woman" as "the embodiment of the Scottish nation in formation, both its real and historical legacies as well as its fantasized and imagined potentialities." The masculine homosocial extension of the scheme, mentioned by Hoeveler, receives full treatment later in this volume in Oliver Buckton's case study of *The Bride of Lammermoor*.

Meanwhile Kenneth McNeil's essay, grappling with the challenge of teaching Scott to nonmajors, also pursues the national theme, focusing now on the fate of ethnic rather than gender difference. If gender difference, as Hoeveler shows, must be carried forward for the narrative of modern nation formation to work, the sociological and cultural differences codified by an emergent science of anthropology are relegated to a vanishing past. Scott's late short story "The Two Drovers" revisits with scathing intensity the great questions of modernization, nation formation, and "internal colonialism" broached in the Scottish Waverley novels. McNeil shows how the tale's staging of a tragic collision between the imperatives of (Romantic) cultural diversity and (Enlightenment) universal law in the modern liberal state can be brought urgently home to students who may have little concern with the study of literature for its own sake.

Scott was a professional lawyer, and several of his works feature the law as the central institution of Scotland's modern, postnational civil society. In her essay Clare Simmons demonstrates the exemplary part Scott's novels, with their persistent reflection on the historical evolution and symbolic resonance of modern legal systems, may play in an interdisciplinary course on law and literature. Her analysis of competing versions of law in *Ivanhoe*, finely attentive to the historical contexts invoked by Scott as well as to his status as a Scots lawyer interrogating the early history of English legal institutions, provides illuminating suggestions for teaching this and other Waverley novels in a range of instructional contexts.

Each of the remaining essays presents a case study of a particular novel or pair of novels. Caroline McCracken-Flesher revisits the gateway position occupied by *Waverley* in approaches to Scott. Her tribute to the wisdom of students, often more open to Scott's aesthetic of confusion and disturbance than their category-fixated elders, is thoroughly in the spirit of this volume. *Waverley*, McCracken-Flesher insists, remains very much alive in its resistance to commentators' schemes; her pedagogy seeks to recover the critical scrutiny that Scott's novel may cast on us, rather than the other way round. Next, Antony Hasler suggests ways in which the controversial edge of Scott's great novel of state violence, terrorism, and radical religious insurgency, *Old Mortality*, may be brought into the classroom. Then David Hewitt shows how the profound questions of law, justice, and interpretation mobilized in *The Heart of Mid-Lothian* can still be made compelling—and discomforting—for students. Buckton's account of *The Bride of Lammermoor* uncovers a recalcitrance of suppressed queer energies violent enough to wreck both the conventional marriage plot and the national allegory that rides on it. Here is a pedagogical strategy that helps students think against the grain by showing how Scott's novel does so before them. Graham Tulloch considers together *Ivanhoe* and *Kenilworth*, resplendent romances that did much to shape the modern ideas of medieval and Elizabethan England in the popular imagination. His essay supplies a crucial dimension of Scott's innovative achievement in historical fiction that falls outside the Scottish history covered by Mack and Gilbert. Lastly, Tara Goshal Wallace calls our attention to another aspect of Scott's achievement outside the domain of Scottish history, his role as one of the first romancers of the globalizing British Empire. Scott's Scottishness, Wallace argues, allowed him to assume a cosmopolitan perspective that casts the imperial enterprise—whether historically British (in *The Surgeon's Daughter*) or allegorically Christian (in *The Talisman*, second of the *Tales of the Crusaders*)—in an unexpectedly dissident light.

These discussions of particular novels take up many of the issues raised in earlier chapters. McCracken-Flesher's account of the systemic instabilities of *Waverley* extends Sorensen's characterization of the unstable linguistic medium of Scott's narrative. Hasler's discussion of *Old Mortality* develops several points in the historical survey given by Mack and Gilbert, offering practical suggestions for re-creating in the classroom the debate about the legacy of the Covenanters stirred up by Scott's novel: assigning rival tales by the Scottish Romantic authors John Galt and James Hogg, for instance, which directly challenge Scott's depiction of a modern civil society founded on a war between liberal and "fundamentalist" worldviews. Hewitt's discussion of the contest between different versions of law and justice in *The Heart of Mid-Lothian* offers a powerful complement to Simmons's essay on teaching Scott in a law and literature course, as does McNeil's focus on the trial in "The Two Drovers"; all three restage Scott's trial scenes in the classroom. Simmons's review of the relation between Regency-era legal debates and competing versions of medieval law, historicized in the late-twelfth-century setting of *Ivanhoe*, also resonates with Tulloch's discussion of Scott's medievalism. Tulloch too resumes issues of linguistic usage raised by Sorensen—here, Scott's brilliant (and notorious) pastiche of ancient English styles mined from literary and antiquarian sources. Hoeveler's scrutiny of gender roles in *The Heart of Mid-Lothian* and the three major "Jacobite" novels opens onto the treatments of *The Heart of Mid-Lothian* by Hewitt and *The Bride of Lammermoor* by Buckton. Wallace's analysis of "Scott's global vision," focused on British enterprise in the East, complements McNeil's account of the predicaments of internal cultural and ethnic diversity in the multinational British state in "The Two Drovers."

Likewise, readers of this volume can follow the treatment of a particular Scott novel in essays besides those devoted to the title in question. *Waverley* is discussed by Mack and Gilbert, Langan, Edwards, Duncan, Hoeveler, and Gottlieb; *Guy Mannering* by Duncan; *The Antiquary* by Sorensen and Gottlieb; *Old Mortality* by Mack and Gilbert; *Rob Roy* by Mack and Gilbert, Sorensen, Duncan, and Hoeveler; *The Heart of Mid-Lothian* by Mack and Gilbert, Sorensen, and Hoeveler; *The Bride of Lammermoor* by Edwards; *Ivanhoe* by Simmons; and *Redgauntlet* by Mack and Gilbert, Duncan, and Hoeveler.

GENERAL APPROACHES

Scottish History in the Waverley Novels

Douglas Mack and Suzanne Gilbert

Walter Scott lived in a world of emerging modernity, a world shaped by the American and French revolutions, by the Napoleonic Wars, by British imperial consolidation within the British Isles, and by British imperial expansion abroad. This chapter will discuss the ways in which some of his major novels approach themes of revolution, empire, and modernity from the perspective of Scottish history.

Scott's understanding of the processes of history had been shaped during his education at Edinburgh University by the insights of the Scottish Enlightenment. Particularly influential here was Adam Smith's famous theory that there are four stages in the development of human society: nomadic hunting, shepherding, agriculture, and commerce. This theory had first been set out by Smith in a series of lectures on jurisprudence at Glasgow University, as part of an examination of the development of the rights of property. Bearing this context in mind, we should see Smith's four stages as a conceptual scheme rather than as an attempt to describe the detail of actual historical developments. But for Scott, as for Smith, history was to be understood in terms of the progress of society from one stage of development to another. Both men regarded the law-abiding and commerce-based modern Lowland Scotland in which they lived as being well on its way to becoming a fully evolved society, one in which civilized values and high culture could be expected to thrive.

The assumptions underlying Scott's major Scottish historical novels are based on the Enlightenment-influenced view that the emergence of Scottish modernity had been made possible by two crucial events, the so-called Glorious Revolution (1688–89) and the union between Scotland and England (1707). Many of the potted histories available to students do not satisfactorily explain the significance of the Glorious Revolution and the union from a Scottish perspective, but understanding these events from that perspective will enhance and enrich a reader's response to Scott's novels.

In the Glorious Revolution a Stuart king was deposed because the parliaments of England and of Scotland were driven to reject the traditional assertion by the Stuarts of their right to rule with unfettered royal authority. The Stuart dynasty, having ruled in Scotland since 1371, had come to power in England in 1603 when James VI of Scotland inherited the English throne (as James I) on the death of Queen Elizabeth. Many decades later, in the Glorious Revolution, King James VII (in Scotland) and II (in England) was deposed, first by the English parliament, and later by the Scottish parliament. There was a religious dimension to this: James was widely distrusted in both countries because of his Roman Catholicism, and in the Glorious Revolution he was replaced in both Scotland and England by his Protestant son-in-law William of Orange. After the Glorious Revolution William reigned jointly with his wife, James's daughter Mary, who had been brought up as a Protestant. Following Mary's death in 1694, William reigned in his own right in both Scotland and England. When William himself died in 1702, the Protestant succession was maintained in both countries by Anne, another Protestant daughter of James VII and II. Meanwhile James had died in 1701, at which point his son (also James, a half-brother of Queen Anne) became the exiled Catholic claimant to the two thrones, a man regarded by his Jacobite followers as the de jure King James VIII and III.[1] In Scott's view, the Glorious Revolution opened the way to law-abiding, commercial modernity by abolishing the arbitrary power of monarchy. From now on, real power would be in the hands of parliaments elected by property-owning gentlemen, to whom the right to vote was restricted. Scott regarded this as an eminently satisfactory settlement, which could be kept in place so long as the efforts of the Jacobites to reestablish the old regime could be defeated, and so long as radicals failed in their efforts to establish the mob rule of democracy. Late in his life, Scott strenuously opposed the agitation to extend the right to vote in the lead-up to the Reform Bill of 1832.

For Scott, the path to modernity had also been opened by the Treaty of Union of 1707. In 1703 the Scottish parliament, under Jacobite influence, had passed the Act of Security, which asserted its right to name Queen Anne's successor on the Scottish throne, in the event of her death without issue. The Act of Security opened the way for the eventual restoration to power in Scotland of the Catholic Stuarts—a decidedly unhelpful development in the eyes of Protestant England, then engaged in a struggle with pre–Revolutionary Catholic France. Faced with this possibility, anti-Jacobite forces engineered the signing of the Treaty of Union, under which the separate countries of England and Scotland combined to form a new multination state, Britain. This treaty was negotiated and implemented with a view to safeguarding the Protestant succession, and after Queen Anne's death in 1714 the British throne passed to a Protestant German aristocrat, the Elector of Hanover, one of whose ancestors, some generations previously, had married a daughter of the Scottish King James VI. These were the circumstances in which, in 1714, George I came somewhat precariously to the throne of the seven-year-old British state, as the first of what turned out to be a long succession of Hanoverian British monarchs. Scott in some ways deeply regretted the loss of Scottish independence caused by the union of 1707, and he particularly regretted the dilution of Scottish cultural traditions and practices that resulted from union with a much larger, wealthier, and more powerful neighbor. Nevertheless, he believed that the union made a necessary contribution to the development of modernity, by ensuring the ultimate defeat of Jacobite attempts to reverse the outcome of the Glorious Revolution. From Scott's perspective, the union was also to be valued because it had helped to provide a secure basis for the development and success of what was now the British (no longer simply the English) Empire. As England's junior partner in running the British Empire, Scotland had to adjust to English cultural norms and had to accept English priorities and English power structures. In a sense, under the British Empire Scots became both colonizers and colonized. For Scott, however, the internal colonization of Scotland within Britain was in the end a price worth paying: he believed that, as well as securing the advance of modernity, the union also gave Scotland access to the wealth generated by Britain's external empire.

During the early decades of the eighteenth century Scottish Jacobites attempted to secure the return to power of the exiled Stuart dynasty, a return that they assumed would end the still-fragile union of 1707. An unsuccessful Jacobite rising of 1715 followed Queen Anne's death in 1714, and in 1745 Prince Charles Edward Stuart (a grandson of James VII) arrived in Scotland to lead another rising. Although the prince came with few companions, he did arrive with promises of support from pre-Revolutionary Catholic France. Charles found a ready response among his Scottish supporters, who were mainly Episcopalian and Catholic, although he was strongly opposed by Scottish Presbyterians. A Jacobite army was raised, which quickly gained control of Scotland, and subsequently began an invasion of England. However, the hoped-for widespread English support for the Jacobite cause did not emerge as the prince's army moved toward London, and the promised assistance from France likewise failed to materialize. This resulted in a retreat into Scotland by Charles and his followers, and devastatingly final defeat followed at the Battle of Culloden in 1746.

Scott's major Jacobite novels (*Waverley*, *Rob Roy*, and *Redgauntlet*) grow out of his complex attitude to the Jacobite cause. At an emotional level his sympathies had been strongly Jacobite since childhood, but his letters indicate that rational judgment in due course pointed him toward support for the status quo of Hanoverian Britain (see *Letters* 1: 343, 3: 302-03). In 1813, a year before the publication of *Waverley*, he wrote to Miss Clephane:

> Seriously I am very glad I did not live in 1745 for though as a lawyer I could not have pleaded Charles's right and as a clergyman I could not

> have prayed for him yet as a soldier I would I am sure against the convictions of my better reason have fought for him even to the bottom of the gallows. (3: 302)

Scotland's ancient (but deposed and exiled) Stuart royal family had a romantic appeal that made strong claims on Scott's sense of history and on his sense of patriotic loyalty. Nevertheless, he was sufficiently a product of the intellectual climate of the Scottish Enlightenment to believe that progress and modernity lay with commercial, postunion, Hanoverian Britain. In tune with Smith's four-stage theory, Scott saw Highland Scotland (presented as a heartland of Jacobitism in *Waverley*) as a society at an early stage of development, as a precommercial society of heroic violence and atavistic tribal loyalties. This old society had its own powerful emotional appeal, but for Scott the future lay elsewhere. A parallel might be drawn with the attitude to American history to be found in some classic Westerns. In *Shane*, for example, the film ends with the heroic gunfighter, his era at an end, riding off into the sunset to a haunting, lamenting cry of "Shane, Shane." A new and law-abiding modernity is replacing the freedom and heroic violence of the old West—and although this process is felt to be necessary and ultimately desirable, it is also felt to involve a significant loss.

Waverley, the first of Scott's Jacobite novels, was published in 1814, a year before the battle of Waterloo finally brought the Napoleonic Wars to an end. In this novel the central character, Edward Waverley, is a young English cavalry officer in the army of Hanoverian Britain, who happens to visit the Scottish Highlands on the eve of Prince Charles's Jacobite rising of 1745. Swept up in the "romance of his situation" (78), Edward transfers his loyalty to the returning prince. In due course, however, reason prevails over the forces of romance, and when Edward eventually abandons the Jacobite cause we are told that "he felt himself entitled to say firmly, though perhaps with a sigh, that the romance of his life was ended, and that its real history had now commenced" (283). Now returned to the Hanoverian fold, the wavering Waverley at the end of the novel begins a new life of prosperous and uneventful domestic tranquillity in what (Scott implies) is the best of all possible worlds, the Britain of the later eighteenth century.

Waverley's view of the significance of the events of 1745–46 is summed up in the scene in which Edward first enters the Highlands. He is accompanied by Evan Dhu Maccombich, a Jacobite Highlander dressed "in his full national costume" (73), and as they enter the Highlands by the pass of Bally-Brough, Evan speaks to Waverley:

> "See, there is an earn, which you southrons call an eagle—you have no such birds as that in England—he is going to fetch his supper from the Laird of Bradwardine's braes, but I'll send a slug after him."
>
> He fired his piece accordingly, but missed the superb monarch of the feathered tribes, who, without noticing the attempt to annoy him, continued his majestic flight to the southward. A thousand birds of prey, hawks,

> kites, carrion crows, and ravens, disturbed from the lodgings which they had just taken up for the evening, rose at the report of the gun, and mingled their hoarse and discordant notes with the echoes which replied to it, and with the roar of the mountain cataracts. (76)

Evan's unsuccessful shot provides a memorable image that encapsulates *Waverley*'s view of the nature and significance of the Jacobite rising. Evan fires at "the superb monarch of the feathered tribes," but he misses, and the monarch of the skies soars on his way, untroubled. According to *Waverley*, in 1745–46 the gun of an outmoded Highland society can and does stir up a good deal of unpleasantness by rousing many hawks and carrion crows, but it cannot begin to disturb the secure and serene authority of the eagle, the embodiment of the majesty and power of the Hanoverian monarchs of modern imperial Britain. Scott's novel takes the view that the Jacobites, in their rising, are attempting to hit a target well beyond their range. On this view, the clock cannot be turned back, and the modern world is secure from the archaic threat of Jacobitism and the old regime.

In *Rob Roy*, Scott's second Jacobite novel, the focus is on the rising of 1715 rather than the rising of 1745–46. Once again, as in *Waverley*, a young Englishman travels north from modern, civilized, and commercial England into the wild northern regions of the island of Great Britain, where he becomes embroiled in plans for a Jacobite rising. The young Englishman who travels north in *Rob Roy* is Frank Osbaldistone, the poetical son of a prosperous London merchant and the descendant of an ancient landed family in the north of England. When Frank arrives at his family's ancestral Osbaldistone Hall it becomes apparent that he has in effect moved far backward in time from the emerging modern world of Hanoverian Britain in which his father successfully operates and has arrived in the midst of a disturbingly archaic Jacobite world. In this novel the center of the Jacobite plot is placed in northern England rather than Highland Scotland. Nevertheless, Frank has to travel into Scotland in order to challenge Jacobite schemes that threaten his father's commercial empire.

In Scotland, Frank encounters two Scotsmen who, although kinsmen, sum up marked differences between contrasting strands in the fabric of Scottish life. One of these, Bailie Nicol Jarvie, is a Lowlander and a Glasgow merchant and is in effect the Scottish equivalent of Frank's father. A staunch Hanoverian, Jarvie is an eloquent supporter of the recent union, which (he argues) has promoted Scottish prosperity by opening the way for Glasgow merchants like himself to trade with England's (now Britain's) American colonies. Jarvie says:

> There's naething sae gude on this side o' time but it might hae been better, and that may be said o' the Union. Nane were keener against it than the Glasgow folk, wi' their rabblings and their risings, and their mobs, as they ca' them now-a-days. But it's an ill wind blaws naebody gude—Let

> ilka ane roose the ford as they find it—I say, Let Glasgow flourish! whilk is judiciously and elegantly putten round the town's arms, by way of by-word. —Now, since St Mungo catched herrings in the Clyde, what was ever like to gar us flourish like the sugar and tobacco-trade? Will ony body tell me that, and grumble at the treaty that opened us a road west-awa' yonder? (312)

Jarvie is part of the new and prosperous postunion commercial world of the British Empire, the world of "the sugar and tobacco-trade" with North America. Even the limes for his brandy punch, he tells Frank, "'were from his own little farm yonder-awa,' (indicating the West Indies with a knowing shrug of his shoulders)" (295). However, Jarvie's cousin, the Highland outlaw Rob Roy, is a man from the very different old world of preunion Scotland. Rob, rather like the gunfighter in *Shane*, is the embodiment of an era that in some ways is deeply attractive but whose time is almost over. In the introduction he wrote for the 1828 Magnum Opus edition of this novel, Scott writes about the historical Rob Roy as follows:

> He owed his fame in a great measure to his residing on the very verge of the Highlands, and playing such pranks in the beginning of the 18th century, as are usually ascribed to Robin Hood in the middle ages,—and that within forty miles of Glasgow, a great commercial city, the seat of a learned university. Thus a character like his, blending the wild virtues, the subtle policy, and unrestrained license of an American Indian, was flourishing in Scotland during the Augustan age of Queen Anne and George I. Addison, it is probable, or Pope, would have been considerably surprised if they had known that there existed in the same island with them a personage of Rob Roy's peculiar habits and profession. (Introduction 5)

The "wild virtues" of Rob's world offer a primeval, liberating energy that has the potential to energize the somewhat etiolated Augustan refinement of the postunion British imperial center, as embodied by Joseph Addison or Alexander Pope. Just as Jarvie's commercial acumen embodies a contribution that Scotland will be able to make to the British imperial cause, so Rob's resourcefulness, honor, loyalty, and primitive energy point forward to the contribution Scottish Highland soldiers will make as the British Empire fights its way to world dominance at Waterloo and elsewhere. *Rob Roy* asserts that Scottish cultural traditions still have an important part to play in the postunion and post-Jacobite world of British modernity (see Duncan, "Primitive Inventions").

Redgauntlet, the last of Scott's major Jacobite novels, centers on a fictional Jacobite rising twenty years after the 1745–46 rising. Here, the thrust of Scott's novel is to emphasize that, by the 1760s, the time of Jacobitism is utterly past. Prince Charles returns to Britain to lead another rising, and through the efforts of Hugh Redgauntlet he is able to gather together some followers. However, the Jacobites can now be dispersed by the Hanoverian government without recourse to physical force. In the great closing scene of the novel, General Colin Campbell of the British army walks into a meeting of Prince Charles and his supporters and tells them that, despite their meditated rebellion, they are free to go. This applies even to the prince, the "last heir of the Stuarts":

> "You, sir—all—any of the gentlemen present," said the General—"all whom the vessel can contain, are at liberty to embark uninterrupted by me; but I advise none to go off who have not powerful reasons, unconnected with the present meeting, for this will be remembered against no one."
>
> "Then, gentlemen," said Redgauntlet, clasping his hands together as the words burst from him, "the cause is lost for ever!" (373 [ed. Wood])

The political settlement under which Scott lived had been established by the Glorious Revolution and the union, and in his Scottish historical novels he defends that settlement by asserting that Jacobitism belongs to a departed past. In supporting the current British political settlement, these novels oppose what Scott regarded as the arbitrary royal despotism of Jacobitism and its ally, pre-Revolutionary France. They also oppose what Scott took to be the mob rule of democracy, as offered by the French and American revolutions. In Scott's view, the Glorious Revolution in Scotland and England had curbed the tyranny of the old regime's unfettered monarchy by locating decisive power in parliaments whose members were elected by property-owning gentlemen. For Scott, this arrangement not only restrained arbitrary royal power, it also offered a bastion against the dangerous innovations proposed by radicals and democrats.

Scott's antiradical views find expression in his novels of the Covenanters, most notably in *Old Mortality*.[2] Here, as in *Redgauntlet*, Scott goes out of his way to locate a potentially subversive and dangerous movement firmly in the past. In the frame narrative of *Old Mortality* we are invited to contemplate the quiet graves of some Covenanters:

> The monuments . . . are half sunk in the ground and overgrown with moss. No newly-erected tomb disturbs the sober serenity of our reflections by reminding us of recent calamity, and no rank-spring grass forces upon our imagination the recollection, that it owes its dark luxuriance to the foul and festering remnants of mortality which ferment beneath. (6–7)

The Scottish Covenanters were a seventeenth-century religiously motivated popular movement, named for their support of the principles of the National Covenant of 1638 and the Solemn League and Covenant of 1643. These covenants were based on widespread opposition of Scottish Presbyterians to attempts by the state to control the Scottish church in the interest of royal power.

Following the Restoration of Charles II in 1660, there were major armed risings in 1666 and 1679, in which the Covenanters attempted to assert the rights of the people against arbitrary royal power (see Stevenson). The narrative of *Old Mortality* centers on the rising of 1679—a politically sensitive subject during the radical agitation of the second half of the 1810s, because most lower-class Lowland Scots of Scott's generation remembered the Covenanters with respect and affection as people prepared to die defending the rights of the people in the face of aristocratic oppression.

Attempting to read *Old Mortality* through the lens of the English Civil War without insight into the history of seventeenth-century Scotland is bewildering. The origins of the Covenanters lie in the Scottish Reformation of 1560. In England the Reformation was instigated by royalty (Henry VIII), and its Anglican character preserves many aspects of Roman liturgy and ceremony, while also reflecting high regard for royal authority. In Scotland, however, the Reformation legislation was passed by the Scottish parliament against the opposition of the Catholic monarch, Mary Queen of Scots. Mary's power was effectively undermined both militarily and theologically through the influence of reformers such as John Knox and George Buchanan, and, in sharp contrast to the English Reformation, the Scottish Reformation emerged as Calvinist, egalitarian, and Presbyterian.

The Regal Union of 1603, with James VI of Scotland moving the court to London and becoming James I of England and Ireland, produced even deeper divisions. Believing that he had a divine right to rule both the state and the church, James instituted policies that deeply angered the Scottish Presbyterians, who took the view that Christ, not the king, was the head of the church. Controversially, he imposed a system by which bishops under his control governed the Scottish Kirk. With James's death in 1625, his son Charles I continued and intensified his moves to anglicize Scotland, in a process that could fairly be described as internal colonialism within the island of Great Britain. Charles's insistence on introducing the English Book of Common Prayer into the Scottish Kirk in 1637 met with great resistance in Scotland, and the following year this resistance manifested itself in the signing of the National Covenant at Greyfriars Church in Edinburgh. Essentially a contract with God, this document was signed not only by ministers but also by nobles and by very large numbers of ordinary people. While agreeing to loyalty to the monarch, the covenant more tellingly promised to resist any royal attempt to control the Kirk's form of worship.

Charles I had dissolved the English parliament in 1629 and ruled alone for over a decade, but in 1642 civil war broke out between the royalists and the Puritans, led by Oliver Cromwell. The English parliament needed military assistance for the Puritan cause and turned to the Scottish parliament, who agreed to help if the English agreed to reform their church along Scottish lines. The English parliament acquiesced and in 1643 the Solemn League and Covenant was signed. Initially, the war went well for the royalists, but in 1646 Charles I had to surrender to the Scottish Covenanter army. At this point the alliance between the parliaments was strong enough to undermine the king's attempts to sow dissent between them, and the Scots turned over their captive to the English. The fragile alliance crumbled, however, when the English parliament failed to keep the promises they had made in the Solemn League and Covenant. In 1649 Charles I was executed, and a commonwealth was set up that would govern England for the next eleven years. Scotland went its own way, declaring loyalty to Charles II as king after he had signed the National Covenant. The English and Scottish parliaments, so recently allied, were now bitter enemies, and when Cromwell's forces marched into Scotland they met with strong resistance. The Scots' covenanted king, however, had to make a quick escape to France.

With the Restoration of the monarchy in 1660, Charles II returned to England. He asserted the supremacy of the king over the church, renouncing his commitment to the Covenant. Along with placing restrictions on the English nonconformists who might oppose him, he set about imposing episcopacy on the Scottish church and undermining the power of the Scottish parliament: again, this can be seen as a process of internal colonialism within the island of Great Britain. The Covenanters refused to submit, and when their form of worship was repressed they organized "conventicles" in the countryside, open-air meetings in which the ministers, who became known for their fiery, uncompromising sermons, preached to enthusiastic crowds, some in southwest Scotland numbering over ten thousand. Full-scale rebellion broke out, and in 1677 martial law was declared. By 1679, the year in which Scott's *Old Mortality* begins, the drive to stamp out the rebels was in full swing. A small group of men led by John Balfour of Kinloch assassinated Archbishop James Sharp, an act that to the government was "but one step away from regicide" (M. Lynch, *Scotland* 294). This event polarized the nation and prompted sharp retribution by the government. Covenanters took up arms and inflicted a surprise defeat of government troops led by John Graham of Claverhouse at Drumclog. Soon after, at Bothwell Bridge near Hamilton, conventiclers amassed in preparation to face the troops again. This time, they suffered a crushing defeat. Oppressive measures continued: the government undertook a campaign of executions and massacres that came to be called the Killing Time.[3] In 1685 James VII and II succeeded his brother Charles on the thrones of both Scotland and England. More overtly supportive of Roman Catholicism than his predecessor, James quickly made enemies, and he was deposed in the Glorious Revolution of 1688–89.

After focusing on the Bothwell Bridge rising in 1679, *Old Mortality* jumps in its concluding chapters to the immediate aftermath of the Glorious Revolution. Written from a safe distance, over a century after the chaotic events depicted, the novel is underpinned by a sense of fear at the consequences of popular insurrection and by a firm commitment to a balanced, rational future for Scotland, made possible by the Glorious Revolution and (applied retrospectively) the 1707 union. Dramatizing the conflict in 1679 allowed Scott to explore the effects of what he perceived to be fanaticism and lawless revolt.

Peter Pattieson, Scott's fictional narrator in *Old Mortality*, claims that his narrative of the Covenanters presents an "unbiased picture of the manners of that unhappy period," a picture based on his researches among "the most authentic sources of tradition, afforded by the representatives of either party" (13). In keeping with this measured tone, *Old Mortality* duly gives a sympathetic account of the actions of its hero, the gentlemanly and moderate Covenanter Henry Morton, as he opposes tyrannical abuses of royal power. However, Pattieson's narrative draws a sharp distinction between Morton's admirable moderation and the position of extremist Covenanters like John Balfour of Burley and Habakkuk Meiklewrath, who are presented as murderously deranged fanatics. This aspect of *Old Mortality* draws on Scott's visceral hostility to the kind of popular revolutionary energy that had found expression in the subversive forces liberated by the French Revolution. In attacking extremist Covenanters as murderous fanatics, Scott's novel articulated the fear and the antagonism felt by members of the British elite of his generation when they contemplated the comparatively recent history of revolutionary France: the storming of the Bastille, Robespierre, the Jacobins, and the Terror.

Morton is, in effect, more a man of Scott's own time (1810s) than of the seventeenth-century milieu of the novel. The hero of *Old Mortality* is positioned as the way forward out of the darkness, the earlier evolutionary stage represented by seventeenth-century turmoil, and into the full sun of the Scottish Enlightenment. His character and actions must be judged against extremes. The Covenanters' extremity is embodied in the murderous fanaticism of Burley, the dangerous primitivism of Meiklewrath, and the futile backwardness of Morton's own family. The Royalist cause draws criticism in, for example, the government dragoons' blatant disregard for ordinary people, dramatized in the invasion of Milnewood by troops under Serjeant Bothwell (who represents Charles II) and in Lady Margaret's nostalgia for the old days and "his sacred majesty King Charles" (and his "royal visit" [24]). Scott's novel also provides a memorable portrait of John Graham of Claverhouse. Demonized as a war criminal by supporters of the Covenanters, Claverhouse emerges from Scott's novel as a Jacobite leader who is no doubt ruthless, but who is also heroic and cultivated.

Old Mortality is a prime example of Scott's anchoring of broad historical themes in particular places, his lifelong interest in places evocative of the crucial events of the past. If Scott had been an American, for example, he would have found Civil War battle sites highly significant and deeply moving. This connects with the resonant use of the Lanarkshire landscape in *Old Mortality*. The tower of Tillietudlem, home to the royalist Bellendens, is based on a real sixteenth-century tower, sited at a pivotal location between the moorland (associated with the chaos, violence, fanaticism, the past) and the fertile upper Clyde Valley (associated with cultivation, civilization, rationality, the future). In the novel Tillietudlem is a focal point for dramatizing shifts in power; at a significant moment, the Covenanters, led by the moderate Henry Morton, capture it. The struggle for Tillietudlem is a struggle for the future.

Scottish Presbyterian opinion was deeply angered by Scott's portrayal of the extreme Covenanters of *Old Mortality*, and this anger was given lucid expression in an influential review by Thomas McCrie. In response, Scott restates his case in modified form in *The Heart of Mid-Lothian*. The narrative action in this novel opens in 1736, and its leading Covenanter (Douce Davie Deans, a veteran of Bothwell Bridge and the Killing Time) is an old man who cannot seem to move beyond the past. His language reflects that sense of being stuck in time; he repeats phrases from martyrs' speeches that in the modern postunion context have been emptied of meaning.

However, in Davie Deans's daughter Jeanie, Scott stresses another, more fruitful, possibility emerging from the conflict of the previous century. In *The Heart of Mid-Lothian* Jeanie Deans embodies the virtues of a religious upbringing: faith, compassion (e.g., in her fight for her sister and her sympathy for her father), adherence to truth, and willingness to take decisive action in the name of truth and freedom. But she is also able to function in the postunion milieu and can mediate between the old world and the new one. She reveres her father, but she also loves Reuben, the moderate minister, a man of modernity and enlightenment.

The treatment of the Covenanters in *The Heart of Mid-Lothian* is more sympathetic than it had been in *Old Mortality*. Here Scott's "hero" is not a young gentleman representing the interests of the property-owning class, but the lowly Jeanie Deans, the devout Presbyterian who has shaken off the damaging characteristics of her covenanting forbears, while maintaining contact with their virtues. A model for maintaining integrity while adapting to the new order, she has overcome the horrors of the past to become a productive member of a new, postunion, post-Revolution society, part of the solution rather than of the old problem. Eventually, with Jeanie's patient guidance, Davie Deans takes a few small steps toward integration into the new world; he joins Reuben's congregation at Knocktarlitie. Jeanie serves as mediator, exhibiting understanding of both her father's entrenched scrupulousness and Reuben's practical modernity (Scott, *Heart* [ed. Lamont] 450; see also Gottlieb, "'To Be'").

Scott's Scottish historical novels confront major issues of revolution and modernity through the lens of Scottish history, and they are driven by a resonantly complex attitude that combines an intellectual Whig commitment to progress and modernity with a deeply felt Tory attachment to the past and to tradition. Influential and contentious in their time, these major novels provoked other major novels written from the perspective of the Scottish Presbyterian tradition. For example, James Hogg's *The Three Perils of Woman* (1823) can be seen as an eloquent egalitarian and "democratic" response to *Waverley*, and John Galt's *The Entail* (published at the end of 1822, but with 1823 on the title page) responds to *Rob Roy* by challenging the values underlying the commercial prosperity of Nicol Jarvie's eighteenth-century Glasgow, a prosperity based on the slavery-driven postunion "sugar and tobacco-trade" with America. Likewise, Galt's *Ringan Gilhaize* (1823) and Hogg's *Private Memoirs and Confessions of a Justified Sinner* (1824) can be seen as responses to *Old Mortality*. All these novels take their place among the outstanding achievements of nineteenth-century fiction.[4]

NOTES

1 *Jacobite* is from Latin *Jacobus* ("James").

2 The Edinburgh and Penguin editions restore the title given in Scott's manuscript, *The Tale of Old Mortality*.

3 The name comes from Wodrow's monumental work on the Covenanters.

4 See Hasler's essay in this volume for more information on how to teach the relations between *Old Mortality* and the fictions of Galt and Hogg.

"Something Glee'd": The Uses of Language in Scott's Waverley Novels

Janet Sorensen

The languages of Scott's Waverley novels can both delight and frustrate students. In these historical novels the language of the dialogue is one of the techniques that produces the authenticity effect underwriting the novels' evocation of place and time. Relishing odd-sounding vernaculars in the English literature classroom—a space often seemingly dedicated to inculcating a normative English—students unfailingly enjoy hearing and sometimes themselves pronouncing the varieties of Scots, non–Standard English, and even the occasional Scots Gaelic on offer in Scott's novels. In some cases, words nearly incomprehensible on the page become, oddly, the students' own as they read them aloud. Alternatively, those same moments of linguistic strangeness can act as narrative road blocks, demanding pauses to consult a glossary at sometimes critical plot junctures and reminding readers of their own outsider status in relation to some of the worlds represented in Scott's texts. If part of the pleasure of reading Scott's Waverley novels, for ourselves and our students, is getting "lost" in the distinct space and time they so artfully construct, the languages of Scott's novels reproduce both the sense of pleasure and of annoyance at being lost. Here are languages that, like most students' or most English speakers' language for that matter, do not perfectly mirror a flawless Standard English—a linguistic space, then, that invites a reprobate identification. But these same languages are precisely and more commonly moments of disidentification—pointedly not the language of any imagined print community most readers will have encountered, and never the language of the novels' narrators. These tensions, I want to argue, are productive ones, helping to illuminate the novels' complex interventions in contemporary linguistic and social theories.

Scott's Waverley novels not only include a variety of languages remote in space or time from the polite language of the period's writing. They also reflect on the debates in which those languages serve as evidence of difference and connection between social and ethnic groups of the past and present. Focusing on language in these novels, then, provides a thread that can pull together an array of critical themes. It is my intention here to situate representations of and reflections on linguistic difference within various contexts as a means of drawing on students' enthusiasm for the distinct languages of these novels and in order to access some of the broad literary, cultural, and political conversations in which these works participate. These include, but are certainly not limited to, Scots, English, and British cultural and political identities and relationships; transformations in print cultures and the shifting status of orality; negotiations of class difference and the position of the servant; the gendering of the customary and the folk; and theories of social development and historiography.

Perhaps the most significant back story to Scott's use of language is the standardization of English that took place in eighteenth-century Britain. Students are often surprised at the relative recentness of the project of establishing and disseminating in print a standard English—and at the realization that what counts as Standard English had to be established at all. They find fascinating, and likely oddly familiar, the middle-class obsession with mastering proper English and the consequent proliferation of grammar guides, dictionaries, and public talks on "correct" elocution at this time. The number of grammar books is itself impressive—over 230 appeared in the eighteenth century, some of them, such as Robert Lowth's *A Short Introduction to English Grammar*, among the best-selling books of the age. Reproducing pages from popular instructional volumes for students is one means of revealing the perceived stakes in constructing and promoting a national standard—and demoting the nonstandard. In his *General Idea of a Pronouncing Dictionary*, John Walker maintains that "rational intercourse with our fellow creatures depends on proper pronunciation" and bemoans "the most disgraceful imitations of the pronunciations of other nations" in England (9). Henry Alford's nineteenth-century update of Walker's work reaffirms that "the common standard dialect is that in which all marks of a particular place of birth and residence are lost" (68). In these grammars and dictionaries, a newly circulating standard English worked to consolidate, while it also, tautologically, served as evidence of, a stable, unified national British culture. Mastery of such a language marked an individual as a linguistic insider, poised for advance in an increasingly fluid class system in which cultivated manners and language—not just family bloodlines and names—signified status.

Not least invested in mastering an authoritative standard English at this time were educated Lowland Scots. The language they spoke, Scots, is a distinct language sharing a common linguistic ancestor with English, and as a result there is much overlap between the two languages. Yet after the Act of Union of 1707, and its complex project of political and cultural consolidation, the eighteenth century saw a vigorous effort to eliminate any hint of Scots language in English. Grammars and dictionaries in Britain relegated specifically Scots terms and grammatical constructions to the status of a local, impolite "dialect"—a term that is itself worth exploring with students. Asking students to research particular entries from Samuel Johnson's *Dictionary of the English Language* can demonstrate the outsider relation of Scots to the newly institutionalized Standard English. Johnson's notorious definitions for words such as *oats* and *plaid* and his proscriptive labels for Scots terms like *bairn* provide evidence of the often overt hostility to Scots. Lowland literati seeking a future in Great Britain, particularly after the migration of parliamentary government and related professional positions south, sought to purge the residue of Scots from their written and, to the extent that it was possible, oral language. Leading lights of the Scottish Enlightenment, including David Hume, published their own lists of "Scotticisms"—Scots words and grammatical constructions—to avoid in proper English.

One of the more surprising and interesting aspects of the "story of English" in this period, however, is the central role played by Scottish figures and institutions not just in imitating but in defining and promoting English and English vernacular literature. In Edinburgh and Glasgow Adam Smith and Hugh Blair taught some of the first university courses to include English literature, and their lectures not only expounded on the beauties of Joseph Addison's writing but also modeled polite English usage. Tobias Smollett called for an English academy that would establish and advocate a proper English and made a point of correcting, in print, the linguistic improprieties of his political opponent, the English John Wilkes. Yet in naturalizing their relation to what was in some ways a foreign linguistic and literary culture, intellectual leaders like Smith and Blair demonstrated their ability not simply to assimilate but to move between and even perform a variety of languages circulating within the British nation. The highly successful lecturer and writer on proper English elocution Thomas Sheridan was himself an actor—as well as being an Irishman. Scott's Waverley novels highlight those performative capacities in some of the more complex Scots characters, as I discuss below. Yet the social history of English instruction and use should alert readers to the estranged, alien quality of even the seemingly "transparent" refined English prose of Scott's narrators, the culmination of these ongoing efforts of adaptation and standardization.

Not all literate Scots, of course, actively distanced themselves from Scots language. Poets from Alan Ramsay to Robert Fergusson, Janet Little, and of course Robert Burns returned to a Scots that had not seen much public printing since the removal of the Scottish court to London in 1603 and the consequent end of patronage of writing in Scots. In a world in which the expansion of print publication coincided with the marginalization of Scots, these writers brandished varieties of Scots in an innovative poetics. By the end of the century, a vernacular revival of Scots in poetry and in ballad collecting recovered the languages of Scotland that an Anglocentric linguistic standardization process had initially devalued. Even Scots Gaelic, the language of Scotland's far-flung Highlands and western islands—and a language the British state, with the help of some Lowlanders, hoped to eradicate from Britain—was getting a second look. Reflective both of an increasingly historicist bent to literary studies and of a politically driven historical philology, "outsider" languages such as Scots and Scots Gaelic gained new interest as evidence of various cultural, literary, and linguistic accounts of British origins. In antiquarian studies these languages were the fodder of hotly contested narratives regarding the earliest settlements of the British Isles. In literary criticism, they provided insights into the newly valued past, and for some they bespoke an inspired vision of societies uncorrupted by commercial development. In both cases, the lately secure position of Standard English allowed a revaluation of once competing languages, but only as those languages were consigned to the past. Alternatively, however, the standardized English print language of the present and the official political structures it facilitated represented, for some, enervated communication and a weakened body politic.

Oral, embodied language and its implied tightly knit community of speakers were part of the mystique not only of a Scottish past (and even present, supposedly, in certain parts of Scotland) but also of England's own myth of an "unwritten constitution."

Scott's Waverley novels, some of the very first to represent Scots and Scots Gaelic languages in prose fiction, would seem to conform to a number of contemporary assumptions about the languages of Great Britain. They do often associate Scots and Scots Gaelic languages with the past and with peoples and places that appear, on the surface, to be outside mainstream commercial relationships, and sometimes, but not always, the closer and more virtuous for it. As Graham Tulloch has stressed (*Language*), it is also significant that Scots, Scots Gaelic, and nonstandard English languages appear only in dialogue, whereas the voice of the present reflecting on the past (the standard English of the narrator and of the scholarly apparatuses of the novels, including prefaces, notes, and appendices) assumes a kind of transparency. An Enlightenment formulation that helped underwrite the valorization of Standard English ascribed an interest-free, universal quality to that standard (a language that was, nonetheless, based on the particular practices of upper-class speakers of London and the Home Counties). Nonstandard languages such as Scots were understood to be irredeemably particular, the language of specific regions and their special interests.

When the novels represent these place-specific languages as very much alive, it is usually in the mouths of less socially elite speakers, especially servants, and their languages are merely "vulgar," to use the term most frequently associated with Scots by the early nineteenth century. *The Antiquary*'s Edie Ochiltree, *Rob Roy*'s Andrew Fairservice, and *The Bride of Lammermoor*'s Caleb Balderstone are a few of the many vagabonds, servants, and laborers who speak comic, digressive, broadly Scots languages in Scott's novels. Yet their language, as difficult as it sometimes is to take seriously—or even penetrate—both contains critical information for the novels' narratives and is the place where key, secret knowledge of local pasts resides. The very particularism of these languages often works toward fierce regional affiliations in the Waverley novels, forging cultural bonds capable, in their appeal to shared histories, of crossing class lines. No less a figure than the Duke of Argyle quotes a Scots proverb to the humble peasant Jeanie Deans in *The Heart of Mid-Lothian*, invoking cultural ties that might unite them despite their class differences. In the Waverley novels, particular, especially regional, languages oscillate tactically between functioning as a sign of vulgar class status and as a sign of cross-class spatially based affiliation. This is a contradictory but unavoidable logic common in the cultural forms of the nation.

Frequently, female characters, repositories of oral languages and lore, become the site through which the spatial identity attributed to Scots supersedes associations with the vulgar. This is perhaps because of their association, regardless of class, with the domestic, the nonpublic space into which standard language and official history had yet, supposedly, to penetrate. In *The Antiquary* Miss Oldbuck, without access to the formal schooling and book learning of her brother, speaks in a markedly oral Scots of local superstitions, saying "she didna ken I had left open a chink o' your window, for forbye the ghaist, the Green Room doesna vent weel in a high wind" (82).[1] The high-ranking Miss Oldbuck, here literally describing domestic space and its hauntings, remains located within regional language, privy to the legends of the past that, in turn, give specific identity to place. Interestingly, however, in Scott's novels the sense of place conjured by oral, often female knowledges and beliefs frequently shades into a menacing, recursive one. The words of *Bride of Lammermoor*'s blind old Alice, of *Heart of Mid-Lothian*'s crazed Madge Wildfire, or of *The Antiquary*'s ancient Elspeth, whose speech is "like the dead speaking to the living" (215), harbor the past's dark secrets or foretell future doom. These instances of uncanny violence recollected and prophesied in women's utterances resolutely belie any reading of Scott's use of regional languages to summon the local as merely nostalgic or sentimental cultural nationalism.

Students can effectively engage in the still-current critical debate about the status of regional and cultural nationalist differences that Scott's use of language helps establish. Are those depictions of difference part of a new multicultural vision of Great Britain as some critics, such as Robert Crawford, have argued (*Devolving*)? Or does the lingering Enlightenment privileging of the general—especially in the "transparent" language of the narrators and some protagonists—compromise those representations of particular difference? That debate is not an easy one to resolve, given that Scott does not simply reproduce conventional understandings and representations of the languages of Britain in this period. More often than not he offers shrewd commentary on divisions between regional and national, particular and general, oral and written. He insists on their interdependence, emphasizing the messy, contested and utterly constructed character of the social meaning of language use and of a historical linguistics aimed at plotting various languages within a schema of nationalist historiography. Print, it turns out, might not be ontologically secure, for instance: Elspeth's (and Madge's) speech is "like a prent buke" (215), a phrase that itself embeds dialect within the valued formality of print. The hackneyed commonplace esteeming blood and indigenous knowledge also does not hold: Old Alice is a transplanted English woman who now knows the local lore better than any of the area's Scots. Further, in the Waverley novels, the languages of both Scotland and England are much more internally stratified and multivalent than any simple division between England and Scotland would suggest. The coarse language in the mouths of the English peasants that Jeanie Deans encounters in her travels to London in *Heart of Mid-Lothian* differs markedly from the "proper" English of characters like Edward Waverley, or even the Highlander Rob Roy. Scots too is inflected with class, regional and less readily nameable peculiarities. In *The Antiquary* the narrator comments on the strong Aberdonian traces in the language of Francie Macraw while the Glaswegian Nichol Jarvie speaks a distinctly urban patter in *Rob Roy*. In *Heart of Mid-Lothian* deranged Madge Wildfire's Scots shares the lexicon and pronunciation but none of the reassuring transparency of Jeanie Deans's "honest" Scots.

Even the linguistic borders between Scots and English are shown to be untenable—in *Rob Roy* the language of the north of England features Scots words and pronunciations. One Northumberland landlord remarks that Scots "are all gentle, ye mun know, though they ha' narra shirt to back, but this is a decentish hellion . . . I trow he's a dealer in cattle" (*Rob Roy* 93). The passage asserts Scots national difference in an Englishman's mixed language that itself undermines hard-and-fast distinctions between English and Scots. Alternatively, the first man Waverley encounters in Scotland, the "natural fool" Davie Gellatly (*Waverley* 40), sings a Scottish ditty with no hint of Scots language or pronunciation: "False love, and hast thou play'd me this / In summer among the flowers? / I will repay thee back again / In winter among the showers" (38). Nor is the language of the butler, Waverley's next acquaintance, particularly marked. And the language of the Scottish Baron of Bradwardine, a heterogeneous mix of English, Scots, French, and Latin, bears far fewer traces of regional difference than that of the English Sir Hildebrand Osbaldistone of *Rob Roy*. Differences often occur instead at more socially connotative and complex, less apparent levels, in distinct meanings for the same words, for example. Waverley learns "in Scotland a single house was called a *town*, and a natural fool an *innocent*" (40).

Nor is Scots the only or most particular of languages; a range of jargons threatens to instate a more insular particularity. The highly specialized languages of legalese and antiquarianism vie for attention in a conversational tower of Babel in *The Antiquary*, for instance, as "the Latin forms of feudal grants were mingled with the jargon of blazonry, and the yet more barbarous phraseology of the Tiend Court of Scotland" (149). In *Rob Roy* the language of Frank's rural Yorkshire relatives is marked both by its distance from "proper" English and by its frequent, sometimes exclusive use of technical sporting terms. Sir Hildebrand, the family patriarch and Frank's uncle, speaks a remarkably casual, colloquial language, even on first meeting Frank: "take thy long body aside, Thornie, and let's see thy brother a bit" (109). He refers to his planned strategy for Frank's instruction in the particular terms of rural gentry sport: "I must ride thee on the curb, or we'll hae some one to ride thee on the halter," a speech that, Frank admits, "was totally unintelligible to me" (122). Yet mastery of "general" English and a polished well-spokeness are no guarantee of character. That novel's devious Rashleigh Osbaldistone "was at no loss for language of every sort" (111), while in *Heart of Mid-Lothian* Effie's sophisticated English is one sign of her moral dissolution.

Revalued in Scott's novels, some particular regional languages encode key information. In *Rob Roy* the Scots gardener Andrew Fairservice has news that the English Frank eagerly seeks, but he tells it in language that withholds that knowledge. Andrew intimates, "Than, if ye maun hae't, the folk in Lunnun are a' clean wud about this bit job in the north here." And a stumped Frank asks, from a position likely shared with most readers, "Clean wood! What's that?" (193). The dialogue goes on:

> "Ou, just real daft—neither to haud nor to bind—a' hirdy-girdy—clean through ither—the deil's over Jock Wabster."
> "But what does all this mean? Or what business have I with the devil or Jack Webster?"
> "Umph!" Said Andrew, looking extremely knowing, "it's just because—just that the dirdum's a' about yon man's pokmanty." (193)

Andrew's knowingness is one of the most important and suggestive aspects of this passage. Unlike the English Frank, Andrew moves between British languages, deploying his polyglot abilities for power and even profit—at one point Frank pays Andrew to translate his expression that Di Vernon is "something glee'd," a Scots term meaning crooked or astray (500), into more specific phrasing: she is, Andrew then says, "a Papist . . . the bitterest Jacobite" (119). The reader shares Frank's sense of bewilderment and desire to decipher—and in the process revalue—the language of a Scots laborer. That language, it turns out, is not easily translated outside its highly specific context.

Andrew's exchange of language for money gestures toward the significance of economics for understanding the reevaluation of languages in Scott's novels. Ian Duncan (Introduction [*Rob Roy*]) and Penny Fielding ("Burns' Topographies") have both helped situate the local within an expanding commercial world system. Indeed, local languages only come to be understood as "local" and to be valued in that sense in the face of a wider network of far-reaching linguistic relations and the imposition of a "general" standard. The forces of economic development move unevenly, creating pockets of "regional" underdevelopment but, at the same time, demanding exchange between all sites. In a reversal of conventional understandings of linguistic mastery and social power, then, Scots characters familiar with a range of languages and dialects—and not the English characters who speak exclusively the king's English—hold the upper hand in many conversational settings. Andrew translates both Lowland Scots and Scots Gaelic for Frank. Evan Dhu McCombich must translate for Edward Waverley. The Duke of Argyle must translate for the queen. These translating figures make the most interesting element of Scott's use of language not the depictions of particular languages but the movement between languages—and, frequently, the unreliability and mutation of meaning in such trafficking, as James Buzard ("Translation and Tourism") and Ina Ferris ("Translation") have shown.

Rob Roy—a Highlander, and therefore isolated and primitive in some social theories—is one of the most mobile of Scott's characters, moving between economic and linguistic zones, deploying his knowledge of multiple languages in a supple movement across linguistic registers. His own son can switch from

Scots Gaelic to English so "that he might not be understood by their followers" (362). And Rob can use language to suit particular audiences, modulating from English with English speakers to Scots Gaelic with his family and compatriots to a familiar Scots—his "Ho's a' wi' you, Dougal?" is a token of strategic intimacy (258). In one conversation the Highlander speaks both a commanding English, "'I do not,' he said, 'carry you there as a prisoner. I am,' he added drawing himself haughtily up, 'neither a messenger nor sheriff's officer; I carry you to see a prisoner from whose lips you will learn the risk in which you presently stand'" and a language that "became more broadly national as he assumed a tone of colloquial freedom—'Muckle wad the provost and bailies o' Glasgow gie to hae him sitting with iron garters . . . that now stands wi' his legs as free as the red-deer's on the outside on't'" (256). Such use of a variety of languages helps disguise his identity from the reader and from his interlocuter, the English Frank Osbaldistone, who describes how Rob "possessed the power at times of laying [the Scottish brogue] aside." This power means that Frank "could assign no exact local or personal associations" to Rob—giving Rob the very abstracting powers usually associated in Scott's time with metropolitan English speakers (273). In Scott's work, however, it is instead a multilingual Highlander, strangely representative of the modern subject, who performs myriad linguistic identities.

Like his more linguistically adept characters, Scott himself demonstrates a canny awareness of the constructedness of markers of linguistic difference and a willingness to play with language's protean, mobile character. In his novels the same Scots character in the same conversation might switch between recognizably English pronunciation and Scots for no particular reason. In *The Antiquary* Edie Ochiltree, speaking to Dousterswivel, uses the word "country" in one sentence and "kintra" in the very next (198, 199). David Hewitt has shown how Scott even used different spellings of the same Scots words—printers and editors took it upon themselves to standardize the Scots spellings—signaling not a commitment to rigid linguistic identities but to a sense of the fluid, uncontrollable motility of language. Such textual practices do not provide much traction for a reading of Scott's use of language as chiefly concerned with representing actual regional and cultural difference. Rather, they emphasize Scott's interest in the techniques and processes endowed with the power to construct such identities. It does not seem of much importance to Scott that his representations of different languages, whether variations of Scots or Scots Gaelic or provincial English, are accurate and consistent so much as that they draw from and elaborate the literary conventions attached to authenticity. Thus, Scott indulges in the literary convention of Scots Gaelic speakers using "she" as a masculine and feminine pronoun, even though this convention bore little resemblance to actual linguistic practice. Linguistic markers of specific regional difference slip into signs of general linguistic otherness. Francie Macraw, Edie Ochiltree's old comrade in *The Antiquary*, pronounces "fat" for "what," in the Aberdeen style, but then shouts, "Ohon, ohon!" (222), meant to convey his Aberdonian roots; the expression, however, as Hewitt points out, "presents rather a Lowland idea of Highland speech than Aberdeenshire" (583).

Still more suggestively, Scott invents his own Scots place-names and proverbial phrases, mingling fabrications freely with historically recorded names and phrases. In *The Antiquary* proverbs such as "knew the measure of a guest's foot" (17), meaning knew a guest's weaknesses, which John Ray recorded in the seventeenth century, appear alongside "right as my glove" (238), a phrase Scott likely created. Actual places, such as Ardoch or Burnswark, appear next to invented ones, as in *The Antiquary*'s "Kaim of Kinprunes" (28)—a name whose own etymological value remains uncertain in the novel. In *Ivanhoe* and his other novels set before 1660, Scott would again fabricate antique terms, weaving them into the lexicon and grammar of his contemporary readers, less concerned with the actual authenticity of the language than with creating the sense of authenticity through his language. These manipulations, however, go beyond Scott's well-known assertion in *Ivanhoe* that "in the historical novel, it is necessary . . . that the subject assumed should be, as it were, translated into . . . the language of the age in which we live" (Tulloch, *Language* 9). Playing fast and loose with the historical accuracy of words, proverbs, and place-names lends itself, in turn, to the fabrication of national histories. In *Ivanhoe*, as Tulloch notes, Scott posits a twelfth-century mixed English and Norman-French language, a pidgin of sorts that gave rise to modern English. Such a linguistic narrative, however, had more to do with a particular vision of the formation of national identity than with historical accuracy. As Tulloch writes, "some such lingua franca or pidgin may have existed (although we have no evidence of it) but it is not the origin of modern English" (Tulloch, "Historical Note" 496).

Scott's fabricated orthographies in the Waverley novels frankly acknowledge the willful—and suspect—use of linguistic evidence for nationalist narratives in the eighteenth century. In that period, language stood as evidence with serious implications for nationalist historiographies that bestowed on words and phrases revelatory powers regarding continuous cultural identities. In these narratives, a place-name or the spelling of a word might divulge key etymological information in contemporary debates regarding the original inhabitants of Britain, as in Mr. Oldbuck and Sir Arthur Wardour's debate in *The Antiquary* regarding the word *penval* (48). Fielding has discussed the significance of the fact that Sir Arthur intuits Celtic origins of this Pictish word, whereas Oldbuck sees its Gothic origins (*Scotland*). For late-eighteenth-century thinkers, establishing such origins might, as Colin Kidd has shown, have some bearing on legitimating current political authorities and legal systems; Celtic origins would thus bolster support of the Jacobite cause, and Teutonic the Whigs'. The arcane etymologies proffered by Oldbuck and Sir Wardour, in their respective competing narratives of Celtic or Teutonic settlement of the British Isles, suggest Scott's own familiarity with the discourse of a politicized philology. Yet the absurdity of some of these debates and Scott's inventions of words and phrases more strongly argue the spurious and unresolvable quality of such linguistic and political histories. Most significantly, in both men's etymologies, the word *penval* is of mixed origin, part Pictish (Celtic or Gothic) and either part Roman or part Celtic. Thus, even the earliest and supposedly "purest" moments of linguistic evidence reveal an inherent syncreticism, and again the emphasis, even at this linguistic point of origin, is on interaction and mobility.

Scott's suspicions of the use of linguistic evidence to establish unvariegated and continuous cultural identities and his insistence on the multivalency and infinite adaptability of linguistic identities are important to keep in mind when considering his language of "local color" and the ascription of political histories to those languages. When in *The Antiquary* the narrator describes Oldbuck reading aloud Chaucer and "giving each guttural the true Anglo-Saxon enunciation, which is now forgotten in the southern parts of this realm," he repeats a belief, popular in some circles, that Scots had the truest connections to the original Anglo-Saxon of Britain (23). Yet the passage alludes to the already questionable promotion of this theory by Lismahago in Tobias Smollett's *Humphry Clinker* and is cagily couched in free indirect discourse, making it Oldbuck's, and not the narrator's, theory. Such location tars the belief with the same brush that renders those others' speculations dodgy.

Similar theories about the continuity and purity of Scots Gaelic circulated at this time, and Frank recapitulates them in *Rob Roy* in terms that, again, deflate such notions. He comments on the courtly tone and manner of Helen MacGregor's English, writing:

> [N]or was there the least tincture of that vulgarity, which we naturally attach to the Lowland Scottish. . . . [T]he language rendered by Helen MacGregor, out of the native and poetical Gaelic, into English, which she had acquired as we do learned tongues, but had probably never heard applied to the mean purposes of ordinary life, was graceful and flowing. (411)

In these observations Frank echoes dominant language theories of the late eighteenth century: first, that Scots Gaelic was a "primitive" and unmediated language, naturally "poetical," an idea popularized in James Macpherson's poems of Ossian (that those poems were themselves "translations" into English already undercuts such theories, just as this passage will) and, second, that writing, in its controlled remove from initial speech, had the capacity to transcend "vulgar" particularities.

Frank comments that Rob's language, at times, shares those qualities:

> Even *his* language rose in purity of expression, as you may have remarked, if I have been accurate in recording it, when the affairs which he discussed were of an agitating and important nature . . . in his case, and in

> that of some other Highlanders whom I have known, when familiar and facetious, they used the Lowland Scottish dialect,—when serious and impassioned, their thoughts arranged themselves in the idiom of their native language, and in the latter case, as they uttered the corresponding ideas in English, the expressions sounded wild, elevated, and poetical. . . . [T]he language of passion is almost always pure as well as vehement, and it is no uncommon thing to hear a Scotchman, when overwhelmed by a countryman with a tone of bitter and fluent upbraiding, reply by way of taunt to his adversary, "You have gotten to your English." (412)

Frank postulates, as many language theories of the period did, that oral speech powerfully expresses universal passions and that Scots Gaelic captures that essential power. But the passage undermines those ideas in multiple ways, starting with the reminder that these are Frank's observations and that his recordings already mediate readers' access to these languages. Additionally, the primacy and elevated eloquence the passage ascribes to orality is itself questioned. Helen's "graceful, flowing" English is a product of her book learning—unsullied by the spoken word. Alternatively, Rob's "purity" stems from his resort to oral language alone. Set alongside each other, as they are, the descriptions of Helen's and Rob's languages undo each other. The reflections on Rob's language are still more complex. At their most "serious and impassioned" Scots Gaelic speakers turn to the "idiom of their native language" (412)—a moment of seeming purity and essentialism. However, Highlanders, inversely, name this moment getting "to your English"—the moment of "passion . . . pure and vehement" is also, for them, a moment of translation. Here, the prospect of moving between languages, between English, Scots Gaelic, and Scots, transforms and denaturalizes the period's conventional understandings of oral and written language and of the essential purity and continuity of native "primitive" languages.

As students grapple with the languages of Scott's Waverley novels, the most productive readings might come from holding in suspension the perhaps fleeting charm of linguistic estrangement and the competing desire to translate. The desire to translate, after all, can be gratified in the glossaries to Scott's novels; in his own antiquarian writings on language, such as his "Ancient History of Scotland"; and even in the writings of eighteenth- and early-nineteenth-century language theorists, and such translations do help place the works within the various fields in which the novels intervene. Scott's writings, however, as often as not foil that desire to translate, offering deep interrogations of the representational systems and narratives by which language comes to stand for stable knowledge of place and history. Scott's Waverley novels unsettle even as they seem to construct tidy regional languages. Linguistic borders, finally, are highly unstable, and meaning occurs most fully in circulation; stories of origins and continuity circulate as open fictions. These novels are less about the past and specific regions than about the emerging relations that will structure the future, particularly the inextricable connections between spaces, and they reflect on the forces of modernization that themselves produce particular representations of cultural, linguistic, and temporal difference.

NOTE

[1] Quotations from *The Antiquary* cite Hewitt's edition.

The Author of *Waverley* and the Problem of Romantic Authorship

James P. Carson

By the time of the Romantic period in Britain, the book marketplace had largely replaced literary patronage. The career of Walter Scott provides an ideal case study for presenting to students the vestiges of patronage in the early nineteenth century and the role of the bookseller in determining both what gets published and how authors are compensated. Scott's career is particularly informative because he is the most popular author of the period and because his works cover the broad range of literary production from periodical criticism, ballad collecting, editorial projects, voluminous histories, lengthy verse romances, and brief occasional poems to the new subgenre of the historical novel. Moreover, his letters, journal, and prefaces supply everything from playful mockery to thoughtful analysis of the conditions of publishing, the role of the author, and his own mode of composition. In addition, Scott was a long-term partner in James Ballantyne's printing firm beginning in 1805 and in the publishing enterprise John Ballantyne and Company from 1809 until its failure in 1813. Scott was the friend, correspondent, or reviewer of many of the most important writers of the Romantic period, including William Wordsworth, Samuel Taylor Coleridge, Lord Byron, Jane Austen, Maria Edgeworth, Joanna Baillie, Charles Robert Maturin, James Hogg, and Robert Southey. He thus provides privileged access to a variety of constructions of the Romantic author—including the high Romantic genius, the world-weary wanderer, the oral minstrel, the peasant-poet, the woman writer, the gothic novelist, and the historical romancer who figured as the Great Unknown. For Scott, the patronage system compromises the author's independence, while the literary marketplace undermines genteel respectability even while it provides only a precarious livelihood, owing to the vagaries of fashion and the vicissitudes of taste. Scott constructs the Author of *Waverley*, his anonymity, and his multiple pseudonyms as a response to the literary marketplace, to the mass public, and to the writer's loss of moral authority even while he may revel in the celebrity of a literary lion. The elaborate narrative frames of the Waverley novels, which students tend to rush past as annoying impediments to narrative interest, should gain new significance through a pedagogical focus on authors and readers.

In a context in which influential criticism of the Romantics has focused on such problems as constructions of authorship, the history of the book (including quantitative studies of literary production and reading practices), and the social contexts for and functions of literary works, students might assess the myths of original, solitary genius and the transcendent imagination through Scott's self-conscious negotiations with the audience and his immense success in the literary marketplace. William St. Clair's recent history of reading in the Romantic period makes abundantly clear Scott's preeminent position in the market for "newly published copyrighted books," admittedly an expensive luxury market that excluded most of the literate population (205). St. Clair makes the striking observation that "Scott and Byron sold more poems in a normal afternoon than Shelley and Keats did during the whole of their lives" (219). Cheap French reprints of their works helped make Scott and Byron the most influential figures in Romanticism as "a European-wide phenomenon" (298). St. Clair notes:

> With novels as with poems, by sales as well as by reputation, the dominant author of the romantic period, and indeed of the Victorian period which followed, was Walter Scott. During the romantic period, the 'Author of Waverley' sold more novels than all the other novelists of the time put together. Even by about 1850 . . . no novel by any other recent novelist, including Austen, had achieved cumulative sales of 8,000, a number which several Waverley novels reached in the first week. (221)

With reference to Mary Wollstonecraft's *Vindication of the Rights of Woman*, now a central text in college and university courses, St. Clair argues that the potential to influence discussion and shape attitudes depends on accessibility to readers:

> With only a few thousand copies of the book manufactured during the whole of the first century after first publication, a figure often surpassed by Scott and Byron on the day of publication, it would have been difficult, and unusual, for anyone, woman or man, to find and read the book. (278)

Scott's quantitative domination of Austen and Wollstonecraft invites an examination of the relationship of gender and genre in the Romantic period. In relation to the Waverley novels, this project has been undertaken most influentially by Ina Ferris, who argues that the literary reviews founded in the early nineteenth century insinuate that "the novel as a genuinely male form . . . has become feminized and so has lost the centrality it supposedly once enjoyed" (*Achievement* 72). The reviews thus opened up a space for the Waverley novels, which, through their claims to historical seriousness and "imaginative and emotional expansiveness," served "not only to legitimate novel writing as a literary activity but to validate novel reading as a male practice" (86, 10). At the same time, especially through the passive hero, Scott expresses an anxiety about the refinement or effeminacy brought about by commerce and characteristic of modernity (89).

Most of the commentary on the Author of *Waverley* has focused on Scott's prefaces, introductions, and narrative frames. Fiona Robertson has compared the frame narratives of the anonymous first editions with the frequently autobiographical introductions and notes to the Magnum Opus edition of the Waverley novels, in order to argue that the two enterprises share a concern with the nature of narrative authority and the origins of stories (142). Frank Jordan and Claire Lamont have both focused on Scott's image of the unmasked harlequin in the introduction to *Chronicles of the Canongate*, first series. Jordan argues that Scott's masks facilitate negative capability, the chameleon imagination, and the art of improvisation, and Lamont suggests that the mask liberates, arouses curiosity, and limits autobiographical identifications, even as Scott's account of unmasking "joins the many tropes for the loss of inspiration in Romantic writing" (63). Seamus Cooney enumerates eleven separate motives for Scott's anonymity and suggests that this overdetermination indicates psychological obsessiveness rather than rational choice (209).

In fact, most novels of the Romantic period, whether by male or female authors, were published anonymously, perhaps because "the publishers and the circulating libraries" sought "to turn novels into uniform and mutually substitutable commodities" (St. Clair 175). The anonymous Waverley novels, however, present a special case—a distinctive and distinguished name brand. As the runaway best sellers of the time, they aroused widespread speculation about the identity of the Great Unknown. Moreover, Scott took pleasure in the mystifications of anonymity and authorial masks, in addition to confronting personal and theoretical issues about the status of the author. Margaret Russett has emphasized Scott's playfulness as he positioned himself in the book marketplace as "the CEO of Waverley Incorporated" (182), as well as in a Scottish context in which a "legacy of imposture," including James Macpherson's Ossian, figured "as a trope of national identity" (155). For an amazingly prolific author, anonymity and the production of authorial personae—such as Peter Pattieson and his editor, Jedediah Cleishbotham, in the *Tales of My Landlord*—helped to prevent "market saturation" (Russett 160).

Jane Millgate focuses on the changing nature of the author function in the shape of Scott's literary career. From the time of his first lengthy verse romance, *The Lay of the Last Minstrel* (1805), "the desire to frame and contextualize," through annotation and through dramatizing authorial and editorial figures, is for Scott "intrinsic to the working of the creative impulse itself" (Millgate, *Walter Scott* 18). For one who possessed a "passion for multiplicity and variety" (Millgate, *Walter Scott* 66), the anonymity of the novels marked off a new field, segregated from the identities of Scott the poet and Scott the lawyer, on which to situate "an inexhaustible game in which he could exploit all the facets of his personality, experience, reading, and fantasies," while challenging readers to pin him down to one "known individual" (67). As the series of Waverley novels grew, ultimately incorporating the *Tales of My Landlord*, Scott explored the sources of narrative authority and maintained a dialogue with readers, from whom he expected an intertextual familiarity with the plots and motifs of the earlier works by the Author of *Waverley* (Millgate, *Walter Scott* 152–53).

The multiple frames, narratives, and notes of the Waverley novels readily lend themselves to the conception of the novel posited by Mikhail Bakhtin as a genre staging a dialogue among various discourses, each marked by its own language. In Bakhtinian interpretations, as Robertson notes, Scott presents "as competing discourses the (several) official voices of authoritative narrators and the unofficial voices of local gossips, incompetent antiquarians, minstrels, poetic or prophetic amateurs" (117). In the remainder of this essay, I propose to supplement these previous accounts of the Author of *Waverley* by drawing primarily on Scott's letters and journal.

Since Scott's political ideology is aristocratic, and since he frequently expresses nostalgia for an economy of paternalism and dependency, one might expect him to be attracted to literary patronage. However, in an 1802 letter about the third volume of the *Minstrelsy of the Scottish Border*, Scott politely informs Anna Seward that he cannot avail himself of the encouragement of her name at the head of his volume, because the work is not, as she assumes, published by subscription:

> Providence having, I suppose, foreseen that my literary qualifications . . . might not, *par hazard*, support me exactly as I would like, allotted me a small patrimony, which, joined to my professional income, and my appointments in the characteristic office of Sheriff of Ettrick Forest, serves to render my literary pursuits more a matter of amusement than an object of emolument. With this explanation, I hope you will honour me by accepting the third volume as soon as publishd . . . and I also hope, that under the circumstances, you will hold me acquitted of the silly vanity of wishing to be thought a *gentleman*-author. (Scott, *Letters* 1: 154–55)

While Scott denies that he wants the status of gentleman author, he is proud to be able to claim independence through inheritance, profession, and appointed office. Thus he need not avail himself of the lucrative but degrading vestigial patronage of publication by subscription, a system in which the author would solicit friends and members of the social elite to purchase copies of an unpublished work and whose names would appear in the subscription list in the book's opening pages. Despite his disclaimer, Scott does want to be a gentleman who engages in gift exchange with friends and fellow authors rather than one who needs to seek their financial assistance. Teachers might point out how Scott reuses such commentary about authorship from his personal correspondence in the Waverley novels—not only in the narrative frames but also, in the case of his letter to Anna Seward, in the conversation between William Lovel and Jonathan Oldbuck about mercenary authorship and the lack of respectability in publishing by subscription (*Antiquary* [ed. Watson] 136).

A more direct mode of patronage appears in the royal gift of the poet laureateship. On the death in 1813 of Henry James Pye, whom he derisively terms "the poetical Pye" (*Letters* 3: 335), Scott was offered the official laurels on the direct instigation of the prince regent. In a socially contradictory way, Scott writes the noble head of his own family, Charles, Duke of Buccleuch, for paternalistic advice on whether and how he might decline this instance of patronage, given that his own literary endeavors and professional employments have raised him above an office that is somehow "ridiculous," especially when he would "make a poor courtier" (3: 324). As Scott notes in a letter to Robert Southey, in whose favor he declined the laureateship, he felt himself to be "incompetent to the task of annual commemoration"—the written-to-order birthday odes for the king (3: 335). To Lady Abercorn, a noblewoman into whose circle Scott was proud to be admitted, he writes (with reference to Thomas Gray, who in 1757 declined the laureateship accepted instead by the obscure William Whitehead) that he hopes the regent will understand "why I should reject the wreath 'profaned by Cibber and contemn'd by Gray'" (3: 339). In still another letter, Scott claims that his political independence would be lost were he to accept this mark of royal favor: "a place in the household is a sort of tie on votes and political conduct" (3: 351). The man whom William Hazlitt mocks as a royalist hero worshipper—as one who finds complete felicity in dining with the king (Hazlitt, "My First Acquaintance" 226)—values his independence as both gentleman author and political actor.

In the light of Scott's insistence that it is the legal profession that has freed him to pursue literature as an amusement, teachers of Romanticism might wish to compare Scott's ideas on authorship with those of Coleridge. In chapter 2 of *Biographia Literaria*, Coleridge defends poets from the Horatian charge of sensitivity to criticism and an insatiable appetite for praise—"Genus irritabile vatum"—by explaining that the public makes a false distinction "between *literary*, and all other property," and proceeding to argue that, were artisans and manufacturers subject to ad hominem attacks in reviews, the irritable genus would be found to include many species besides bards (1: 43). Horace's complaint in epistle 2.2 about having to write for a mutual-admiration society of irritable poets assumes a different force in the Romantic context of reception by a broad public and anonymous reviewers. In the 1827 introduction to *Chronicles of the Canongate*, Scott no doubt has Horace in mind when he defends his past decision to publish anonymously by claiming that anonymity facilitated moderation in the pursuit of fame:

> I felt some alarm that I might acquire those habits of jealousy and fretfulness which have lessened, and even degraded, the character of the children of imagination, and rendered them, by petty squabbles and mutual irritability, the laughing-stock of the people of the world. (9–10)

Although Coleridge criticizes "the manufacturing of poems" in a culture in which a superabundance of books is both cause and consequence of the mechanization of language (1: 38–39), he incidentally defends authorship as a profession; thus, it is no very "culpable case, that he who serves at the altar of the muses, should be compelled to derive his maintenance from the altar"

(1: 43). At the beginning of chapter 11, however, Coleridge attributes to William Whitehead, Colley Cibber's successor as poet laureate, this advice to youthful poets: "NEVER PURSUE LITERATURE AS A TRADE" (1: 223). In the state of the language in which stereotyped elements are available for assembly, anyone can make a poem "so as to delight the many" (1: 39). Since original works of genius, however, are scarcely to be produced under conditions of compulsion, it is advisable for "every scholar, who feels the genial power," to "devote his *talents* to the acquirement of competence in some known trade or profession, and his genius to objects of his tranquil and unbiassed choice" (1: 224). Mere talent—"the faculty of appropriating and applying the knowledge of others"—exercised in a profession will supply the necessaries of life, thus enabling the noncompulsory exertions of genius, which bring "the whole soul of man into activity" (1: 31, 2: 15–16). Although it may be permissible to receive compensation for serving "at the altar of the muses," Coleridge finds service at the altar of the established church to be the ideal profession for those with literary ambitions (1: 226).

Writing to Maria Edgeworth from the Court of Session in 1815, a place where he composed more than a few of his letters, Scott comments on the advantages of his own profession: "I am writing while specially attending my duty as a Clerk of Court—a fine occupation for a literary man combining a comfortable salary, light attendance, and no labour or responsibility" (*Letters* 4: 31). Scott goes even further than Coleridge in insisting on a profession for a literary man. According to J. G. Lockhart, Scott consistently maintained the view "that literature ought never to be ranked on the same scale of importance with the conduct of business in any of the great departments of public life" and that, in particular, his own achievements were unworthy of praise in "the age that had produced Watt's improvement of the steam-engine, and the safety-lamp of Sir Humphry Davy" (3: 272, 5: 84). Scott's views are partly to be attributed to his conception of the gentleman author, for whom literature "can only be gracefully executed as an occasional avocation" (*Letters* 4: 204–05). A profession frees the author from alternative modes of dependence: "either on patrons or booksellers and the former will be regulated by their own caprice the latter by their interest and the caprice of the public" (4: 137).

Scott recognizes, of course, that in the sphere of literary production commerce has made the patron increasingly irrelevant. Early in his career, Scott regrets that vulgar commercial society fails to support men of genius. In 1802, he laments the "painful" situation of the poet Thomas Campbell, who is forced "to mendicate [his] way through life and solicit the Merchants of Liverpool to subscribe to what they neither can read nor understand" (1: 136). The slave traders of Liverpool epitomize for Scott the insensitive "new men" to whose opulence, after the decline of aristocratic patronage, genius must look in vain. In a world in which human beings are bought and sold, what chance is there that the work of art can escape reduction to its market value? For Scott and Coleridge, an author who has another profession than writing has the chance to free aesthetic value from implication in the market. By attending to Scott's ambivalence toward the market and modernity in his letters and prefaces, students will be better able to explore the way that the Waverley novels establish oppositions between commercial effeminacy and martial masculinity, between the individual merit of the professional classes and the social bonds of patronage and deference in aristocratic society.

The British Romantics were faced with the new reality of a mass reading public. One response is the kind of contempt for "the devotees of the circulating libraries" that appears in the famous footnote on mass culture in chapter 3 of the *Biographia Literaria* (Coleridge 1: 48n). As William Hazlitt remarked when Wordsworth dismissed Matthew Lewis's gothic drama *The Castle Spectre* for fitting "the taste of the audience like a glove," such an assessment was far from praise for this severe new school (Hazlitt, "My First Acquaintance" 225). For Wordsworth and Coleridge, the responsibility of the artist was not to cater to but rather to elevate the taste of the public. According to Wordsworth, "every Author, as far as he is great and at the same time *original*, has had the task of *creating* the taste by which he is to be enjoyed" (657–58). While awaiting such appreciation, Wordsworth and Coleridge tended to console themselves with the praise of what John Milton termed the "fit audience . . . though few" (*Paradise Lost* 7.31). Both early and late in his career, Scott, too, occasionally expresses contempt for the mass public. Often Scott adopts such an attitude in an ad hoc manner—for example, when consoling a friend for a stylistic or commercial failure. Scott seems, however, to have been sincerely convinced of the mutability of public taste. This conviction helps explain the shape of his literary career: from ballad collecting to writing verse romances to abandoning poetry altogether in becoming the Author of *Waverley*, once Byron's poems began to approach his own in popularity.

Scott, however, is a much more populist writer than Wordsworth or Coleridge. James Ballantyne—Scott's friend, literary consultant, and business partner—thought that Scott had no sense of the success or failure of his works independent of popular favor or dislike: "it is a singular fact, that before the public, or rather the booksellers, had given their decision, he no more knew whether he had written well or ill, than whether a die thrown out of a box was to turn up a size or an ace" (qtd. in Lockhart 5: 26). Despite the occasional elitist expression of contempt for the "mob," and the occasional statement that a commercial failure has met with the approval of the most capable judges, Scott may have relied on the market for his sense of the value of his own works. He is not a Romantic author on the model of John Keats, who would continue to write even if the "night's labors should be burnt every morning" (*Selected Letters* 148)—a phrase that appears in the famous letter to Richard Woodhouse, a letter in which the opening sentence provides yet another reflection on how the irritable race of poets relishes praise. Despite his fondness for outlaws and pirates as heroes, Scott, unlike Byron, was no alienated Romantic artist. Scott frequently criticized Wordsworth for his unwillingness to appeal to public taste: "Not that I think the amiable Bard of Rydale shows judgement in chusing such subjects as the popular mind cannot sympathise in" (*Journal* 259). In his own search for sympathy, however, Scott may have conceived of an audience other than the mass reading public. In an effort to avoid reducing aesthetic value to market value in the manner of the political economy of Adam Smith and the Scottish Enlightenment, Scott may have nostalgically constructed his authorial identity as minstrel or, once he became the Author of *Waverley*, as oral storyteller.

Even if the construct of the minstrel or the anonymous storyteller enables Scott to evade in part the demands of the market, by the Romantic period the modern economy and the dominance of the bookseller were irresistible facts. As Scott confides to his journal late in life, "being hackd what is it but another word for being an author" (548). Moreover, money facilitated identities that were even more important to Scott than that of the Author of *Waverley*: namely, those of antiquarian collector and Laird of Abbotsford. While Scott might be acquitted of the Horatian charge of belonging to the touchy race of poets, while he may have been free from authorial vanity, his impulsive purchases and his ambitions for the building of Abbotsford might well remind our students of modern habits of consumption and even the rise of the "McMansion." H. J. C. Grierson provides this critical assessment of Scott's character:

> What Scott wanted he must have at once, whether a wife, a property, or an antiquity. It is true that his success never made him vain or other than generous, but it is not true that it did not affect his mind in other ways. A little more literary vanity might have been better than such unlimited social ambitions. (*Letters* 3: 287n1)

Ironically, what Scott sought to purchase were articles that embodied tradition and Scottish history and a social status that instantiated the paternalistic, precommercial values celebrated in the Waverley novels.

The position of the Author of *Waverley* is thus riven with contradiction. The self-deprecatory nature of most of Scott's remarks on his writing derives from the paradoxical position of one who writes for money to construct an identity other than those available in commercial society. Scott writes for money and invests in the publishing business to gain the status of a landed proprietor. Then, after his bankruptcy early in 1826, owing to the failure of business ventures with the publisher Archibald Constable and the printing firm James Ballantyne and Company, Scott writes to preserve the status of a man of honor, which, in his view, requires him to pay off his debts in full, instead of negotiating a composition to pay his creditors only a few shillings in the pound. Thus, early and late, Scott's favorite images for his writing are those of a turnspit (a dog forced to run in a mill in order to turn a roasting spit), an automaton, an oarsman (perhaps a galley slave), and a counterfeiter. To gain or retain status or honor, Scott finds himself to be dehumanized or criminalized. This royalist and Scottish patriot ironically compares the incessant labor of writing to the murder of a Scottish king. Apologizing to his Highland friend Miss Clephane, Scott attributes his deficiencies as a correspondent to the amount that he must write in other capacities:

> You must with your friendly goodness excuse the laziness of my fingers in consideration of the hard duty to which they have been lately subjected in their editorial authorical and official capacity. At times the quantity of ink which I am obliged to shed weighs on my conscience like Lady Macbeth's sea of blood and the spot on the upper side of my middle finger seems as indelible and as worthy of execration as the stains of Duncan's gore. (*Letters* 2: 337)

Criminalized and feminized by both his profession and the book trade, Scott in his authorial degradation might once again remind students of Coleridge's views on how in the progress of literature books have suffered a decline in moral authority, from "religious oracles" to "venerable preceptors," "instructive friends," "interesting companions," and ultimately "culprits" at the bar of anonymous criticism (Coleridge 1: 57). When, as Scott writes in the introduction to the Magnum Opus edition of *The Fortunes of Nigel*, it is no longer viable to believe "in the moral utility to be derived from fictitious compositions" (*Prefaces* 178), the author loses any claim to high rank and becomes a mere entertainer like an actor or buffoon, who has scarcely more independence than a menial servant or a literary hack.

Less than two weeks after beginning the journal that he would keep until incapacitated by the strokes that would lead to his death, the writer who advocated an alternative profession for an author expresses his dislike of task work and suggests that he will need to fool himself into thinking that his daily duty is an exercise of freedom: "I think this Journal will suit me well; if I can coax myself into an idea that it is purely voluntary it may go on—*Nulla dies sine linea*" (Scott, *Journal* 23). "No day without a line" is a fitting motto for the voluminous, versatile, and obsessive professional writer who wants to coax himself into the idea that he is a gentleman author.

Teaching the Waverley Novels: An Intertextual Approach

Samuel Baker

For those of us so enchanted by Scott, or so adept at dispelling his enchantments, that we make reading him a main part of our professional lives, it can be easy to forget how forbidding, pointless, and inert his works can seem to the uninitiated. Luckily, however, we have our students to remind us of such difficulties. Even when carefully guided, students typically find reading Scott's novels a frustrating experience at best, a distasteful one at worst. Often the most dedicated English majors object most vociferously to Scott's fiction. Turning the tables on their instructors, they torture us by castigating the Author of *Waverley* for what they perceive to be long-winded periphrases, flat characters, and self-indulgent plots. In their time, the Waverley novels may have sold themselves, but in our time, it takes a clever teacher to make the sale. Unless one prepares to argue the case for Scott's fiction, a syllabus that features it can turn out to be a recipe for disillusion.

How best to argue for the worth of reading Scott? One answer emerges when we reflect on how we ourselves came to appreciate his work. No doubt a few of us were weaned on Scott, reading family-heirloom editions at fabulously young ages like latter-day Victorian prodigies. Others among us first encountered Scott on a secondary or primary school curriculum, particularly if we grew up in a region where Scott's works were taken to speak to the local heritage. But most of us probably came to Scott's fiction in advanced university classes, and then generally less as an end in itself than as a means to understanding the history of the novel, of the Romantic period, or of historical narration. By and large, we first study Scott not for his own charms but because of his historical significance. Reading Scott is even a means to an end for many who read Scott on their own recognizance, whether studying for field exams or keeping up, as autodidacts, scholars, or teachers, with the trend toward emphasizing Scott's importance. So in general, we who now teach Scott's fiction came to study it for how it might illuminate literature and society more broadly, and we continue to enjoy how knowing it helps us navigate the broader intertextual network of modern fiction, broadly construed. To read Scott is to discover a planet whose presence explains what might otherwise seem disturbing anomalies in the literary system.

While our students may not yet approach our breadth of reading (although in their own favored genres and media their knowledge of course surpasses ours), we can bring them to take pleasure as we do in the opportunities that reading Scott's fiction affords for intertextual discovery and explanation. We can propose that if they understand Scott, they will understand a major shaping influence on the broader literary field that we plot for them—and on many of the representational subcultures they map on their own besides. Then, once lured in by such a notion of Scott's usefulness, students will as likely as not be ensnared by Scott's intrinsic charms. And these charms, they will discover, involve how Scott inlays fascinating intertextual webs within the very same novels that are themselves so densely woven into the fabric of literature since. Moreover, on investigation, it becomes evident that Scott does not entirely control the stories and images he works into his texts—far from it. Nor have readers and writers since seemed to have much control over how Scott's materials become theirs. So while an intertextual approach to Scott may well start with accounts of Scott's influence on other writers and his impact on society, it can lead students to a more profound appreciation of how the themes, ideas, and characters that flow through literature are not only channeled by authors but overflow such channels to move through other routes, including those we study under the rubric of history.

To make this approach concrete, I'll describe a lesson plan I've used successfully to introduce Scott to my upper-division undergraduate students at the University of Texas, Austin. Most of these students are English majors. They are fairly well read in American literature; less sure-footed in English literature; and generally unaware of the most basic facts about Scotland and how its literary traditions relate to English, British, American, and world traditions. They are open to learning about Scott and his work but need reference points that will enable them to connect his fiction with their own nascent conceptions of literary history. To this end, I sometimes begin class by projecting, on one of the overhead document projectors that we have available in our classrooms, a plain book illustration of a half-sunken boat. The picture is captioned simply "The Wreck."

Having kept the book containing this illustration carefully wrapped in brown paper (as befits its sometime status as banned literature), I ask the students to raise their hands—without saying anything—if they can identify what I'm showing on the screen. (No student has as of yet immediately identified the picture, but I want to be sure at the start to enlist in my riddling anyone who could otherwise keep the exercise from playing out.) Then I ask people to say what they see. It's a boat, comes the response. A ship. A shipwreck. A sinking boat. After prompting them to note that it is a picture of a boat, and not a boat itself, I ask them if they can say what boat is depicted and if they have encountered this boat before. Puzzlement ensues. After some time they place the illustration in the nineteenth century and recognize the boat depicted as a river boat. I then zoom out to include a few lines of surrounding text, which give the game away: "Well, before long, here comes the wreck, dim and dusky, sliding along down! A kind of cold shiver went through me, and then I struck out for her." At this point at least a half dozen students instantly recognize the narrative voice of *Huckleberry Finn* (Twain 91). (Thanks to the good work of Project Gutenberg, the illustration and surrounding text can be seen online [www.gutenberg.org/files/76/76-h/p3.htm#c13-107].)

But the question remains, What is the boat? Does anyone remember? All but a handful of students in the class will have read *The Adventures of Huckleberry*

Finn, which stands, as Jonathan Arac has superbly shown, as the "hypercanonical" text par excellence in contemporary American culture and education. Few of them will remember, however, one of Huck's less-celebrated escapades, in which he prevails on Jim—for the sake of "an adventure" worthy of Tom Sawyer—to land on a wrecked steamboat that turns out, sure enough, to harbor a dangerous gang of thieves intent on murdering one of their cohort. I remind them that Huck escapes from the boat, and I then describe how Huck tries to engineer the unfortunate thief's rescue by enlisting a local ferryboat watchman to help. Improvising a tale about a family improbably marooned on the wreck, Huck pleads with the watchman to rescue them. I turn the page, and put Huck's dialogue with the watchman on the screen:

> "I broke in and says:
> "They're in an awful peck of trouble, and—"
> "*Who* is?"
> "Why pap, and mam, and sis, and Miss Hooker; and if you'd take your ferry boat and go up there—"
> "Up where? Where are they?"
> "On the wreck."
> "What wreck?"
> "Why, there ain't but one."
> "What, you mean the *Walter Scott?*"
> "Yes."
> "Good land! what are they doin' *there*, for gracious sakes?"
> "Well, they didn't go there a-purpose." (89)

More lies ensue; Huck insinuates that a great reward awaits whoever should save the unfortunates trapped aboard the *Walter Scott*; and the ferryboat watchman hastens to prepare to rescue them—although, soon afterward, Huck sees the wreck come drifting along in the current, sinking, and realizes that his efforts to save those aboard have been for naught.

At this point, the lesson can be clearly stated for the class. *Walter Scott* names an imaginative place they've already visited, many times, "a-purpose" perhaps, but without knowing its name. Although only at most a handful of my students will have previously encountered Scott directly, he and his works, they learn, have been an abiding presence in the stream of literary history that they have been learning to navigate. This point leads to several possible further topics for lecture and discussion: among them the centrality of Scott to the modern Anglo-American literary imagination, the genre of the historical novel, the problem of the literary representation of history, and the general question of how to understand intertextual links across genres and periods. Lingering a moment longer with *Huckleberry Finn* provides an excellent opportunity to exemplify how a familiar author handles Scott's influence. The episode from Mark Twain's novel I gloss for them figures *Walter Scott* as at once commonplace (a generic name for a steamboat) and sensational (a ruined vessel for the imagination of adventure). As such, it links Scott with the mode of trivial, failed, gothic adventure, which is associated with Tom Sawyer. This mode takes over (and some think ruins) the novel in the painfully drawn out concluding "evasion" episode, in which Tom engineers the "imprisonment" of Jim. I remind my students of this, while remarking on how the wrecked steamboat episode begins shortly after Huck reflects on what he has learned from his father about stealing, and leads directly into an account of Huck "read[ing] considerable to Jim about kings, and dukes, and earls and such" from books pilfered from the wreck, books that sound like they might be Waverley novels (*Ivanhoe* and *Kenilworth* come to mind) or imitations thereof. Bringing his main characters to the *Walter Scott*, Twain is evidently working through his own troubled relation to his disavowed literary forbearer. (Judith Wilt evokes Twain's ruined vessel at the outset of her classic 1981 article on what English novelists from Thackeray to Woolf made of Scott; for the latest word on Twain's struggle with Scott's influence, see Susan Manning's 2002 article on Twain's agon with his predecessor.)

Here I insert a brief lecture on Scott's popularity and influence, the outlines of which many readers of this volume will find easy to imagine. I explain that Scott's novels were, after the Bible, the most widely read books of the nineteenth century, with, as Andrew Hook notes, an estimated half million copies of his novels already circulating in the United States by 1825; that a hundred years ago critics regularly paired Shakespeare and Scott as the twin fountainheads of literature in English; that Scott did much to help develop many of the devices most integral to modern—and postmodern—storytelling; and that in particular he is known for having crafted the modern genre of the historical novel. I describe Scott's penchant for elaborate, self-referential frame narratives, and I outline the norms associated with historical fiction since Scott: a setting that takes place several generations in the past and during a moment of national crisis, as well as imagined main characters who navigate real events and who observe famous historical personages making cameo appearances in the narrative. Picking up on the final point, and tying the lecture together with its opening gambit, I point out that *Huckleberry Finn* is itself something of a disguised, or evasive, historical novel (with Tom Sawyer burlesquing the role of historical personage already known to the novel's reader), and I have the class brainstorm a list of narratives that might still better fit the model I describe Scott as having pioneered. Some students will mention *Gone with the Wind*, others the novels of William Faulkner, of the magic realists, or of popular writers such as James Michener. Inevitably, some students will mention period costume dramas (Jane Austen films, say) that don't bear the same connection to Scott, but it is useful to sort out why that is and to contrast such works with others—the novels of Patrick O'Brian, for example, and the movie *Master and Commander: The Far Side of the World*—that more closely approach the generic rules we associate with Scott's practice. Many students will bring up texts of which I am only dimly aware, an inevitability that yields a pedagogical opportunity. Highlighting how no one in the room, the teacher included, has anything approaching a full command of the range of texts shaped by Scott's novels, I propose to my students that in a similar way no one, the author included, could have a full command of all the texts to which he makes reference *within* those novels. In this way I give them permission to enjoy, for its own sake, the effect of literary plenitude, which Scott's myriad citations and allusions create and to see the novel at hand as an opportunity to glimpse literary terrain that would have been terra incognita for Scott's original readership as well.

As we brainstorm texts in the main tradition traceable back to Scott, questions inevitably arise about what counts as authentically "historical" narrative and to what degree this authenticity requires hewing to conventions of the historical novel such as the presence in a supporting role of real historical figures. Such questions provide opportunities for laying the groundwork for the critical analysis of the particular Scott novel on which we are about to embark. Meanwhile, the vexing general problematic of historical representation will have come into view. My Texan students who know *Gone with the Wind*, for instance, typically know it through a sentimental family attachment to the novel or film, but they also typically know enough not to defend it in public, given how it romanticizes the old South, slavery, and resistance to Reconstruction. Should I wish to highlight progressive elements of Margaret Mitchell's achievement in her book, I can always mention how she makes her heroine a protagonist whose initiatives would have shocked Scott (even if, or especially because, Scarlett O'Hara seems in many ways a relative of Effie Deans); I can also note how Mitchell cleverly displaces Scott's "light and dark heroines" motif onto Ashley and Rhett, who are the men of the piece, and how, in a further twist, Scarlett settles down with the dark hero. (Alexander Welsh's *The Hero of the Waverley Novels* provides a useful inventory of the stock characters and themes of Scott's that recur in such far-flung literary locales, as does Northrop Frye's *The Secular Scripture*.) Finally, I let the students take the lead in an area of their own special expertise by having the class address how the state history texts that my students have read in high school offer celebratory tales of minor individuals that owe much to Scott's fables of union, progress, rebellion, and commercialization. We recall how, before Texas became party to the largest rebellion in United States history—the Civil War—it had been party to the greatest union in United States history: in 1846 it gave up its independence and became the twenty-eighth state. Widening our scope to take in United States history more generally, we touch on how, in ways that Andrew Hook, Susan Manning (*Fragments*), and Robert Crawford (*Devolving*) have explored, American national consciousness drew heavily on Scottish precedents for ways to resist English hegemony while making use of English resources.

When the theme of nation-building emerges, it gives me my opening to distribute photocopies of Twain's famous jeremiad against Scott in *Life on the Mississippi*, where Twain blames Scott for causing the Civil War by bequeathing to the southern United States the romanticized idea of chivalry. While reminding my students of Twain's penchant for exaggeration, I ask them to bear in mind as they read Scott the question of what kind of readership could go beyond enjoying his romances to attempting their reenactment. This prepares us for later classes when, as we read Scott closely and parse the ironies with which he drapes his historical representations, we think about how irony does not always debilitate the visions it frames but sometimes serves to keep those visions in view (much as, to cite a theoretical formulation of Slavoj Žižek's, ideology works through the disavowal of belief, not through belief itself [*Sublime Object* 33–35]). In conclusion, I am always sure to mention one final well-known intertextual connection: that between Scott's works and modern fantasy literature, especially J. R. R. Tolkien's universally familiar *The Lord of the Rings*—a three-decker novel composed to look like the redacted reflections of a series of old hobbits on the events of sixty years since. Proposing this connection, I ask to what extent Tolkien's work speaks to an era that must retreat to fantasy literature to fully enjoy a mode of racialized history, and I point out that Scott's novels once provided his audience this history in relation to supposed historical reality. Can we, in reading Scott, find (even if we don't take to it) what Tolkien refuses us—namely, palpable links between some past "Middle Earth" of purer ethnic difference and our own mixed-up modernity? How do we receive Scott's offer of such links, the claim that we meet in these novels Highland and Lowland Scots, Normans and Saxons, Dutchmen and Gypsies, all representing racial types from whom some of us can believe ourselves to descend?

Having established the general case for the intertextual significance of Scott's influential fiction, I finish out the hour by suggesting particular intertexts relevant to the text at hand, or, at least, by urging the students to keep the possibilities of such connections in mind. Such possible connections are myriad and generally well known, although they are perhaps now more talked about than analyzed in writing, a quarter century after J. H. Alexander and David Hewitt published *Scott and His Influence*, the proceedings of a conference on the topic. *Waverley* provides a template for the American national tales of James Fenimore Cooper (however much he may have protested the connection from the first, when he sought with his own sea novels to outdo Scott's *The Pirate*) and for subsequent bildungsromans exploiting the gap between storybook romance and the harshness of actual combat, up to and beyond Leo Tolstoy's *War and Peace*. The postcolonial romance of *Guy Mannering* also exerted a vast influence, although one perhaps more difficult to trace; Pleydell has been identified as an early literary detective, and the novel's themes of astrological prediction and predestination resonate in science fiction plots of time travel. *The Antiquary* became a crucial text for Virginia Woolf and (as an object of polemic) for E. M. Forster. *Rob Roy*, with its title character's Strider-like introduction as a disguised traveler at an inn, has always seemed to me a probable favorite of Tolkien's, and its influence on American outlaw fiction is indubitable. *The Heart of Mid-Lothian* inaugurated the project of representing the urban mob that Charles Dickens and Victor Hugo would take up with *A Tale of Two Cities* and

Les misérables, while, as a bleak moral tale of region and class, it seems decisive for how George Eliot and Thomas Hardy engaged with Scott. *The Bride of Lammermoor* sets a mood of gothic tragedy that the Brontës both evoked and rebelled against. *Ivanhoe* importantly recasts Scott's influential plot of nation formation across a wider sweep of time; both that novel and *Kenilworth* gave rise to endless stage and screen adaptations that in turn shaped modern ideas of medieval and Renaissance aristocracy. (When teaching *Ivanhoe*, it is amusing to show the first three minutes of the Elizabeth Taylor version, which feature, in a jolting change from the novel's narrative structure, a jolly Richard the Lion-Hearted returning from war. Students who have seen the classic Errol Flynn *Adventures of Robin Hood* are often surprised to discover that in some ways it follows Scott's story more closely than the titular adaptation.)

A main danger of this intertextual approach to introducing Scott's fiction is that it risks monumentalizing Scott's achievement without sufficiently accounting for his own extensive borrowings, or for his literary identity as a master *bricoleur*. It is for this reason that I want to stress, in conclusion, the importance of making the pivot described earlier from brainstorming texts that draw on Scott to considering the range of texts on which he draws, as well as how other works seem to enter into his own. This pivot occurs naturally enough as we move into the text, but it helps if in so doing I highlight scenes of reading and writing therein. This allows students to grasp how the phenomenon of intertextuality connects the life of Scott's works in the world with the worlds that live within his work. In leading my students to this insight, I urge them to approach Scott's fictions and their fortunes as open texts, taking those fictions' experience of how uncontrollably Scott's influence can be seen to have proliferated as a model for considering how loosely, if effectively, he controls his transmission of the works that influence him. The seemingly careless fluency with which Scott weaves ballad, folklore, legend, and history together with romance, novel, and biography makes his works as allusive as they are alluded to—and as we move between the extensive and the intensive dimensions of Scott's intertextual reference, my students come to feel not only a new level of competence in literary study but also a new intimacy with the creative process. Scott's relation to Shakespeare can be particularly compelling for students to trace (this is one area where I rely on students to make connections that I myself, far from a Shakespeare expert, fail to see), and in a Romanticism course Scott's frequent use of Robert Burns, William Wordsworth, and Samuel Taylor Coleridge can make for exciting moments of recognition. But I ask students also to avail themselves of their encyclopedias (a word they hear as an antiquated term for "search engines") to track down and learn about select intertexts that are new to them. Without a doubt, I tell them, in doing so they follow in the footsteps of many of Scott's earliest readers—and many of the most learned of them.

We could never keep track of all the strands of cultural endeavor that have emerged from Scott's projects, nor could we ever hope to track down all the strands of previous culture that Scott weaves into them. But as a practical matter, by encouraging students to identify with Scott as a literary redactor, we can help them appreciate the plethora of references, languages, and dialects he provides, an abundance that they might otherwise find bewildering. Students who learn to locate Scott in an extensive intertextual web become primed to appreciate the intertextual architecture within Scott's works. Once students see how Scott has influenced other writers they admire, they better appreciate why Scott should so often pay tribute to the writers who influenced him. Furthermore, in tracing the web of literary connections to be found within and without a given Scott novel, students begin to move beyond a simple model of literary "influence," in which one author imitates or chooses not to imitate another. They grasp instead how writers can echo one another without intending to do so, through the force that constraints of genre, technique, and situation exert on their work. So all the tactics retailed here redound to further an overall strategy of teaching Scott for his own sake and for the sake of literary study as such. The connections I encourage my students to make may draw them into Scott's web, but what holds them there is Scott's own way of letting past and future stories dwell within his own narratives.

COURSE CONTEXTS

"The Poetry of Pure Memory": Teaching Scott's Novels in the Context of Romanticism

Celeste Langan

> It was in many a winter walk by the shores of Ullswater, that he acquired a more complete mastery of a spirit tamed by adversity, than his former experience had given him; and that he felt himself entitled to say firmly, though perhaps with a sigh, that the romance of his life was ended, and that its real history had now commenced. (*Waverley* 283)

By virtue of this passage alone, the value of including *Waverley*—or several other of the Waverley novels in which "romance" and "real history" are similarly opposed—in a course on the Romantic period ought to be apparent. In a powerful theorization of Romanticism, *The Literary Absolute,* Philippe Lacoue-Labarthe and Jean-Luc Nancy ground their discussion in what they call the "mediocrity" of the category:

> As it is usually understood—or not understood—this name is quite inaccurate, both in what it evokes as an aesthetic category (which often amounts to an evocation of evocation, so to speak, to evocation of flowing sentimentality or foggy nostalgia for the faraway) and in what it pretends to offer as an historical category (in a double opposition to classicism and to realism or naturalism). (1)

What they call the "mediocrity" of the term is thus meant to underscore the fact that Romanticism tends to be read as a midpoint, or medium, positioned between—or, better, "wavering" between—aesthetic alternatives and historical periods, and perhaps too between concepts of the subject (as determining and determined). Always positioned on a threshold even when it is not set in a borderland, the Romantic "epoch," as Lacoue-Labarthe and Nancy describe it, is less a period than a moment of self-interrogation, whether it concerns the spatial and temporal determinants of that self or the medium—the language—of its self-interrogation.

More recently, in *England in 1819*, James Chandler characterizes Romanticism as a "somewhat remote period in the history of British literary culture" (1). By thus qualifying its remoteness, Chandler suggests, like Lacoue-Labarthe and Nancy, that Romanticism belongs entirely neither to the archaic past nor to modernity. What is perhaps most valuable about describing the Romantic period as "somewhat remote," occupying a kind of middle distance, however, is that doing so thoroughly captures Romanticism's own attempt simultaneously to mark and to mute its difference—"somewhat remote" being the temporal equivalent, as it were, of the Near East, that favorite oriental landscape of Romantic writers, or of the Scottish Highlands, which constitutes a kind of "Near West" in relation to Ireland or the Americas. Even William Wordsworth's interest in the "somewhat remote" periods of childhood and youth—identified in book 9 of *The Prelude* as a partial defense against the too-near contemporaneity of the French Revolution—belongs to this trajectory. But it is too easy to derive from this pattern a conclusion that Romantic representations of "somewhat remote" periods and places allegorize the traumatic rupture of revolution, that Romanticism is about the French Revolution, and that Scott's Jacobites are really Jacobins (the difference so often escaping first-time readers of *Waverley*). Instead—and this is Chandler's advance beyond new-historicist accounts of Romanticism—our attention is drawn to the process of periodization itself. Not merely determined by a given historical event, nor even the "peculiar eventfulness" of the period, Romantic writers also demonstrate the human capacity to mark endings and determine beginnings—to periodize, to give measure to time. And, according to Chandler, "Scott's is the literary form in which the problem of what it means to 'be of one's age' was given its fullest and certainly its most influential realization" (378).

Scott's representation, in 1814 (might we call it the midpoint of the Romantic period?), of the rather anticlimactic moment of Waverley's education by the shores of Ullswater seems to me to gloss this theorization, as well as other important accounts of Romanticism as aesthetic movement and historical period, in extremely productive ways. I foreground three dimensions of Scott's work that illuminate what I call Romantic "mediocrity," which might be adduced to help students interrogate such accounts—and their own understanding of Romanticism—critically. I try to locate *Waverley* as the self-conscious midpoint at which Scott ends his career as a brand-name poet and commences one as an anonymous novelist, a shift represented in *Waverley* as a kind of refusal to choose, a decision to write "neither a romance of chivalry, nor a tale of modern manners" (4) and to narrate his story in a prose that our students are not the first to complain of as "mediocre," or unremarkable, especially when contrasted to the varieties of speech contained within or set off from the narrative by quotation marks. In that context, I take up the question of *Waverley*'s famously mediocre hero, one who, liable to "fits of absence" (31), is not altogether distinguishable from the novel's other poet-figure, Davie Gellatley, himself identified with "neither idiocy nor insanity . . . but something of a compound of both" (38). Finally, I consider Scott's decision to set the action of his novel in "borderlands" (not only the borders of England and Scotland but also the internal "border" between Highland and Lowland) and in a "somewhat remote" historical period as an attempt to use the critical distance that setting provides to think about the nature of literary language. Each case, I hope, will enable students to think differently about what it means to read in the Romantic period—especially, to read (rather than hear) poetry. For that is the primary question, I argue, that Scott raises by enclosing oral forms in his book.

It is with a sigh—that characteristically "Romantic" evocation or evocalization of nostalgia—that the notoriously "mediocre" Edward Waverley supposedly bids farewell to "romance." We recall the ending of Keats's "Ode to a Nightingale": "Adieu! The fancy cannot cheat so well / As she is famed to do" (lines 73–74).[1] Yet the form of Waverley's farewell should also give us pause, cause us to reflect on the status of poetic "utterance" itself. This is an especially important consideration given the extent to which Romanticism is positioned—positions itself—between a lost and lamented oral culture and a new hegemony of prose "information." We should notice, in other words, that in chapter 60 of *Waverley*, Edward does not actually *say* his adieus, that the speech act itself, however "firm" or manly it is imagined to be, appears to remain virtual, a form of free indirect "speech" that makes a better-known debut in the novels of Scott's contemporary, Jane Austen. We are told only that Waverley "felt entitled" to announce an end to an era, the commencement of another—in short, to mark a period. One imagines, in other words, that the only sound that escapes him is the sigh itself.

How might we understand this virtual speech act and the escaped sigh that is its only phenomenal manifestation in relation to the "mastery of spirit" Waverley is said to have acquired? The possibilities are equivocal. On the one hand, since maturity and mastery are associated with saying "firmly," the sigh might seem to mark a residual infirmity, femininity, or adolescence. On the other, insofar as "mastery of spirit" is itself associated with domestication in the passage (Waverley is "tamed by adversity," less a sovereign than a subordinated subject), it is possible to read the sigh that escapes as a remnant of freedom, the now interiorized "freedom of thought" (or feeling) as the last refuge of individual sovereignty or national feeling after an otherwise total submission to a new hegemony. Scott suggests the relevance of such a reading in chapter 2, when, to explain the capitulation to Hanoverian rule of Edward's father, he cites "the words of an old song": "Passive obedience was a jest, / And pshaw! was non-resistance" (6). Here the interjection "pshaw" is the equivalent of Edward's sigh, with the difference that the former marks the *failure* of conscience—freedom of thought—to count, to make any "real" difference between obedience or nonresistance on the one hand, and defeat or submission on the other.

In this context the *brilliance* of Scott's analysis of mediocrity becomes apparent. Waverley poised between the firmly said and the infirm sigh points to a central question of the Romantic period: what *is* the "spirit of the age"? Is it—as E. P. Thompson posed the problem so long ago—one of "disenchantment" or one of "default"? If one supposes (as Hazlitt and Shelley do) that poets are the representatives of this spirit, their poetic effusions or sighs its (barely) material expression, what does their cultural status or power tell us about the relative reality or illusoriness of the "creative" imagination? These questions pervade Romanticism: consider the well-known passage written by another frequenter of the shores of Ullswater, Wordsworth. Similarly concerned with "to what point, and how, / The mind is lord and master—outward sense / The obedient servant of her will" (*Prelude* [1850], bk. 12, lines 221–23), Wordsworth argues that the composition of poetry—the imposition of meter or measure, the marking of language's time—is proof of the mind's (the subject's) sovereignty. But this "argument"—undertaken in a condition of "deliberate holiday" not unlike Edward Waverley's forced sojourn near Ullswater—remains, like Waverley's, virtual, unpublished during his lifetime. It falls to Scott, to the historical novel (along with Byron and the "novelized" epic *Don Juan*) to meditate in public on the question that, as David Scott has recently argued, is implicit in the Romantic assumption that "spirit" has different ages, different stages: "Are historical events to be understood as principally the outcome of the action of individuals imposing their sovereign wills upon the world, or the result of external and impersonal forces determining the direction of individual action?" (36).

One cannot help thinking, however, that Scott's choice of the Lake District as setting for Waverley's sojourn and new feeling of entitlement to announce an end and a beginning is meant to allude to the famous enunciation—some sixty years hence—of a new era in *literary* history, the *Lyrical Ballads* of 1798 (and its subsequent preface). When, in the 1829 general preface to his novels, Scott, reflecting on a turning point in his own life, claims that "it makes no part of the present story to detail how the success of a few ballads had the effect of changing all the purpose and the tenor of my life" (351), he of course alludes not to *Lyrical Ballads* but to his own highly successful foray into literary authorship with *Minstrelsy of the Scottish Border*. But the anonymously published *Lyrical Ballads* seems to stand as a precedent for the anonymously published *Waverley*; in both cases, the authors' sense that the work "was an experiment on the public taste which might very probably fail" partly motivated the anonymity (355). Moreover, the experiment with hybridity is a crucial feature of both; indeed, *Lyrical Ballads* may have suggested to Scott that his own farewell to poetry, a farewell supposedly announced with the publication of *Waverley*, need not be complete. For if *Lyrical Ballads* is not quite a farewell to romance, or to "flowery-bowery poetry," one can nonetheless read in the volume a kind of narrative "progress" from "The Rime of the Ancient Mariner" to "Tintern Abbey," poems that offer, respectively, a supernatural and a natural account of how one becomes, like Edward Waverley, "a sadder and a wiser man" (Coleridge's line is quoted prominently in *Waverley* [296]). This implicit narrative of progress from supernatural events and enchanted time to the natural and historical ("July 13, 1798") is, like Scott's distinction between romance and "real history," a generic one. The first "stage" is marked as "primitive" by its ballad meter and archaic vocabulary; the concluding poem (which announces or inaugurates "real" history) adopts a "conversational" blank verse barely distinguishable from prose. But it is also, therefore, not *simply* a question of genre. As John Guillory points out, "the 'real language of men' and the 'language of prose' are *equivalent terms* in Wordsworth's argument," even though " 'prose' is a practice of writing and it is only the bourgeois gentleman's learned error to think that conversation is prose" (130). How to represent forms of speech—from the ballad to the "gibberish" of Scots dialect to the Gaelic charm to the literate sigh—within the medium of print literature? *That* is the central formal dilemma of the Romantic period, as Scott affirms in *Waverley*'s concluding chapter: "It has been my object to describe these persons, not by a caricatured and exaggerated use of the national dialect, but by their habits, manners, and feelings" (341).

If the status of speech, the sound of the sigh, seems far removed from the question of historical agency, of the spirit of the age, Scott helps us connect them. His novels—especially *Waverley*—continually remind readers of the manifold senses of "disenchantment" in the Romantic period. On the one hand, this term relates to the project of Enlightenment, the "disenchantment of the world" represented, for example, in Thomas Paine's dismissal of the "metaphor" of the crown (314). When Edward Waverley attributes his relatively rapid cure from wounds received during the hunt neither to the Latinate "gibberish" pronounced over him nor to the Gaelic charms pronounced over the herbs but rather to the "opiate" chemical properties of those herbs, he evinces the same demystifying skepticism he later applies to the Bodach Glas, or "Grey Spectre," in which Fergus MacIvor reads the prophecy of his death. Waverley believes the specter to be either "a Cumberland peasant in his ordinary dress" or "the operation of an exhausted frame and depressed spirits" (277)—in short, either material or immaterial. But there is a more "mediocre" solution: the specter is the (im)material difference of repetition.[2] Repeating the violence of his forefathers, and recalling the past, Fergus perceives a pattern and a probable outcome. Thus Scott helps us understand the peculiar logic of Romantic prophecy, which so often takes the form, as in *Prometheus Unbound*, of "recalling" the past. (Hazlitt would call Scott himself "a *prophesier* of things past" [qtd. in Chandler 236].) That this form is often "spectral," or phantasmatic, suggests the intervention of *aesthetic* distance. The act of (self-)quotation allows Prometheus (and "select classes of poetical readers," as Shelley says in his preface to *Prometheus Unbound* [232]) to recognize in the verbal form of the imperative ("All that thou canst inflict I bid thee do," "Rain then thy plagues upon me here") a complicity with Jupiter's reign, with the forms of empire, and so to liberate himself from this regime, albeit with a sigh: "Ah no! I pity thee" (act 1, lines 263, 266, 53). It is, arguably, repetition itself—"many a winter walk"—that Scott identifies as the mechanism of art, of "that internal sorcery, by which past or imaginary events are presented in action, as it were, to the eye of the muser" (17).

But how can such "internal sorcery"—the phrase Scott uses to describe Edward Waverley's "castle-building" in chapter 4—be allied with *dis*enchantment? One might turn here to Scott's curious account of that celebrated elegist of the "age of chivalry," Edmund Burke: "Burke appeared, and all the *gibberish* about the superior legislation of the French dissolved like an enchanted castle when the destined knight blows his horn before it" (Scott, *Letters* 11: 455). Paul Hamilton, who draws our attention to this passage, points out that "Burke, as 'destined knight,' is a character in the romance he is there to demystify" (129); Romantic "disenchantment" remains incomplete, since it operates chiefly by opposing one representation to another. But this is merely to reiterate a point that Shelley makes in the *Defense of Poetry*: literature can "defeat the curse which binds us to be subjected to the accident of surrounding impressions" (698), *either* by making the unknown familiar ("mark[ing] the before unapprehended relations of things" [676]) *or* by defamiliarization, by "strip[ping] the veil of familiarity from the world" (698). "Real history," in this account, is merely the as-yet-unrecognized "romance" or illusion of the present. Edward Waverley's exercises in chapter 4's "castle-building," we then recall, occur after "hours exhausted in listening to the oft-repeated tale of narrative old age" (15), the "dry deduction of his line of ancestors" (16). Edward, in short, is a reader bored by history, and so reads "between the lines," as it were, for its "poetry." Contemporary readers of Scott, by contrast, are more likely to be readers bored by poetry.

When Scott figures the genre of romance as so much "gibberish"—a loaded term in his novels, associated as it is with the Samuel Johnson–like denigration of Gaelic and Scots dialect (in *Waverley* it is the John Bullish Colonel Talbot who exhibits this prejudice [282])—he reminds us as well that the history of language, like the history of literature, can be read as a narrative of "disenchantment" in possibly its most literal sense: as the cessation of the activity of chanting, of what Wordsworth called "the animated or impassioned recitation" of poetry ("Preface to *Poems*" 752). Given the influence on Scott's thought of Scottish historiography, in which whole societies move through "stages" or "states" (savage, pastoral, agricultural, commercial), one might expect that poetry—a form of "orality"—would be associated with the primitive and (in the end) abandoned as insufficiently modern. What's effective about pursuing this line with students is that they are likely to share its premise, baldly stated by Scott's contemporary, Vicesimus Knox: "Poetry is not one of the necessaries of life. The information it conveys may be conveyed in prose" (qtd. in Price 83). Knox's implicit suggestion is that prose not only conveys the same information as poetry does but also that it does so more efficiently, thus rendering poetry unnecessary, obsolete. Yet Scott's literary career suggests a more complex attitude toward genre and medium. Consider his career as Maureen McLane and I recently mapped it:

> [A]s if Scott was determined to prove the efficacy of Marshall McLuhan's maxim, that the content of one medium is another medium, ballad texts, manuscripts, oral recitations, and legal documents provided the "content" for his *Minstrelsy of the Scottish Border*; ballad material and minstrel figures the content of his romances; and romance structures and historical inquiry the content of his novels. (256)

Rather than *replace* another genre or medium, as in Knox's argument, Scott in practice produces a dialectical synthesis.

It is of course true that many readers of Scott's novels tend to skip the poems, quotations, and verse fragments that might seem more or less to "ornament" his novels, and they may grow annoyed at having to flip to the endnotes to have various Scottish ballads or other poetic allusions identified for them. But to focus on this conflict in readerly desire—indeed, to elicit it—seems to be Scott's purpose, and may suggest to students the necessity of reexamining definitions of prose or of poetry, of *literature*, as a medium of "information." For if readers desire to race through a text toward its end or outcome, they also must acknowledge, given the frequency with which certain plots are repeated (not only the marriage plot but also the education plot of the "sadder and wiser" man), that the end is in some sense beside the point. (Readers of *many* Scott novels will certainly feel the force of this point.) Scott himself draws attention at the beginning of chapter 24 of *Waverley* to the conflicting rationale of the novel (which Pierre Macherey has described as "a procrastinated anecdote" [19]): "Shall this be a long or a short chapter?—This is a question in which you, gentle reader, have no vote, however much you may be interested in the consequences" (115). Here again the question of mastery, of sovereignty and subjection, is linked to language, and our attention is directed to the difference made by the "virtual" speech act of writing. Elsewhere, Scott also appears to anticipate his readers' displeasure at his particular way of procrastinating anecdotes: "The baron's story was short, when divested of the adages and commonplaces, Latin, English, and Scotch, with which his erudition garnished it" (299).

Regarding the relation between poetry and "information," Scott is ambivalent.[3] *Waverley* evinces this ambivalence when it describes the manner of the wandering poet Davie Gellatley. Quoting Robert Southey's *Thalaba*, Scott emphasizes the untimeliness of poetry: "still his speech was song" (83). In other words, though the rest of Scotland, perhaps, is under the sway of prose, Davie Gellatley is a kind of anachronism. Yet the oft-repeated lesson of Scott's novels is that those characters (and readers) who agree with Edward Waverley's initial assessment of one of Davie's verses—"This contained no information" (38)—do so at their peril. Like Wordsworth's "Idiot Boy" (Scott refers to the poem on page 301), who is the agent of Susan Gale's "cure" despite his being incapable of delivering straightforward "information," Davie may seem to be an untrustworthy messenger (Waverley wonders if he is capable of delivering a letter, and the gardener "would hardly trust him with a long message by word of mouth" [39]), but he is the medium by which the freedom of Baron Bradwardine is preserved. Moreover, this preservation is effected through citation or parody: Davie puts on the baron's cloak, "majoring and looking about sae like his Honour, that they [the soldiers who have espied Bradwardine] were clean beguiled" (301). The suggestion, I believe, is that Davie's poetic effusions, like his successful physical impersonation of the baron, are to be understood not as information but as its citation, its quotation.

Davie is thus the figural form of Scott's practice in the novel. Only in later novels would Scott develop the habit of providing verse epigraphs for most of his chapters, but anyone scanning the pages of *Waverley* will find ample evidence of the extent to which Scott's new, "hybrid" form of novelistic discourse is marked, even typographically, as a prose frame set around poetic fragments. This practice can in turn be linked to Scott's interest in the relation between word and image—an interest most fully developed in *The Bride of Lammermoor*, where Scott celebrates the traditional pub sign, marked by what Chandler usefully calls "the redundant conjunction of word and image" (337). It is an elegiac celebration, for the narrator criticizes a contemporary "illiberal measure of economy" that dispenses with the image and makes do with the written word. What the literate subject might experience as "redundancy," however, those unfamiliar with the alphabet find *necessary*: they rely on the image's "symbolical representation" to locate "a pot of good ale" (*Bride of Lammermoor* [ed. Alexander] 5). In *Waverley*, redundant conjunction more often takes the form of word and music, word and setting: Flora MacIvor worries that "a Highland song would suffer still more from my imperfect translation, were I to introduce it without its own wild and appropriate accompaniments" (106). Yet redundancy is exactly the point: a poem beginning "[t]here is a mist on the mountain" requires for its full effect the "setting" of mist and mountain stream.

By contrast, Davie Gellatley's poetic language is not only untimely; it is also unlocalizable. Like many Romantic visitors to Scotland, Edward Waverley wants to imagine Davie's verses as "belong[ing] to old Scottish poetry" (106)—in other words, to imagine them as a local product, indigenous, organic. But Rose Bradwardine reports that Davie had a college-educated brother who, like the writer of "[l]ines, left upon a Seat in a Yew-Tree," returned home with disappointed expectations. "We think that from him Davie gathered many fragments of songs and music unlike those of this country" (55), she tells Waverley, thus upsetting any simple version of "bardic nationalism." To extrapolate once more from Davie Gellatley to Scott himself, we should remind students that, unlike the nationalist Baron of Bradwardine, whose knowledge of poetry is almost entirely Scottish, Scott collects and displays poetry of various genres, periods, and national traditions.

When Katie Trumpener, in *Bardic Nationalism*, criticizes the treatment of Scott by Georg Lukács in *The Historical Novel* and Edwin Muir in *Scott and Scotland*, she cites in particular their "displacement of formal or generic analysis in the service of a national-historical reflection theory" (130). Evidence of this displacement might be found in the passage she quotes from Muir: a fascinating passage that might usefully provoke students into thinking critically about the "very curious emptiness"—the lack of vital interest I've identified with mediocrity—that students often attest to in reading Scott's novels. Attributing this emptiness to that fact that Scott "spent most of his days in a hiatus, in a country, that is to say, which was neither a nation nor a province," Muir comments:

> A people who lose their nationality create a legend to take its place. The reality of a nation's history lies in its continuity, and the present is its only guarantee. . . . But where national unity is lost, the past is lost too, for the connection between past and present has been broken, and the past turns therefore into legend, into the poetry of pure memory.
>
> (qtd. in Trumpener 129)

I have tried in this essay to offer a kind of advance illumination of that phrase, "the poetry of pure memory," which Muir opposes to "the reality of a nation's history" in a way precisely reminiscent of *Waverley*'s category of "romance." I have tried to suggest that there is no such thing, or rather that as one tries to imagine a "poetry of pure memory," it turns into two entirely different things. On the one hand, it is the inarticulate sigh, a mark of loss or a "strange [fit] of absence" within utterance. "Purified" of historical content, this poetry would approximate the "gibberish" that Gaelic has become to those now under the sway of England and English. It would be represented in the novel by Edward's naive "worshi[p] of the Celtic muse" because "he does not understand a word of her language" (106). On the other hand, perhaps a "pure" poetry would be that which no longer bore the marks, sounded the shibboleth, of its historicity. At first, Scott appears to worry that the affective power one associates with the sigh would be lost in this process of purification, and that Waverley's modernizing translation of oral performance might be an improvement on a par with the "illiberal economy" of the pub sign. Describing the experience of hearing Rose Bradwardine sing, Scott writes:

> The sweetness of her voice, and the simple beauty of her music, gave all the advantage which the minstrel could have desired, and which his poetry so much wanted. I almost doubt it can be read with patience, destitute of those Advantages. . . . (60)

Since we know that the verse she sings is Scott's own, we should pay attention to Scott's identification of this poet as one "who, noteless as the race from which he sprung, / Saved others' names, but left his own unsung" (59). Here "noteless" seems to connote "lacking fame": the poet (Scott himself) remains anonymous. Yet, given Scott's famously tin ear, and the fact that his name is described as "unsung," it is possible as well to construe "noteless" as "without music"—that is, as referencing a *literate* poetry, "pure" in the sense that it eschews accompaniment, the potentially "redundant conjunction" of its words with music or image. Only then do we recognize the extent to which *Waverley*—in using a "mediocre" prose narrative to demonstrate the power of language to mediate both sound and image—has disenchanted the "internal sorcery" that is reading.

NOTES

[1] *Evocalization* is a term coined by Stewart to describe the effects of voice that linger in silent reading.

[2] Compare Wordsworth's "version" of the Grey Spectre in book 8 of *The Prelude*: "By mists bewildered, suddenly my eyes / Have glanced upon him a few distant steps, / In size a giant, stalking through thick fog" (lines 264–66 [1850]). As many have pointed out, Wordsworth's representation here of a "supernaturalized" Cumberland shepherd owes something to James Thomson's *The Seasons*.

[3] Though long-winded himself, Baron Bradwardine seems a likely buyer of one of Vicesimus Knox's "elegant extracts"; despite his familiarity with the "classics" of Scots poetry, Scott suggests he would have preferred to have "the historical narratives" and moral lessons that such poems contained "presented to him in the form of simple prose" (108).

Home and Away with Walter Scott

Simon Edwards

If my title contains a football allusion (or soccer, as the game is known in the United States), it is to insist on the essentially popular nature of Scott's fiction. At the time of writing, Heart of Midlothian, the only football team to take its name from the work of a novelist, are tied for first place in the Scottish Premier League. The Edinburgh team is mounting the first serious challenge in the last quarter of a century to the traditional hegemony of Glasgow Celtic (Catholic) and Glasgow Rangers (Protestant). The sectarian passions of Scottish football carry of course a rich reminder of the very stuff of Scott's work, deeply enfolded as these passions still are in the economic, social, political, and cultural life of the modern nation. Hearts' Edinburgh rivals are aptly enough named Hibernian. The ferry loads of Irish supporters who attend every Glasgow home game serve also to remind us that Scott's revolutionary transformation of the art of the novel took its shape in the fertile soil of the Irish "national" fiction (e.g., Edgeworth, Owenson, Maturin) that followed in response to the 1800 Act of Union.

The ramifications of the act may be thought to determine not merely the political culture of Scott's own age but British political life down to the beginning of the twenty-first century. The great cycle of Scottish novels from *Waverley* onward is in part an engagement with the struggles, the losses and gains, that were a consequence of the earlier 1707 Act of Union between England and Scotland. These novels contain all the issues with which we remain painfully familiar: ethnic and religious rivalry and hatred, played out, to adapt Karl Marx and Friedrich Engels, in "uninterrupted, now hidden, now open fight" (79). While Georg Lukács, from the perspective of the Moscow "show trials" of the 1930s, had found in Scott an epic dramatization of the history of class struggle, we may now take a darker view of a historical process that moves almost in defiance of those universalist Enlightenment strains still to be found in Marx's thought. This is not to contend that Lukács was wrong about Scott's grasp of the scope and nature of class conflict but rather to suggest Scott's even more profound insight into the national inflections of the conflict. Those same national inflections, forged under local conditions and then bloated into the nationalist ideologies of the nineteenth century, also help us understand exactly how and why Scott's example was so readily and widely appropriated throughout not only Europe but the world. The map of Europe and the map of the world have both proved infinitely friable. Scott's assiduous attention to *territory*, the fault lines of community and belief within structures and patterns of uneven economic development, anticipates our contemporary need for subtler forms of comprehension in order to overcome the recurring shortfalls and deficits of modern politics. To read Scott today is not simply to engage with the most finely documented version of the prehistory of our political landscape but to engage with it at a level of human sympathy and understanding that is more commonly attributed to Scott's heirs among the nineteenth-century novelists.

For the past several years I have offered a third-year undergraduate class, Romanticism and the Novel, to be taught over two twelve-week semesters. Scott's fiction lies at the center of both semesters. The first nearly always recruits well—it includes, after all, both Jane Austen and Mary Shelley among a range of European and American fiction. Embedded in this is usually *The Bride of Lammermoor*, followed immediately by James Fenimore Cooper's *The Last of the Mohicans*. I choose *Bride* partly because it is the shortest of the major Scottish novels, partly because its putatively tragic structure offers some discussion of matters of genre, and partly because of the gothic dimension of some aspects of its plotting.

The class is carefully prepared in the preceding weeks. We try to imagine or recover a culture in which reading was a central activity and one that determined the sources and circulation of information more generally. Some of the novels on the way will have included Johann Wolfgang von Goethe's *The Sorrows of Young Werther*; Ann Radcliffe's *A Sicilian Romance*, perhaps in conjunction with Jane Austen's tribute/riposte *Northanger Abbey*; William Godwin's *Caleb Williams*; Charles Brockden Brown's *Wieland*; the Marquis de Sade's *Misfortunes of Virtue*; Maria Edgeworth's *Castle Rackrent* and *Ennui* (mercifully still available together in Marilyn Butler's Penguin volume). Cooper will be followed by, perhaps, James Hogg's *Confessions of a Justified Sinner*. To preserve the international dimension, I will include some of E. T. A. Hoffman's tales, Honoré Balzac's *Père Goriot*, and a final excursion into Aleksander Pushkin's verse novel *Eugene Onegin*.

We take seriously Sade's contention in his 1800 "Reflections on the Novel" that the gothic romance is a symptom of the revolutionary period through which humankind is now living. We see this statement as complementing and anticipating Lukács's claim in *The Historical Novel* that the new genres of the period reflect the entry of the masses into history and political consciousness. Indeed the sheer proliferation of embryonic fictional genres that the course explores is seen as consistent with the categories of "experiment" and "project" to be found in the social thought and activity of the period.

Thus in the approach to *Lammermoor*, Goethe provides clues to the valorization of an Ossianic Scotland. But he also provides, in his use of Homer, a more general justification of the Doric virtues identifiable with the Rousseauesque invocation of noble savagery and the Roman Republican patria. Werther will identify the emotional violence of his response to his travails with that of an oppressed nation seeking to free itself from tyranny. Goethe's admiration for Johann Gottfried von Herder's early theorization of national identity, based on Herder's encounter with the rich fabric of Slavonic life and culture that surrounded his posting as Lutheran minister in the east Prussian marches, will find a curious echo in Edgeworth's glossary to *Castle Rackrent*. Here, suddenly, is cited an untraceable popular Estonian rhyme, articulating the analogous "resistance" of the Irish peasantry to the feudal impositions of an ethnically and culturally alien landowning class (128). The preface to *Rackrent* (conventionally attributed to Edgeworth *père*—Maria's father, Richard Lovell Edgeworth) also contains the risible prediction that

> [n]ations as well as individuals gradually lose attachment to their identity, and the present generation is amused rather than offended by the ridicule that is thrown upon their ancestors. . . . When Ireland loses her identity by an union with Great Britain, she will look back with a smile of good-humoured complacence on the Sir Kits and Sir Condys of her former existence. (128)

Richard Lovell Edgeworth ended up, for whatever reasons, voting in the Dublin parliament against the union. A comparable division between Scott's avowed unionism and his palpable Jacobite sympathies is manifest in *Lammermoor* by the competing claims to the Ravenswood estates in the Scottish borders. Edgar's redundant claim of feudal custom is of necessity overturned by the long arm of modern law, invested with script and contract, represented in Sir William Ashton. Scott's novel shows how the victory of a particular economic interest group drives the political embrace of the union, while it marks richly and sympathetically the ideological and cultural, the sheerly human, costs of the process.

Werther also provides an early instance of the key motif of the community of readers anxious to share or defend their tastes. This is apparent not only in the dedication of the book itself—"let this little book be your friend" (23)—but also in the critical exchange between Lotte and Werther on the merits of Oliver Goldsmith's *The Vicar of Wakefield.* We can trace this through Austen's *Northanger Abbey* (or indeed her *Sense and Sensibility*, one of the alternative Austen texts from the course), to Edgeworth's idealized mixed-sex "reading group" of Lady Geraldine and Cecil Devereux in *Ennui.* The ambiguous function of the solitary bourgeois reader, consoled but vulnerable, as with Lucy Ashton's perhaps anachronistic taste for "romance," is as much a topic of Scott's novel as it is a real issue in the period's means of fictional production. We are thus able to explore the conflicted constructions of male and female readerships, as well as those related contrasts between male and female spheres of activity. Hunting, shooting, matchmaking, politics, and the rites of hospitality are in fact never as clearly gendered in Scott's model of the past as they will become in the Regency world he inhabited. Lucy's loyalties are divided between love for her hardheaded, practical lawyer-father and for the embodied relic of a tale-telling feudal culture in Edgar Ravenswood. That Scott himself was both lawyer and businessman, as well as regaler of Scottish song and legend, significantly enriches his account of the "risks" of the heightened female sensibility that preoccupied so many novelists.

Radcliffe, Sade, and Godwin all provide significant variations on the presentation of patriarchal power, which is depicted both as a function of political oppression and in very specific forms of physical and mental violence. Again Scott extends dialectically these narrative strategies. Lady Ashton's appetite for political and social power is set as boldly against her daughter's typical passivity as Sade sets his Juliette against the parodic feminine idiocy or innocence of her sister Justine. When Lady Ashton, rather than Lucy, leads the wedding dance with the virile figure of her son-in-law Bucklaw, we may sense Scott's perception of a sublimated sexual power that is akin in purpose to the serial exploitations of Sade's wicked "common sense" heroine. Both are perhaps cognate with Maria de Vellorno, the stagey sex-crazed duenna of *A Sicilian Romance*. Both Sade and Scott, however, are interested in more than the traditional mythic role of the femme fatale.

From Godwin too emerge important insights into the masculine dimensions of patriarchy. The extended and profoundly Hegelian romance of master and slave in *Caleb Williams* is perhaps specifically echoed in Scott's choice of name, Caleb Balderstone, for Edgar's ever-loyal retainer. Without Caleb, Edgar is virtually nothing, a mere body looking for an otherwise no-longer-available recognition. Caleb's piratical raid on the village of Wolf's Hope for food to entertain Edgar's guests articulates perfectly the culture of what Scott elsewhere describes as "feudal waste," a paradoxically predatory system that fails to rationalize either production or distribution for its members, yet one that is rich in human bonds. Herein also lies the political heart of the novel, its persistent attentiveness to the struggle for control of the means of material production in its simplest forms of food and shelter. Caleb's characteristic loquaciousness, his commitment to good "crack" (i.e., conversation), his valuation of narrative invention invite comparison with Edgeworth's impersonation of the voice of Old Thady in *Castle Rackrent,* as well as her caustic dismissal of Joe Kelly the Irish rebel manservant who briefly but dangerously seduces Glenthorn's political attention in *Ennui*.

So, as I have suggested, we come reasonably carefully prepared for the encounter with Scott. We have accessed some feminist, some cultural materialist, some queer readings. Just before their first anxious foray into border territory, class members are alerted to the "difficulties" of Scott's opening chapters. A week or so before the class, news breaks of long-standing hospital appointments, unexpected family crises, not-to-be-missed job interviews. Undismayed, we await what I still hope will be the "conversion" experience. The slow, masterly unfolding of a plot that realizes the full complexity of human motive still has the capacity to surprise and reveal. For those who have struggled, but not quite fallen, we focus on the second chapter. First we attend to details of landscape in which economic conditions are reflected as finely as any picturesque perspective. Then we gloss the broad but precise overview of British history, the history of the Scottish union in the wake of the Irish, before considering Scott's carefully weighed reflections on monarchy, tyranny, absenteeism, constitutionalism, and corruption. We consider the first indications of Lady Ashton's character in relation to the politics of the family and the relations between the family and the interest group. We speculate about the continuing political potency of such kinship networks. Finally we wonder about the precocious responsibilities thrust on Edgar Ravenswood, "a youth of about twenty years of age," and how Scott intended us to rethink issues of identity and inheritance as they are found in Shakespeare's *Hamlet* (Scott, *Bride* [ed. Alexander] 20). Thus we can examine the tension between an older idea of character as an ideal, if divided, accompaniment to a particular social role and the emergent Romantic concept of character as a dynamic and personal process of growth and education. Indeed, given Scott's explicit mobilization of not just *Hamlet* but also both *Romeo and Juliet* and *Macbeth*, the relations between stage character and the "characterization" techniques of the novel are available for discussion.

This in turn will lead those who have finished the work of reading to account for the extraordinary social range of Scott's "characters" and for how the political articulacy of Johnny Mortsheugh, Ailsie Gourlay, and the villagers of Wolf's Hope—the sheer fullness of their representation—serves as an echo of the popular revolutionary aspirations of the epoch. This excess of representation with all its demands on the reader's attention (often in a formidably broad Scottish vernacular) has its latent political energy. Students more familiar with later realist fiction will be able to recognize how some of that energy and articulacy is fitfully, if not systematically, eroded in the century that follows.

The more palpable thrills of Cooper's *The Last of the Mohicans*, the following week, perfectly establish the dominant role of the genre initiated by Scott and the alternative uses to which it will be put. The bloody implosion of Brown's ideal colonial community in *Wieland* has already prepared us for a close examination of the contradictions to be found in the putatively progressive project of these American representatives of the "international" bourgeoisie (more profoundly, perhaps, than *Frankenstein*). We are able to focus boldly on questions of ethnicity, violent conquest, and the formation of national identity and myth. The shift from tragic plot to that of epic and romance in Cooper's novel anticipates usefully the terms on which the second part of the course will be conducted.

The first part of the course concludes with two out of three further novels, each distinctive for its sheer brio, and these in some sense continue to anticipate the second part. Hogg's *Confessions of a Justified Sinner* perfectly complements in its chronology and themes *The Bride of Lammermoor*: feckless aristocracy pitted against puritan ambition and cunning just before the 1707 union. It gives a rich flavor too of the cultural and class (as well as the remarkable persistence of theological) divisions that characterized the Scottish literary scene of the period, reflecting, as it may, the troubled bonds that tied Hogg and Scott in mutual friendship and rivalry. It beautifully consolidates our perception of the radical democratic potential of Scottish letters and the uneasy roots of these within the covenanting traditions of popular belief. Its formal and metaphysical bravura extends the work of both *Wieland* and *Frankenstein*, while it lays some of the seeds for the more detailed study of Scott's *Old Mortality* that lies with all its terrorist menace in the wings.

From here we move either to Pushkin's *Eugene Onegin* or Balzac's *Père Goriot*. Pushkin's extraordinary verse novel is of course sui generis. In one sense it prepares us, as do Scott and Cooper, for Pushkin's *The Captain's Daughter* and Nikolai Gogol's *Taras Bulba* in the second part of the course. But it also activates in the most provocative way questions of the constitution of a national literature, whereby international cultural signs and forms enter a heterogeneous milieu, are transformed locally, and then return in the guise of a wholly new genre. Nevertheless Tatanya's readings and misreading in literature and life throughout *Onegin* make for interesting comparisons with those of Lucy (as does her complex rapport with a feminized folklore), just as Edgar's rigid but troubled sense of the obligations of class propriety suggests parallels with Eugene's only apparently youthful insouciance. Balzac's novel, on the other hand, manifests the ways in which the realist novel of post-Revolutionary Parisian life takes not only its dramatization of the processes of class struggle from the model of Scott but also much of its raw mythic energy from Cooper. Ever since the execution of Louis XVI fictional form has been vexed by a crisis in patriarchy. In Balzac this is made wholly explicit. We have witnessed too, not least in the example of Scott, the exposure of authorship—and thus cultural authority—to both the opportunities and traumas of the marketplace. Balzac's ambiguous recoil from newly aggressive developments in the marriage market generates a new kind of sexually sophisticated female character. Such developments in turn serve to reinforce that strain of homosocial bonding, now named in the figure of Vautrin, that we have had cause to trace through the course thus far.

Above I invoke the hope and expectation of a "conversion" experience in reading Scott, a return to the conditions of his heyday. I may cite here the exemplary case of a sports-science major who discovered a key difference in the narrative structures of *Waverley* and *The Last of the Mohicans*. While Waverley is often allowed to sleep at the end of chapters before waking to his "dream," every attempt at rest in Cooper is violently interrupted, with the effect, in this case, of sustaining an extended dreamlike state of arousal in the reader. Similarly, students from ethnic-minority backgrounds are likely to find, buried in Scott's only apparently alien narratives, provocative but sympathetic treatment of highly charged questions of confessional and linguistic identity under "modern" conditions. In this hope, the second half of the course makes only a flimsy attempt to conceal, under the title Romanticism and the Novel 2, its real subject and subtitle, The Historical Novel. It recruits sufficiently perhaps one year in three a gallant crew of readers who signed on for the whole voyage out, plus a couple of late entrants who have caught the sense of adventure and risk from a favorable run before the wind in the first semester.

So we start, of course, with *Waverley*. Rather than let the novels simply read one another as in the first part of the course, we take onboard some of the critical evaluation of the genre: Lukács, for the boldness of his assertions; the opening chapters of George Dekker's *The American Historical Romance* (for the sheer lucidity of its exposition of the historiographical models); Franco Moretti's *Atlas of the European Novel, 1800–1900*, for its perversely suggestive ingenuity; William Hazlitt's essay from *The Spirit of the Age*, for its virtuoso celebration of Scott's anti-ego. At some point we draw on Richard Altick's *The English Common Reader*, as well as Philip Bolton's magisterial compilation *Scott Dramatised*. Thus we can measure the sheer scale of Scott's achievement in transforming both the material conditions of the novel and its broader reception within the culture of the period. We proceed now at a more leisurely pace appropriate to epic, digressing at ease, reflecting and sometimes researching questions of history, politics, economic development, military strategy, theology, justice, and penal reform as these seem to determine the lives of the characters. We try to account for the narrative power of these novels, but we are also ready to acknowledge the slacker sequences when our Homer nods.

Usually I follow *Waverley* with *Old Mortality*. This novel seems to bear most closely on our contemporary world of linked but disparate economic and theological systems, the intransigence of their agents, the recurrent outbreak of terrorist acts and the concomitant reprisals, the curiously familiar invocation of a hostile military terrain, the competing codes of a professional soldiery and those of a potentially self-immolating popular resistance, arbitrary arrest and judgment, and torture. I have used both *The Heart of Mid-Lothian* and *Rob Roy* in the past to some effect. Both novels raise and eloquently test related issues of loyalty, courage, endurance, honor, revenge, cowardice, and mercy. They test these in a climate that is represented, not unsympathetically, as one of secular calculation and self-interest that includes romantic desire. If doors open onto the historical past, illuminating, as Lukács insisted, the nature of class struggle as its effective engine, they also open onto a living present.

If we had a graduate program in the field, I should certainly want to add *Redgauntlet*, *Ivanhoe*, and *Quentin Durward* for students to encounter the full range and subtlety of Scott's art. Meanwhile we move on to a brace of Cooper's Leatherstocking tales: *The Prairie* and *The Deerslayer*. The epic impulse may be even stronger in Cooper than Scott. In the earlier novel we find an apparently primal and featureless landscape, something like Locke's version of America as tabula rasa, haltingly made over into Western consciousness and thus into a form of possession. The role of its indigenous inhabitants as it takes fuller and fuller shape toward the end of the novel serves as the living embodiment of what is both a recognition and refusal of the morally grubby outriders of a process of imperial conquest that is relentless and inevitable. Here the form of the historical novel turns into a fantastic and grotesque pastoral, an account of a promised land for which, with the death of Natty Bumppo and after the extinction of its native people, there may be no worthy claimants. *The Deerslayer* returns us to Natty Bumppo's youth, offering another version of this fall, redeemed only finally by Hawkeye (as he "becomes" in the novel through his first act of killing) and his honoring of his parole. If Scott compels us to consider the full complexity of how European civilization is developed and contested, with his novels' external dramas of combat and interior dramas of choice and conscience, then Cooper seems to return us to the question of the formation of civilization ab initio. He gives us starkly secular tales of pagan dignity and energy, interwoven with fragments of Old Testament biblical narrative in which the New Testament code of redemption and salvation hardly seems to figure at all. To illustrate this we compare passages culled from both Genesis and Exodus, from some of the more vengeful of the psalms, as well as from the *Iliad*. Just insofar as Cooper distances himself from actual history his fiction may be thought to raise a series of purely philosophical issues.

It is, alas, unlikely that undergraduate students will find the appetite for Alessandro Manzoni's *I promessi sposi*. A key testimony to the rapid dissemination of the genre and its explicitly political function in the formation of an Italian national consciousness and culture, it is equally notable for precisely what Scott ironizes and Cooper refuses, its insistence on the power of Christian regeneration. First Fra Cristoforo and then L'Innominato are redeemed. The sainthood of Cardinal Borromeo is taken as seriously as are the issues of Enlightenment health care during a providential visitation of the plague. We can offer only the briefest account of the Manzoni phenomenon: the painstaking rendering of the text into modern Tuscan and its subsequent role in the Italian school system; the Milanese milieu that gave us Gaetano Donizetti's *Lucia di Lammermoor*; the political meanings of the nineteenth-century operatic repertoire, north as well as south of the Alps; the incorporation of the story of national liberation and unification into the mainstream of Western liberal thought.

Thus our next move into Russian imperial territory has to be understood as less than wholly typical of Scott's legacy. Pushkin's *The Captain's Daughter* provides the most elegant and suggestive reprise of Scott's work there is, and students will always embrace its magnificent economy. But we also note the extraordinary—one is almost tempted to say miraculous—strength of its movement toward reconciliation between people and power, between children and parents, between romance and reality. Its understated insistence on the violence that sustains the project of progress may stop us in its tracks as it is very literally "brought home." Gogol's *Taras Bulba*, on the other hand, is experienced as horrible: in its ethnic hatreds, its palpable misogyny, its sardonic invocation of patriarchal brutality. We may read it alongside Cooper, but we can (must) also read it alongside our buried knowledge of the dark centuries of European history that succeed it and continue to determine our own: the movement of peoples through swathes of territory where the natural frontiers of nineteenth-century nation-state theory are wholly absent and where invading armies can recruit locally. The question now arises whether we are to read Gogol the Ukrainian or the Russian novelist. The owner and backer of Heart of Midlothian, the football club with which I began, claims a Lithuanian identity that is his as far as his patronym of Romanov allows.

The course will conclude with Charles Dickens's *Barnaby Rudge.* This is the novel that Dickens had long on his stocks as "Gabriel Varden: The Locksmith of London," evidence of his aspiration as would-be novelist rather than the producer of the spectacular popular improvisation that underwrote his fame and wealth. The pervasive violence of its imagination of the father-son relationship together with its rootedness in the "real" historical record of late-eighteenth-century London ("tis sixty years since," of course) suggests Dickens's wealth of oedipal indebtedness to Scott as his unacknowledged master of the English language novel. By now the form reeks of an unconditional contempt for the barbaric English past, not least its capital code. A certain kind of Biedermeier smugness appears to inherit the earth in the form of the morally and politically cleansed Varden household at the end of the novel, replacing the ruthless gentility of what is clearly intended to be an account of England's ancien régime. Up to this point, on either course, we have had little to do with the ideological presumptions of "narrative closure." If Dickens has the capacity to bully us a little in that direction, it nevertheless remains true that under the liberty of Scott's "masterful shadow" we find as perhaps nowhere else in his work an unapologetic working-class eloquence in the figure of Hugh, a Michelangelesque hero who brings to the scaffold an emboldening but subversive rhetoric that recalls the trial of Evan Dhu in *Waverley* or Mause Headrigg's rebuttal of Lady Bellenden's feudal exactions in *Old Mortality.*

We stop here, but provisionally. Next year, or the one after, the campaign will reach *War and Peace.* Was it only under particular cultural conditions that it became axiomatic that this was the masterpiece of the greatest novelist ever? And how do we measure Tolstoy against the putative English majesty and range of the Scott-riddled George Eliot, rewriting *The Heart of Mid-Lothian* as *Adam Bede*? "experimenting" disastrously with *Romola*? finding a "Polish" source of moral and sexual renewal in Will Ladislaw in *Middlemarch*? imagining a new-old nation-state as the resolution of *Daniel Deronda*?

This "old" canon has received its quittance. We have plenty of contemporary "historicist" fiction that gratifies and exploits our curiosity about the past. It is often as entertaining as it is well researched. The historical novel itself is a mere bastard popular form. I first read Walter Scott not only alongside the work of Lukács but also with Bertolt Brecht's critique of Lukács in view. When I began to write about him, the Marxist terrain had been occupied by high theory and Scott's textual self-consciousness seemed susceptible to poststructural readings. The rich historical-textual apparatus was as central as imagined speech in the construction of the novels. All the novels seemed to invite multiple interpretations. William Hazlitt's essay had announced "the death of the author" well before Roland Barthes and Michel Foucault. Yet, despite this abundant "play" of meaning, the novels remained rooted in representations of the conditions of labor, the often harsh material lives of their characters. Perhaps "character" after all was not a redundant critical category but an essential part of a politically radical aesthetic.

But Scott can prepare us for many other fresh encounters. Teachers in British universities have in the last twenty years had access to a wider world of English studies supported often generously by European Union funding in the form of Erasmus and Socrates exchange programs. However generous the official funding, it is unlikely to match the hospitality and welcome of academic hosts whom I have met all over Europe. Against this convivial background, I have had countless opportunities to teach and lecture on Scott and the historical novel to students at home in more than one literary and cultural tradition. Each invitation to teach becomes an invitation to find out more about each national literature; each national trajectory of nineteenth-century development; each variation on the example of Scott, explicit or otherwise. Sometimes these lectures must seem like willful acts of exhumation of a cultural "unconscious" that is both local and pan-European. Elsewhere there are far more exciting lecture tours and readings by living writers, courtesy of the British Council. More exciting for us in Scott studies, however, may be the prospect of whole bodies of work, sometimes yet to be translated, from literatures that take their shape and themes from the continuing revolution of Romanticism. For the moment I can only recommend that there is a project of comparative literature in which Scott will have a central role. We can read his legacy everywhere. We read it not just in the mountain ranges where the bandits mutated into liberators, in the provincial towns reclaimed as capital cities where the young lawyers plotted sacrifice and struggle, in the squares of those cities with their ubiquitous statues of both the writers and the soldiers of the revolution. We also read it in the long, often loose and baggy, even clumsy, novels and poems that attempted to invoke some compelling national story, to convey some rich dignity to the labor and the aspirations of peasant people speaking a multiplicity of languages. As teachers and scholars of Scott we have the opportunity and privilege of a dialogue beyond that of the conventional preoccupations of Anglo-American letters.

For me the dialogue has been enriched in Sofia by the encounter with Ivan Vasov, author of *Under the Yoke*, a tale of the abortive Bulgarian revolt of 1873, of which, in an introduction to an anonymous English translation, Edmund Gosse observes, "it is like seeing *Old Mortality* written by Morton, or finding the autobiography of Ivanhoe" (xi). In Timisoara and Cluj-Napoca there are grainy photographs on the walls of the Philology departments of, among others, Liviu Rebreanu, the author of a Tolstoyan trilogy of novels that figure the belated twentieth-century formation of the Romanian state. In Brest, just outside of which Breton is still a living language, there is the prospect of reengagement with *Les Chouans*, the first novel Balzac published under his own slightly spurious name of "De Balzac." At IULM University in Milan I knew it was possible to invoke Manzoni's novel in all the fullness of its institutional afterlife and read it against Scott and Cooper, with their greater frankness in dealing with violence as act rather than mere threat. In Catania, just around the corner from the Verga museum, we can consider how the relative poverty of western Sicilian literary culture nevertheless generated one sure masterpiece in Giuseppe

Tomiasi di Lampedusa's *The Leopard.* Leipzig, in the center of the Saxon plain, provides the topography for Heinrich von Kleist's precocious novella *Michael Kohlhaas,* adumbrating as it does many of Scott's essential themes and reminding us of his rootedness in German literature from the outset of his translation of Goethe's *Goetz von Berlichingen.* At Graz, Leopold von Sacher-Masoch collected a chair in history at the age of twenty-three. From here came a whole cycle of historical novels, buried now under his infamous reputation as author of *Venus in Furs.* If Masoch understood some of the power with which Scott endowed so many of his female characters, there is an important sense in which Scott, in what otherwise might be thought of as minor work like *The Talisman,* was already deploying the paradoxical extremes of the sexual relations that earned the term *romantic* as enduringly as did the political and cultural revolutions we all inherit.

"What a list of names! What a host of associations! What a thing is human life! What a power is that of genius! What a world of thought and feeling is thus rescued from oblivion!" (Hazlitt, "Sir Walter Scott" 230)—so Hazlitt remarks in his peroration on the Waverley novels. He points to a whole world of reading pleasure, "a new edition of human nature." The work of reclamation, which finds purpose and productivity in that pleasure, has only just begun.

Scott, the History of the Novel, and the History of Fiction

Ian Duncan

Occupying, indeed constituting, a turning point in the history of the genre, Scott's novels can crown an eighteenth-century-novel course, open a course on the nineteenth-century novel, or form the keystone of a course on Romantic fiction—productively set, if the instructor wishes, alongside the more usual candidate for these positions, Jane Austen (see Gottlieb's essay, in this volume). As a representative Scott title many teachers choose *Waverley*, which after all personifies a certain kind of romanticism in its dreamy protagonist and allegorically rehearses a "rise of the novel" through rival discourses of romance and history. Personally, I have found *Waverley* quite hard to teach to undergraduates, in part because it takes so long for the story to take hold, and the historiographical and metafictional preliminaries can try the patience of readers new to Scott. (*Waverley* goes better in graduate courses or upper-level seminars, where students approach it with some prior experience.) I look at *Rob Roy*, my preferred Scott novel for courses in the novel and Romanticism, in the last part of this essay. *Redgauntlet* works beautifully in an eighteenth-century-novel course, as its subtitle, *A Tale of the Eighteenth Century*, promises. I have taught *Ivanhoe* and *The Heart of Mid-Lothian* as first offerings in courses on nineteenth-century fiction: the first for its invention (and critical scrutiny) of an imperial myth of English origins that still shapes the popular conception of the Middle Ages, the second as prototype of a distinctive form of the Victorian novel, with its multiple plots, tumultuous heterogeneity of languages and genres, pan-British geographic and social range, and, not least, its pioneering placement of a working-class heroine and critique of a social order through trials of fallen maternity and female virtue (developed in later novels such as Elizabeth Gaskell's *Ruth*, George Eliot's *Adam Bede*, and Thomas Hardy's *Tess of the D'Urbervilles*).

The typical account of Scott's importance, following Georg Lukács, understands him as the father of the historical novel. Scott did not merely establish a distinctive subset of the novel, defined by a clearly marked period setting; he made the novel as such historical and in doing so equipped it to be the dominant literary medium, throughout nineteenth-century Europe and its colonies, for imagining collective forms of identity under the pressures of modernization. Other essays in this book, notably Simon Edwards's, discuss that great achievement. Recent scholarship has refined, revised, and in some cases challenged Lukács's identification of Scott's originality with an invention of historical realism, calling our attention to precursor genres such as earlier French and English historical novels (Maxwell, "Inundations"), gothic fiction (Duncan, *Modern Romance*; Robertson; Watt, *Contesting the Gothic*), Jacobin and anti-Jacobin novels (Trumpener, "National Character"), and the Irish national tale

(Garside; Ferris, *Achievement*; Trumpener, *Bardic Nationalism*), as well as variant generic frameworks such as the bildungsroman (Moretti, *Way of the World*) and the eighteenth-century forms of "romance revival" (Duncan, *Modern Romance*). Attention to these literary-historical contexts can help students reflect not so much on the antiquarian dissensions of current scholarship as on the contested rather than settled terrain of the novel in Scott's own day, epitomized in the opening chapter of *Waverley* (discussed in McCracken-Flesher's essay in this volume).

The national tale, developed by Irish women writers in the early decades of the nineteenth century, provides an especially provocative case for comparison. Its recent critics have made claims not only for the overlooked priority of (notably) Sydney Owenson's (Lady Morgan's) *The Wild Irish Girl* in establishing some of the formal and thematic innovations ascribed to *Waverley* but also for a more radical nationalist tradition that was eclipsed by Scott's critical and commercial success (see Trumpener, *Bardic Nationalism*, 128–57). *The Wild Irish Girl* establishes the "allegory of union" in which a private marriage plot articulates the national historic theme of a cultural reconciliation between the modernizing Anglo-British core (in the person of a polite English tourist) and an archaic Celtic hinterland (in the person of a dispossessed Irish heiress). Owenson's novel, modeling a regional autonomy of social and cultural forms within the framework of British union, supplies a dissident, sentimental, feminist alternative not only to Scott but to the Irish precursor who was acknowledged by Scott in the postscript to *Waverley*, Maria Edgeworth. Edgeworth's tales invoke the Scottish Enlightenment programs of political-economic and moral "improvement" addressed in the Waverley novels, although in neither case are those programs adopted or applied in any simple way. *Ennui* makes for an especially resonant comparison with *Waverley*, since it too tests a chronically indecisive protagonist in the historical crisis of rebellion and works out a plot in which a primitive national identity has to be discovered and destroyed in order for that protagonist to come into his own as a modern British gentleman. It's worth asking students to weigh Edgeworth's complex and subtle artistry alongside her apparent conservatism in comparison with Owenson, as well as with Scott, and to think about the relations between fiction and didacticism as well as fiction and history in all three authors. (My own view: for all that Scott took from the Irish national tale, in neither Owenson nor Edgeworth do we read the emergence of history and fiction—as discrete, autonomous, but dialectically conversant terms—that takes place in Scott and that constitutes his originality.)

The present essay addresses Scott's famous invention, historical fiction, from the other side of the equation. Where most recent commentary has fastened on history as the key to the innovative force of the Waverley novels, I suggest that Scott remade the novel into the typical literary genre of modernity by associating it with the categorical autonomy of fiction—that aspect of the novel that distinguishes it from history and specifies it as such. Here I am indebted to

Catherine Gallagher's argument that "the rise of fiction is not coterminous with the rise of the novel" and that fictionality, "the novel's most important formal trait," achieves full articulation only in the second half of the eighteenth century (164, 173); even then, I contend, the formal equivalence between fictionality and the novel is not fully realized until Scott historicizes it in *Waverley* and its successors. As a teacher, I find that this line of inquiry can help students repossess the distinctive pleasures of reading Scott—pleasures mislaid over the last hundred years or so through the vicissitudes of the history of taste, but to be relished all the more keenly once rediscovered. At least in the classroom I try to make that recovery of a form of pleasure take precedence over literary history for its own sake (however pleasurable, in the relative privacy of scholarship, we may find literary history for its own sake).

In a course on eighteenth-century fiction Scott's novels obligingly do much of the pedagogical work of situating themselves in relation to their predecessors. *Redgauntlet* presents itself as an anthology of the literary genres digested in the novel in the course of its "rise," including the polite letter, law case, criminal autobiography, family history, gothic tale, and the vernacular forms of regional popular tradition such as folktale and song collection. (Wandering Willie's musical exchange with the captive Darsie Latimer makes clear the status of the "national air" as an item in a *collection*.) *Redgauntlet* starts out as an epistolary novel—a genre canonized, at the time the novel is set, by Samuel Richardson (whom Scott had recently been editing), although largely obsolete by the 1820s (see Watson; Price; K. Sutherland). Scott puts this material to work as follows: Two young men, Alan Fairford and Darsie Latimer, exchange letters in which they liken themselves to the rakish correspondents Lovelace and Belford in Richardson's *Clarissa*. The second volume opens with an abrupt abandonment of the epistolary form and the onset of an impersonal "narrative" recounting Darsie's disappearance. A few chapters later, Darsie resumes his narration, but now in the form of a journal written in captivity. Instead of a Lovelace, in other words, Darsie has turned out to be a Pamela—a destiny fulfilled near the end of the novel when he is forced to dress in women's clothes. In the last chapters all the novel's intrigues converge on Father Crackenthorpe's inn, a carnivalesque compound of all the inns in novels since *Don Quixote*: the sanctioned site of storytelling, chance meetings, crossed intentions, mistaken identities, and the confusion and resolution of plots. Here, the historical plot that has been brewing—the second return of Prince Charles Edward Stuart for a final attempt to seize the British throne, twenty years after the 1745 Jacobite rising—fizzles out, without the tragic eruption we have been expecting. The Hanoverian general who appears in the midst of the conspirators reveals that he has known all about it all along, and he won't take any further action if the gentlemen simply go home. The failure of the Jacobite plot to enter public life and become history reinforces its status as Scott's own fictional invention—no such secret return of Charles Edward took place in the summer of 1765. Scott made it up. With its dissolution into a register of fiction that affirms all the more powerfully the present dispensation of historical reality, the ending of *Redgauntlet* affords perhaps the most concentrated, thematically distinctive, and richly pleasurable example of the aesthetic that Jerome McGann has called "Scott's romantic postmodernity." I like to ask students to reflect on our enjoyment and recognition of this wonderfully satisfying anticlimax. Is what Scott is doing here "postmodern"—and, if so, in what sense? How does this resonate with the metafictional and counterfactual turns we have come to know so well in more recent narrative?

One strategy I use to help students reflect on what Scott is up to is to supply a philosophical as well as historical context, by turning to David Hume's *Treatise of Human Nature*, a work that founded the intellectual project of the Scottish Enlightenment transmitted to the European novel through Scott. Invoking Hume works well in courses that emphasize historical context—eighteenth-century and Scottish—but the example can just as effectively be presented in its own terms. I ask students to read the famous conclusion to book 1 of the *Treatise*. Here the philosopher suddenly steps forward as a character, in a confessional, dramatic, novelistic mode of representation, reflecting on the subjective stakes of the argument he has been making. Skeptical reason, exposing as imaginary the metaphysical foundations of reality, provokes a crisis that is not just intellectual but social, moral, and psychological:

> I am at first affrighted and confounded with that forelorn solitude, in which I am plac'd in my philosophy, and fancy myself some strange uncouth monster, who not being able to mingle and unite in society, has been expell'd all human commerce, and left utterly abandon'd and disconsolate.

The crisis resolves itself in a spontaneous reentry into "the common affairs of life":

> Most fortunately it happens, that since reason is incapable of dispelling these clouds, nature herself suffices to that purpose, and cures me of this philosophical melancholy and delirium, either by relaxing this bent of mind, or by some avocation, and lively impression of my senses, which obliterate all these chimeras. I dine, I play a game of backgammon, I converse, and am merry with my friends; and when after three or four hour's amusement, I wou'd return to these speculations, they appear so cold, and strain'd, and ridiculous, that I cannot find it in my heart to enter into them further.
>
> Here then I find myself absolutely determin'd to live, and talk, and act like other people in the common affairs of life. (Hume, *Treatise* 316)

Intercourse with others, "the commerce and society of men" (317), produces the everyday reality in which we live. Reason, rigorously applied, will expose this everyday reality as a work of fiction: "The memory, senses, and understanding" are "all of them founded on the imagination" (313), which fills in the gaps between discrete sense impressions and writes phenomena into an intelligible text of experience. What stabilizes this work of imagination, and gives the fiction its "reality effect," is its shared, customary status. "[All] our reasonings concerning causes and effects are deriv'd from nothing but custom" (234): custom, the socializing force of repetition and habituation, weaves together an intelligible, familiar world and our identities in it.

Hume's *Treatise of Human Nature* provides what we might call the intellectual plot of Enlightenment, an epistemological analogue to the historical scheme of modernization tracked in Scott's novels. Skeptical reason dismantles a traditional world of metaphysical illusion, but that dismantling, with its psychic effects of disenchantment, is only half the story. What completes it is the dialectical return to reality in a sentimental rather than rational commitment to "common life," a social medium we are obliged to share by the very impulses—the passions and affections—that make up human nature. Our commitment to common life is strengthened rather than subverted by our intermittent awareness (a novel reader's awareness) that it is an imaginary construction of reality sustained by custom. Hume's plot of Enlightenment gives us the complex dialectic of modernization that structures *Waverley*. Toward the end of the story Scott's narrator tells us that the hero "felt himself entitled to say firmly, though perhaps with a sigh, that the romance of his life was ended, and that its real history had now commenced" (283). This reflection has too often been taken literally as an authoritative summary of the novel in which it appears. Far from disappearing from the narrative at this moment of chastened self-reflection, however, fictional devices intensify to rescue Waverley from the consequences of treason and reward him with a bride and estate (that estate itself marvelously redeemed and restored; see Duncan, *Modern Romance* 92–105; Lee 23–24). *Waverley* narrates, thus, not only the emergence of modern civil society through the final conquest of an ancient regime (Catholic, Jacobite, feudal, tribal) but also the Humean dialectical progression from "metaphysical" illusion through melancholy disenchantment to a sentimental and ironic reattachment to the world. A key part of that story is the story of the novel itself: *Waverley* unfolds an internal allegory of the rise of the novel as modern national form, in which the movement from archaic imaginary modes of "romance" through an empirically exigent "history" yields a third, synthetic term, the combination of romance and history that is realized in the novel we are reading. The historical novel constitutes the vantage point of modernity as it produces the plot of its own production. Scott's novels, reflexively insistent on their fictional status, mobilize skepticism rather than faith as the subjective cast of their reader's relation to history. As in Hume, this is a moderate or conservative skepticism that underwrites the legitimacy of a modern political order founded on custom, on the weight of historical circumstance accreted over generations, rather than on any appeal to foundational principles.

Following Hume, then, Scott made fiction the art of a liberal ideology, one that stakes its modernity on the claim of having superseded "fundamentalist" modes of ideological identification—the Enlightenment terms for which are *superstition* and *fanaticism*—through its capacity to help us stand apart from and reflect critically on historical modes of being. Scott more thoroughly explores the equivalence of modernity with fictionality in his second novel, *Guy Mannering*, in which a full-scale reanimation of the traditional tropes and figures of romance stabilizes the fracturing, alienating shifts of modernization, represented here on a world-historical scale, from the coast of southwest Scotland to India. Scott does not simply cast romance as the medium of premodern forms of value and allegiance, although, influentially, he does that. The novel performs a marvelous domestication and renovation of the cultural resources of what Fredric Jameson (in *The Political Unconscious*) calls "magical narrative," so perilous in the theater of colonial struggle, whether in India or at home; it does so by converting romance from ancient magic to modern fiction, an acknowledged act of the imagination (see Duncan, *Modern Romance*). The Gypsy matriarch Meg Merrilies turns her curse on the new order into a benison and helps restore the lost son to his inheritance; in doing so, dying, she cedes her authority to the enlightened Edinburgh lawyer, Pleydell, who invokes the decorum of fictionality, irony, and play:

> Look ye, Dominie, if you speak another word till I give you leave, I will read three sentences out of the Black Acts, whisk my cane round my head three times, undo all the magic of this night's work, and conjure Harry Bertram back again into Vanbeest Brown. (308)

Melancholy tempers delight at the close of *Guy Mannering*—so I encourage students (as Scott encourages them) to recall what has been lost, the price that has been paid, to bring us to the comic conclusion. In successive novels Scott keeps troubling a liberal-conservative solution that may seem easy or complacent only in critical summaries of it. I turn now to the Scott novel I have taught most successfully in courses on Romantic fiction, *Rob Roy*. The status of *Rob Roy* as Scott's only full-length novel narrated in the first person makes it especially accessible to students—mitigating the dryasdust, ironical and pedantic style that many of them find off-putting in Scott. My main agenda in teaching *Rob Roy* is to help students see how Scott invokes the historical sciences developed in the Scottish Enlightenment, such as anthropology and political economy, in order to subsume them into a distinctively novelistic access to the world-historical order of modernity. Scott's novel offers a knowledge of modernity that unsettles the historical schemes—such as a national history organized in progressive evolutionary stages—it is supposed to serve.

Rob Roy appears to exemplify what influential recent commentators have ascribed to Scott: the imperialist plot of modernization, nation formation, and internal colonialism, marching across the uneven cultural spaces of the new

United Kingdom (see Trumpener, *Bardic Nationalism*; Makdisi; Moretti, *Atlas*; and the essay by Mack and Gilbert in this volume). (The maps of *Waverley* and *Rob Roy* in Moretti's *Atlas* are especially helpful for classroom discussion—ask students what's missing from the *Rob Roy* map, i.e., Glasgow, and what difference its replacement makes to Moretti's thesis.) London and Glasgow represent different states of commercial modernity, the core of the new multinational British Empire, and thus its future. The Jacobite backwater of rustic Northumberland and the wild Highlands—Rob Roy's country—represent a past fated to vanish with the consolidation of the modern state, their concrete forms of social life sublimated into aesthetic trophies for the polite classes, who are the beneficiaries of this process and who are reading the work of fiction—in short, us.

To stop with this insight, however, is to reduce Scott's wonderfully alive and untidy novel to a didactic formula. I encourage students to reflect on the ways that Scott characterizes the novel's different regions and aligns them with particular historical, cultural, and aesthetic associations (these are identified in the notes to my Oxford World's Classics edition): he draws on Defoe's *Tour through the Whole Island of Great Britain* to evoke the emergent mercantile energies of Glasgow, for example, while the Highland chapters are seeded with allusions to barbaric, pagan, or savage cultures, notably of North American Indians. Critics often describe the novel as divided between two characters that constitute opposite poles of cultural and ethical value: one is Rob Roy MacGregor himself, and the other is the Glasgow merchant and magistrate Nicol Jarvie, who personifies (with magnificent comic eloquence) the ascendant commercial virtues of creditworthiness and civic duty (see Mack and Gilbert, in this volume). During Frank's sojourn in Glasgow Jarvie provides a set-piece analysis, according to the principles of Scottish Enlightenment political economy, of the history underpinning this historical novel. Students are quick to notice the disappearance of Jarvie's authority, along with the explanatory force of his analysis, once he and Frank leave Glasgow for the Highlands ("a wild kind of warld by themsells" [300]). It is Rob Roy, the persecuted outlaw, who displays far greater mobility, adaptability, and linguistic and cognitive command as he traverses the different territories of the new United Kingdom, changing his appearance with a preternatural skill. At the end of *Waverley*, the state execution of the chieftain Fergus MacIvor represents the end of clan society and the extinction of an entire glamorous but doomed archaic world. Here, though, Rob Roy outlasts the end of the story after which he is named, and Scott reminds the reader—in defiance of Jarvie's prophecy—that he will not be hanged but die peacefully in bed. In the novel's sole episode of military violence the clan MacGregor defeats a troop of disciplined redcoats. The scene belongs to the theater of colonial struggle, in which an indigenous guerilla force, composed mainly of women and youths, exploits their home terrain to overthrow alien invaders. Scott's readers (it is worth pointing out to students) would be reminded not only of the raising of Highland regiments in the British army to fight imperial wars abroad but also of Britain's recent support of Spanish guerilla troops against Napoleon in the Peninsular campaign. The difference is that these Highlanders cannot be drafted—they remain outlaws, ferocious in their resistance to the military and legal apparatus of the British state.

I encourage students, then, to see how Scott's insistent identification of the Highlanders with "savage" peoples in *Rob Roy* actually disrupts the teleological scheme of an unfolding national modernity that it might seem, on a casual reading, to reinforce. Rob Roy himself, with his freakishly long arms and "fell of thick, short, red hair" (374), bears an uncanny resemblance to that creature stationed at the ambiguous border of the human in late-Enlightenment and Romantic natural philosophy, the orangutan. In this he embodies the emergent anthropological category of the primitive, as it breaks loose from the historical chronology of pastness that at first frames it and reaches toward its later nineteenth-century destiny in a biological discourse of vitalism and "eternal return." Providing students with handouts on the Romantic orangutan (see Simmons) as well as a discussion of subsequent mutations of the figure can be helpful here. Having not arrived at that later scientific destiny, Scott's primitive is not yet confined there, either: the fiction finds imaginative life in the unsettling of fixed knowledges rather than in their new settlement. The Jacobites, exemplified by Diana Vernon's wraithlike father, occupy the historical past in the novel, which they define in terms of an ideological obsolescence. Unbound by ideology, Rob Roy represents a potent synthesis of organic honor and alienated opportunism; he is at once pre- and posthistoric, and his aptitudes for secrecy, shape-shifting, robbery, and homicide ensure his survival in the uncertain order of the present. The opposition between Rob and Jarvie, cousins after all, articulates a relation of complementarity and complicity fixed in the blood, rather than a binary antagonism in which one (Jarvie) must supersede and cancel the other. Both of them constitute the new kind of world of which modern Great Britain is a part—an imperial, immanently global political economy in which jaggedly uneven times and spaces, from commercial hub to wild hinterland, are bound in a complex web by trade and military force.

The novel itself is the peculiar instrument through which we view this world. Instead of opening a window onto the past, *Rob Roy* shows its readers the obscure, occult, bewildering shapes and forces of the present—a present not yet amenable to the perspective of historical analysis, and so more authentically sensed through the symbolic techniques of romance. The historicity of the modern world system becomes legible in the novel's derangement (but not its disintegration) of an Enlightenment historicism by primitive forms and figures. Far from disabling storytelling from the power to represent modernity, Scott's reactivation of these primitive forms produces the cognitive fitness of the novel as the genre of modern life. This cognitive fitness is found in those devices that are most notoriously novelistic and least reducible to other discourses: the disclosure of relations and connections through the formal turns of plot (coincidence, reversal, doubling) and symbol (metaphor, allegory), the evocation of psychic states of anxiety, dread, wonder, bafflement, hilarity, longing—all part of the complex of strange pleasures that fiction affords but officially dismissed from the faculty of cognition. In my introduction to the Oxford World's Classics edition of *Rob Roy* I quote a contemporary reviewer's characterization of the novel's plot as a "mass of confusion and improbability":

> The author himself, as he goes on, finds himself so thoroughly involved in the meshes of his plot, that seeing no legitimate extrication, he clears himself at last by the most absolute, we had almost said the most tyrannical, exercise of the empire which authors must be acknowledged to have over their personages and events, which we recollect, even in the annals of that despotic class of sovereigns. C'est un vrai coup d'état – and one which we should have expected rather from an Asiatic writer, than from a novelist "in this free country."[1] (xxvii–xxviii)

Scott's novel, as the reviewer complains, enthralls its readers in the barbaric political psychology of world empire, instead of admitting them to the rational transactions of civil society, as a British novel is meant to do. The work of fiction, in this light, bears a perverse resistance to the nation-building ideology with which Scott is too often and too easily credited.

NOTE

[1] The review is reprinted (see "Unsigned Review" 215) and was originally published in *Quarterly Review* in October 1821.

Sir Walter and Plain Jane: Teaching Scott and Austen Together

Evan Gottlieb

When Scott published *Waverley* in 1814, Byron may have been the year's best-selling poet—*The Corsair* sold 10,000 copies on its first day alone—but the fiction market belonged to women. Jane Austen's *Mansfield Park*, Mary Brunton's *Discipline*, Frances Burney's *The Wanderer*, Maria Edgeworth's *Patronage*, and Sydney Owenson's *O'Donnel: A National Tale*—to name just a few—were all published in 1814. Writing novels in the Regency era, then, necessarily meant engaging with the works of female authors. Accordingly, in his general preface to the Magnum Opus edition of the Waverley novels, Scott famously credits Edgeworth's Irish fictions for providing a model of how to write about regional characters and themes for a British audience (*Waverley* 352–53). Elsewhere, in the Magnum Opus introduction to *Saint Ronan's Well*, Scott's sole novel of present-day manners, he praises his female contemporaries while acknowledging that he is poaching on their territory:

> The ladies, in particular, gifted by nature with keen powers of observation and light satire, have been so distinguished by these works of talent, that reckoning from the authoress of *Evelina* [Burney] to her of *Marriage* [Susan Ferrier], a catalogue might be made, including the brilliant and talented names of Edgeworth, Austin [sic], Charlotte Smith, and others, whose success seems to have appropriated this province of the novel as exclusively their own. (1)

Teaching Scott together with any (or all) of the above-mentioned female authors can be highly productive. Teaching Scott alongside Austen, however, offers distinct advantages for both students and teachers. For students, a relative familiarity with Austen's work (most will have at least heard of her, if only by way of Hollywood remakes and spin-offs) can help ease them into Scott's more exotic fictional worlds. For instructors, pairing Scott and Austen makes excellent sense on many levels, including the historical, the stylistic, and the theoretical. In the first part of this essay, I draw primarily on recent scholarship to review in general terms what can be gained from pairing Scott and Austen in the classroom. In the second, I focus on two sets of novels that exemplify the benefits of teaching Scott and Austen together: *Waverley* and *Persuasion* and *The Antiquary* and *Northanger Abbey*.

The Not-So-Odd Couple

Students are often surprised to learn that, although Austen is better known to contemporary audiences, Scott was by far the more famous writer in their day.

Indeed, Scott helped significantly raise Austen's profile with the reading public by penning the first important appraisal of her fiction in the *Quarterly Review*. When assigning this piece to students (usually in the middle of the course, after they have had a chance to read something by both novelists), instructors should ask them to consider above all Scott's claims that Austen primarily excels at "the art of copying from nature as she really exists in the common walks of life," such that "we never miss the excitation which depends upon a narrative of uncommon events" (Rev. of *Emma* 63). Scott's appraisal, by establishing Austen's reputation as "the realist par excellence" (Galperin 96), allows students to consider how Scott limits her fictional talents to representing the quotidian and the domestic. (Privately, Scott self-deprecatingly compared his "Big Bow wow strain" to Austen's "exquisite touch which renders ordinary common-place things and characters interesting from the truth of the description and the sentiment," a talent Scott admitted "is denied to me" [*Journal* 132]). By contrast, Scott understood himself to be writing a kind of synthetic genre, a cross between Austen's new realism and the older "romance" tradition of which he was famously fond. Accordingly, students should note that, after praising Austen for writing fiction from which "the youthful wanderer may return from his promenade to the ordinary business of life, without any chance of having his head turned by the recollection of the scene through which he has been wandering," Scott concludes by reminding readers

> of that once powerful divinity, Cupid, king of gods and men, who in these times of revolution, has been assailed, even in his own kingdom of romance, by the authors who were formerly his devoted priests.
> (Rev. of *Emma* 68)

Whereas female writers like Austen can no longer be counted among Cupid's followers, in other words, Scott casts himself as one of the few author-priests to remain faithful to Cupid and, by extension, to old-fashioned romance, understood here as both genre and principle of starry-eyed idealism.

The danger of taking Scott's review of *Emma* as authoritative, however, is that it reinforces many students' initial impressions of Scott and Austen as highly dissimilar writers. On the level of content, for example, students tend to underestimate the complexity of Austen's tightly focused family- and female-centered narratives, while feeling overwhelmed and frustrated by Scott's broad plots and extensive casts of characters; on the formal level, they tend to assume that Austen's intimate narrative voice can be straightforwardly equated with her personal subjectivity, while becoming lost and confused by Scott's use of multiple authorial and editorial personas. After framing these sorts of initial juxtapositions, however, instructors can begin to focus on Scott's and Austen's similarities. After all, both authors were clearly committed to the novel as the most effective literary form for reaching a national public, and their stylistic choices were equally highly influential on subsequent generations of novelists. The latter point may need some emphasis; while students tend to recognize quickly Austen's use of free indirect discourse—traditionally defined as "characterized by a shifting, elusive interplay of the voices of narrator and depicted character" (Shaw, *Narrating Reality* 117)—as a precursor of more contemporary forms of stream-of-consciousness writing. for example, instructors should also call attention to what Jerome McGann calls "Scott's Romantic postmodernity," that is, the ways in which Scott, like many of today's experimental writers, "make[s] the subject of tale-telling an explicit and governing preoccupation of the fiction" (119). Indeed, students should consider the possibility that, despite an old-fashioned predilection for Latin terms and abstruse asides, Scott's habit of "put[ting] the reader in the most self-conscious relation to the whole fictional enterprise that the books are unfolding" makes his ludic narrative strategies just as pioneering as Austen's use of free indirect discourse.

Students should also be aware of changes to the critical understanding of both authors' political leanings. For much of the twentieth century, Scott and Austen were considered "post-1789 Burkean Tor[ies], asserting (or shoring up) a traditional conservative sense of national and familial identity in direct reaction to the spread of Enlightenment and Jacobin thinking into English political discourse" (D. Jones 3). More recently, however, the time-honored Tory status of each author has been challenged. One way to encourage such revisionary interpretation in the classroom is to assign lesser-known works that push canonical boundaries and assumptions; in this vein, Emily Auerbach "recommend[s] sampling [Austen's] flamboyant, risqué adolescent works" to dispel the popular image of Austen as "prim, proper, and priggish" (41), while James Watt demonstrates that Scott's later novels (like *The Talisman* and *The Surgeon's Daughter*) evince much more sympathy with alien cultures than the orientalist productions of most Romantics ("Scott"). Even when reading more canonical texts, however, instructors can stress the self-consciousness that Austen and Scott bring to their conservative postures. Miranda Burgess, for example, has drawn attention to "Austen's national myth . . . that legitimate social order can be produced by romance-reading in a chain of homes across Great Britain" (185), while Yoon Sun Lee has argued that Scott's so-called conservatism is infused with—indeed produced by—deliberate irony (74–104).

The theoretical gap between these two novelists has also recently been narrowed. Critics have long recognized that, however lightly he wore his learning, Scott was heavily influenced by the sociological and historical theories of the Scottish Enlightenment, and he built their notions of cultural evolution and civil society into the foundations of his historical fictions (see Garside; Forbes; McMaster). More recently, critics have also begun to recognize Austen's similar, albeit less obvious, philosophical background, with Peter Knox-Shaw describing Austen as "a writer of centrist views who derives in large measure from the Enlightenment, more particularly that skeptical tradition within it" (5). Furthermore, the once-common claim (first established by Scott, as we have seen) that Austen had little interest in events beyond the domestic sphere no longer seems defensible. From Edward Said's (in)famous claim that *Mansfield Park* must be read as colluding with British imperialism (*Culture* 80–97) to Deidre Shauna Lynch's more recent observation that Austen, like Scott, was keenly aware of "the new tasks of historicizing and of periodizing that literature was being called on to perform after 1815" (x), critics have finally begun to dissolve the largely illusory barriers between the domestic and historical branches of the novel (for refutations of Said's position, see Trumpener, *Bardic Nationalism* 162–63; Fraiman). By encouraging students to think through the ramifications of these recent critical insights, instructors can help bring out the commonalities of Scott's and Austen's novelistic projects.

Waverley *and* Persuasion

Scott's first and Austen's final fictions make a wonderful pair for teaching purposes. Both feature main characters who must learn to deal with disappointment, even betrayal, as they strive for happiness and fulfillment. Moreover, as products of their time, both novels align their characters' fates with the national crises taking place around them. Scott, of course, sets Edward Waverley's development from boy to man alongside the rise and fall of the 1745 Jacobite rebellion, fusing the bildungsroman and the national tale to create the historical novel as we know it. Students should be aware that *Waverley* was published (on 7 July 1814) almost two months to the day after Napoleon's original abdication. Its concluding chapters, which detail the reconstruction of Tully-Veolan and the union of Anglo-Scottish interests in the marriage of Waverley and Rose Bradwardine, reflect Britons' elation at what they believed was revolutionary France's final defeat and the restoration of the old regime in Europe. *Persuasion*, the most explicitly historical of Austen's novels, takes place in the temporary peace between Napoleon's first exile to Elba and his sensational return to the Continent. (Perhaps not coincidentally, Austen's novel is also set during the months of the first publication and reception of *Waverley* itself.) The hopefulness of Austen's narrative, then, is tempered by the reader's knowledge that, unbeknownst to the characters, the war is not really over. Accordingly, *Persuasion* ends not with Scott's optimistic account of continual historical improvement ("like those who drift down a smooth river, we are not aware of the progress we have made until we fix our eye on the now distant point from which we set out" [*Waverley* 340]) but with the recognition that, facing an uncertain future, the present becomes ever more vital: "Anne was tenderness itself, and she had the full worth of it in Captain Wentworth's affection . . . the dread of a future war was all that could dim her sunshine" (203).

In addition to their mutual interest in the spirit of the age, *Waverley* and *Persuasion* share noteworthy structural conjunctions that students should be encouraged to identify and explore. Despite Jane Millgate's discerning observation that *Persuasion* repudiates Scott's favorite device of the long-lost heir ("*Persuasion*" 192–93), the two novels are equally invested in recovering a usable past, albeit in different registers. For Scott, this means reconciling English and Lowland Scottish interests while consigning the Highlanders to the historical record; for Austen, this means allowing Anne and Wentworth to renew their relationship by coming to terms with their past failures and misunderstandings. Furthermore, each novel's plot turns on the fact that, at a critical moment, its main character allows himself or herself to be "persuaded" by an older, more charismatic character. In Waverley's case, Bonnie Prince Charlie temporarily convinces him to join the Jacobite cause; in Anne's, Lady Russell has already convinced her to break off her first engagement to Wentworth. In both novels, moreover, such persuasion must be overcome for the main characters to proceed with their lives: Waverley must recognize that the Jacobite cause is untenable and obsolete, and Anne must come to see that, despite good intentions, Lady Russell was mistaken in separating the young couple. (At the same time, Anne remains convinced that she was right to submit to such persuasion.) Yet these similar narrative movements are simultaneously indicative of opposing authorial affinities. On the one hand, when Waverley repudiates Jacobitism along with his love for the bewitching but unreachable Flora MacIvor, he is finally and decisively putting away childish things: "he felt himself entitled to say firmly, though perhaps with a sigh, that the romance of his life was ended, and that its real history had now commenced" (283).[1] On the other hand, when Anne admits to herself that she still loves Wentworth, she is recognizing that youthful hopes and passions should be cherished for as long as possible: "How eloquent could Anne Elliot have been . . . on the side of early warm attachment. . . . She had been forced into prudence in her youth, she learned romance as she grew older—the natural sequence of an unnatural beginning" (30). Thus, although the name of Anne's selfish and vain father, Sir Walter Elliot, may be Austen's subtle dig at another Walter's perceived penchant for self-promotion, it is the author with the reputation for nostalgic romance who appears to stand for prudence and maturity in his first work of prose fiction, whereas the supposedly hardheaded realist seems to side with true love and the retention of youthful idealism in her last completed novel.

The Antiquary *and* Northanger Abbey

On the surface, Scott's third novel and Austen's first completed mature work (albeit last published, along with *Persuasion*) appear to have very little in common. *The Antiquary* concerns the quotidian adventures of its eponymous hero, Jonathan Oldbuck, a cantankerous but sympathetic character who spends his days expounding his pet theories about Scotland's Roman past, arguing with his neighbors, and being waited on by his "womenfolk." Its quasi-gothic plot concerns the restoration of the missing heir of the local Catholic gentry, whom Oldbuck has unknowingly befriended, and who eventually marries the daughter of Oldbuck's best friend, Sir Arthur Wardour. *Northanger Abbey*, by contrast, is a more straightforward bildungsroman that traces the development of its sheltered but resilient heroine, Catherine Morland, who learns above all to overcome her gothic fixations through a series of social (mis)adventures, first at Bath and then at the abbey after which the novel is titled. Yet even these brief synopses reveal a common element: both works reflect on the gothic novel craze of the 1790s. Consider, for example, Scott's description of the haunted "green room" in which Lovel is forced to spend the night at Oldbuck's estate:

> [The Antiquary] led the way through many a dusky and winding passage, now ascending and anon descending again, until he came to the apartment destined for his young guest. . . . The guest, thus separated from the living world, took up the candle and surveyed the apartment. . . . It was hung with tapestry. . . . The bed was of a dark and faded green, wrought to correspond. . . . The large and heavy bottom-stuffed chairs, with ebony backs, were embroidered after the same pattern, and a lofty mirror, over the antique chimney-piece, corresponded in its mounting with that on the old-fashioned toilet. (Scott, *Antiquary* [ed. Hewitt] 95–97)

Now recall Henry Tilney's parodic description of the room where he tells Catherine she will sleep at Northanger:

> While [the rest of the family] snugly repair to their own end of the house, she is formally conducted by Dorothy the ancient housekeeper up a different staircase, and along many gloomy passages, into an apartment never used since some cousin or kin died in it about twenty years before. Can you stand such a ceremony as this? Will not your mind misgive you, when you find yourself in this gloomy chamber—too lofty and extensive for you, with only the feeble rays of a single lamp to take in its size—its walls hung with tapestry exhibiting figures as large as life, and the bed, of dark green stuff or purple velvet, presenting even a funereal appearance? (161)

Written almost two decades apart, these passages are remarkably similar, from the labyrinthine hallways through which the hero/heroine is led into isolation to the menacing tapestries on the walls of the chamber in which they must pass the night to the very color (green) of the rooms themselves.

Once students see that Scott and Austen are employing similar well-worn conventions—thus simultaneously honoring and surpassing the work of Ann Radcliffe, whose gothic romances ruled the 1790s—they also need to recognize that such tropes are being deployed for rather different purposes by each novelist. In *The Antiquary*, Lovel *is* in fact visited by a ghost during his night in the "Green Room," an encounter that proves important for the novel's resolution, since the specter alerts Lovel to Oldbuck's family motto—"Kunst Macht Gunst" ([85] translated by Oldbuck as "Skill wins favour" [87])—which in turn inspires Lovel not to give up his courtship of Isabella Wardour. Since Scott is too savvy to offer readers straightforward gothic thrills, however, he also has Oldbuck pour cold water on Lovel's enthusiasm by providing a rational explanation for his supposed visitation (131), thus allowing readers a safely skeptical vantage point from which to enjoy the book's supernatural elements. Moreover, the motto "Kunst Macht Gunst" is more ambivalent than it initially appears, since as David Punter indicates, "*Kunst* can also refer to trick, knack, artifice, sleight-of-hand, while *Gunst* as 'favour' can also figure in phrases like 'courting a favour' or 'doing a person a favour'" (109). Like Oldbuck's multilayered family motto, then, Scott's gothic motifs are not necessarily what they seem. Although the German-adept Dousterswivel turns out to be a trickster rather than a member of the Illuminati, and the Kaim of Kimprunes is revealed to be a drainage ditch rather than the ruins of a Roman encampment (as Oldbuck had hoped), the crypt beneath the ruined Saint Ruth's Priory really is the burial place of the Countess of Glenallan, whose death sets in motion the chain of events that reveals Lovel to be the presumed-dead heir of the Glenallan fortune.

Where Scott's use of the gothic is self-consciously artificial, Austen's is overtly disparaging. Catherine's great weakness, of course, is her fondness for gothic fictions, which Henry mercilessly takes advantage of when he builds every gothic cliché available into his description of the bedroom that awaits her. Indeed, since Henry purposefully inflames Catherine's desire for gothic experiences of her own, it seems almost cruel that he should later shame her for entertaining morbid fantasies surrounding the circumstances of his mother's death. This is especially unfair given that Catherine's suspicion of General Tilney's character turns out to be not entirely unfounded: although no murderer, he is certainly guilty of being selfish, manipulative, misogynistic, and tyrannical. Thus, while most students initially assume that *Northanger Abbey* criticizes gothic novels for being overly fantastical and untrue to human emotions, it is probably more accurate to say that Austen faults the gothic, not for going too far, but rather for not going far enough; as Claudia L. Johnson writes, "by showing that the gothic is in fact the inside out of the ordinary, that the abbey does indeed present a disconcerting double image . . . *Northanger Abbey* does not refute, but rather clarifies and reclaims, gothic conventions in distinctly political ways" (34). The target of Austen's parody in *Northanger Abbey*, in other words, is not gothic trappings themselves, but rather the ways those trappings tend to blind readers like Catherine to the real—albeit systemic and unsensational—abuses suffered by women in a patriarchal society.

Besides asking students to consider Scott's and Austen's reformulations of the gothic, *The Antiquary* and *Northanger Abbey* should also be presented as historical novels. *Northanger Abbey*, while not as overtly historical as *Persuasion* in its setting or concerns, has an unusual publishing history (it was not published until nearly two decades after it was originally written), qualifying it as a historical novel: as Austen writes in the advertisement, "thirteen years have passed since it was finished, many more since it was begun . . . during that period, places, manners, books, and opinions have undergone considerable changes" (36). This accords well with Scott's advertisement to *The Antiquary*, in which he states that his third (and, at the time, potentially final) novel "refers to the last ten years of the eighteenth century" (3). Both novels, then, are set in the late 1790s, and both deal with their Revolution-inspired anxieties by staging them satirically. For his part, Scott concludes *The Antiquary* with a French invasion scare, in which the burning of Dousterswivel's fraudulent machinery is mistaken for a signal fire, whose alarm spreads up and down Scotland's coast before the mistake can be cleared up. In *Northanger Abbey*, Catherine Morland and Eleanor Tilney get into a misunderstanding about the potential for "something very shocking indeed [to] soon come out of London" (126); Catherine is talking about another gothic fiction, but Eleanor thinks she means a riot (and Henry, as usual, takes it upon himself to explain the women to themselves). For both Scott and Austen, the mechanism of an averted crisis becomes a strategy for reassuring readers that they have little to fear in the present. The more one teaches Scott and Austen together, the more one recognizes the ways in which Sir Walter and "plain Jane," for all their differences, make a very fitting couple indeed.

NOTE

[1] On the multiple implications of this pivotal statement, however, see the essays in this volume by Duncan, Hoeveler, and Langan.

Teaching the Female Body as Contested Territory

Diane Long Hoeveler

I routinely teach Scott's novels in my graduate and undergraduate courses on Romanticism and gender, frequently pairing them for contrast with Jane Austen's novels: *Pride and Prejudice* with *Waverley* or *Northanger Abbey* with *Bride of Lammermoor* or *Persuasion* with *Redgauntlet* or *Sense and Sensibility* with *Heart of Mid-Lothian* or *Emma* with *Ivanhoe* or *Mansfield Park* with *Rob Roy*. Obviously, I do not have the space here to discuss all those novels or the many rich themes that emerge from these pairings, but I would encourage instructors to experiment with Austen and Scott in tandem in their own upper-level or graduate seminars (see Gottlieb's essay, in this collection). I have never taught more than one of Scott's novels in a course, so my discussion of the novels here is not intended to suggest that instructors would teach all these novels in one course (unless, of course, they were offering a specialized seminar on the novels of Walter Scott). Rather, what I hope to provide here are some points of theoretical departure that could be used to address the sometimes contested and constructed roles and identities of female characters in some of these novels.

To begin with my overriding approach: my course shows that the female body in the novels of Scott is most frequently presented as a bifurcated figure, a split woman who embodies both positive and negative aspects of a fairly stereotypical notion of "femininity" (what Nancy Goslee has identified as the "witch or pawn" syndrome in Scott). But to nuance this device and allow students to see that Scott frequently complicates this dichotomy, I demonstrate how in some novels the female characters are sometimes meant to be read as the embodiment of the Scottish nation in formation, both its real and historical legacies as well as its fantasized and imagined potentialities. Sometimes the female body is the privileged site of reproduction and future life, and therefore a topic of intense anxiety and control by the male power-elite. At other times in Scott's novels the female body is scarred and wounded, a site of national disgrace and ignominy. In some novels the female body is an object, almost a fetish, that is exchanged between men to consolidate male control of property. And finally, at other points the woman is a veiled screen, a performance of gender, and the male characters associated with her may clothe themselves as female in a sort of ritualized, or mock, gender display. These various approaches to the female body suggest, of course, some of the most basic ways that male authors have traditionally presented "the feminine" in their works. Scott is certainly no exception in dealing in gender stereotypes; the fact is that his depictions of women and appropriate gendered behaviors were tremendously influential during the early nineteenth century, in Britain, America, and throughout Europe. At the same time, gender was not a simple or unilateral sign during the period, just as it isn't in our own time, and in many ways Scott's novels complicate, challenge, and even innovate a variety of gender constructions that were circulating in his society.

I begin my presentation of gender dynamics in Scott's works by providing Ina Ferris's very useful approach to the subject:

> *Waverley* reading offered a compelling alternative both to female reading and to feminine writing. In particular, in this period of conservative reaction, evangelical revival, and the domestic-didactic novel, *Waverley* and its successors licensed a nostalgic male-inflected romance of history that offered the satisfaction of emancipation from the necessary restraints of civil society even as it effectually absorbed male subjectivity into those restraints. And central to that sense of liberation, the reviewers suggest, was release from a feminized space. . . . Even as it was marked by unfeminine "vigour," masculinity shared with femininity the "purity" that guaranteed its "healthiness," so that both genders were constructed under the sign of restraint and both in a sense lived on deferment. (*Achievement* 91–92)

As this passage suggests, masculinity during this period was constructed in at least two ways: as self-control (the idealization of the "pure" man) and as the bold and unrestrained man (the heroic, warrior ideal). Femininity was also constructed in at least two ways, as a paradoxically contradictory sign for emotion ("human sympathy") and self-control (abnegation and self-sacrifice). I also introduce the argument outlined in Nancy Armstrong's *Desire and Domestic Fiction*:

> Men were no longer political creatures so much as they were the products of desire and producers of domestic life. . . . [T]he difference between male and female was understood in terms of their respective qualities of mind . . . that had formerly determined female nature alone. (4)

In short, the virtues of women, or domestic *virtú*, now became the source and standard for modern civic morality, so that idealized representations of nineteenth-century male literary characters were frequently presented as androgynous or feminized (see Armstrong, *Desire*; Hoeveler).

One of the most basic approaches to teaching the female body as a contested site of meaning is to introduce students to the concept of the "virgin-whore dichotomy" typically found in male-authored literature (not to say that it also isn't found in female-authored texts as well, e.g., Rossetti's "Goblin Market"). The composite figure of the split woman, one pure and one fallen (*Heart of Mid-Lothian*), one blonde and one dark (*Ivanhoe*), one victim and one victimizer (*Bride of Lammermoor*), is a long-standing device in Western culture. Students can readily understand the figure as troping anxieties toward the sexualized body of the female in contrast to the idealized presentation of a virgin, frequently depicted as having almost miraculous powers. In analyzing the split woman one could resort to Sigmund Freud or Julia Kristeva for theoretical background, but I have found it most useful to simply locate the origin of the syndrome in the Bible. Students are familiar with two of the most dominant mythic depictions of the idea: the Old Testament Eve (fallen and sinful) contrasted with the New Testament Virgin Mary (the mother of the redeemer) or the Virgin Mary (miraculous mother of Jesus) contrasted with Mary Magdalene (whore reformed by Jesus).

The clearest example of the device can be seen in the Deans sisters of *The Heart of Mid-Lothian*. Effie and her sister, Jeanie, represent the potential of Scotland, as if Scotland were a female body to be colonized and controlled either by its own native traditions (David Deans; his surrogate Butler, Jeanie's husband; and, at the top of the patriarchal pyramid, the Duke of Argyle) or by a corrupt English aristocracy (George Staunton, who is the seducer of Madge and father of her murdered child as well as the eventual husband of Effie and the father of Effie's feral and parricidal child "the Whistler").[1] The history of the Deans sisters is remarkably rich and entertaining (Jeanie's "honesty" and her journey to England to plead for her sister's life before two other women, the queen and the king's mistress, and Effie's contrapuntal journey from seduced maiden to English lady). The conclusion of the novel may be hopelessly melodramatic, but it is important for developing the destinies of all the characters: the "pure" Jeanie's happiness, prosperity, and fertility contrasted to the "fallen" Effie's confinement in a convent.

To present to students some interpretive strategies for understanding Jeanie's journey to redeem her sister, I reprint a series of passages from Judith Wilt's discussion of Jeanie as a "Prince Errant" (*Secret Leaves* 129–42). Wilt's approach relies on a knowledge of *Waverley* (which I attempt to summarize for students who have not read the novel), as well as the allusions in the novel to *Pilgrim's Progress* (which students, at least my students, have not read, so I am once again summarizing the text as a context for them). Wilt usefully reads Jeanie as the hero/heroine of the novel:

> As heroine her job is to incarnate the still center of the turning world, the blond domesticity that goads and rewards the hero for his journey of self-discovery and self-limitation. As hero, her job is to take that Waverley journey from "romance" to the "real history of her life." (134)

Halfway through the journey south,

> Jeanie encounters her own particular Apollyon again, and undergoes at her/his hands a complex version of the typical Waverley hero's self-discovery—kidnapping, outlawing, escape back to the law with the power to destroy the outlaws, which, out of hidden sympathies, she does not use. Apollyon, falsehood, tempts her on the public road north of Grantham. (138)

Charting the steps of Jeanie's journey as stages in an archetypal pilgrimage or quest-romance (from the initial challenge to temptations to final apotheosis) allows students to see how Scott adapted and transformed gendered stereotypes, creating a masculinized heroine who fully inhabits the historical novel in new and innovative ways.

Also important is Scott's depiction of another female pair, Madge Wildfire and her mother, Margaret Murdockson, alternately called "Mother Blood" or "Mother Damnable," dark doubles of the Effie-Jeanie configuration. Although the Deans sisters are Scottish, both venture onto English soil—one to redeem her sister's life and one to live as the wife of an English aristocrat. The fact that Effie's son, who should have been the embodiment of a reconciliation between classes and nations, kills his father and loses himself among the American Indians speaks to the challenges that faced England and Scotland as they sought at once to merge and retain their separate traditions. Students can be fruitfully directed to recognize the many aspects of the contested female body throughout this novel, displayed, for example, in the songs sung by both Effie and Madge ([ed. Lamont] 98, 303) or the gendered confusion of Madge's clothing and its assumption by George (306).

Jeanie's quest southward is punctuated by an attempted assault, captivity among thieves in a Gypsy's barn, and encounters with George and his father. I focus student attention on one particular episode of the journey: the church scene in which Madge dishevels Jeanie's clothing and hair to make her appear to be a madwoman and then leads her "in captivity up the whole length of the church" (323), kicking and punching her throughout the service. As Wilt has noted, in this "remarkable humiliation scene, pitched somewhere between farce and melodrama, the sensible unromantic Jeanie is fully 'womanized' at last, reduced to 'dishevelled hair, downcast eyes, and a face glowing with shame'" (324). The scene forces readers to see a "sisterhood" between Madge and Jeanie (Wilt, *Secret Leaves* 139), just as there is a sisterhood in seduction between Madge and Effie and a more literal sisterhood between Jeanie and Effie.

The split woman also functions in Scott's first novel, *Waverley*. In this novel I focus student attention on the female body as a sign under which the author can examine the temptations of nationalism and revolution as embodied in Flora MacIvor, a "Jacobite *femme fatale*" (Irvine 176), in contrast to the stability and promise of Lowland reconciliation with England represented by Rose Bradwardine.[2] Caught up in the events of the 1745 Jacobite uprising, Scott's quixotic hero Edward Waverley finds himself torn between his affections for Rose and her father the Baron of Bradwardine on the one hand and Flora and her brother Fergus on the other. In his various travels (again explained to students as a version of the archetypal quest-romance) and changes of heart, Waverley also enacts a nationalistic split that represents what I see as the logic of an embodied and homosocial politics. Rose and her father (as well as their estate Tully-Veolan) represent an idealized vision of a new community on the border between Lowlands and Highlands, a new, professionalized Scotland successfully absorbed into a modernized, commercial, and capitalistic England. Flora and her brother, in contrast, represent a seductive family romance in which Edward is attracted as much to the gothically reactionary brother as to the sister. By the conclusion of the novel Scott appears to have erased the wild, homosocial Highland spirit; Edward has supposedly renounced his attraction to a Scotland that is rabidly and irrationally nationalistic, incapable of assimilation into Britain because of its seductive gothic legacy (the "Grey Spectre"): clan-based, barbarous, lawless, and isolationist. ("[H]e felt himself entitled to say firmly, though perhaps with a sigh, that the romance of his life was ended, and that its real history had now commenced" [283]). To explain the cultural contexts here, I spend some time summarizing Eve Kosofsky Sedgwick's theory of the "homosocial" and Norbert Elias's theory of the "civilizing process" that took place when the middle class imitated, demonized, and gradually replaced the aristocracy as the dominant class.

Students can see the contrast between romance and history most clearly by considering the novel's conclusion in a companionate marriage between Edward and Rose, in which Edward is firmly entrenched in a domestic sphere, not a public or political one, at the close of his "romantic" adventures. This emphasis has caused a number of critics to position the novel within the private sphere and to see its real subject as the domestication and feminization of the hero. For instance, Robert P. Irvine has noted that the

> governing opposition here is not between one type of politics and another, but between politics and domesticity; and . . . that opposition no longer coincides with a gender division, for domestic virtue is now as proper to the male as to the female. (182)

But *Waverley* also addresses both the conflicting claims of public and private domains and the proper alignment of both for the newly emerging upper-middle-class man. Edward ultimately marries into the "modernized," or "civilized," aristocracy by his alliance with Rose and her father and estate, but he has to face temptations, captivity, and trials before he can be restored to his rightful situation and identity.

One of the most blatant ways of illustrating to students the contrast between old and new versions of masculinity can be found in the portrait that Edward has commissioned of himself and Fergus. The two of them represent opposed masculine types (much like the Laird of Solway and Darsie in *Redgauntlet*), and their relationship throughout the novel is often strained. The portrait, in fact, stands in sharp contrast to the content of the novel: "It was a large and spirited painting, representing Fergus Mac-Ivor and Waverley in their Highland dress, the scene a wild, rocky, and mountainous pass, down which the clan were descending in the background" (338). Whereas the painting presents a sentimentally homosocial image of clan life and the hero's adventures, as Edward would nostalgically prefer to imagine them, the novel makes it clear that the actual experiences of Edward and Fergus and by extension the processes of modernizing Scotland were far from idyllic.

Rob Roy concerns the 1715 revolution, the earliest event in the historical chronology of Scott's Jacobite novels, and once again features the device of the split woman.[3] In this work, however, the two primary female characters are decidedly more ambivalent in their function as objects of exchange between men who contend for property and wealth over the bodies of women. Rob Roy's wife, Helen McGregor, is an Amazonian figure, a woman who literally takes to the battlefield and kills:

> She might be between the term of forty and fifty years, and had a countenance which must once have been of a masculine cast of beauty; though now, imprinted with deep lines by exposure to rough weather, and perhaps by the wasting influence of grief and passion, its features were strong, harsh, and expressive. She wore her plaid, not drawn around her head and shoulders, as is the fashion of the women of Scotland, but disposed around her body as the Highland soldiers wear theirs. She had a man's bonnet, with a feather in it, an unsheathed sword in her hand, and a pair of pistols at her girdle. (349)

Wilt calls Helen a "Christian princess reverted under stress to a pagan deity" with a "savage Druidical nobility" about her (*Secret Leaves* 68). Her transgressive violence is explained by an earlier sexual assault on her, gingerly broached by Scott not within the text of the novel but in his later 1829 author's introduction:

> It is said that [the] diligence of the law, as it is called in Scotland, which the English more bluntly term distress, was used in this case with uncommon severity, and that the legal satellites, not usually the gentlest persons in the world, had insulted McGregor's wife, in a manner which would have aroused a milder man than he to thoughts of unbounded vengeance. She was a woman of fierce and haughty temper, and is not unlikely to have disturbed the officers in the execution of their duty, and thus to have incurred ill treatment, though for the sake of humanity, it is to be hoped that the story sometimes told is a popular exaggeration. (Introduction 17–18)

In fact, according to local historical records, Helen was not only evicted and raped but also branded with hot irons; her rage against the English stems from this assault on her body and her honor.

In contrast, Diana ("Die") Vernon is presented as something of a virginal object of desire by the hero, although the reader can see that she may also be a compromised schemer, a Catholic and Jacobite rebel. In league with her mysterious father, Sir Frederick Vernon, who sometimes masquerades as a priest, she plots to overthrow the Hanoverian line and return Britain to its feudal,

Catholic past. Wilt notes that her nickname, Die, suggests both a "keenness of spirit [that] comes from a life lived at the edge of a kind of dying . . . and the dice determining her fate" (*Secret Leaves* 64). Diana says to Frank, "I should be rather like the wild hawk, who, barred the free exercise of his soar through heaven, will dash himself to pieces against the bars of his cage" (43). Students are familiar with the nineteenth-century representation of women as "birds in gilded cages," so they are able to understand Diana's more masculinized character; she is a frustrated quester who rebels against the limitations that the endogamous marriage market seeks to impose on her (a forced alliance with her odious cousin Rashleigh).

As Irvine has noted, one way to understand the differences between the two women in *Rob Roy* is to focus on their use of language and their conversations with others (Helen's eloquence as originating in the savage and Diana's recalling the *Spectator*'s discourse of politeness and finances [164–67]). Students could fruitfully oppose this observation with the introduction to the Oxford World's Classics edition of the novel, in which Ian Duncan reads the two women in relation to the master discourse of the novel, economics:

> The ordeal of a masculinity beset by eloquent Amazons—the lovely Die Vernon, the terrifying Helen MacGregor—culminates not in any clarity of action or self-possession but in a remarkable fit of hysteria, as an archaic feminine energy overwhelms the hero from within. (xvii)

Frank's "hysteria" occurs when he meets Diana on the road at night in the Trossachs and she hands over a packet of letters of credit before she leaves. Focusing on this scene and Frank's reaction to it as almost a voyeur of a sexualized exchange of goods, students may see how anxious the male establishment was about women gaining access to the public realm of economics and finance (through the free circulation of their "goods," i.e., sexuality).

Frank Osbaldistone's attraction to Diana is similar to Edward Waverley's attraction to Flora MacIvor, except that here the hero is allowed to claim his errant love object and redeem her in a marriage that returns him to his paternal estate. The differences in the endings of the novels can partially be accounted for by the presence of a father rather than a brother in Diana's history. If one were to look for excuses for Diana's revolutionary and conspiratorial behavior, one could claim that a dutiful daughter is much more acceptable to Scott and his readers than a willful sister in league with an uncontrollable and attractive brother. That Diana can pass directly from her father's control to Frank's makes her an acceptable object for matrimony, an unsullied object of exchange between men. Much has been made of the complete obliteration of the Osbaldistone brothers, which clears the way for Frank's inheritance of the estate; his marriage to Diana, a cousin and coequal heir, legitimates Frank's identity as lord of the Osbaldistone manor.

Redgauntlet, the last of Scott's Jacobite novels, concerns a fictitious revolutionary threat that in fact never occurred in 1765.[4] The novel focuses on versions of contested manliness: Hugh Redgauntlet, the "Laird of the Solway Firth," represents an anachronistic form of masculinity doomed to extinction in the new Scotland (legalistic, professionalized, modern), while his nephew Darsie Latimer undertakes a journey that remasculinizes him and prepares him for survival in his rapidly changing society. Containing two particularly curious representations of the female body, *Redgauntlet* sets "the Green Mantle" (the feminine promise of fertility and new life) between the novel's two heroes, Alan Fairford and Darsie Latimer, suggesting the homosocial dynamic analyzed by Sedgwick in *Between Men*. Later in the novel, Green Mantle is revealed to be Lilias Redgauntlet, Alan's eventual wife and Darsie's sister—after she has functioned as a blank screen onto which Darsie projects his unknowingly incestuous desire.

In the second example of curious gender dynamics, Darsie himself undergoes a humiliating feminization. His uncle Hugh Redgauntlet, seeking to use Darsie as a pawn in his ill-conceived Jacobite plot, forces him to dress in female clothing:

> Darsie permitted Cristal Nixon to place over his face, and secure by a string, one of those silk masks which ladies frequently wore to preserve their complexions, when exposed to the air during long journeys on horseback. He remonstrated somewhat more vehemently against the long riding-skirt, which converted his person from the waist into the female guise, but was obliged to concede this point also. The metamorphosis was then complete. (310 [ed. Sutherland])

Once under his uncle's control, Darsie is then stripped of his female clothing and ceremonionally remasculinized:

> I restore you to yourself, and trust you will lay aside all effeminate thoughts with this feminine dress. Do not blush at having worn a disguise to which kings and heroes have been reduced. It is when female craft or female cowardice find their way into a manly bosom, that he who entertains these sentiments should take eternal shame to himself for thus having resembled womankind. (367)

Redgauntlet's words constitute a performative speech act, language that does what it says. This entire scene provides an opportunity to introduce students to Judith Butler's theory of the "performative," in (admittedly) a simplified manner for undergraduates. Drawing on the philosopher John Searle, Butler notes, "within speech act theory, a performative is that discursive practice that enacts or produces that which it names" (*Bodies* 13). Butler redefines gender as

> *a corporeal style* . . . an act which has been rehearsed, much as a script survives the particular actors who make use of it, but which requires individual actors in order to be actualized and reproduced as reality once again. ("Performative Acts" 272).

Understanding gender as constructed and performed in order to impose heteronormative standards on individuals, Butler endorses a freedom from any essentialist understandings of gender or sex.[5] In *Redgauntlet*, Darsie is extremely uncomfortable at the "feminization" he is forced to assume at the hands of his uncle, which exemplifies the performance of gender and its restrictive categories and codes.

This scene can also be used to demonstrate to students Scott's use of historical allusion. The cross-dressing scene would have recalled, for Scott's original readers, the story of Charles Edward Stuart's assumption of a maid's clothing to escape after the battle of Culloden in 1746 (K. Sutherland xx; *Redgauntlet* [ed. Sutherland] 461). This performance of gender by the would-be king might also have reminded Scott's readers of the tactic employed by the French rebels of dressing as women to storm the Bastille and rampage through the streets of Paris during the Revolution. Scott had used this association of men assuming female clothing when Robertson (the alias assumed by George Staunton) wears the female dress of Madge Wildfire to raid the Tolbooth prison in a failed attempt to free Effie in *The Heart of Mid-Lothian*. The bodies of women as well as their clothing take on transgressive and violent powers in all these examples. Although Hugh Redgauntlet's words appear to condemn women for "craft" or "cowardice," the passage suggests that when women cannot be demonized as witches ("craft") or pawns ("cowardice"), they are dangerous and antisocial forces to be reckoned with in the new nation.

Teaching the contested female body in Scott's novels allows students to see gender as a fluid sign in his as well as in our own society. The language and length of Scott's novels may be a challenge for them, but, by focusing on how gender defines and constrains the major characters and their interrelationships, students can see that Scott has preserved for future generations of readers a sweeping portrait of how one nation, Scotland, came to modernize itself while also memorializing its best imaginings and legends of its past.

NOTES

1 There are many secondary articles on *The Heart of Mid-Lothian*, but I place on reserve for students Duncan's discussion of the novel (*Modern Romance* 146–76); J. Thompson; Morgan; and McCracken-Flesher ("Narrating").

2 Of the many secondary sources available on *Waverley*, I place on reserve the discussion of the novel in Wilt (*Secret Leaves* 26–36); Hennelly; and Ferris (*Achievement* 94–104).

[3] An excellent listing of secondary sources on the novel is available in Duncan's edition.

[4] An excellent listing of secondary sources on the novel is available in K. Sutherland's edition of this text. The most detailed discussion of gender in *Redgauntlet* can be found in Irvine 200–15.

[5] A useful pedagogical overview of Butler's theories and approaches to teaching them can be found in Felluga.

Proof and Truth: Teaching the Waverley Novels in the Law and Literature Class

Clare A. Simmons

Law and literature intertwine in both Scott's life and his works. Although Scott's fortune was largely derived from his literary career, his reputation as a poet and editor probably helped in his appointment as sheriff-depute of Selkirk, a position that Scott held for thirty-three years; in 1806 his political connections enabled him to hold the additional position of a principal clerk at the Court of Session in Edinburgh.[1] Scott's closeness to law and awareness of legal problems in the Waverley novels make him the ideal author for a class titled Law and Literature.

Although many prelaw students may be attracted by course titles of this kind, the objective of Law and Literature is not to teach students law but rather to interrogate both the legal discourse and themes found in creative works and to recognize and analyze the rhetorical impulses of legal language. In Richard Posner's 1988 *Law and Literature*, ominously subtitled *A Misunderstood Relation*, Posner suggests that the "study of law and literature seeks to use legal insights to enhance the understanding of literature, not just literary insights to enhance understanding of law" (1).

In a useful overview of law and literature studies, Julie Stone Peters connects the movement's rise with "residual anxieties and disciplinary shifts in both literary and legal studies" (443). Peters categorizes shifts in thinking about law and literature under the categories of the "humanism" of the early years of the interdisciplinary connection, when literature appeared to offer a humanist corrective to the pragmatics of law; the "hermeneutics" of the 1980s, where literary theory provoked lawyers such as Posner by challenging interpretation; and the "narrative" focus of the 1990s, where both lawyers and literary scholars alike investigated the rhetorical power of story (444).[2] Peters's own narrative provides helpful ways of viewing shifts in the focus of law and literature, yet even in her characterization of the 1980s, where she suggests that literary critics may have been looking to law for the certainty that their own discipline lacked, her three historical moments assume that literature provides the interpretative lens. In the classroom, students may more directly ask how law is going to help them interpret literature.

I would therefore suggest that the undergraduate law and literature class may take a number of different approaches to the intersections of the two fields of study. First, the connection may be thematic: the class can read and discuss texts where law is relevant to the theme of the work. Second, a class can use a literary work as a case study and debate the legal questions that it presents. Third, literature can provide a focus for debating the nature of law and what it means to live under a specific legal system. And finally, legal discourse itself can be analyzed as literature, providing an opportunity to explore the relation between rhetoric and factual presentation.

As the interdisciplinary field of law and literature gains in recognition, the question arises of which texts best serve its purpose. Since humanities students, especially at the undergraduate level, cannot be expected to know much about either law codes or legal language, novels that explain their legal aspects through narrative are a valuable resource. Students in law and literature classes tend to be self-selecting, many having chosen the course because they are thinking of pursuing law as a career. The pragmatics of this choice have some consequences for the instructor. First, the instructor should emphasize that this is not a law course, even if the students glean some snippets of law in group discussion of specific examples. Yet to meet the expectations of students who want "some law stuff," the instructor will need to ensure that law remains part of the discussion.

Many of the Waverley novels will be effective teaching tools in the law and literature classroom. Complaints found in other classes, such as that the Waverly novels are too long, will, one hopes, be less of an obstacle to students committed to thinking about the interrelations between literature and law. Yet even in the law and literature classroom, different emphases are possible. *Redgauntlet* would be a good choice for a course focusing on the legal profession. *The Bride of Lammermoor* might lead to fruitful discussion in a class focusing on property law and how legal processes define and affect families.

I have tended to focus on the nature of evidence in law and literature–themed classes. An analysis of how we know what we know in a story does not require specialized legal knowledge (although of course it may require knowledge of genre), yet it helps students think about how evidence can be used and interpreted. Ironically, one of Scott's best-known novels with a thematic focus on evidence, *The Heart of Mid-Lothian*, may actually be overdetermined for this purpose. The conflict between Jeanie Deans's sense of truth and the law's reliance on "presumptive evidence" for proof not merely of Effie's actions but also of the supposed intent behind them are so central to the narrative that students may need reminding not merely to retell the story (213 [ed. Hewitt and Lumsden]). The novel nevertheless has other significant legal dimensions; Marie Hockenhull-Smith's essay on *The Heart of Mid-Lothian* in Michael Freeman and Andrew D. E. Lewis's *Law and Literature* focuses on the Porteous riots. I here use *Ivanhoe* as a familiar example from the Waverley series that repeatedly interrogates codes of laws. This novel, moreover, includes a major trial scene that complicates ideas of judicial evidence by suggesting that notions of what can be true are not universal but determined by historical circumstances.

Ivanhoe was Scott's first novel to venture into English history. By the story's conclusion, the Saxon and Norman peoples have united as the English under their king and under English law. Critics such as Judith Wilt have argued for a continuity between *Ivanhoe* and the Scottish Waverley novels, but because of its resoundingly English theme, Scott's perspective as a Scot has been less discussed in relation to *Ivanhoe* than to any of his other major works. Although

Scott masks himself by his anonymity and his fictional English narrator Laurence Templeton, *Ivanhoe* may be presented in the law and literature class as the work of a Lowland Scottish lawyer with an outsider's perspective on English law. *Ivanhoe* points to the inherent dangers of interpretation in local law and gently implies an alternative in common law, both commonly applied and based on common sense.

Students will need a little background for their discussion. Unlike English common law, which traditionally claims a perfection through time-tested interpretation and ultimately from its derivation from nature, Scottish law acknowledges its hybrid origins and the inherent limitations of system put together over ages. Scottish law complicates the notion of innocence as the opposite of guilt through the verdict of not proven. Whereas in English law, a verdict of not guilty means that a person is innocent in the eyes of the law and that all other versions of what truly happened become irrelevant, the decision of not proven suggests a truth that the law has failed to uncover. According to David Hume, the advocate, Scottish juries rarely use the word *innocent*. Hume explains, "not uncommonly, the phrase *not proven* has been employed to mark a deficiency only of lawful evidence to convict the pannel [defendant], and that of *not guilty*, to convey the jury's opinion of his innocence of the charge" (*Commentaries* 2: 439–40). Scottish law, then, embodies in its verdicts an awareness of the imperfection of law in uncovering the truth, something that, even in dealing with minor disputes, Scott had to acknowledge in his own legal career (Chisholm 147).

England too was recognizing problems with the law. Between 1688 and 1815, the number of offenses punishable by death rose from about fifty to over two hundred (McLynn ix). If the law so frequently needed to be revised, then the makers of the law were openly implying its imperfection, or at least the inadequacy of common law to cover all the exigencies of modern life.[3] Moreover, those charged with offenses were reliant on the workings of local justice: a sympathetic jury who considered that the offense did not warrant the mandated punishment might simply acquit, while a justice or jury hostile to certain types of offenses might be inclined to make an example of a defendant even in the face of dubious evidence. Although the huge expansion of statute law might seem to make law more definite than common-law tradition, in fact it had the opposite effect of creating laws without precedents for interpretation.

Interpretation not merely of laws but also of facts was a current concern in English legal theory. Around 1810–12, Jeremy Bentham compiled a vast collection of commentaries on the law of evidence in England; in the 1820s, the teenaged John Stuart Mill edited these into the *Rationale of Judicial Evidence* (1827).[4] Since Bentham's theory of utility is based on the intersection between self-interest and common interest, witchcraft provides the extreme example of the difficulty of declaring anything improbable, being the key instance of a charge in which no kind of evidence, circumstantial or testimonial, can be valid: it is "not capable of being rendered probable by any quantity of testimonial evidence" (3: 392). Witchcraft is for Bentham, then, the charge in which his reader cannot possibly believe, the ultimate contradiction of natural evidence and common sense. In his *Letters on Demonology and Witchcraft*, Scott was to agree with Bentham's characterization of witchcraft as a charge in which modern readers cannot believe. Although Scott would not go as far as Bentham in claiming to be writing at a crisis point in English law, *Ivanhoe* may be read as providing a commentary on the imperfections of law by suggesting that English law has encountered crises in the medieval past.

From the perspective of later legal history, *Ivanhoe* is set at the last vague point in the history of English law. In legal parlance, "time immemorial," the point where common-law tradition fades into the unknown, is supposedly 1191, or when the accession of Richard I took place. When the supposed editor, Laurence Templeton, reminds his readers of the difference between that time and their own, he draws the distinction in legal terms: the modern reader, with the comforts of home,

> is not half so much disposed to believe that his own ancestors led a very different life from himself; that the shattered tower, which now forms a vista from his window, once held a baron who would have hung him up at his own front door without any form of trial; that the hinds, by whom his little pet-farm is managed, a few centuries ago would have been his slaves; and that the complete influence of feudal tyranny once extended over the neighbourhood village, where the attorney is now a man of more importance than the lord of the manor. (16)[5]

Templeton's reading of Richard's reign sets the tone for a world in which law functions in a different way. Whereas in modern society, the attorney, the interpreter of the law, is more important than the lord of the manor, the former upholder or even maker of feudal law, legal interpretation is a constant problem in the world of *Ivanhoe*. Characters in *Ivanhoe* seem constantly to need to remind one another of the law, and almost invariably when the matter of law is raised, a debate ensues about how to interpret it. Throughout the story, competing systems of local law readily identifiable by students are in operation, and they cause the characters doubt, fear, degradation, and physical danger.

Students should be able to find examples of codes of law that require interpretation. *Ivanhoe* assumes that its readers have a general awareness of the concept of the Norman yoke, according to which, as English radicals had argued at least since Renaissance times, Norman feudal oppression replaced Saxon constitutional freedoms (Hill 60). The story opens in the domain of the "out-law." The forest, though, later proves not to be a space outside the law but to have its own laws, which function with more definition than the systems operating outside it. Locksley tells the Black Knight, "in these glades I am monarch." The "out-laws" divide up their spoils according to a strict system, and Richard is astonished to observe that

> men, in a state so lawless, were nevertheless among themselves so regularly and equitably governed, and all that he observed added to his opinion of the justice and judgment of their leader. (351)

Robin Hood and his men hence model good law to the man who has failed to protect it at a national level.

Yet the main responsibility for the state of law falls on Richard's brother John. John is regent, yet he himself does not seem quite sure of how to interpret the laws. Before the tournament, John points out that he must appoint a "Sovereign of Love and of Beauty" (99). A debate ensues about whether a Jewess can take this role; the laws prove negotiable when De Bracy suggests that the tournament champion should choose her (100), and the herald adds this to the laws. All the tournament laws, "calculated in some degree to abate the dangers of the day" (142), are announced verbally by the herald: an advantage that the tournament holds over most of the legal systems in *Ivanhoe*, then, inclusive of the English constitution, is that the laws are stated in words. Ivanhoe takes part in the tournament not under his own or even an assumed name but under a legal title: his shield bears "the Spanish word *Desdichado*, signifying Disinherited" (106). Bois-Guilbert and Ivanhoe draw their swords, but the "marshals of the field" remind them that the "laws of the tournament" do not permit it (109).

Prince John fails to change the laws of the tournament; he is next confronted with a problem of English law. Ivanhoe's father disinherited his son for recognizing Richard as his feudal overlord, but Richard gave him a "castle and manor" that Prince John subsequently bestowed on Front-de-Boeuf. John claims as his "right" the authority "to confer the fiefs of the crown upon the faithful followers" who will carry out feudal obligations rather than go to the Crusades (152).

John also usurps the fatherly role that Cedric holds as Rowena's guardian. In Cedric's territory, Saxon law is still partly in force, and, in contrast with the radical idealization of the laws of Alfred as the foundation of English constitutional freedom, it is here heavily associated with the laws of the father. Yet Saxon law is in decline, so that even Cedric does not seem quite sure himself how Saxon law works. His son Ivanhoe has left home to join the Norman court, contrary to his father's "wish and command," and Cedric claims that "in the days of Alfred that would have been termed disobedience—ay, and a crime severely punishable" (166). The laws of Alfred include the Ten Commandments, one of which is to honor one's parents, but do not explicitly mention obeying one's parents. They do state that someone who strikes or curses his father should be put to death but make no mention of obedience (Liebermann 1: 31). Moreover, while in theory Saxon law was severe, most capital offenses were remittable through fines, and it seems unlikely that sons were ever executed for striking or cursing their fathers. Even if the novel is tacitly calling into question the traditional reading of Saxon law as the foundation of English freedom, Cedric seems here to be projecting his own parental feelings onto Saxon law in contradiction with the written record.

Parallel to the Saxon laws of the father are the Jewish laws of the father. Scott's general sympathy toward the Jews in *Ivanhoe* has been extensively discussed elsewhere;[6] students may be interested to note, though, that the novel creates parallels between the Saxon law that many Britons so admired in Scott's time and the seemingly alien Jewish law. Like the laws of Alfred to which Cedric appeals, Jewish law is based on biblical commandment. For both Cedric and Isaac, for example, the custom of hospitality functions almost as a law (63, 124). Isaac states that he has "duly kept every jot and tittle of the law of Moses" (125). Yet, like Cedric, he can be challenged on the interpretation of the law. He later tells Rebecca, "by our law we may not deal with the stranger and Gentile, save for the advantage of our commerce." Rebecca here appeals to the law of common humanity: "we may not indeed mix with them in banquet and in jollity; but in wounds and in misery, the Gentile becometh the Jew's brother" (293). She further adds that if Ivanhoe dies because they have not helped treat his wounds, "we are indeed answerable for his blood to God and to man" (294).

Readers are clearly expected to sympathize with Rebecca's humane reading of what is right, the point where the laws of God and human law coincide, and to retain this sympathy in the major legal scene of this legislation-obsessed novel, Rebecca's trial for sorcery. Even though Rebecca learned her healing skills from the shadowy figure of Miriam, who was killed as a witch, the novel makes clear that Rebecca's healing abilities are skills, not magic, and that she only uses them for good.[7] Yet Scott is careful not to suggest that because the trial of Rebecca is unjust, all medieval law is simply bad. The grand master of the Templars states that since Rebecca "hath flung her enchantments over a brother of the Holy Temple, assuredly she shall die the death" (395). Albert Malvoisin begins to say, "But the laws of England," when Beaumanoir interrupts him: "The laws of England . . . permit and enjoin each judge to execute justice within his own jurisdiction. The most petty baron may arrest, try, and condemn a witch found within his own domain" (396). Students may wish to guess what the rest of the preceptor's sentence would have been. The laws of England certainly do not permit someone to be condemned without a fair trial, and Beaumanoir is assuming Rebecca's guilt beforehand. Some of Scott's readers may additionally have been aware that witchcraft was not a separate offense in Britain until after the Reformation, although William Blackstone notes that English law, "both before and after the conquest," ranks "this crime in the same class with heresy," hence punishable by burning (4: 60). In theory, Rebecca could have been tried for heresy, but this is not how Beaumanoir presents the case.

Beaumanoir's assertion of local authority serves not merely to enforce the law but in effect to create and carry through a unique code of laws. Yet even though, as the preceptor cynically observes, a "trial moves rapidly on when the judge has determined the sentence beforehand," the court has not allowed for the person of Rebecca herself. When she hears she is to be tried, she praises God and states that "the name of a judge, though an enemy to my people, is to me as the name of a protector" (400). In the court the grand master is both judge and prosecutor as he endeavors to try Rebecca for the crime of sorcery and Brian de Bois-Guilbert for breaking the laws of the Templars at the same time. Beaumanoir has already shown his inclination to apply local authority to Rebecca's case; for Bois-Guilbert the difficulty is that laws that the Templars normally overlook, such as chastity, are here being applied in the literal way that Cedric had read the laws of Alfred.

But Rebecca knows how to appeal to the law. Given that the prosecutor-judge has decided before the trial that at least Rebecca is guilty, a surprising amount of effort is put into producing witnesses. Malvoisin has prepared two soldiers to give the same evidence "which would have been, in modern days, divided into two classes—those which were immaterial, and those which were actually and physically impossible" (411). It is not clear that this court is obligated to find two witnesses who agree, but the implied need to find coinciding testimony itself ironically recalls Jewish law, while at the same time it puts Rebecca in a similar situation to Christ in the Gospels.

At this point, the narrative directly distances the reader from the historical setting, describing the "circumstances of their evidence" as "in those ignorant and superstitious times, easily credited as proofs of guilt" (412). Just as Bentham makes the initial assumption that his reader does not believe in witchcraft, so Scott assumes not merely that his reader will utterly reject the possibility that Rebecca is a witch but also that his reader believes that circumstantial evidence is not legal proof. Rebecca, however, believes that truth is absolute and that God provides proof. She appeals to God as judge between Bois-Guilbert and herself, and the book leaves open to interpretation whether God indeed judges her situation.

At first consideration, the wager of battle in *Ivanhoe* seems to mark a distinction between medieval justice and that of Scott's own period, although as both Mark Schoenfield and Gary Dyer have shown that as recently as 1817, the courts had deliberated whether a defendant could still claim the right of wager of battle.[8] As Bruce Beiderwell has noted, *Ivanhoe* conforms to the medievalist evocation of the past in suggesting that in the world of romance, justice will persist, and Bois-Guilbert's death not at Ivanhoe's hands but as "a victim to the violence of his own contending passions" leaves the reader free to agree with the grand master's verdict that "[t]his is indeed the judgment of God" (*Power* 84–95). If that is the case, the medieval law of might, supported by the law of God, may be able to prevail. It is dangerous to conclude that this is Scott's own judgment, though, since it is spoken by the grand master, whose own judgment of Rebecca has been from the outset clearly wrong. A more concrete example of medieval law as wishful thinking might in fact be the grand master's own prompt withdrawal on Richard's arrival and the execution of the Malvoisin brothers (496). Even Saxon law is modified by the end of the story, since Cedric accepts Richard as ruler and, in the symbolic free space of the forest, gives Gurth his liberty. By the end of the story, we see optimism for equal laws equally applied, and just as most novels end with the hope of peace and happiness in the next generation, so the story concludes with hopes of true English law.

Students may, however, be confronted with the problem of whether different codes of law can exist in the same place and time. At the conclusion of the story, Rowena advises Rebecca to exchange one code of law for another: "O, remain with us—the counsel of holy men will wean you from your erring law, and I will be a sister to you" (501). Educators may rejoice in Rowena's faith that law is teachable, yet given the story that has preceded it, the reader must suspect some irony in this appeal to the authority of holy men. Rebecca herself seems to accept that to continue the code of law on which her identity depends, she must leave England. A final question for a law and literature class might thus be whether a code of law must exclude those who place a value on other systems of law. In its persistent presentation of law's challenges to interpretation, *Ivanhoe* is one of several Waverley novels that are model texts for the law and literature classroom.

NOTES

[1] On Scott's eagerness to have public recognition in the law, see J. Sutherland 109–11.

[2] For another useful overview of law and literature, see Ward 3–27. See also Julius ix–xxv.

[3] In his introduction to Bentham's *Rationale of Judicial Evidence*, John Stuart Mill argues that the system "ought to be reformed thoroughly, and one a comprehensive plan; not piecemeal, but at once" (xiii). In fact, by the time this book appeared in print, Robert Peel was already making extensive penal reforms that would permanently change Britain's use of capital punishment.

[4] Alexander Welsh has discussed the implications for narrative of Bentham's theory of circumstantial evidence (*Strong Representations* 16–42).

[5] Citations to *Ivanhoe* are from Duncan's edition.

[6] See, for example, Ragussis (*Figures* 94–115).

[7] It is unclear whether Miriam was killed as a witch or simply as a Jew, the narrative noting that "the fate of Miriam had indeed been to fall a sacrifice to the fanaticism of the time" (295). Beaumanoir later states that she was killed as a witch (392), but his determination to kill Rebecca for the same reason seems to make the charge of witchcraft merely a cover for the charge of being Jewish.

[8] On the legal implications of wager of battle, see Schoenfield; Dyer.

The Limits of Diversity: Using Scott's "The Two Drovers" to Teach Multiculturalism in a Survey or Nonmajors Course

Kenneth McNeil

Critical attention to Scott's novels has seen a revival of late as critics have realized that the questions of national and ethnic identity, cultural difference, and cross-cultural exchange with which we grapple in the twenty-first century were also very much the concern of lettered Scots in the late eighteenth and early nineteenth centuries. Yet renewed scholarly interest in Scott has not always translated into renewed interest in teaching Scott in the undergraduate classroom. This is perhaps because the reputation of his work is one of inaccessibility. The plots of his novels are assumed to be interminable and improbable, and few student readers, especially nonmajors, are thought to have the patience to wade through the multiple frame narratives that characterize Scott's work. Also, even when readers arrive at the story proper, they immediately are confronted with a rush of historical references and footnotes that only serve to heighten the alienation between them and Scott's historical settings.

To address this problem and to return Scott to the undergraduate classroom, I suggest that we offer students not a novel but a short story. "The Two Drovers," published relatively late in Scott's career, provides a superb introduction to the themes and ideas of the Waverley novels, particularly in its concise and dramatic exploration of the dynamics of ethnic diversity and cultural difference within a modernizing society. Its brevity, relatively fast pacing, and the absence of the complicated frame narratives and detailed historical references that attend many of Scott's novels make "The Two Drovers" wonderfully accessible to a wide range of students.

In "The Two Drovers," Scott highlights the contrast between Gaelic-speaking Highland and Lowland Scottish and English cultures to explore the dynamics of cultural encounter, particularly between "primitive" and "civilized" peoples. In doing so, Scott charts not only the imperatives of progress and modernization and the concomitant decline of an indigenous culture but also the ongoing internal divisions that fracture a supposedly settled, unified national society. Scott's tale explores the complexity and ambiguity of an emerging imperial consciousness that is alert to the nuances of cultural difference yet reserves for itself the power to impose a universal set of standards by which to arbitrate seemingly irreconcilable differences between competing cultures. "The Two Drovers," like much of Scott's fiction, is grounded in the juxtaposition of contrasts, in the clash of cultures. It poses both the possibilities and the limits of diverse cultures living in proximity to one another and therefore lends itself to a more generalized discussion of the contemporary possibilities and limits of multiculturalism.

The philosophical underpinnings of Scott's exploration are provided by the eighteenth-century inquiry into the development of human society associated with the Scottish Enlightenment. Scott reveals his debts to Adam Smith; Adam Ferguson; Lord Kames; and others as his story quickly establishes an anthropological frame of reference, setting the actions of its principal characters, one English and the other from the Scottish Highlands, within the framework of their cultures. Thus, in its first few pages, not only do we receive a lesson in eighteenth-century cattle-driving, or "droving," practices; we also learn that Highlanders are masters of the trade. This lesson initiates a litany of generalized traits that establish the Highlander as a distinct cultural type. We learn, for instance that "a Highlander was never so happy" as when he was driving cattle:

> There was a variety in the whole journey, which exercised the Celt's curiosity and natural love of motion; there were the constant change of place and scene, the petty adventures incidental to the traffic, and the intercourse with the various farmers, graziers, and traders. . . . (125)[1]

Such a summation expresses two related assumptions: that what is true of one Highlander, Robin Oig McCombich, is true for all Highlanders and that culture makes the man—the motives and conduct of individual characters are dictated by their social formation. The first few pages of the story are replete with ethnographic observations that establish the exotic quality of the Highlands and the authority of the narrator to speak on behalf of the natives. We discover that a Highland dirk is properly a *skene-dhu*, or "black knife"; that a *doch an-dorroch* is a Highland parting cup; that the goatskin purse Robin wears over his kilt is called a *sporran*; that the *Taishataragh* ("second sight") of Highland women is not to be dismissed lightly; and so on.[2] In short, Scott adumbrates an emerging set of categories that would make up the formal field of anthropological inquiry in the nineteenth century: costume, language, traditions, rituals, beliefs. Moreover, these descriptions of Highland ways are followed by the description of Robin's fellow drover, the Englishman Harry Wakefield:

> In countenance and temper, Wakefield was the model of Old England's merry yeoman, whose clothyard shafts, in so many battles, asserted her superiority over the nations, and whose good sabres, in our own time, are her cheapest and most assured defence. (129)

It is important to note that Scott here does not set up English character as some normative standard by which all cultures can be measured. Instead "Englishness" functions as simply one more ethnic category—one that has established its dominance over others to be sure—but one that is no less distinctive than its Scottish Highland or Lowland counterparts.

The plot of "The Two Drovers" departs from Scott's other Highland fiction. *Waverley*, for example, unfolds a romantic adventure plot in which a normative

English hero ventures into the exotic primitive space of the Highlands. As he travels north, the Anglo-British subject embarks on a fascinating journey into the past, where he gains a temporary glimpse of the primitive vestiges of the modern world that he otherwise inhabits. In "The Two Drovers," however, it is the Highlander who ventures into the world of the English, and not in the vanguard of an invading Jacobite army but following the cyclical everyday routine of the business of cattle droving. The story's northern English setting is as much a part of Robin's world as it is a part of Harry Wakefield's, and the fields surrounding the Doune market are a kind of polyglot border zone in which English and Highlander come together. At this point in the story, Scott highlights interaction and mutual interdependence, as the friendship between Highlander and Englishman is based on their shared livelihood. Shared economic interest seems to transcend cultural difference, and Scott seems to be setting up a kind of "feel good" cultural relativism, an early-nineteenth-century affirmation of the benefits of tolerance and cultural diversity. In any case, the world of "The Two Drovers" is recognizably modern, as the story concisely sketches the dynamics of a transnational culture that is situated in the borderlands and initiated by the demands of a complex interdependent market economy.

But this initial mood of mutual tolerance and a friendship that crosses cultural boundaries quickly gives way to an ultimately disastrous sequence of events. After a misunderstanding that leads to a confrontation between the two drovers in a bar, Harry Wakefield is dead, stabbed in the heart by his Highland friend, who is then put on trial for the murder, convicted, and sentenced to death. "What happened?" I ask my students. Contrasting the beginning of the story with its ending highlights its horror and tragedy, and I ask them to trace the trajectory of events that led to such a conclusion. Students offer several possible lessons of the story, including the inevitable danger of too much "trash talk" after tossing back a few, a danger only fueled by the egging on of bar patrons who make it difficult to back down from confrontation. Students have also suggested that the story reveals the limitations of an overdeveloped sense of masculine pride and honor, which compels the two men to fight each other, despite the personal inclination of both combatants to avoid conflict.

All these readings are valid and worth exploring, but I also point out that the story anthropologically frames the motives and outcome of the conflict. For example, the bar confrontation reveals the ugly racial ethnic stereotypes that erupt when tensions begin to heighten. Most crucially, incompatible notions of personal honor compel Harry to coldcock his Highland friend and the Highlander to return to the inn several hours afterward, *skene-dhu* in hand, to stab his English friend in cold blood before a dozen astonished onlookers. For Harry, the unintended slight that Robin had given him earlier in the day can only be repaid by hand-to-hand combat, so that the Englishman can save face among his drinking companions—after which, honor restored, both men can continue their carousing and their friendship. For the Highlander, for whom (Scott reminds us) a bare-handed attack constitutes an unforgivable slur on his manhood, the intended slight of his English friend requires him to seek out Hugh Morrison (the Lowlander to whom Robin had given his knife as a precaution earlier) and return to the bar several hours later to kill Harry. The stain of dishonor can only be washed away with blood.

After his murderous deed, Robin simply waits to be taken into custody. Peeling back the napkin that covers the face of Harry's corpse, the Highlander exclaims, "He was a pretty man."[3] At the point of Robin's utterance, however, there is a curious syncope in the narrative and then a quick shift, which many students notice and which is worth examining. The narrator remarks, "My story is nearly ended," which abruptly motions to its conclusion, even though the tale still has a few pages to go. Why this pre-ending? The very last line of the story is given to Robin, who, as he is taken away to execution declares, "I give a life for the life I took . . . what can I do more?" (146). Yet between this statement and the narrative stop, there is an extended description of the trial, most of which is taken up by the judge's speech to the jury, which spans five long paragraphs. This brings on a radical change of style, as the judge's oratorical, Latinate rhetoric replaces the rich dialogue full of dialect for which Scott was celebrated. This shift in narrative voice is significant in what it says about who gets to frame the meaning of the story for the reader. In the legalistic voice of the judge, Scott rehearses what are by the 1820s clichéd assumptions about the nature of Highland society—that the isolated mountainous regions of Scotland produced a primitive but noble tribal people who were given to war and internecine strife and whose notion of justice was "wild and untutored," grounded in acts of bloody vengeance. Scott's judge—following Smith, Ferguson, and other writers of the Scottish Enlightenment—compares Highland society with that of other warlike primitives, the Cherokee and Mohawks of North America.[4] Yet in keeping with the mood of cultural sensitivity established in the beginning of story, the judge argues for a kind of cultural relativism, suggesting that the cultural codes of the Highlands ought to remove Robin from reproach. Given the Highland code of vengeance, the judge suggests, Robin's actions are perfectly understandable and mark him as an honorable man.[5] However, and this is the big "however" in the story, the judge condemns Robin to death because, as he says:

> The first object of civilization is to place the general protection of the law, equally administered, in the room of that wild justice, which every man cut and carved for himself, according to the length of his sword and the strength of his arm. (146)

In other words, if the judge were to let Robin off for the sake of some misguided notion of cultural tolerance, "you may unsheathe, under various pretences, a thousand daggers betwixt the Land's-end and the Orkneys" (146). This line arguably signals the final message of the story: when cultural differences *cannot* be accommodated, when competing notions of justice cannot occupy the same national space, the dominant culture must and will prevail, by force if necessary.

Many of my students have seen this as a clear illustration of the imperial mindset. As more than one of them has remarked, if the story had taken place in the Highlands or if it had been Highland society that had had the more powerful army to enforce its notions of justice, the proceedings and results of the trial would have been completely different. Yet the certainties of these students are often tested when one invites analogous comparison with cultural conflict in our contemporary world. For example, returning to the comparison offered by Scott with Native Americans, I cite examples when Native American notions of justice have been at odds with the laws in different states, the most useful example being cases where tribal elders have prescribed banishment for tribal members convicted of criminal offenses.[6] If they had been the judge arbitrating in such a case, I ask my students, how would they have ruled?

What "The Two Drovers" says to us is that, contrary to the assertions of many, cultural diversity is a messy business that often poses profound challenges to the social status quo.[7] Framed in the context of Scott's time, the story complicates our picture of early-nineteenth-century "internal colonialism," the process by which the supposed English "center" brings the Celtic "fringe" into its hegemonic sway before moving beyond Britain's shores to engulf the rest of the world.[8] Scott's stance on the clash between dominant and minority cultures is ultimately ambivalent, in the postcolonial sense, and connotes a more complex Scottish relation between colonizer and colonized, a relation that recent critics have begun to recognize.[9] By putting the final pronouncement in the mouth of one of his characters, Scott forecloses a final, objective position on the fate of minority cultures and the beneficence of establishing standardized "civil" notions of justice for all members of a culturally diverse society. As a writer with a keen sense of his own multivalent identity as borderer, Scot, and Briton; as one who made a career of articulating and exploring cultural difference; and as one who acutely felt the passing of old ways and was in his later life increasingly skeptical of social improvement and progress, Walter Scott was ideally suited to investigate in his fiction the dynamics of cultural diversity and of cross-cultural exchange, in the era of emergent globalization. "The Two Drovers" provides a brief, accessible, and unforgettable entry into Scott's imaginative exploration of these issues.

NOTES

I would like to give special thanks to the students in my fall 2005 British Romanticism class for their helpful input and for allowing me to test out the ideas I describe in this essay.

1 All page references are from the Penguin edition of the *Chronicles of the Canongate*, which includes "The Two Drovers" in addition to "The Highland Widow" and *The*

Surgeon's Daughter. The Penguin paperback is based on the definitive Edinburgh Edition of the Waverley Novels (EEWN) and presents "The Two Drovers" for the first time since its publication in 1827 in the *Chronicles of the Canongate* collection. (For a brief discussion of the history of the text, see Lamont, "Note." For a more complete account, see her "Essay on the Text" in the EEWN.) "The Two Drovers" appeared in the sixth edition of the *Norton Anthology of English Literature* but was dropped from subsequent editions. The story appears in *The Oxford Book of Scottish Short Stories*, edited by Dunn, but I know of no other recent anthology that includes the story.

[2] As Scott himself was careful to state several times, his own experience of the Gaelic-speaking Highlands was limited to summer visits as a boy and occasional travel. Scott's knowledge and use of Gaelic was quite limited, and his rendering of the English of native Gaelic speakers is generally crude. For a complete analysis of Scott's linguistic renderings, see Tulloch (*Language*).

[3] Scott already had glossed the meaning of "*pretty* man" in *Waverley* in 1814, which for the Highlander signifies, he writes, "not handsome, but [a] stout warlike fello[w]" (142).

[4] In the 1829 Magnum Opus introduction to *Rob Roy*, Scott himself writes that the celebrated Highlander's character blends "the wild virtues, the subtle policy, and unrestrained license of an American Indian . . ." (5). Scott offers an alternative cultural comparison in an 1816 essay, describing the "curious points of parallelism between the manners of the Afghaun tribes and those of the ancient Highland clans" (Rev. of *The Culloden Papers* 288).

[5] The sympathetic cultural relativism of the judge's pronouncement is echoed in Scott's writing elsewhere. In *Waverley* the presiding judge at the trial of Evan dhu Maccombich, Fergus Mac-Ivor's loyal henchman, makes a similar argument. Scott reiterates the case for Highland exculpation in his own history of the 1745 Jacobite rebellion in *Tales of a Grandfather*.

[6] For example, in November 2003 the Alaskan assistant attorney general Dean Guaneli sought to strike down the Alutiiq village of Perryville's banishment of one of its residents, who had a long record of assault and drunk driving convictions. "One or two individuals can disrupt a small community," Guaneli is quoted as saying in an *Anchorage Daily News* piece, "but there is only one criminal justice system in Alaska. It's the state system, and it's for all Alaskans" (Toomey).

[7] Walter Benn Michaels, for example, argues that the contemporary focus on "celebrating" cultural diversity and tolerance in the United States distracts from the more troubling and intractable problem of economic inequality.

[8] For a definitive account of internal colonialism, see Hechter.

[9] For recent rethinking of the internal colonialism model in the context of British literary culture, see Trumpener (*Bardic Nationalism*) and Sorensen (*Grammar of Empire*). For a discussion of colonial ambivalence, see Bhabha, who writes that ambivalence strikes at the very heart of colonial discourse, threatening to undermine its stability. Since colonial discourse, he writes, poses a colonial subject that is "at once an 'other' and yet entirely knowable and visible," it reveals its desire for a "reformed, recognizable Other, as *a subject of difference that is the same but not quite*" (126). This process of colonial "mimicry" reflects the ambivalence of colonial discourse, insofar as, "in order to be effective, mimicry must continually produce its slippage, its excess, its difference" (126).

APPENDIX

Below is a brief outline of suggested strategies and approaches to teaching "The Two Drovers" in the context of multicultural and diversity issues for a survey or nonmajors course.

"Retry" the Highlander in the class. Require that students take a stand on Robin's guilt and either agree with the judge's sentence or argue for some alternative solution.

Examine the anthropological or sociological construction of characters. For example, list the elements (language, costume, manners, etc.) with which Scott delineates his characters. Such a listing can reveal the categories by which Scott identifies ethnic categories and the centrality of these categories in determining character behavior and motives.

Discuss imperialism and the uneven power relations between "primitive" cultures and "civilized" ones. With a little background and supplementary information, the class could examine the formation of the "noble savage." This discussion is often aided with parallel examples of the noble-savage theme in representations of Native Americans. Such a discussion can shed light on anthropological parallels that Scott and others drew between Highlanders and other indigenous peoples around the world. (I, for example, have used visual examples gleaned from eighteenth- and nineteenth-century American art.)

Establish the contemporary relevance of Scott's themes through the use of current-day analogies. Native American legal issues work particularly well for this comparison. (See the example in note 6.)

Compare and contrast the treatment of the encounter between civilized and primitive society in "The Two Drovers" with those in other texts. Using the new definitive Penguin edition of the story, which brings together all the stories in the *Chronicles of the Canongate* for the first time since their initial publication, allows one to juxtapose the story with "The Highland Widow" or the short novel *The Surgeon's Daughter*, which is set in India.

CASE STUDIES

"'Twas Thus the Latest Minstrel Sung": Listening to *Waverley* with an Un/Conventional Ear

Caroline McCracken-Flesher

In "The Lay of the Last Minstrel," Walter Scott emphasizes the productivity of minstrelsy. Both the minstrel, toward the end of his life, and the wizard Michael Scott, after his death, continue to tell tales and disturb the lives of those who think their time has passed. There is always a tale to tell. Moreover, because the audience shifts with the times, it thereby makes even the oldest tales different and new. What seems to be last—an end—is also the latest thing, and always up-to-date.

In our classes, however, we are cautious about naive student encounters with literary texts. We work hard to banish the formulations "I believe," "I think," "I feel"—and especially "it's my opinion" and "it reminds me of." Yet it can be worth our effort—though near to impossible—to offer our students the experience of a primary encounter with a literary text. In 1814, after all, *Waverley* was the latest thing because it was the newest. And Scott sets up his text to produce and privilege an uneasy relationship between reader and novel. *Waverley* forces readers to become involved in the making of meaning and thus to question whether meaning can be made in any consistent or lasting fashion. If we yield to its confusions, in the end this is a text that empowers its readers. From this perspective, the generations of criticism that have accumulated to facilitate the encounter between reader and text may actually undermine it. So in this Approaches volume, full of important ways to connect our students with the history and expanding horizon of criticism, I suggest the virtue, at least for a moment, of doing what Scott suggests and bringing reader and text into a more direct conjunction.

Of course, what I am recommending is functionally impossible. On the one hand, even student readers are never completely naive; on the other, Scott's contemporaries brought expectations to his novels that our students cannot hope to access. Still I have found this strategy productive when exercised alongside more conventional approaches, and have had success with it in standard novel courses and in more experimental classes. In each, it has the effect of giving students an interactive yet critical relationship with a text, one that can speed less experienced students to innovative thinking and the more seasoned to important research. It has been especially productive in courses with an exploratory mandate. At my institution, Scottish literature falls within the "emerging fields" category in our curriculum. Through this approach, students with little formal training in the novel or Scottish literature and little grasp of history find themselves grappling with complexity and, potentially, expanding a field. This approach pushes students to become active researchers, directly engaged with their texts, and perhaps capable of redirecting a critical discourse.

I here suggest a sequence of moves that may be enacted, as time allows, to offer this direct and dynamic experience. A class might begin by reading criticism oppositely—not as a model for practice, but to identify its insistences. The class might then turn to contemporary criticism, to see if it carries the same certainties. In Scott's case, the issues turn out to be the same, but (as recent critics increasingly appreciate) they are sources of anxiety. The stage is then set for the turn to the text. The novel now tests the criticism, rather than vice versa; as students ask, what so disturbed Scott's contemporaries that his successors tried to box it within rather narrow, and oddly matched, critical terms? And here, students may discover that Scott worked to resist categorization and keep a lively, creative relationship with an uneasy reader.

Obviously, time often *does not* allow. Thus, some of the moves to peel away early layers of critical patina might be sidestepped: students might go straight to our fourth stage—but Scott's first—where the author undoes his novel even as he writes it and denies his reader the comfort of critical perspective. Or there may be time on hand, and a teacher might introduce students to primary materials that hint at the contemporary context within which Scott appeared new in 1814. The question for the teacher might be, how uncomfortable do we want our students to become, and about what? How far do you need to go with a pedagogy of perplexity to become productive?

First Move: Reading against the Tide of Criticism

Scott is a good candidate to demonstrate this kind of approach, because he can benefit from it specifically. More than most authors, Scott has been placed in traditions both literary and political. For much of the twentieth century, he was figured (primarily through *Waverley*) as crucial in the development of the novel, in the formulation of the nation, and in the depiction of history. But such prominence is problematic. Scott is often viewed retroactively, from the disciplines he himself expanded, as wanting: *Waverley* is thus considered originary, yet not so good; national, yet not so helpfully Scottish; historical, but unfortunately romantic. Scott has been woven into traditions he may have produced but in which he does not fully belong. Indeed, he has at times been locked into binary formulations of past versus present, history versus romance, literature versus politics. This is ironic because Scott himself called such oppositions into question.

Step one, then, is not to read the novel but to evaluate the criticism that foregrounded Scott within literary and political traditions, or the discourse of history, and that yet may have miscategorized and confined him there. Here, students read criticism not as a road map for their subsequent encounter with the text but as a subject for analysis. Instead of considering criticism authoritative and determinative for student readings of *Waverley*, we track the emphases and thus the anxieties criticism betrays in the context of Scott's novel.

There is a vast archive of Scott criticism, any of which would be relevant here. Still, a few texts stand out. These can be read in full or excerpted, as appropriate to the class and the time frame, allowing a range of students to appreciate how much our reading of Scott is a constructed and historical phenomenon. Such an assemblage would allow students to see how often Scott is read within binary patterns but how the emphasis of a given binary falls differently over time. In 1937, Georg Lukács reads Scott across the opposition between romance and history, seeing in him "a renunciation of Romanticism, a conquest of Romanticism, a higher development of the realist literary traditions of the Enlightenment" (33). He thus identifies the author with history against mere fiction—both as romance and Romanticism. By contrast, F. R. Leavis's 1948 declaration that "[o]ut of Scott a bad tradition came" places the author at the beginning of Leavis's tradition of great novelists, yet sees Scott as locked into eighteenth-century romance and thus as against a growing tradition and not good enough for it (14). Alexander Welsh's 1963 extension of the binarisms of romance and history across Scott's leading men and women encourages Welsh to note the gender contraventions of Scott's anxious heroes yet to conclude that "[t]he Waverley novels [as a group] are romance . . . the kind of fiction that projects a moral and dreamlike arrangement of things" (*Hero* 264).

But in 1919, G. Gregory Smith sensed in Scott a different set of opposing terms—in fact, he identified a structure of dualism stretching back through Scottish literature. Smith encouraged readings of Scott and others that presumed cultural and political divides in their work. He saw these divides as both demonstrated and delimited in their use of landscape, language, and character. "The Scot," he determined, "presents two aspects which appear contradictory. . . . We may dwell on these incongruities, the better to explain their remarkable synthesis in Scottish literature" (5). Smith read Scott as the most accomplished author in depicting this oddity and purveying it as ethnic to a non-Scottish audience. But Smith's enthusiasms spurred a criticism that saw Scott as a national problem. While Smith thought Scott had made his land "a place of pilgrimage, as no other literary man has done before or since" and rejoiced "that Europe eagerly claimed to share in the lesson" (274–75), later Scottish authors read through Smith's terms to see here a more dangerous containment of Scotland within a different binarism: Scottish versus English nations and literatures. Edwin Muir lamented in 1936 that Scott's binarisms manifested a static culture and unproductive literature: "A people who lose their nationality create a legend to take its place" (160–61). "In ranging through history," Muir wrote, Scott "merely went on repeating again and again an image of [past] society"; "reluctantly perhaps, but firmly, order, the established order, is reinstated again" (167–68). Scott's supposed oppositions between past and present, England and Scotland, romance and history, and so on delimited Scottish culture, binding Scotland in the romanticized past against the present of a living nation.

These views persist in literary and political analysis that tries to shift the discourses of criticism. In *After Britain*, written after Scotland gained a devolved parliament and published at the millennium, Tom Nairn traces to Scott's nostalgia the difficulty of a current Scottish politics. He writes, "[Scott] learned to set off ineffectual (hence emotionally exaggerated) regret against a 'level-headed' (and all too effective) acceptance. . . . Most alarmingly, such traits soon came to be incorporated into Scottish 'national character' and were eventually awarded ethnic status" (230). By contrast, "New nationalism is . . . in quest of new air to breathe" (241). In the most stimulating of such arguments, Cairns Craig observes that Scott's fictions, especially *Waverley*, struggled to express "simultaneity"—Scott actually resists the confinements of one time, discourse, or genre over another. Nonetheless, by the pressures of narrative, Scott's novels turned backward, and their plots became recursive. Since every novel ended in civilization but began anew in barbarism, they pushed Scotland "out of history." So Craig looks for an imaginative space set apart from the opposition between history and romance, past and present—a place "not *after* history, or *before* it, but *beyond* it." This is not, we infer, a place that can be found in Scott (224).

Any handful of these examples reveals a layered mapping of oppositions: Scott is the author of history against romance, romance against history, past versus present, imagination versus nation, and so forth. From these shifting binarisms, students can easily identify anxieties about what the novel should be; the relative authority of romance and the real; the need for continuity but the desire for momentum in all politics, whether literary, gendered, or national. It is not hard to see that a novel tradition in formation requires its origins and ends, its insiders and outsiders, or that a nation in search of relevance might want to find a cause for its perceived powerlessness that it might then escape.

Second Move: Reading within the Critical Current

Once students are aware how criticism has brought a range of its own literary, political, and historical emphases to bear on Scott, they are ready to turn to recent scholarship. Given the context of critical absolutes and opposites that flip their terms in an almost predictable routine, students will find the work of the past twenty years encouraging. Recent analysts see little certainty, and they struggle with anxiety and imprecision. As Katie Trumpener suggested in 1993, it was time to recontextualize Scott ("National Character"). Trumpener pried open the terms of romance and history, and, increasingly, a more exploratory view recognized how criticism had hitherto strained to restrict Scott within categories he was oddly thought to have delineated. Ian Duncan (1992) focused on *Waverley* to argue that in Scott, "the old commonplace of an antithetical relation between romance and reality, invoked by the novel in its own apologies of origin, produces a new, dialectical figure of romance as the fulcrum against which . . . reality can be turned around" (*Modern Romance* 2). In "Translation from the Borders," Ina Ferris wondered if the move between worlds (and, in her *The Achievement of Literary Authority*, between audiences and genders) contains peoples and genres—an English audience will always appropriate a Scottish text, a masculine audience a feminine form. Yet such containment can never be complete; rather, it gestures toward an excess that escapes description. In 1997 she concluded, "Translated texts [one culture's story told to another] are not captured once and for all [by the receiving discourse], and their particular history . . . is not necessarily erased. . . . [T]ranslation . . . [is] a more ambiguous and troubled activity than is often recognized." And criticism itself has become troubled. Still operating within the discourses of romance and history, recent critics sense (if I may plunder Ferris) that "something goes on in the peripheries as well" ("Translation" 206). From this step, students can see themselves as criticizing the critics, yet nonetheless participating in a recent (if oppositional) critical perspective.

Third Move: Reading Scott's Readers

If students recontextualize *Waverley*, as Trumpener suggests, they will discover that early critics, coming to the book for the first time and unburdened by the weight of a criticism derived from and set against the author, often focused on this indefinable "something." It disturbed them deeply. Students who go beyond the necessarily conventional selection in John O. Hayden's *Critical Heritage* volume will see that Francis Jeffrey's assessment of *Waverley* in the *Edinburgh Review*, while admiring the novel's "force and truth and vivacity of its colouring," found its success odd. In fact, Jeffrey insisted that "[i]t is wonderful what genius and adherence to nature will do, in spite of all disadvantages." He noted the novel's inadequacies and unfortunate choices at some length:

> Here is a thing obviously very hastily, and, in many places, very unskillfully written—composed, one half of it, in a dialect unintelligible to four-fifths of the reading population of the country—relating to a period too recent to be romantic, and too far gone by to be familiar. (203)

And, devastatingly, he concluded, "The passages in which the author speaks in his own person, and assumes the smart and flippant style of modern makers of paragraphs, are also considerably below mediocrity" (242).

Moreover, the national aspects of Scott's writing that twentieth-century critics categorize easily disturbed not only Jeffrey the Scot but also the American critic in the *Port Folio* and the Englishman reviewing in the *Critical Review*. These last had to fight down their own national politics to evaluate the book. The *Critical Review* huffed, "Had the work been less national . . . we think it would have proved as acceptable to English novel readers as it must doubtless be to those on the other side of the Tweed" (Rev. of *Waverley* 297), while the *Port Folio* became entangled in Scott's historicizing of Fergus's punishment, declaring that "we have a distinct recollection of similar 'scenes,' and similar 'sentiments' toward more than one of the British dependencies" (Rev. of *Waverley* 331).

J. Merivale in the *Monthly Review* typified the contemporary response to the difficulty of *Waverley*: "without wasting any more time in saying what it is *not*, we shall proceed by a few extracts to shew [sic] what it *is*" (280). That is, early critics located *Waverley*'s oddities but could not quite analyze them, so they made way for the text. They thus spotlighted for our students what was truly unusual about Scott's novel while leaving it open for their analysis.

Fourth Move: Scott Reads the Reader

So what is *Waverley*? Students will find out if they listen to those parts of the text that bothered contemporary readers and that twentieth-century criticism often read with too much confidence in its own terms.

Criticism of *Waverley* as novel, character, and national discourse hangs on the hero's declaration that "the romance of his life was ended, and . . . its real history had now commenced" (283), and it obsesses over the imagery of his portrait (338). But Scott teaches early on and through the entire text that we should trust no ideas of coherence in character or novel (not even portraits). Waverley, we are told repeatedly, is an unreliable observer of events—students could usefully map the number of times that Scott undermines his protagonist's authority as the point of view for the novel. Further, Waverley's portrait is of a piece with his inadequate realization of what goes on around him: it was painted in London, taken from a spirited sketch by a different artist, includes a dead friend, and is set against scenery that is a product of the studio.

In fact, we should not invest in the narrative voice that troubled Jeffrey. In those pieces of the text most extraneous to the plot (and thus themselves a test of our reading commitment), Scott on the one hand sets up a map for misreading, and on the other dares us to participate in reading as strategic interaction. Scott appended to his novel "A Postscript, which should have been a Preface." Few read prefaces, we might presume, but most read postscripts. Here, Scott points to actual histories and persons and gives the nod to Maria Edgeworth and Henry Mackenzie—thus placing his novel between local color and sentimental romance. Yet this is only the second move in a complex parenthetical construction: Scott also wrote a chapter titled "Introductory." In it, he anonymously challenges a literary history yet to come by situating his work not as subject to generic expectation or to direction from character or narrator but as a negotiation across the gap between playful author and anxious reader. Together, narrator and reader participate in a process, instead of mining for a meaning.

While twentieth-century critics have often insisted that *Waverley* constitutes either history or romance and belongs most surely within either literary or political traditions, Walter Scott very directly tells us what it is not. Scott runs through alternative titles (3–4). With "a Tale of other Days," "must not every novel-reader have anticipated a castle scarce less than that of Udolpho?" Had the novel been subtitled "a 'Sentimental Tale,'" "would it not have been a sufficient presage of a heroine with a profusion of auburn hair, and a harp?" *Waverley* is neither a gothic nor a sentimental novel. Yet Scott does not tell us what it actually is. Rather, he has established a discourse of what it is not.

Students may find a perverse pleasure in listing Scott's negative assertions, piling up their double negatives, and vainly searching for positives throughout the text: Waverley, we will eventually discover, is not a hero; Fergus we will see constructing himself as a hero, so he cannot be one; Flora is too theatrical for a heroine; Waverley is always not quite aware of what is going on—and what is going on is not what he thinks. And importantly, the opening sentences of *Waverley*'s introductory chapter set the discourse:

> The title of this work has *not* been chosen *without* the grave and solid deliberation which matters of importance demand from the prudent. Even its first, or general denomination, was the result of *no* common research. (4; my emphases)

Scott sets his reader the impossible, proto-Derridean task of sifting through what his novel and its hero are not in search of what they are.

In *Legitimate Histories*, Fiona Robertson notes that over the years, criticism has "obscured [Scott's] firm belief in the role of the reader." Scott, she considers, had almost "a theory about contracts of expectation between writers and readers" (62). By turning directly to Scott and by listening to what he actually tells us—which turns out to be a lot of nots—students may find themselves subject to, and able to argue for, Scott's investment in the writerly text. Readers are challenged to involve themselves in the meaning making of the text and thus to see both how meaning is made and the impossibility (despite the critics) of achieving any meaning that is stable. Scott produced texts that invited and rewarded the kind of exploratory strategies favored by a new student reader.

And since Scott is thus his own best context, where time is limited, instructors may find it most useful simply to turn to the text and to follow his discourse of what is not.

Fifth Move: What Did Scott's Readers Read?

If time is available, situating Scott within a few of his contemporary and later worlds can offer students some of the contextualization that has both invited readers' and critics' investment in his works and made that investment so problematic over the years. Jane Millgate observes that in *Waverley*, "Mystery becomes a device for disrupting narrative sequence and obliging the reader to bring together all the Tully Veolan episodes for interpretation through superimposition" (*Walter Scott* 44). Where the text insists on what it is not, we are encouraged to search around its peripheries for a clue to its mysteries. In so doing, we risk being seduced into extraneous considerations and at worst might find ourselves restricting Scott's novel within discourses not its own. But at best students can appreciate how Scott's texts operated in the past and continue to operate now as discursive sites that presume, sometimes set up, and generally welcome the eruptions of meaning allowed by active reading. Students might themselves attempt what Scott invites: "interpretation through superimposition."

Even as he opened gaps in his text, Scott imagined a knowledgeable reader for *Waverley*. He gestures to events outside the novel; with George IV's 1822 visit to Edinburgh, he retroactively provided a context for his story; and by inviting readers into his texts, he ensured that the most recent of events will always echo through it. Indeed the gaps in Scott's tale particularly invite such contextualization. The contexts given below supplement Scott's textual gaps and the critical problems they arouse. But they are by no means exhaustive. Rather, they are meant to suggest how expansive classroom analysis of Scott's novel can usefully become if it not only follows the text's enthusiasms and emphases but also delves into its rifts and fissures. By undertaking such research—which stands a real chance of originality—students will have mapped Scott's favorite dictum. They will have let "every herring hang by its ain heid."

APPENDIX: CONTEXTS FOR READING *WAVERLEY*

Romance versus History

Review of *Waverley* in *Scots Magazine* (July 1814: 524–33; print), blends romance and history.

Walter Scott, introduction to *Tales of the Crusaders* (see *The Betrothed*), 1825. The Author of Waverley pits history against romance, but history is found to be fictive itself.

Walter Scott, *Tales of a Grandfather*, first and second series, 1828 and 1829. Scott's history of Scotland for children.

Marinell Ash, *The Strange Death of Scottish History* (Edinburgh: Ramsay Head, 1980; print). Considers Scotland as composed in history, Scott's history writing, and his relations with historians.

The Portrait of Edward and Fergus

Henry Raeburn's portrait, exhibited in 1812, of Alasdair Ranaldson Macdonell of Glengarry, National Galleries of Scotland, and viewable on the gallery's site. Glengarry may have modeled, or modeled himself after, Scott's image of the chieftain (see *The Lady of the Lake*).

Contemporary representations of Scott (e.g., portraits by Thomas Lawrence, Henry Raeburn, David Wilkie; bust by Francis Chantrey).

Scott's opinion of sitting for those portraits and of how they turned out (see letters indexed in James Corson, *Notes and Index to Sir Herbert Grierson's Edition of the Letters of Sir Walter Scott* [Oxford: Clarendon, 1979; print]).

The National Portrait Gallery in London, its establishment and nature. Note the involvement of the Scottish author Thomas Carlyle (www.npg.org.uk/live/history.asp).

Analyses of nineteenth-century British-history painting (e.g., Roy Strong, *When Did You Last See Your Father?* [London: Thames, 1978; print]).

The Prince's Visit to Edinburgh

Portraits of Charles Edward Stuart. See Robin Nicholson, *Bonnie Prince Charlie and the Making of a Myth: A Study in Portraiture, 1720–1892* (Lewisburgh: Bucknell UP, 2002; print).

George IV's 1822 visit to Edinburgh, partly staged by Scott. See John Prebble, *The King's Jaunt: George IV in Scotland, 1822* (London: Collins, 1988; print) and, for an academic view, Caroline McCracken-Flesher, *Possible Scotlands: Walter Scott and the Story of Tomorrow*, chapter 3 (Oxford: Oxford UP, 2005; print).

The Scottish Parliament's Opening Day (Scottish Parliament, 1999; videocassette). The parliament opened to muted pageantry.

The Baron's Body Service to the Prince

For the traditions of exchange between monarch and subject in Scotland, see Louise Olga Fradenburg, *City, Marriage, Tournament: Arts of Rule in Late Medieval Scotland* (Madison: U of Wisconsin P, 1991; print).

Scott's reconstruction of this scene at George IV's 1822 visit to Edinburgh. See McCracken-Flesher, *Possible Scotlands* 96–97.

London alderman William Curtis and his service to George IV in Edinburgh. See McCracken-Flesher, *Possible Scotlands* 98–99, 109–10, 112, as well as the print of Curtis in Prebble.

Scotland's Destiny (Scottish Parliament, 2000; videocassette). The queen chose not to walk with Scotland's children and politicians to parliament.

Waverley's Wanderings

Tobias Smollett, *The Expedition of Humphry Clinker*, 1771. The Scottish Smollett sends a Welshman on a British tour. Scotland turns out better than expected.

Samuel Johnson, *A Journey to the Western Islands of Scotland*, 1775. Johnson travels north, finds Scotland barren, but has a good time talking about it.

Dorothy Wordsworth, *Recollections of a Tour Made in Scotland*, 1803. The Wordsworths and Coleridge view Scotland according to their characteristic perspectives.

John Carr, *Caledonian Sketches or a Tour through Scotland in 1807*, 1809. Belatedly takes on Samuel Johnson.

Robert Louis Stevenson, *Kidnapped*, 1886. A Scot is lost in Scotland.

Women

Sentimental biography of Scott's youthful romance (e.g., John Buchan, *Sir Walter Scott* [London: Cassell, 1932; print]).

Flora's self-construction as art. See Gill Perry and Michael Rossington, eds., *Femininity and Masculinity in Eighteenth-Century Art and Culture* (Manchester: Manchester UP, 1994; print).

Flora MacDonald and the practical circumstances by which she saved Bonnie Prince Charlie. See Theo Aronson, *Kings over the Water: The Saga of the Stuart Pretenders* (London: Cassell, 1979; print), 164–66.

Rose's omissions (as she talks to Waverley, when she nurses Waverley). See Martha Vicinus, ed., *Suffer and Be Still: Women in the Victorian Age* (Bloomington: Indiana UP, 1973; print).

Elizabeth Grant of Rothiemurchus, *Memoirs of a Highland Lady*, 1898.

Rosalind K. Marshall, *Virgins and Viragos: A History of Women in Scotland from 1080 to 1980* (Chicago: Academy Chicago, 1983; print).

Esther Breitenbach and Fiona Mackay, eds., *Women and Contemporary Scottish Politics* (Edinburgh: Polygon, 2001; print).

Framing the Covenanters (Again): Teaching *Old Mortality* in Context

Antony J. Hasler

Scott's *Waverley* and *The Tale of Old Mortality* both find a place on the edges of historical traumas—atrocities that trouble representation and so breed what Nicolas Abraham and Maria Torok identify as "transgenerational phantoms" (165–76). *Waverley*, of course, skirts Culloden and its aftershock in the annihilation of Highland culture. It was, however, *Old Mortality* and its prehistory of the Killing Time of 1684-85 that caused a firestorm of controversy, provoking literary responses from both John Galt and James Hogg. When I first taught The Scottish Experience: From Burns to Stevenson, I was offering the first Scottish literature course my department of English had ever seen—an experience, I suspect, familiar to many readers of this volume. I started with a simple desire to reveal to my students the fascination of the material. Courses, however, have a habit of changing under one's eyes, and in teaching *Old Mortality* and its fictional ripostes, Galt's *Ringan Gilhaize* and Hogg's *Private Memoirs and Confessions of a Justified Sinner*, I soon found that the historiographical strife around Scott's novel supplied an essential focus for classroom thinking about the play of cultural and political forces in Scott's time and place.[1] As I rethink my course, I also find myself considering how far the contention surrounding *Old Mortality* speaks to several twentieth- and twenty-first-century analogues, not all of them safely distanced by time and fiction.

In 1821, William Aiton, the sheriff-substitute of Hamilton, published an account of the covenanting victory over government troops at Drumclog in 1679, which includes some reflections on *Old Mortality*. Aiton's work is a fascinatingly contradictory mix, and a few sections can be of immense classroom use. Since the Drumclog skirmish was literally close to home for Aiton (whose ancestors, like those of other Lanarkshire gentlemen, had been directly involved on the covenanting side) the Covenanters are celebrated as protodefenders of civil liberties against tyranny—in a word, they are heritage. Yet there is also a deep distrust of the populist energies that to landowners like Aiton connected the Covenanters with the radicals of his own day (see Mack and Gilbert, in this volume). The link had become very apparent in 1815, when thousands of textile workers marched to Drumclog, both to commemorate the covenanting victory and to show support for Napoléon's escape from Elba.

Aiton praises *Old Mortality* in general terms but lists a string of (mostly topographical) errors, which call for the fiction police to step in:

> [S]ince the author has written a sort of medley between the true History and a Novel, there is danger of the Tales being received by many as the

> correct account of these transactions; which renders it necessary to have a line drawn between fact and fiction. . . . (85)

He also pours due scorn on the Freemasons and artisans who interpreted the Drumclog victory in their own class terms; they become dull illiterates, led astray by Whig politicians just as their ancestors were by the assassins of Archbishop Sharpe, and so themselves mistaking details of event, terrain, and relevance. Their reading of history is scornfully dismissed as ironic misreading. What is interesting here is the parallel: as Aiton describes them, the revisions imposed by Scott's "fancy" are not so very different from the infinitely more pernicious distortions of the Drumclog marchers.

This, of course, is not quite what we hear nowadays, when Scott is all too likely to figure in undergraduate courses on Romanticism (if at all) as the uncomplicated embodiment of an imperialist and expansionist Britain. While Scott's elaborate framing narratives are of course a crucial element in his version of history, the implication is often met that Scott, deeply unsympathetic to contemporary radicalism, "framed" his Covenanters in other ways too. Angus Calder supplies what is probably the majority view for modern readers: while Scott called both sides in his conflict "cruel and bloody bigots" (Scott, *Letters* 11: 59), "the Cavaliers are people one might find amusing company, whereas the 'western zealots' are so dour and devoted that . . . only distant admiration and perhaps a small measure of intellectual sympathy are available to the reader" (Calder 26). Aiton, however, tells a different story. For this lawman—and pace some Scott critics—Scott's Covenanters offered a mimetic space where imaginative fiction was not so very far from political sedition.

As Ina Ferris's fine account shows, such immediate energies were embroiled in a larger cultural debate about history and its relation to fiction, in particular Scott's own canonizing of the genre of the historical novel (*Achievement*). Early opponents of Scott's novel, in particular Thomas McCrie and the *Eclectic Review*'s Josiah Conder, took exception both to Scott's disabling of Covenanter history's sacred truth—in a sense, they defend the Covenanter's own turf of scripture and folk memory—and to his more general problematizing of the boundaries between truth ("the faithful page of history" [McCrie qtd. in Ferris, *Achievement* 157]) and fiction. Such a move threatened not only to supplant "true" records with a more palatable alternative but also to expose a not-so-latent instability in the very genre of history, since while archival verifiability "may rule out certain forms of writing as unhistorical . . . it cannot distinguish among competing stories made out of archival materials" (Ferris, *Achievement* 151). Scott's fiction suggests that narrative proliferation is the inevitable principle of written history and that no account can ever claim single and fixed authority. Scott's Covenanters may be restricted by their visionary or comic textualism—bound, in Ian Duncan's words, by "monomaniacal, logarchical possession by a single discourse . . . until they themselves are figures locked within it" (*Modern Romance* 95). And yet the formal experiment within which they have their being allows them a paradoxical emancipation, which in turn enables the answering, oppositional innovations of Galt and Hogg. Any bid to teach Scott's texts, at whatever level, cannot rest content with platitudes about Scott's "conservatism"; it needs to address the context of his historical figures, a context that looses even as it binds. Hence the need, in the classroom, to set the framing devices of his novels alongside other frames, including those supplied by the works answering his own, and to open them up to student interpretation.

But how to go about such reframing? A key point of reference for *Old Mortality* is of course Scott's paradigmatic historical novel, *Waverley* itself. The course's first part, "After the 'Forty-Five: Reading the Highlands," approached it by some oblique paths: excerpts from Ossian, from the stadial anthropology of Adam Ferguson and Hugh Blair, and also some of the poems of 1745 included in Derick Thomson's *Gaelic Poetry in the Eighteenth Century: A Bilingual Anthology*. Some of *Waverley*'s ideological patterns thus became visible, as Edward Waverley moves through a history vanishing into loss and memory and mirrors that history's suppression and disappearance in his own progress. (The Gaelic poetry restored a voice to Scott's stylized Highlanders.) A second unit, "Religion and Revolution: Writing the Killing Time," explored *Old Mortality* and *Ringan Gilhaize* alongside the historical materials and contemporary reviews already mentioned. Robert Burns's sophisticated play with folk diabolism in *Tam O'Shanter* and Hogg's *Three Perils of Man* prepared the way for *Confessions of a Justified Sinner*.

Establishing a wholly unfamiliar historical context is not easy. I relied on many handouts, "cast lists" of Scott's novels noting not merely characters but also their political and religious affiliation, and in the case of *Ringan*—I'm sorry!—a plot summary keyed to a timeline of covenanting history as the novel recounts it through the Gilhaize generations. There was a punitive initial week of lecturing and quizzing, as well as a showing of Peter Watkins's film *Culloden*. The movie provides a useful stimulus to discuss not only its content but also historical narrative in general, provoking reflections germane to Scott on the ironies of "true" history (here figured as documentary) and spectatorship (of which more later) as well as on the movie's Vietnam-era interrogation of the relation between imperialism and journalistic "objectivity" and on its double-edged critique of British genocide in the Highlands and of Jacobite posturing.

Equipped with some grasp of history and the *Waverley* paradigm, students were ready to address parallel aspects of *The Tale of Old Mortality*: the hero "inadvertently" caught between conflicting historical principles, the often startling genderings that mark these contrasts (Rose Bradwardine / Flora and Fergus MacIvor, Edith Bellenden / Balfour of Burley), the "Shakespearean" comic subplots. Moving beyond first-order responses to plot and character (does Morton jump or is he pushed?), we considered broader literary and cultural implications: what aspects of the book especially aggravated William Aiton, Thomas McCrie, and Josiah Conder? Ferris's emphasis on Scott's framing techniques points a way here. The pedant Cleishbotham introduces the (already dead) Pattieson; Pattieson is caught up in the character Old Mortality's "converse among the dead" (*Tale* 10); the latter's own work of restoration is "hastening, like all earthly memorials, to fall into ruin or decay" (13). And yet the vehement debate that followed the novel's publication suggests that reports of the Covenanters' deaths may have been greatly exaggerated. The Killing Time, as I reminded my class, is still divisive; the historian's skepticism about the actual numbers of the victims runs alongside the languages of martyrology (reprinted "Tales of the Covenanters" can still be found in evangelical bookstores or ordered from the scattered remnant's last refuge in cyberspace) and commodified national heritage (covenanting graves and monuments are still tourist sites and a good source of visual aids). Through discussion of the purposes of monuments and memorials, we examined how Scott's novel gains its fictional life from a careful thematizing of entropy and decay. Fiction is like the "rank-springing grass . . . that . . . owes its dark luxuriance to the foul and festering remnants of mortality which ferment beneath" (6–7), a negative life powerfully evoked in Pattieson's very denial of its presence. The final appearance of Miss Buskbody, reader of "the whole stock of three circulating libraries" (349), to adjudicate Pattieson's work reveals historical fiction as novelistic commodity. The multiplication of narrators diffuses history's "faithful page" into the fictive realm Scott's critics feared.

It is by reaching out to frame a text by which they are framed that Scott's characters show us where they belong in history. The Covenanters are presented as a series of rhetorics, from the "indulged" latitudinarian Poundtext to the comically ponderous (Kettledrummle), terrifying (Burley), and affectively powerful (MacBriar) Cameronian to the sublimely unhinged (Meiklewrath). Unleashing these figures on students is illuminating on many levels; at present, I simply note that it was useful to ask where the characters seem to script alternative endings to the history in which they are caught and so to script different versions of future historical memory. Thus John Graham of Claverhouse—a born-again Cavalier poet like his own Serjeant Bothwell, the bearer of royal blood in eclipse—offers a fatalistic bravura ("the memory which the soldier leaves behind him, like the long train of light that follows the sunken sun—that is all which is worth caring for" [268]). He is in turn trumped by the supposedly dead Meiklewrath, who rises from the floor, "a gory figure" (268), to foretell the exile of the Stuarts and Dundee's own doom. Both look to the Glorious Revolution—for Scott the decisive historical abolition of absolutism and popular revolt alike. Yet 1688–89 appears in *Old Mortality* as a gap, the end of Morton's ten-year exile, after which a curiously broken conclusion relegates Morton to the shadow world of the dead with which the narrative began. I asked students to compare the final sequence of *Old Mortality* with that similarly ironic and self-conscious instance of "framing" in *Waverley*, the portrait of Fergus MacIvor in full Highland dress on the wall at Tully-Veolan. Several found a troubling bleakness in *Old Mortality*'s final disintegration. Here, Scott's "very curious emptiness" (Muir 12) denotes not some imputed deficiency but a strategic and thoroughly disquieting acknowledgment of the insufficiencies of narrative closure.

Scott's Claverhouse prophesies his own death at Killiecrankie, "pressing one day some well-fought and hard-won field of battle, and dying with the shout of victory in my ear" (268). Galt's *Ringan Gilhaize* too builds up to this moment, but it is the outcome of a very different prophecy. The class looked hard in Scott's novel at narrative temporality and duration: the clear and precise sequence of events in the main body, the disjoined final episodes, the slow emergence and fading out of various frames. In *Ringan*, "frames" become remarkably difficult to define. Ferris speaks of the book's patriarchal narrative order (*Achievement* 165–85); it is a story of fathers and grandfathers, pervaded by an Old Testament sense of patrilineage and, it most unexpectedly turns out, ultimately anchored in the Declaration of Arbroath, the baronial assertion of Scottish autonomy directed to the papal curia in 1320. If in Scott collisions of culture and class issue in the ironic transcendence of a riven national past through literature and lending libraries, Galt seems to insist that Scotland's covenanting inheritance is the true heart of the nation.

As I took pains to stress to my class, however, Galt's relation to his novel is a complex one. The date of his birthday coincided with that of John Knox's 1550 arrival in Scotland, and Galt even ensured that his novel appeared on the same date in 1823. Yet he also insisted more than once that his viewpoint was not to be simplemindedly identified with Ringan's. How, we asked, do Scott's frames compare with Galt's narrative devices? In *Ringan*, voice and duration are constantly unsteady: Ringan's viewpoint and perspective meld with those of his forefathers; some events receive close attention, while extended passages of history rush past at a distance; the Gilhaize family's life is now the main clause and now a subordinate clause in the narrative syntax; and moments of messianic import ("John Knox is come!" [91]) slither indistinctly into local detail, minor characters, and anecdotes. (*Ringan Gilhaize* trivia—who are Icener Cunningham and Tobit Balmuto?—can be a somewhat disturbing classroom game.) I asked students to look especially hard at the description of Michael Gilhaize, Ringan's grandfather, and his meditations after the burning of the priest Walter Mill (Myln). The passage shifts tenses consistently, as the elder Gilhaize's anguished failure to find words for the remembered horror itself arouses his grandson's "implacable enmity" toward "papistical cruelties." Ringan's eager zeal impresses his grandfather:

> Then he would lay his hand upon my head, and say, the Lord had not gifted me with such zeal without having a task in store for my riper years. His words of prophecy, as shall hereafter appear, have greatly and wonderfully come to pass. But it is meet that for a season I should rehearse what ensued to him, for his story is full of solemnities and strange accidents. (32)

The "task" is the assassination of Dundee, the Man of Blood, and the passage is exemplary in its movement between emotion and exhortation, patriarchal prophecy and the discrete incidents that are Galt's "strange accidents." Throughout the novel's first part, Michael Gilhaize's espionage on behalf of the Lords of the Congregation puts him at every major historical event (one student memorably called him the Forrest Gump of the Scottish Reformation). These "accidents" rise, however, from the constant rhythm of circumstantial detail, not all of which is available to a providential reading.

The ultimate effect of Galt's book is, as we were able to observe, paradoxical. One side of *Ringan* does indeed answer to Ferris's model of a paternal, undifferentiated, quasi-biblical time. The novel, however, also conjures up the diffuse, seemingly random quality of Galt's earlier novels *The Entail* and *The Provost*, where close-to-the-ground empiricism (the "accumulation of small but decisive incidents") seems in Katie Trumpener's view to critique the grand moments of historical metanarrative and to complicate and "camouflage" agency (*Bardic Nationalism* 155). Even on the strength of this novel alone, students could see that Ringan's spiritual and divinely articulated narrative is distanced within the text by Galt's evocation of a plethora of material it will not quite absorb.

One incident exemplifies such internal distantiation. Ringan's narrative builds toward Dundee's death at the moment of Jacobite triumph. Critical too, however, is the earlier episode when a captive Ringan finds himself face-to-face with the severed head of his son, carried on the other side of the window of the Edinburgh Tolbooth. The shock of this "unfruitful thing" (*Ringan* 393) drives Ringan's fellow prisoner to flinch Ringan, loosening the bars to which he is clinging and enabling his companions to escape. The moment is jolting; near-hallucinatory horror folds into a clunking contrivance of providential plotting. While the récit of *Ringan* unequivocally labels Ringan's son's execution a tragedy, the narrative's overall formal investment in the moment, characterized as an appalling yet thrilling spasm of recognition, suggests something close to jouissance, here the father's enjoyment at the son's mortification. Galt responds to *Old Mortality*'s own phantasmagoric recalling of such matter, not least in the chilling night piece at the Drumshinnel farmhouse where the Cameronians exultantly prepare to sacrifice Morton, the convenient "ram caught in the thicket" (*Old Mortality* 261). The conjunction of horror and of plot coincidence that is self-advertising and divinely ratified suggests the obscene enjoyment that may lie in Covenanter lore, with its profound fascination with the Abrahamic sacrifice of sons ("the mystery of the required sacrifice was brought into wonderful effect" [*Ringan* 393]). As the prison bars break, *Ringan* destroys its patrilineal scaffolding, killing the son while still proceeding to its promised end, oblivious to mere event. My point is not that my undergraduate classroom was bubbling with conversations about Jacques Lacan (though I did hint at such possibilities through Freud's *Totem and Taboo*); it is rather that the class was able to perceive the tension between different modes of narration and to explore it productively.

After such an approach, Hogg's novel virtually taught itself. I have more than once included *Confessions* in other classes, and for readers familiar with the serial-killer genre Hogg's terrifying psychological exploration of Wringhim's antinomianism is immediately accessible. Students home in immediately on the novel's central epistemological question of Gil-Martin's true identity; coming to this problem from the novels by Scott and Galt, however, provoked a more precise response, which clarifies Hogg's reaction to the historiographical debate.

I began this section of the course by introducing the anonymous letter that Hogg wrote to *Blackwood's Edinburgh Magazine* to prepare a market for his novel. The letter, insisting on the topographical reality of a "suicide's grave," abolishes mediacy, as Hogg removes the safe distance between a comfortably remote, aesthetically swaddled historical past and the literary culture of his own present. With this unsettling proximity, however, comes a radical unknowability. Scott's editorial layers, as well as Galt's presentation of a self-enunciation where to say "I" *is* to speak one's forefathers, give place to splits and doublings. Instead of a single protagonist, Hogg supplies a fiction divided between two narrators, a Scott-like post-Enlightenment editor and Robert Wringhim, the "justified sinner." Scott's carefully tempered framing fictions and his apparatus of notes are parodically replicated by the editor's perplexed pursuit of unstable sources. The editor stands bewildered by the object of this history ("the rage of fanaticism in former days" [64]) and by a confessional narrative that itself doubles up, as Wringhim calls into being the diabolical Gil-Martin.

For a class acquainted with Scott's and Galt's work, much in the *Confessions* carried a special shock of recognition. It was also clear, however, that Hogg's novel, like Galt's, effects not a simple break with Scott but a loosening of one strand in Scott's meticulous synthesis that ultimately threatens to unravel the whole. After reading Scott, the class was better able to appreciate a work that recasts editorial detachment as incomprehension and that induces readerly panic by presenting the subjectivities of the past and the idea of historical truth as inaccessible. I began by speaking of transgenerational phantoms; the class understood that for Hogg the past as object of investigation is animated by a spectral violence that resists easy intelligibility and assimilation. And—not least with Aiton's fixation on topography and truth in mind—students could understand the force of that familiar locus in recent Hogg criticism, the hilltop grave where the editor, here explicitly associated with Scott's circle, is brought up against historical remains at their most aggravatingly material. Encountering Scott on his own terrain, Hogg literally decomposes the historical novel, while his own projection, the Ettrick Shepherd, confronts the body-snatching literati with a dry distaste for those "ganging to houk up hunder-year-auld banes" (170). At the center of Hogg's history lie a half-decayed body and a "damp, rotten and yellow" pamphlet mouldered into "one solid piece" (173). The experience of historical understanding is here displaced by the exhuming of a past beyond interpretation.[2]

I offer a few anecdotal (Galtian?) conclusions of my own. I teach at a Catholic university, to whose culture I, as a displaced Brit of fairly secular disposition, maintain a respectful and involved but not wholly intrinsic relation. When I first taught this course in 1998, the release of the violent and homophobic *Braveheart* lay in the relatively recent past. The familiar film gave a real charge to a class that counted among its members Irish American Catholics highly conscious of their own national-cultural heritage. (They brought much to the course, not least because the very differences in the experiences of two "internal colonies" under English hegemony were valuable in pedagogical terms.)[3] Against this background, what became visible was the unfettered, free-floating quality of images and rhetorics. While *Braveheart* had evidently struck a blow for a certain kind of Scottish nationalism, it had also been appropriated by other political groups; students would show me broadsheets sporting the image of a plaided Mel Gibson, the slogan "Freedom!" standing for a fierce loathing of central government. During the reading of *Old Mortality*, it became apparent that something curiously similar was happening to the covenanting rhetoric of the Drumclog chapters. When Ephraim MacBriar's biblical eschatology met with an ideology of "freedom" from English domination, many of my students were able to recognize the familial and generational resentments and doctrinal alignments with which they themselves had grown up. Elements that might have been thought decisive—covenanting contempt for "papistry" and its works, scriptural fundamentalism, all the evidence that Scott's oppressed Presbyterians were ideologically about as far from Irish Catholics as could be imagined—did not at first make much difference. It is easy to dismiss this initial classroom response as simple misrecognition, and the lability of historical signifiers it bespeaks goes perilously far; if radicals of 1815 could recognize the Covenanters as ancestors, today a glance (not for the faint hearted) at Web sites like *Crown of Christ* make it clear that William Wallace is not the only historical figure up for grabs by the American right. Yet I wonder—tentatively, I hope not sentimentally—whether Scott's Covenanters do not justify the response of 1815, and indeed of my students, and whether in liberating fiction from a discourse of historical truth Scott also confers other kinds of emancipation. I refer to the political utopianism that makes MacBriar's Isaiah-derived apotheosis ("the banner of Reformation is spread abroad on the mountains in its first loveliness, and the gates of hell shall not prevail against it" [*Old Mortality* 155]) strangely akin to Ernst Bloch's revelation of immanence ("the morning threshold, a threshold believed to be reached, of something which has come close" [3: 1264]).

It is suggestive that the same students were not able to make this mistake with *Ringan Gilhaize* and were accordingly offended. When we discussed it, I tried to bring out the narrative techniques that create this impression. It is purely because of Scott's vast and unacknowledged influence that of the three novels under discussion, his looks the most conventional to a historically uninformed reader. It is the one most easily apprehended by today's readers as a "novel"; its capacious embrace of multiple plotlines and subsidiary characters, its discursive signposting and editorializing, all project Scott's Covenanters as one among several allegiances a fictional hero, who may also be a surrogate reader, can inspect. Galt's own mode of artifice—elision of distinctions between narrative foreground and background, deviations that erode differences between "major" and "minor" events, the historically documented and the fictionally interposed—took away the guardrails and meant that Ringan's parti pris couldn't be sidestepped; it had to be met on its own terms, and loved or loathed accordingly.

Such classroom controversies point, however distantly, to the reasons that this course is in a state of transition. The novels discussed here articulate concerns that in the last few years have become especially urgent. Covenanters and royalists together raise definitional and ethical issues surrounding religion, "terrorism," and state violence, and we might extend this focus to take in a number of questions. Can comparisons be drawn between the "state of exception" (Agamben) that legitimizes the egregious measures carried out by modern democracies in the name of counterterrorism and the activities of both sides in these novels? Does the telos set in place by the Glorious Revolution impose its own order of necessity on the action? Does Scott's Morton figure as prototypical liberal humanist confronted with his own limits or as Žižek's "liberal fake" (*Iraq* 67–74), a "moderate" participant in history who controls our view of the Covenanters' "radical [attempt] to 'step outside'" history (81–82)? Is Morton—as has been said of Edward Waverley—a historical tourist, who beholds crises, emotes, and departs, the appalled observer of a history that is essentially spectacle (Buzard, "Translation")? How do the protagonists of Hogg and Galt compare with him? Complex lines of force also run from Scott's harrowing deployment of this fiction to Jean Baudrillard's much-maligned claims that terrorism ("international," of course) and war have become a media event, a welter of simulacra that mask the event (*Gulf War*) but that can also, paradoxically, resurrect it (*Spirit*). Scott's thoroughly self-conscious "packaging" of a violent history comes from an early-nineteenth-century Edinburgh whose aesthetic institutions included journalism, and while I do not suggest some crude identity between Scott's fictions and modern media, the relationship invites classroom exploration.

Such questions should open rather than resolve class discussion, and they appear because Scott's own text opens them. Scott's writing, as I have noted, is too often presented as monolithically impervious to differing perspectives, and a final glance at the relation between *Old Mortality* and *Confessions* may be in order here. Critics have observed that while the structures of Hogg's novel render history indecipherable, they also offer an apprehension of the tormented and fanatical protagonist that cannot be made available any other way (Mack, "Revisiting"; Petrie). As he contends with Scott, Hogg leaves behind the eighteenth-century tropes of sympathetic identity to provide instead an object lesson in the ethics of difference. Yet it is Scott's achievement that *Old Mortality* makes room for, and in the end even solicits, the replies of Hogg and Galt.

NOTES

[1] No student-friendly edition currently exists of *The Brownie of Bodsbeck* (1818), the Hogg novel most immediately relevant to *Old Mortality*.

[2] My debt to Duncan ("Shadows of the Potentate" and "Upright Corpse") and Mack ("Revisiting") will be obvious here.

[3] The phrase is Hechter's.

Teaching *The Heart of Mid-Lothian*

David Hewitt

"Would you lie to save your sister?" I have opened seminar discussion of *The Heart of Mid-Lothian* in this way on several occasions. The question is explosive. Most students say yes without hesitation, arguing that it would be wrong to hang Effie for a crime she did not commit, that the law is unjust, that an unjust law should not be obeyed. There are always some who, rather more tentatively, say no, arguing for their part that one can't lie, that one's doing so would be perjury, that one would have sworn on the Bible. Most say that Effie is a victim of both a man and a patriarchal legal system; others call her selfish, demanding an unacceptable sacrifice of her sister to get her out of a situation she herself has created in getting pregnant and in refusing to escape from jail when the door was open. The argument can become heated.

It is because the argument can become heated that seminar discussion of *The Heart of Mid-Lothian* is an ideal way of engaging students in Scott. In the Waverley novels individual choice is culturally determined, compromised by politics, religion, race, social class, financial status: the young are often resistant to this way of seeing things. But it is the consideration of cultural determinism that makes the Waverley novels necessary reading for students, and through arguing about *The Heart of Mid-Lothian* they surprise themselves into a discovery of the hugely controversial public issues raised by Scott and thereby come to appreciate the intellectual relevancy of the Waverley novels.

Most of the participants in the "would you lie for your sister" debate exhibit a variety of honestly held prejudices, all of which are pertinent to the discussion of *The Heart of Mid-Lothian*, but they are usually unable to tease out the intellectual implications of what they are saying. They should be challenged to find textual support for the positions they take up, and as *The Heart of Mid-Lothian* is rich in dramatic discussion it is not difficult to locate suitable passages.

In the park, Jeanie argues with Robertson, who is trying to impress on her the need to lie in court:

> "But," replied Jeanie, whose judgment was too accurate not to see the sophistry of this argument, "I shall be man-sworn in the very thing in which my testimony is wanted, for it is the concealment for which poor Effie is blamed, and you would make me tell a falsehood anent it."
>
> "I see," he said, "my first suspicions of you were right, and that you will let your sister, innocent, fair, and guiltless, except in trusting a villain, die the death of a murderess, rather than bestow the breath of your mouth and the sound of your voice to save her."
>
> "I wad ware the best blood in my body to keep her skaithless," said Jeanie, weeping in bitter agony, "but I canna change right into wrang, or make that true which is false."

> "Foolish, hard-hearted girl," said the stranger, "are you afraid of what they may do to you? I tell you, even the retainers of the law, who course life as greyhounds do hares, will rejoice at the escape of a creature so young—so beautiful; that they will not suspect your tale; that, if they did suspect it, they would consider you as deserving, not only of forgiveness, but of praise for your natural affection."
>
> "It is not man I fear," said Jeanie, looking upward; "the God, whose name I must call on to witness the truth of what I say, he will know the falsehood."
>
> "And he will know the motive," said the stranger, eagerly; "he will know that you are doing this—not for lucre of gain, but to save the life of the innocent, and prevent the commission of a worse crime than that which the law seeks to avenge."
>
> "He has given us a law," said Jeanie, "for the lamp of our path; if we stray from it, we err against knowledge—I may not do evil, even that good may come out of it." (141–42; 160)[1]

In this interchange both sides can find support. Jeanie's declaration, "I canna change right into wrang, or make that true which is false," is the central point. It is powerfully phrased; it is backed by an appeal to the law of God (even the godless can recognize the force of the law of God); and it makes truth telling a categorical imperative. The other party will point to Robertson's appeal to "natural affection" (arguing that love of one's sister *should* come before the consideration of the public good) and to his recognition that in hanging Effie the law will commit a worse crime than her concealing a pregnancy. The first party will counter and say that although Robertson has some good points they are devalued by the way in which he uses them (he makes them instruments to rectify his own wrong actions) and that in any case his hysterical personality suggests that he is unable to distinguish clearly the difference between right and wrong. The other party may accept this but argue nevertheless that the narrative rhetoric is used in furthering a bad cause: in other words, Scott is wrong.

But can an authoritative position be identified? Jeanie is the heroine, and readers, naively, expect to approve of the principal character. She is heroic: when she realizes that there is another way of saving Effie, she takes it. Readers recognize that in terms of the novel she is not able to be other than what she is: she is a product of the culture to which she belongs and understands the Old Testament commandments in a simple and literal way. "Thou shalt not bear false witness" means you must not lie (Exod. 20.16); however, sympathy does not necessarily imply endorsement.

Jeanie makes telling the truth in court central to her existence. But as Ratcliffe seems about to molest her, she tells him a lie about the whereabouts of Robertson (162, 184–85). She lies to the footpads about how much money she is carrying (259, 295). When the queen asks if she had any friends "engaged in the Porteous mob" (340; 386), Jeanie is evasive, "happy that the question was so framed that she could, with a good conscience, answer it in the negative" (340; 386). It has from time to time been suggested that Scott has been inconsistent in having Jeanie tell untruths, but the text is as it is, and Jeanie's lies and evasions undercut confidence in her moral clear-sightedness. They should make readers ask whether Jeanie is motivated solely by her reverence for the law of God.

In the passage above, Jeanie says, "I wad ware the best blood in my body to keep her [Effie] skaithless." The pronouncement is deeply uncomfortable: Jeanie is prepared to die to keep Effie from harm, but not to tell a lie. When Jeanie visits Effie in prison before the trial, she says, "[H]ow could ye conceal your situation frae me! O, woman, had I deserved this at your hand?—had ye spoke but ae word—sorry we might hae been, and shamed we might hae been, but this awfu' dispensation had never come ower us" (186; 211). In the chapter where Jeanie visits Effie in jail, it seems that Jeanie feels more pity for herself than for her sister, and the epigraph from *Measure for Measure* (3.1.133–36) at the head of the chapter implies a parallel between Isabella's narcissistic righteousness and Jeanie's rectitude.

Would it have been "false witness" had she lied in court? The answer must be yes, but the law of Moses is less simple than Jeanie supposes. "Blood must have Blood," Robertson tells Butler (60; 70), a view that is both proverbial and has biblical support. David Deans says, "an eye for an eye, a tooth for a tooth, life for life, blood for blood—it's the law of God and it's the law of man" (94; 109). Such vengeful statements come straight from the Bible—from Exodus 21.24, Leviticus 24.20, and Deuteronomy 19.21—and their invocation makes modern readers recognize that we are apt to be selective about the biblical texts that we countenance. Jeanie and her father read the Bible differently, and we must ask why Jeanie is right and David is wrong.

While Jeanie should have been able to recognize the ambiguities of her own behavior and could have acknowledged the difference between her own and her father's understanding of scripture, she can have no intellectual understanding of the complexities of the legal system. Here the seminar leader may demand that the class consider why Scott should have placed the trial of Effie in the context of the Porteous riot. Certainly they are contemporaneous, but what does their juxtaposition mean? Butler argues with the rioters who drag Porteous to his death, saying:

> You cannot have, by the laws of God or man, power to take away the life of a human creature, however deserving he may be of death. If it is murder even in a lawful magistrate to execute an offender otherwise than in the place, time, and manner which his sentence prescribes, what must it be in you, who have no warrant for your interference but your own wills? (60; 70)

To Butler, in other words, justice is coincidental with the formulations and procedures of the law. In practice, this too is Jeanie's position. But the law that condemns Effie is manifestly unjust: there is no problem in making the concealing of a pregnancy an offense, but it is clear that from the eighteenth century to the present day the punishment prescribed in statute has been considered totally disproportionate to the crime.[2] Scott removes all the ambiguities that surrounded the trial for child murder of Isobel Walker, Effie's original. Effie conceals her pregnancy and is not known to have asked for assistance at the birth; she is condemned to death for these reasons, not for murder. The prosecution is not required, and does not try, to prove that a murder has been committed. We believe she did not murder her baby, and there are extenuating circumstances in that she suffered from puerperal fever. No reader in reviewing Effie's case can possibly endorse the law, and all pronounce the law unjust. In so doing, they invoke an extrajudicial idea of justice. This is exactly what the rioters do when lynching Porteous: "we are those whom heaven and our righteous anger, have stirred up to execute judgment" (62; 72); and this is what Robertson does in the park when telling Jeanie to lie. Scott brings together two near-contemporaneous legal cases, which set up conflicting models of justice and which provoke contradictory responses in the readers.

Further, Scott makes sure we see that the law and the legal system are politicized. Middleburgh says, "The crime has been too common, and examples are become necessary" (166; 188), and Argyle repeats this view in nearly the same terms: "The crime has been but too common—the Scots crown-lawyers think it is right there should be an example" (320; 364). In other words, the enforcement of the law is an act of state policy. The legal system in Scotland is repeatedly represented by characters in the novel as a means of maintaining the rule of a government lacking popular support. During the riot Robertson tells Butler that "a corrupt government" protected Porteous (62; 72). David Deans consistently maintains that the state is not properly constituted in that it does not recognize the theocracy of 1642 to 1650, which to him is the model of right government (see esp. 173; 196). Jeanie herself cannot betray Robertson to the government to save her sister because it "would be considered as an act of treason against the independence of Scotland" (314; 356). And Scott alters the historical record so that the Porteous riot is less a riot than an act of rebellion (see Hewitt and Lumsden 585–88). In these circumstances, where is justice?

Jeanie, and what Jeanie stands for, can be deconstructed. But some may feel that this is a reading against the grain, for the narrator is clearly "on Jeanie's side." For instance, in the passage above, Robertson's argument is called "sophistry." While that cannot be denied, the overall position of the narrator is less clear. The nominal narrator, Peter Pattieson, is telling a story "founded upon the conversation of the evening" he spent with Hardie and Halkit (20; 25). He does not appear to sift evidence and take a political stance as he does in *The Tale of Old Mortality*. There are gaps and contradictions in the narrative, such as Madge's running away (160; 182) and then being produced from prison the next morning (168; 190); the editors of the Edinburgh edition of the Waverley novels took the view that these were mistakes, but it is possible that such discrepancies were intentional, deliberate gaps that force readers to recognize their part in making the narrative coherent. The concluding moral, "the paths of virtue, though seldom those of worldly greatness, are always those of pleasantness and peace" (468; 532), is so strikingly inept—it is manifestly wrong to say that all that Jeanie goes through as a result of a family catastrophe is pleasant—that readers are bound to conclude that the narrator is unreliable and weak. And the alert may notice that in the Bible it is not "the paths of virtue" but the paths of wisdom that are "always those of pleasantness and peace" (Prov. 3.17). While the narrator makes passing comments, he has no overview and often seems to be unaware of the implications of the story he is telling. It is plain that the "editor," Jedidiah Cleishbotham, feels no responsibility for the tale he publishes: he has merely misappropriated the literary remains of his colleague Peter Pattieson and become rich. But the fictional absence of control makes for a very open narrative that allows the reader to respond directly to the debate without the mediation of a directing intelligence.

The heterogeneity of the literary material also makes for an open narrative. There is much dialogue, and some of that dialogue constitutes straightforward debate on the nature of justice. Despite Mikhail Bakhtin's arguments on the double-voiced nature of dialogue in fiction, positions in the novel are formulated so strongly that they tend to override narratorial coloring and make a claim to be considered alongside some of the great philosophic debates in Plato's *Republic* and the philosopher David Hume's *Dialogues concerning Natural Religion*. The first volume is dominated by historical writing, the second by the narrative of court proceedings in exactly the form used in the records of trials before the High Court of Justiciary, the highest criminal court of Scotland. The third mimics *The Pilgrim's Progress*, and the last a ballad in its beginning and a gothic novel in its ending. The adoption and the transformation of a variety of texts facilitate the recognition that each implies its own conception of "truth": historical narratives interpret events, while court records put down in due form the statements of witnesses; *The Pilgrim's Progress* is the allegorical story of Christian and Christiana's journey to the new Jerusalem. In the gothic novel there is a kind of ideal distribution of justice in accord with psychological demands.

The narrative is impregnated with intertexts, which introduce perspectives on justice from popular songs and proverbial sayings, the Bible, *Measure for Measure*, *The Pilgrim's Progress*, the two volumes of *Commentaries on the Law of Scotland Respecting Crimes* by the jurist David Hume (nephew of the philosopher), while quotations from Tobias Smollett and George Crabbe relate the debate on justice to social and economic issues. In the quotation with which this chapter opens, for instance, Jeanie reasons as a member of a church whose teaching is biblical, and her words reflect the authority of the Bible, for she paraphrases Proverbs 6.23: "For the commandment is a lamp; and the law is light; and reproofs of instruction are the way of life." Her whole outlook is structured in the belief that the law of God is knowable and unequivocal. Robertson on the other hand says that all that is required of her is a word, mere breath. His persuasion initially sounds facile, the petulant response of someone to whom a lie is nothing, but another biblical intertext strengthens his position, for Psalm 33.6 reads, "By the word of the Lord were the heavens made; and all the host of them by the breath of his mouth." The psalmist is talking of God, and the message from Robertson is that words create reality.

Since Plato, Western philosophers have sought objective values; Jeanie believes that the law of God is a knowable objective reality. Robertson, however, is more "modern" in assuming that there is no reality other than how things are represented. And this seems a dominant view in the novel. Had Effie "spoke but ae word" (186; 211), she would not have made herself liable to the law. Ratcliffe tells Jeanie "three words of your mouth would give the girl a chance to nick Moll Blood" (189; 215). After the trial Effie bitterly upbraids Jeanie: "What signifies coming to greet ower me, when you have killed me?—killed me, when a word of your mouth would have saved me" (224; 255). When Jeanie appeals to the queen for a pardon for Effie, she says that "a word of the King's mouth" might restore her to her father (340; 387).

In *The Heart of Mid-Lothian*, the *word* possesses hugely creative power, as is indicated by the most important of all the promptings on the nature of language, Mrs. Saddletree's declaration: "Then, if the Law makes murders . . . the Law should be hanged for them" (47; 55). Comic though it seems at first, it is, nonetheless, the fundamental challenge to the idea of justice. In the novel, Wilson is hanged; Porteous kills members of the crowd and is himself lynched; Renwick and many other Covenanters were executed during a civil war; Meg Murdockson is hanged; Madge is ducked as a witch and dies subsequently; the Whistler kills his father, Sir George Staunton. The list of killings brings out the truth of Mrs. Saddletree's observation: "murder" is a matter of classification; "murder" is created by law. In the end, then, *The Heart of Mid-Lothian* is a novel that hinges on a profound epistemological insight, that much of what is normally considered "reality" does not have an objective existence but is determined by the words we use.

The Heart of Mid-Lothian is one of the greatest of novels, not because it tells readers what justice consists of, but because it generates debate that cannot be confined to a discussion of the text alone. Yet almost every idea about the nature of justice that is likely to rise in argument finds its counterpart somewhere in the novel, so that the intellectual controversy generated by the question, Would you lie to save your sister?, can be textually based. The novel does not offer any solution other than the mercy of God, to which there are repeated appeals. Butler exhorts the rioters to spare Porteous: "In the name of Him who is all Mercy! shew mercy to this unhappy man, and do not dip your hands in his blood, nor rush into the very crime which you are desirous of avenging" (60; 70). While Madge in a sad misapplication of John Bunyan sees herself as Mercy and Jeanie as Christiana going to visit the house of the Interpreter, Jeanie sees in the king the figure of Justice and Mercy. Yet even the suggestion that justice cannot be achieved by human means is compromised by the nature of the narrative, a family chronicle covering about eighty years but rolled up in itself so that past and future are present in the story of the events of the nine months September 1736 to May 1737. The idea of justice, like everything else, is not abstract but historically determined. The theocratic ideas die with David Deans; the great seventeenth- and eighteenth-century codifications of Scots law that represent justice as the product of a system of rules and procedures seem to prevail. And yet they do not, for the culmination of the novel is an act of parricide. We may speculate on which anthropological interpretation of parricide might be most apposite, but to a reader there is something dramatically just in the criminal father's being killed by extrajudicial action such as he himself had engaged in and defended in 1736.[3]

NOTES

[1] The first set of page numbers are from Hewitt and Lumsden's edition of *The Heart of Mid-Lothian;* all quotations are taken from this edition. The second set of page numbers are from Inglis's edition, which may be more easily available to readers.

[2] For an analysis of attitudes to this law in the eighteenth century and for an account of Scott's treatment of his sources, see Hewitt and Lumsden 588–92.

[3] This article is less an account of how to teach *The Heart of Mid-Lothian* than a kind of summary of many stimulating seminar discussions. I wish to acknowledge with gratitude the insights into *The Heart of Mid-Lothian* that I have gained from my students.

"This Monstrous Passion": Teaching *The Bride of Lammermoor* and Queer Theory

Oliver S. Buckton

The Bride of Lammermoor has long been recognized as departing from the conventional narrative structure of the Waverley novels, especially in its renunciation of the marriage-plot formula that is used frequently elsewhere in the series. When I assign the text in an undergraduate course on the nineteenth-century British novel—the context in which I most frequently teach Scott—*Bride* appears on the syllabus between *Pride and Prejudice* and *Jane Eyre* or *David Copperfield*, novels in which narrative closure is achieved through the convention of marriage, or what E. M. Forster irascibly termed "that idiotic use of marriage as a finale" (38). In the case of Scott, the marriage plot usually involves the "prudent" union of the hero and an exemplary, rational, and desirable heroine: the classic example being *Waverley*, which, as James Buzard argues, "will attach its hero to the daughter of a gentleman"—in other words, Rose Bradwardine—and thereby provide "the assurance of an ultimate closure" (*Disorienting Fiction* 93, 92). Moreover, as Alexander Welsh points out, such a marriage achieves the consolidation of property through its continuation within the family or restoration to the rightful heirs (*Hero* [1992] 82). In both these respects, *Bride* departs from the usual pattern: the hero, Edgar Ravenswood, does not marry his betrothed, Lucy Ashton, and fails to achieve the reconciliation between the Ashtons and Ravenswoods that such a marriage would enable. Edgar, moreover, dies before his ancestral title—forfeited as a result of his father's supporting James II's cause in the civil war of 1689—can be restored to him.

Hence, *Bride* affords an invaluable opportunity in such a course to examine both how the hegemony of the familiar marriage plot may be resisted in fiction and how the tragic outcome of this particular novel is connected to the failure to resolve the historical conflicts represented in the narrative. One of the theoretical positions I seek to convey throughout this course is that the nineteenth-century novel is a profoundly ideological form, as Fredric Jameson argues, "with the function of inventing imaginary or formal 'solutions' to irresolvable social contradictions" (79). Marriage, of course, is one of the "solutions" most frequently offered by nineteenth-century novelists to resolve social contradictions. It instantiates, in Lee Edelman's phrase, the "compulsory narrative" of a commitment to "reproductive futurism" (21). In its "refusal to embrace the genealogical fantasy that braces the social order," *The Bride of Lammermoor* poses a threat not only to "life's vital machinery" but also to the very function of the novel as ideological form (Edelman 44). In this essay, I argue that the transgressive passions of the protagonist—in particular the surfacing of homoerotic attachments that disrupt marital intentions—offer a compelling pedagogical tool with which to examine the collapse of the marriage plot and its "prospect of a future" (Edelman 53).

At the outset of the section of the course on *Bride*, I emphasize that Scott's narrative dwells at length on Edgar's erotic ambivalence, for example, in a passage in the eighth chapter, where the conflict between his familial loyalty and sexual desire is first broached:

> There already existed in his bosom two contradictory passions—a desire to revenge the death of his father, *strangely qualified* by admiration of his enemy's daughter. Against the former feeling he had struggled, until it seemed to him upon the wane; against the latter he used no means of resistance, for he did not suspect its existence. (97; 70; emphasis added)[1]

Hinting at an unconscious desire, the narrative ascribes Edgar's resistance against romantic attraction to Lucy to his enmity with Lord Ashton. Moreover, Edgar's "contradictory passions," I point out, raise the issue of the formal dilemma or ambivalence of the narrative itself. The outcome of this war between the passions within Edgar will determine the form that the novel will take.

Yet Edgar's heterosexual desire is no less "strangely qualified" by the animation of homoerotic affiliations engendered within a context of revenge. In particular, the novel's suppressed Jacobite subplot provides a homosocial milieu in which Edgar's homoerotic desire is at once fostered and resisted. Eve Kosofsky Sedgwick's theorizing of "the potential unbrokenness of a continuum between homosocial and homosexual" desire is useful in alerting students to the possibility that the homosocial context of the Jacobites might include forms of sexual activity that are similarly outlawed (1). *Bride* provides "an example of how homosocial environments are powerfully seductive but potentially unsettling for those who are ambivalent about their sexuality" (Chatterjee and Horan 130). Such a reading is supported by the language used to depict revenge, itself presented as an eroticized passion in the novel, the illicit and perverse nature of which leads to its designation as "monstrous."

Early in the class's discussion of *Bride* I emphasize the importance to the plot of Jacobitism and the recurring efforts to restore the Stuarts to the British throne. As the narrative begins, Edgar's father, Lord Ravenswood, has supported the Stuarts following the "Glorious Revolution" of 1689, thus causing the loss of the family's ancestral title. Subsequently, the family's property has been appropriated by Sir William Ashton, thereby exacerbating the poverty and humiliation under which Edgar suffers. The Jacobite cause surfaces, in debased form, through the Machiavellian presence of Craigengelt, an agent of the exiled Stuarts, who recruits the malcontent Hayston Bucklaw as his accomplice. Together, in secret, the two men plot the political entrapment of Ravenswood, who has been enraged by William Ashton's attempt to suppress his father's Episcopal funeral service.

There are clear grounds for reading Edgar's involvement with the Jacobites as a form of homoerotic investment, particularly in the novel's vocabulary of "passion" and "vice." Scott refers to Edgar's "passion which was, and had long been, a prevalent vice in the Scottish disposition" (31; 19), a phrase that may refer in the nineteenth century to revenge and same-sex desire. The association of such vice with the upper classes is affirmed by the relationship of Ravenswood and Bucklaw in *Bride*. As the only son of a deceased and disgraced Jacobite, Edgar is an easy target for the seductions of Craigengelt and Bucklaw. As "the heir of this ruined family" (26; 15), Edgar is viewed as an object of desire by these outlaws, as "such an acquisition [will] sound well both at Versailles and Saint Germains" (71; 49). Following his humiliating failure to kill Lord Ashton, Edgar apparently breaks off his homosocial association with the Jacobites, yet without resolving the powerful and disruptive passions it has engendered. Lacking any outlet of the kind that Scott developed in the fully fledged Jacobite plots of *Waverley* and *Redgauntlet*, the homosocial bonds between Edgar, Bucklaw, and Craigengelt are destined to reemerge as a covert form of same-sex desire, mediated by a rivalry for Lucy Ashton.

The disruptive narrative force of Edgar's homosocial desire is manifested when Bucklaw, provoked by Edgar's "insolence" (76; 54), pursues the master as he leaves Tod's Hole and challenges him to a duel with the words "I always thought and said you were a pretty man; I should be sorry to report you otherwise" (78; 55). In the ensuing combat, Edgar displays powerfully ambivalent feelings toward Bucklaw: having first called him a "hot-headed bully" (76; 54), Edgar then addresses his antagonist as "a generous fellow" and offers an apology (79; 56). When Bucklaw is warned that Craigengelt has been "taken" by government forces, Edgar spontaneously extends an invitation to his new friend: "[R]ide home to Wolf's Crag with me. There are places in the old tower where you might lie hid, were a thousand men to seek you" (79; 56). Bucklaw's presence at Wolf's Crag thus becomes a "secret" that Edgar proposes to hide from prying eyes. Bucklaw's pursuit of Edgar and their subsequent cohabitation at Wolf's Crag precipitate an intimacy that is suggestive of the uncanny relation between protagonist and "double," identified by Sedgwick as a recurring homoerotic motif of the gothic novel. This motif involves a protagonist "who is not only persecuted by, but considers himself transparent to and often under the compulsion of, another male" (91). Sedgwick, examining the gothic as "an exploration of the perverse," specifically links same-sex desire with gothic fiction, describing it as "the first novelistic form in England to have close, relatively visible links to male homosexuality" (91).

The intimacy between Bucklaw and Edgar illustrates just such "transparency" and "compulsion," as Bucklaw reveals an uncanny knowledge of the Master's intimate secrets, charging Edgar with having "nursed in your bosom one great goodly snake that has swallowed all the rest, and is . . . sure to devour you" (81; 58). The phallic symbolism of Bucklaw's metaphor is glaring, yet Edgar claims ignorance of this "snake," asking, "What, to speak without a metaphor, do you call this monstrous passion, which you charge me with fostering?" (81; 58). Though Bucklaw's response is direct ("Revenge, my good sir, revenge"), the attempt "to speak without a metaphor" is a futile one: same-sex passion cannot be represented in nonmetaphoric or nonsymbolic terms, since it defies political or social articulation. Moreover, the instinct for "revenge" invokes the death drive, that "inarticulable surplus that dismantles the subject from within" and that "names what the queer, in the order of the social, is called forth to figure: the negativity opposed to every form of social viability" (Edelman 9).

Bucklaw here reveals knowledge, if not approbation, of the secret "passion" that has come to isolate Ravenswood from the social order. The identification of this passion as "monstrous" suggests Scott's association of powerful desire with destructive forces, representative of a culture in which, as Welsh points out, "morality was typically constructed in terms of prudence, restraint, suppression" (*Hero* [1992] 112). Without the homosocial context of Jacobitism, which would make his revenge public and historically legible, Edgar is obliged to disavow his passion as a form of inadmissible perversion: "I deny the purpose. . . . I had no such intention; I meant but to confront the oppressor ere I left my native land, and upbraid him" (81; 58).

Edgar's transparency to Bucklaw is not the only aspect of their liaison that suggests the dynamic of homoerotic "doubling." Just as the Jacobite conspiracy is formed "in the most private apartment of a small obscure inn"(69; 48), the homosocial intimacy of Bucklaw and Edgar is itself shrouded in secrecy, as Edgar informs his servant Caleb that Bucklaw is "under hiding" (89; 64) and instructs that he be accommodated in the "secret chamber . . . assigned for this purpose" (90; 66). Bucklaw, thus confined, continues to reveal his intimate knowledge of Ravenswood's secret passion, asking, "[H]ave you been able to give battle valiantly to your bosom-snake?" (93; 67).

At this point in the class, I suggest that this interweaving between same-sex desire; male antagonism/rivalry; and secrecy, or suppression, is also dramatized in several other Waverley novels. By placing *Bride* in the context of the homoerotic dynamics in other Scott novels, I encourage students to recognize the queer aspects of the narrative as part of a larger pattern, rather than as an isolated instance of textual deviance. For example, in *The Fortunes of Nigel*, Scott at once hints at and suppresses the homosexuality of King James I of Great Britain (VI of Scotland), representing a predominantly male, sexually dissident court that resists the heterosexual closure generally required of the heroes of the Waverley novels. The novel's protagonist, Nigel Oliphaunt, is however permitted to depart the court and secure his marital union. The exclusion of women from the royal circle is repeated in *The Talisman*, where, however, the text's homoeroticism does implicate the protagonist himself, Sir Kenneth, who, following his banishment from the crusader camp, disguises himself as a Nubian slave, subsequently becoming an object of King Richard's desiring gaze. Unlike Edgar Ravenswood, whose same-sex attachment confirms his inability to marry and reclaim his hereditary title, Kenneth's desirability for men is rewarded, as King Richard, commanding that Kenneth "[h]ere terminate his various disguises," proclaims, "The adventurous knight, Kenneth, arises David, Earl of Huntingdon, Prince Royal of Scotland!" (304). Yet it is in *Ivanhoe* (published in 1819, the same year as *Bride*) that Scott most strikingly replays the connection between repression and homoeroticism that I have encouraged my class to observe in *Bride*. In *Ivanhoe* Scott represents the conflict between the titular hero and the Knight Templar, Brian de Bois-Guilbert, as oppositional structures of male identity that resemble the eroticized tension between Edgar's restraint and Bucklaw's aggression. Ivanhoe's passivity, his prolonged immobilization due to a wound, his disguises, and his heterosexual liaisons are contradicted and offset by his nemesis Bois-Guilbert, who embodies a violent and homoerotically charged masculinity. However, in apparent contradiction of Welsh's claim that for Scott "repressed individuals made better members of society and led happier lives" (*Hero* [1992] 114), the demise of Bois-Guilbert is directly ascribed to the excessive repression of desire. Scott writes of Bois-Guilbert, "Unscathed by the lance of his enemy, he had died a victim to the violence of his own contending passions" (*Ivanhoe* [ed. Tulloch] 392): a crisis, I point out to my students, closely resembling the repressed conflict between "two contradictory passions" that destroys Edgar Ravenswood.

Yet Bucklaw—whose very name suggests rebellion against patriarchal authority—refuses compliance with the repressive agenda that Edgar proposes, as is revealed when the two men share the aristocratic pursuit of stag hunting. Bucklaw's participation in the hunt releases his "natural" violent energies, the narrator describing the chase as a pastime that "seems rather to be an inherent passion in our animal nature, which levels all differences of rank and education" (107; 78). Bucklaw indulges the savage impulses that Edgar is restrained from, and he is soon depicted with "naked arms up to the elbows in blood and grease, slashing, cutting, hacking, and hewing" (111; 81).

However, Bucklaw's subsequent exclusion from Wolf's Crag by Caleb spells the end of his homosocial intimacy with Edgar and precipitates the return of Craigengelt. No sooner has Bucklaw decided to "break off the union" with Edgar (121; 89) than Craigengelt appears to reclaim his place in Bucklaw's affections—the Jacobite "shook him by the hand in the warmest manner possible . . . and no sooner had Craigengelt felt the pressure of his fingers than he knew the terms on which he stood with him"(121; 89).[2] This grasp suggests the physical intimacy between the men, while it also indicates the resurrection of the Jacobite fraternity from which Edgar is now excluded.

Many students will recognize the transgression of gender roles represented by Lady and Sir William Ashton, apparent, for example, in the way that Lady Ashton assumes the dominant role in the household by determining a suitable match for Lucy. In contemptuously rejecting Edgar's claim to Lucy—a claim to which William Ashton had acquiesced—Lady Ashton asserts "the full interest of a parent in Miss Lucy Ashton, which I have disposed of irrevocably in behalf of a worthy person" (288; 222), leaving Ashton to write a conciliatory letter to Ravenswood, thereby adopting the role of "the weaker party" in the marriage (289; 223). While responsive to the text's gender issues, some students are nonetheless resistant to the notion that the novel represents homoerotic intimacy between Edgar and Bucklaw. As a way to address this resistance, I link the homoerotic aspects of the text together with the failed marriage plot, in which Lucy ultimately—and fatally—refuses to mediate desire "between men."

The rupture of the bond between Bucklaw and Edgar has a catastrophic effect on the marriage plot of the novel, thwarting the formation of the erotic triangle that mediates and legitimates desire between men by channeling it through a woman. Following René Girard, Sedgwick theorizes "the relation of rivalry between the two active members of an erotic triangle" in which "the bond that links the two rivals is as intense and potent as the bond that links either of the rivals to the beloved" (21). The relevance of this triangle to *Bride* is apparent, as William Ashton seeks to use Lucy to cement a self-interested bond with Edgar: "He desired to hold the Master of Ravenswood bound, but wished that he himself should remain free" (212; 161). Yet Edgar balks at formalizing the triangle with Ashton, because of "his internal reluctance to wed with the daughter of his father's foe" (204; 154). Rejecting Lucy because of her ties with another man, Edgar refuses the only terms on which he might possess her. If, as Sedgwick argues, access to a homosocial relationship with men may only be accomplished by "the fiction of desiring women" (99), then the reverse also applies: access to a desired woman may be gained only by the game of triangulation with another man: "Fathers and guardians . . . have to be met with on the same terms as brides" (Welsh, *Hero* [1992] 78). Hence, in this erotic scenario the "normative man uses a woman as a 'conduit of a relationship' in which the true *partner* is a man" (Sedgwick 26).

Edgar's sexual transgression is apparent as he avoids the patriarchal "traffic in women" while accepting the emasculating identification with a woman at the expense of his own interests. The alternative "partner" with whom Edgar might accomplish the "triangulating [of] his homosocial desire through women" is Bucklaw (Sedgwick 102), who follows the same aristocratic code of honor as Edgar. Shut out from the triangulation of homosocial desire offered by Bucklaw and excluded from the plot of revenge, Edgar becomes passive and ambivalent again when he is turned away in disgrace by Lady Ashton from his father's former home (244; 186–87). Leaving Scotland on a mysterious assignment that may bolster his political fortunes, Edgar is subject in his absence to the machinations of Bucklaw and Craigengelt, who inform Lady Ashton of the plan to marry Lucy to the Master. Bucklaw thus takes advantage of the absence of Edgar to supplant him in the marriage plot. Indeed, Bucklaw's inheritance and success in gaining Lucy's hand superficially conform to the conventional protagonist in the Waverley novels. But if marriage is part of the ideological formula that keeps Scott "from collapsing into simple despair at the loss of the past" (Shaw, *Forms* 356), then the *failure* of marriage is connected to the premature thwarting of homosocial passions between men. The traumatic image of the crazed, passionate Lucy, and her final words—"So you have ta'en up your bonny bridegroom" (338; 260)—make a mockery of the aborted marriage plot. Lucy's savage appearance "with her bloody fingers [and] frantic gestures of an exulting demoniac" (338; 260) echoes Bucklaw's demeanor at the hunt. Yet it is Edgar who falls victim to "the fatal spot" (347; 267), consumed by the "monstrous passion" that the narrative and protagonist have at once acknowledged and failed to master.

NOTES

This essay has its (distant) origin in a paper I delivered as part of the panel Queer Walter Scott at the 1998 MLA Annual Convention in San Francisco. The paper was subsequently presented at the 1999 quadrennial conference on Sir Walter Scott, held at the University of Oregon. I would like to thank my fellow panelists, Mark Scroggins, Clare Simmons, and Paul Kelleher, as well as the organizer of the Oregon conference, Ian Duncan, for their wide-ranging insights into queer aspects of Scott's fiction, which have helped me as I developed my own thinking about sexual dissidence in the Waverley novels more broadly.

[1] The first set of page numbers are from Robertson's edition of *Bride*, which is based on the Magnum Opus edition and from which quotations are taken; the second are from Alexander's edition, which is based on the Edinburgh edition of Scott's novels.

[2] *Union* is of course a term that carries political connotations in the novel. The first edition of *The Bride of Lammermoor*, published in 1819, is set shortly before the Act of Union between England and Scotland, which occurred in 1707. However, Scott's revised Magnum Opus edition of *Bride*, published in 1830, introduced changes that set the action immediately after the union instead of before it. In both editions, however, the word *union* serves as a useful pedagogical tool to illustrate the combining of the political and erotic discourses in the novel.

Imagining the Middle Ages and Renaissance in *Ivanhoe* and *Kenilworth*

Graham Tulloch

Until quite recently *Ivanhoe* and, even more, *Kenilworth* suffered from a trend in twentieth-century criticism that can be summarized in David Daiches's claim that "[t]he novels on which Scott's reputation as a novelist must stand or fall are his 'Scotch novels'" ("Scott's Achievement. . . (Part One)" 84). It was not always thus: in the nineteenth century *Ivanhoe* was one of the most popular and influential of novels, and *Kenilworth* followed not far behind, fulfilling for a while J. G. Lockhart's prediction that "it continues and, I doubt not, will ever continue, to be placed in the very highest rank of prose fiction" (5: 49). After their fall from grace, both novels attracted relatively little attention, apart from some interest in Scott's treatment of the Jews in *Ivanhoe* (e.g., Mergenthal; Ragussis, *Figures* and "Writing"; Rosenberg), although more recently the novels have proved to be open to postmodern, postcolonial, and cultural-memory approaches. On the other hand, insofar as there is now any popular perception of Scott, it is of him as a medievalist, and this is obviously a good starting point for introducing students to *Ivanhoe*. Less obviously this perception can also be used in approaching *Kenilworth*. In this context students could do worse than starting (probably after rather than before reading the novel) with Scott's thoughtful discussion, in the dedicatory epistle to *Ivanhoe*, of the issues raised by his move five centuries earlier than the setting of any of his previous novels.

It is important for students to realize that Scott's approach to re-creating the past combines both minute detail, as in his description in *Ivanhoe* of Bois-Guilbert's horse "fully accoutred for battle, with a chamfrom or plaited head-piece upon his head, having a short spike projecting from the front" (25; 36–37), and the broad picture—as in, from the same novel, the claim that "[f]our generations had not sufficed to blend the hostile blood of the Normans and Anglo-Saxons" (16; 26).[1] Readers are often unaware of the amount of precise and verifiable historical detail in these novels, especially when it is not simply factual information. To cite just one instance, Sussex's claim in *Kenilworth* that "[w]ere war at the gates, I should be one of her [Elizabeth's] white boys" might seem like Scott's invention (152), but it is drawn from an identifiable historical source (Robert Naunton's *Memoirs of Robert Cary, Earl of Monmouth*, which Scott edited in 1808). Scott also paid close attention to the choice of an appropriate language for his dialogue, as the dedicatory epistle makes clear. To be historically accurate, Scott would need to show his characters in *Ivanhoe* speaking early Middle English, Norman-French, and Latin. Only the last was possible for his contemporary audience to read, and he was able to deploy Latin sparingly but effectively among the religious characters. For the rest he was obliged to use a hybrid language with a few earlier English and French terms, poetic archaisms, biblicisms, and historically appropriate oaths. This is the style of language that is disparagingly referred to as "tushery," but it is important not to attach to Scott the criticism that his imitators deserve. In any case, instead of spending time criticizing this artificial language, which Scott actually developed and used with some skill, students would do better to give attention to the discussion of the differing names of animals in the field and on the table in the first chapter of *Ivanhoe*. Justly famous as a perfect example of the interaction of language and society, it neatly embodies the sociolinguistic situation in England at the time, which Scott in general presents with reasonable historical accuracy, although he chose to ignore one important historical fact known to him—that Richard I spoke little or no English—because the picture of a king at ease with his subjects was essential to the novel's underlying political message. In *Kenilworth* Scott faced an easier task. Elizabethan English was neither unknown nor particularly unintelligible to early-nineteenth-century readers. What is more, Scott was immensely well read in both Elizabethan literature and contemporary historical sources. The notes in J. H. Alexander's edition reveal just how many borrowings from Shakespeare and other Elizabethan dramatists Scott was able to pack into the speech of characters like Lambourne and Gosling. Their language is, of course, a pastiche, a mixture of the archaic and the contemporary, a good example being Lambourne's speech to Amy that begins, "Hark ye, most fair Callipolis" and features inventive reworking of Shakespeare's "duke of dark corners" from *Measure for Measure* (311; 4.3.157). On a larger scale it is worth considering how Scott has used the Templar rule in *Ivanhoe* and Laneham in *Kenilworth* to enrich the dialogue and narrative of each text.

Our awareness of the sources of such borrowings can give us pleasure, but it is not central to our reading and understanding of the novels. More important is recognition of the main elements of the other aspect of Scott's presentation, the broad picture. These elements fall into two main categories: broad historical movements and features that separate the past from the present. In *Ivanhoe* Scott's major historical theme is the move from Anglo-Saxon primitivism and freedom to Norman feudalism and culture; at the same time, the novel foreshadows the future combination of these into a new English consciousness. The distinctive features of the medieval setting are chivalry, Catholicism, and feudalism. Among these, chivalry offers a particularly good entry point, not least because Scott conveniently provides us with a set-piece debate between Rebecca and Ivanhoe on the topic (249–50; 315–17). Who wins this debate? To some readers Rebecca may seem to win, but does Ivanhoe's chivalrous defense of her in the trial by combat give final victory to his arguments? Or does the fact that Ivanhoe only wins because Bois-Guilbert has a heart attack call chivalry's effectiveness into question again? Discussion around these questions can be combined with consideration of Scott's ambivalent portrait of the chivalric king, Richard, that "generous, but rash and romantic monarch" (401; 502). Chivalry also connects with the broad movement from Saxon (to use Scott's terminology) to Norman to English. Chivalry is a Norman preoccupation, but the most thoroughly chivalric character is the Saxon Ivanhoe; Scott is perhaps suggesting that the primitive virtues of the Anglo-Saxons can be harnessed in the cause of chivalry so that the best of Saxon and Norman can be combined. He is, however, ever conscious of the contradictions within chivalry and of chivalry's tendency to degenerate into the fantastic and absurd—see his sardonic comment on the tournament at Ashby that, despite four killed, thirty wounded, and several disabled for life, the tournament is "always mentioned in the old records, as the Gentle and Free Passage of Arms of Ashby" (115 [ed. Tulloch]), a comment made even more pointed by the later emendation of "Free" to "Joyous" (149 [ed. Duncan]).

The tournament is one of the many splendid scenes in the novel, but it is also an example of historically inaccurate detail: the tournament, confined within the lists of a clearly defined tiltyard, belongs to a much later period; tournaments in Richard's reign ranged freely over the countryside. Scott was not bothered by anachronisms and happily admits, in the dedicatory epistle, that "it is extremely probable that I may have confused the manners of two or three centuries" (12; 21). Despite this acknowledgment of his practice Scott was regularly criticized in the nineteenth century for such chronological conflations, especially with regard to his portrayal of Cedric as living a fully Anglo-Saxon lifestyle in the late twelfth century. But while spotting anachronisms of this kind might offer some innocent amusement, it is much more useful to understand how they allow Scott to create a composite picture of the medieval period that includes all its iconic features. One way to illustrate this is to ask students to name all the features they associate with the Middle Ages and then get them to see how many they can find in the novel: knights, fair ladies, castles, chivalry, tournaments, jolly monks, crusades, Robin Hood, Normans—*Ivanhoe* has them all. If, to create this iconic image, Scott needed to bring the more colorful fifteenth-century style of tournament into a nominally twelfth-century setting, then he was willing to do so, and to do so consciously. Similarly with Richard the Lion-Hearted and Robin Hood: Scott knew very well that the ballads place Robin in the reign of an unspecified King Edward, but in the novel he adopts Joseph Ritson's claim that Robin lived in Richard's reign (1: iv, xvi). Admittedly, Ritson was the best Robin Hood scholar of the day, but his claim was certainly not beyond challenge. Scott has chosen to accept a view that allows him to bring England's most romantic king and bandit into the one medieval setting. Scott, of course, both followed and defined the popular image of the Middle Ages, and, in adopting Ritson's claim in his immensely popular novel, he helped make the association of Robin Hood with King Richard the standard feature of popular versions of the Robin Hood story that it has become today. Interestingly, while scholars after Ritson located Robin Hood much later, the most recent scholarship has taken him back to the early thirteenth century, in striking distance of Richard's reign. Since students are likely to find Scott's treatment of the Jews a topic of interest and debate, it may be helpful to bring that too within the discussion of Scott's re-creation of the Middle Ages. Rebecca and Isaac's retreat to Granada at the end of the novel is anachronistic since, unusually for Moorish Spain, it was not in the 1190s a refuge for Jews. However, viewed as part of a broader picture of the Middle Ages, it reminds us that generally Jews were much better treated in Muslim countries and can also be seen as foreshadowing the later expulsion of the Jews from England. Earlier in the novel, however, Rebecca serves a quite different purpose: Scott's Protestantism does not allow him here to vest moral authority in the representatives of the Catholic Church. Instead, Rebecca takes on the role of moral and religious arbiter by demonstrating a remarkable ability to rise above religious divisions and to find the shared elements in the Christian and Jewish traditions.

Ivanhoe and *Kenilworth* form the two ends of a sequence of four novels, which brings the reader from the Middle Ages and its Catholicism and feudalism to the Protestant Renaissance and its highly centralized nation-state and strong monarchy. Scott began *The Monastery* while still writing *Ivanhoe*. Generally regarded as one of Scott's least successful novels, it nevertheless provides an interesting study of the end of the Middle Ages. Into the world of the declining Catholic Church come the new forces of the Reformation, while the arrival of the euphuist Sir Piercie Shafton introduces the new world, where power depends on the personal favor of the monarch rather than on the inherited status of the old feudal nobility. Scott continues these themes in *The Abbot* (in which Protestantism is mostly triumphant but the feudal nobility is still in power and Queen Mary still Catholic) and concludes the sequence in *Kenilworth* with a Protestant state and queen and power firmly in the hands of the monarch. While few students and, indeed, few teachers are likely to read this full sequence of novels, its existence is worth bearing in mind since it relates to one of the notable aspects of *Kenilworth*, the way in which Scott combines a rich and splendid picture of the Renaissance world with relics of the old world of the Middle Ages. Thus, although Elizabeth's world is firmly Protestant, one minor character (Dame Crank) is Catholic (109–10), and various characters, most notably Anthony Forster, are prone to revert to Catholic oaths in moments of stress. Similarly, knighthood is now an honor conferred in court by the queen for mostly political reasons. The figure of the lonely knight wandering the country rescuing damsels survives only in memory, as when the queen applauds Tressilian's choice of Raleigh to accompany him in rescuing Amy from Cumnor Hall and jokingly remarks that "[h]e is a young knight besides, and to deliver a lady from prison is an appropriate first adventure" (377). In the new postchivalric world, it falls to the servants to play the role of knight-errant—Tressilian is thwarted in every attempt to help Amy himself, and it is his servant Wayland Smith who escorts her to Kenilworth, lamenting that he is "playing squire of the body to a damosel-errant" (254). Leicester's relationship with Amy can be viewed in this context. His sense of responsibility to and for her rests on purely personal considerations—he feels no obligation as a knight, despite his being a member of many noble orders of knighthood whose insignia so impress Amy.

With *Kenilworth*, as with *Ivanhoe*, Scott was criticized for historical inaccuracies including variations from the actual chronology of historical events. Many of these "mistakes," especially those relating to the story of Amy and Leicester, are clearly intended to intensify the drama of their relationship, for example, by having their marriage kept a secret (history records it was not concealed) and by having Amy die during the celebrations at Kenilworth (actually she died fifteen years earlier). Other "mistakes" are analogous to those in *Ivanhoe* in that Scott sets out to present a composite picture of the Elizabethan age. How can we imagine the Elizabethan age without Shakespeare, for example? Scott therefore brings him in and has Raleigh quote his lines well before they were written (176). In terms of broad themes, if *Ivanhoe* foreshadows a future union of the two races of Saxons and Normans, *Kenilworth* shows it complete. This is indeed the theme of one of the pageants held at Kenilworth and viewed by the queen. The presence of these pageants has prompted several writers, most notably and extensively Stephen Arata but also Daiches (Introduction viii) and W. M. Parker (xiii), to liken the whole novel to a pageant. It is certainly suggestive that the writing of these novels from 1819 to 1821 led up to the visit of George IV to Edinburgh in 1822, for which Scott organized the extensive pageantry. It may well prove productive to consider both novels in terms of a pageant. The symbolism of setting so common in pageants is also relevant. Houses in particular are often deeply symbolic settings. Kenilworth Castle, with its buildings ranging from Saxon to Elizabethan times, suggests the pageant of English history that the novel celebrates, and Leicester's wing, "which now lies crushed under its own ruins," is not only "the monument of its owner's ambition" (254) but also an image of the passing of the glory of the Elizabethan age. Similarly the dilapidated Cumnor Hall, which once belonged to the abbot of Abingdon, images the fallen state of the Catholic Church, while Cedric's home in *Ivanhoe* symbolizes both the simple virtues and the failings of the Anglo-Saxons that he represents.

In his otherwise excellent discussion of *Kenilworth* Arata claims that "few readers have ever found the Leicester-Robsart plot terribly compelling" (100). Historically this is surely wrong, and I would suggest there is material of interest to us in their relationship today, much of it suggested through the imagery, as Alexander shows ("Major Images" and Introduction xvii–xx). Francis Hart has much to say on the complexity of both characters (205, 209–10), who also serve to flesh out the main themes of the novel. Arata's comment seems to arise from a common notion that both Scott's own primary concerns and our main interest in Scott lie outside the rather gothic central plots. Fiona Robertson (6–8) and James Kerr (1) are surely right in suggesting that these gothic elements are an integral part of Scott's presentation of history. In *Kenilworth* the typically gothic image of the immured and hidden Amy plays a central role in Scott's examination of the tension between private passion and public ambition. Scott uses this tension to dramatize the ways in which, in Elizabethan England, ambition is only satisfied by public glory, which is achieved paradoxically by personal and partly private interaction with the queen. In *Ivanhoe* there is no such pair of lovers at the center, and the unfulfilled relationship of Ivanhoe and Rebecca cannot compete in intensity with that of Amy and Leicester. However, the gothic images of immured and threatened women are again closely related to a central concern of the novel, chivalry. By paralleling Isaac's frightening confrontation with Front-de-Boeuf and those of Rowena and Rebecca with De Bracy and Bois-Guilbert, Scott underlines how vulnerable the two women are. This is the dark side of chivalry—for errant knights to rescue damsels in distress, the women have to be in danger, and that danger is often the threat of rape. Yet these private stories not only illustrate Scott's broader themes, they also undermine the comfortable resolutions with which the novels might otherwise end. Rebecca's exile counteracts the reconciliation of Saxon and Norman, and Amy's death calls into question the idea of a unified England. (Duncan's introduction to the Oxford edition of *Ivanhoe* explores the "Gothic destabilization" of the novel's portrayal of the "evolutionary resolution of differences" [xxi]). Thus, treating *Ivanhoe* and *Kenilworth* as acts of historical re-creation does not exclude but rather encourages consideration of their more overtly novelistic features, leading ultimately to an approach that encompasses both the gothic and the historical elements of each novel.

NOTE

1 The first set of page numbers is from Tulloch's edition of *Ivanhoe*, the second from Duncan's.

Thinking Globally: *The Talisman* and *The Surgeon's Daughter*

Tara Ghoshal Wallace

Twenty-first-century students encounter Scott (if they encounter him at all) as the author of *Waverley* and *Ivanhoe*—that is, as an interpreter of Scottish history and a weaver of medieval romance. While both *The Talisman* and *The Surgeon's Daughter* provide material to approach Scott from these familiar perspectives (for fine treatments of the Scottish dimension in these novels, see McCracken-Flesher, "Recuperation"; J. Watt, "Scott"), these two novels also reveal Scott's global vision, which considers Britain's relation to the Eastern territories it has come to rule and the cultures it seeks to dominate. By the time Scott was writing the novels, the British had achieved almost complete power in India. The East India Company, established in 1600 for trading purposes, had become a military and political power on the subcontinent. Robert Clive's victories over the French in 1751 and over Sirāj-ud-Dawlah in 1757 had consolidated British rule in the Carnatic and in Bengal, and the Maratha wars of 1803 and 1817–19 had extended British influence in northern India. In *The Surgeon's Daughter*, Scott chooses as his subject one of the few manifestations of sustained opposition from native rulers—the resistance mounted by the sultans of Mysore. Hyder Ali and his son Tipu engaged the British forces in a series of wars from 1767 until Tipu's death in 1799. By the 1820s, British rule in India stretched from the foothills of the Himalayas to the island of Ceylon. The defeat of Napoléon in 1815 not only preserved the overland route to Britain's most valuable colony but also established dominant British presence in the eastern Mediterranean, the gateway to the spaces under contestation in *The Talisman*. In venturing beyond the boundaries of Europe, then, these texts both represent and replicate Britain's imperial adventures; they also enable (perhaps require) us to reexamine the received image of the Scottish romancer, thus opening up our own literary boundaries as we attend to Walter Scott's cosmopolitan imagination.

A logical place to begin is Edward Said's dismissive characterization of Scott's orientalism. Conflating creator and character, Said accuses Scott of sharing Sir Kenneth's rigid adherence to generalizations: "no matter how deep the specific exception, no matter how much a single Oriental can escape the fences placed around him, he is *first* an Oriental, *second* a human being, and *last* again an Oriental" (*Orientalism* 102). Said's formulation can provoke a fruitful discussion not only about the extent to which Scott participates in a dehumanizing orientalism but also about the stated dichotomy between "human" and "Oriental," a dichotomy that implicitly privileges the individual over national or cultural identity. It is useful here to refer students to Georg Lukács, who celebrates Scott's drive to collapse such distinctions and his ability "to portray . . . characters who, in their psychology and destiny, always represent social trends and historical forces. . . . Scott's greatness lies in his capacity to give human embodiment to historical-social types" (34–35).

The passage that provokes Said's criticism (rebutted in Bruzelius, "King of England" 30; McCracken-Flesher, "Recuperation" 206; Pelckmans 98) concerns Sir Kenneth's conviction that Sheerkohf/Ilderim/Saladin, like the rest of his "blinded race," can defeat the Crusaders only with help from the devil (38–39). But students experience no difficulty in separating Kenneth's bias from narrative judgment and can readily trace the growing stature of Saladin, especially when his extraordinary qualities are juxtaposed to the repellent assortment of Crusaders camped outside Jerusalem. The early encounter with Kenneth establishes a "separate but equal" relationship between Oriental and European that steadily skews in favor of the sultan. As the text tells us, "The champions formed a striking contrast to each other in person and features, and might have formed no inaccurate representatives of their different nations" (23–24). The Scotsman's bulky strength and blunt manner set off the Saracen's lean brawn and dignified formality; Saladin's "abstemious" meal contrasts with Kenneth's ample ration of meat and wine (26); and the Christian's romantic worship of his beloved Edith is countered by the Muslim's assertion of "patriarchal privileges" (27). This parity, however, dissipates quickly when the two enter into theological debate. Although the narrator twice asserts the ascendancy of knightly courtesy over religious partisanship (12, 19), we note that Kenneth responds to Saladin's genuine respect for devout Christians with passionate contempt for "the camel-driver of Mecca," an insult that the Muslim deflects with a calm reproof: "Slander not him whom thou knowest not; the rather that we venerate the founder of thy religion, while we condemn the doctrine which your priests have spun from it" (31). Christian fanaticism is even more starkly opposed to Muslim tolerance when the very hermit to whom Saladin has extended "love, favour, and regard" (31) attacks the "infidel dog" for singing "the praise of thy false prophet" (44). On the issue of cultural cosmopolitanism, this text grants the Muslim indisputable superiority.

As if to underscore Saladin's worth, Scott describes a Western army in shambles, and we turn next to the long section that delineates the multiple difficulties besetting the Crusaders. Enumerating the sources of the disarray, the narrative lists "the jealousies of the Christian princes," the desertion of discouraged and disgruntled soldiers, the ravages of an uncongenial climate intensified by "dissolute" behavior, and the successful guerilla tactics of Saladin's army (69–70). Richard, chafing under his forced inaction, proclaims his contempt for his allies, dismissing the king of France as cowardly, the archduke of Austria as stupid, the Templar as criminal, the Hospitaller as venal, and the marquis of Montserrat as both avaricious and treacherous. Unhappily assembled under the leadership of England's king, these brothers in Christianity conspire to commit mutiny and fratricide in order to advance their own secular ambitions. As the plot against Richard unfolds, exposing the rot within the European camp, we find ourselves increasingly aligned with Saladin, who not only admires Richard's valor and faith but also personally saves him from a dangerous illness, "seeing that it neither becomes thy place and courage to die the death of a slave . . . nor befits it our fame that a brave adversary be snatched from our weapon by such a disease" (93–94). At the end of the novel, in a reprise of the opening contest and contrast of skills between Kenneth and Saladin, Richard's massive broadsword cleaves a bar of iron, while Saladin's razor-sharp scimitar slices through silk; when Saladin's weapon subsequently beheads the traitorous Templar, Richard announces that "we have witnessed a great act of justice" (311).

At this point it looks as though Scott has written a fairly straightforward anti-Crusade, anti-imperial narrative, one that amply demonstrates Saladin's incontrovertible right to rule, a right based not only on ethnic and territorial legitimacy but also on military, intellectual, and moral superiority. And we note also that Saladin's advice to Richard—to seek peace and order at home rather than conquest abroad—echoes the sentiments of Scott's other Crusader novels. We remember the opening lines of *Ivanhoe*, in which Richard's return "had become an event rather wished than hoped for by his despairing subjects, who were . . . subjected to every species of subordinate oppression" (15 [ed. Tulloch]), and the strong language of resistance deployed by Hugo De Lacy in *The Betrothed*:

> Such is the airy guerdon for which hosts on hosts have been drawn from Europe to drench the sands of Palestine with their gore—such the vain promises for which we are called upon to barter our country, our lands, and our lives! (314–15)

While the earlier novels concentrate on deleterious effects at home, *The Talisman* takes us to those murderous sands and shows us the futility and immorality of the European expedition in the Holy Land.

If a careful reading of *The Talisman* argues against Said's simplification, however, we must also guard against an equally reductive conviction that Scott unequivocally supports Saladin's cause. Two lines of investigation prove useful in complicating what could become a complacent, one-dimensional interpretation. One area has been explored by Harry E. Shaw, who argues that Saladin's "virtues are undercut because he lacks respect for women" and that his power is compromised when he subsequently participates in male fear of female sexuality ("Scott" 292–94; see also Pelckmans 104–05, on Scott's critique of courtly love). Shaw's analysis also points to a Saladin feminized in comparison with Richard's manly strength and stimulates a discussion of gender, power, and alterity. We can ask our students to consider whether a feminized Saladin, especially in contrast to the aggressive masculinity of Richard, might encode Scott's doubts about the Saracen's capacity to govern, and we can insert here a discussion of Edith and Berengeria as contrasting embodiments of femininity. On the other hand, we might conclude, with Margaret Bruzelius and Lisa Hopkins, that the gender-bending fluidity of Saladin empowers not only the sultan himself but also Kenneth and, ultimately, female readers (Bruzelius, "King of England" 29–30; Hopkins 21).

The issue of gender fluidity leads us to the more general question of shifting identities, and again we find that "meaning" can be as flexible as Saladin's masks. The text clearly asks us to admire the ease with which Saladin inhabits his various guises—and also, by the way, to enjoy the kind of readerly self-gratulation that attends detecting masquerades that impose on characters. But beyond applauding Saladin's mastery of disguises and our own acuity in penetrating them, we need to address how his protean skills connect to the larger issues of legitimacy and power. Do we conclude that Saladin's shape-shifting "is a property of his absolute status" and a mark of his innate power (Duncan, "Scott's Romance" 378)? Or do his multiple identities add up, as Jacqueline Jondot argues, to "[une] chose innommé et innomable, forme vide toujours présente, toujours absente, l'Autre" (195; "a nameless and unnameable thing, an empty form at once present and absent, the Other" [editors' trans.])? Further complicating our assessment of Saladin's multiple identities, the text also addresses a monarch's responsibilities to his subjects. When Richard impulsively proposes single combat "for the possession of Jerusalem" or at least "for the love of honour," Saladin gently rebukes his rashness, reminding him that "[t]he master places the shepherd over the flock, not for the shepherd's own sake, but for the sake of the sheep . . . when the herdsman is smitten, the sheep are scattered" (313). Yet this wise leader, who "seems to have accepted the role of the only adult amongst a bunch of early adolescent schoolboys" (Shaw, "Scott" 295) and who "repudiates chivalric folly" (Hart 154), blithely endangers his own (disguised) body and thereby the Muslim defense of Palestine. His battle with Kenneth and the subsequent attack by Theodorick of Engaddi are almost fatal, and his quixotic foray into the European camp, where violence erupts irrationally as well as frequently, surely results from what Ivanhoe calls "the wild spirit of chivalry which so often impelled his master [Richard] upon dangers which he might easily have avoided, or rather, which it was unpardonable in him to have sought out" (364 [ed. Tulloch]). Saladin, while frequently displaying "the deep policy and prudence" that the introduction ascribes to him (2), seems to revel in romantic but risky adventures.

Scott's portrait of Saladin, then, produces no absolute conclusions about his final judgment on this charismatic and enigmatic figure, though it provides ample evidence that Scott's novelistic imagination was as intensely stimulated by this Eastern monarch as it had been by Richard (*Ivanhoe*); Mary, Queen of Scots (*The Abbot*); Charles II (*Peveril of the Peak*); or Louis XI (*Quentin Durward*)—all written during the post-Napoleonic 1820s, as was his *Life of Napoleon*. Clearly, Scott includes Saladin among this gallery of fascinating though flawed royals; moreover, in constructing a narrative in which European invaders look distinctly inferior to (paler than?) the oriental leader they seek to depose, Scott interrogates the racial-cultural arrogance that forms part of the imperial enterprise.

Two years later, Scott's global imagination travels further east and closer in time. *The Surgeon's Daughter* takes up some of the same issues of otherness and imperial ambition that inform *The Talisman*, but in a form both more compressed and more complex. Here, the romance elements that brightened the earlier tale of futile and feckless pursuit give way to a dark vision of imperial greed and violence, lightened only by flashes of mordant humor. Kenneth's conflict between military duty and romantic love is replaced by Richard Middlemas's contempt for both aspects of chivalry. Middlemas as antihero surpasses even the villainous Templar, since his multiple treacheries encompass the betrayal of the woman who loves him as well as of every political ally who has trusted him. Having traveled to India to acquire wealth and power, Middlemas acknowledges no allegiances and no morality, repudiating every constraint that could inhibit his single-minded quest for personal advancement. He represents, in other words, the kind of imperial adventurer decried by Edmund Burke in his speech on Charles James Fox's East India bill: "Animated with all the avarice of age and all the impetuosity of youth, they roll in one after another, wave after wave . . . with appetites continually renewing for a food that is constantly wasting" (372).

This despicable European provides an interesting parallel to the admirable Oriental in *The Talisman*: Middlemas, like Saladin, occupies multiple subjectivities. Born to a Catholic Jacobite and a Portuguese Jewess, raised by a Scottish Presbyterian, Middlemas deploys his fluid identity as ambition dictates. In Madras, he represents himself as the purebred Englishman Tresham, shedding his name and his biological hybridity; that imposture having caused his eviction from the British colony there, he returns three years later as Madame Montreville's "black domestic" Sadoc (261), deeply engaged in plots against both her and their employer Tipu. His final appearance, in Bangalore, crosses both national and gender boundaries: "in a dress as magnificent in itself as it was remote from all European costume," mustaches curled and "eyelids stained" (280), he presents himself as a feminized Indian courtier. Unlike Saladin, Middlemas dons his disguises only in the service of his own interests, and in this novel, the ability to inhabit multiple selves clearly signals instability of character. If *The Talisman* asks us to weigh the relative merits of fixity and flexibility—we might admire Richard's commitment to his cause even as we note the rigidity that disallows adaptation even to climate—*The Surgeon's Daughter* looks suspiciously on those who, like Middlemas and Montreville, "go native."

Students inevitably wonder, at this point, whether Scott in fact is guilty of the kind of orientalism we have been at pains to dismantle in our discussion of *The Talisman*. Given that the villains in this text take on Indian characteristics, it may seem that Scott participates in the construction of an India that contaminates British colonials. After all, natives in *The Surgeon's Daughter* are hardly uniformly admirable, including as they do the lustful despot Tipu and the "Oriental Machiavel" Paupiah, who is indifferent to "the honour of men, and the chastity of women" (264). It is never my design to minimize the extent to which this text participates in British prejudices about the subcontinent, but it is worth pointing out that both Middlemas and Montreville enter India already morally compromised. It is also important to note that in *The Talisman* only Saladin is differentiated from the mass of Saracens—who constitute both savage "irregulars" and "splendid troop" (285)—while *The Surgeon's Daughter* portrays a range of Indian characters. In marked contrast to the "artful Hindhu" (266), for example, we meet the cosmopolitan fakir Barak el Hadgi, with his "intelligence, his learning, above all, his versatility and freedom from prejudices of every kind" (247). We also encounter Hyder Ali himself, whose swift justice on behalf of Menie Gray reenacts Saladin's instant execution of the grand master. The narrative commentary on this dramatic moment demonstrates, in its indeterminacy, what I read as a respectful refusal to appropriate the mental processes of a cultural other:

> The scene of just punishment which he so faithfully exhibited might be owing to his policy, his internal sense of right, and to the ostentation of displaying it before an Englishman of sense and intelligence, or to all of these motives mingled together—but in what proportions it is not for us to distinguish. (285)

Moreover, Scott makes a point of reminding us that Hyder Ali, like Saladin, has been the victim of European transgression of a truce and endows him with the thunderous rhetoric of vengeance:

> Hitherto I have been in the Carnatic as a mild prince—in future I will be destroying tempest! Hitherto I have made inroads as a compassionate and merciful conqueror—hereafter I will be the messenger whom Allah sends to the kingdoms which he visits in judgment! (284)

Although this Eastern monarch makes a late entrance, his presence in the text is electrifying.

Despite the satisfying climax provided by Hyder Ali, we all recognize this novel's "vision of apocalyptic destruction" (C. Jones 149). The good European Hartley, who rescues Menie and who figures the right sort of transculturation—he studies oriental languages and masters the epigrammatic habits of speech favored by his Muslim interlocutors—achieves neither romantic nor imperial success, succumbing instead to a "contagious distemper" while his beloved returns to Britain "unmarried though wealthy" (285), to live out her years as a "very gentle, but rather tiresome" spinster (156). It is as if the dystopian perspective of this text cannot accommodate even the momentary optimism we find at the end of *The Talisman*. I have argued elsewhere that the bitter ending of *The Surgeon's Daughter* articulates Scott's conviction that misleading (and mischievous) fantasies of imperial grandeur have damaged not only relations with subjected cultures but also British character itself (Wallace 323). In my teaching of Scott's "oriental" tales, I want students to see how these novels problematize Britain's imperial ventures, how his texts "disrupt the expectations that readers brought to a work of fiction dealing with the East" (Watt, "Scott" 100). Most of all, I want students to note that Walter Scott, that quintessentially "Scottish" novelist, was also a deeply engaged citizen of the world.

NOTES ON CONTRIBUTORS

Samuel Baker teaches English at the University of Texas at Austin. He has published articles on William Wordsworth, Matthew Arnold, and Mary Shelley and a book, *Written on the Water: British Romanticism and the Maritime Empire of Culture.*

Oliver S. Buckton is professor of English at Florida Atlantic University, Boca Raton. He is the author of *Cruising with Robert Louis Stevenson: Travel, Narrative, and the Colonial Body* and *Secret Selves: Confession and Same-Sex Desire in Victorian Autobiography*. His essays have appeared in *ELH*, *Victorian Studies*, and *Nineteenth-Century Literature*, among other journals.

James P. Carson is associate professor of English at Kenyon College. He has published essays on Samuel Richardson, Tobias Smollett, Oliver Goldsmith, Mary Shelley, and the gothic novel, in such periodicals as *Criticism*, *The Eighteenth Century*, *Philological Quarterly*, and *Eighteenth-Century Fiction*. He is completing a book entitled *Unsexed Multitudes: Disciplinary Individuation, Gender, and the Crowd in Romantic Fiction*.

Ian Duncan is a professor of English at the University of California, Berkeley. He is the author of *Modern Romance and Transformations of the Novel: The Gothic, Scott, Dickens* and *Scott's Shadow: The Novel in Romantic Edinburgh*, as well as a coeditor of *Scott, Scotland, and Romantic Nationalism* (a special issue of *Studies in Romanticism*) and *Scotland and the Borders of Romanticism*. He has edited Scott's *Ivanhoe* and *Rob Roy*, James Hogg's *Winter Evening Tales* and *Private Memoirs and Confessions of a Justified Sinner*, and (with Elizabeth Bohls) *Travel Writing, 1700–1830: An Anthology*. He is working on a book on the novel and "the science of man" from 1740 to 1870.

Simon Edwards teaches at Roehampton University in London and has lectured and taught widely throughout Europe, East Asia, and the United States. For the last four years he has been involved in a curriculum development project in English studies at Shkodra University in Albania. His most recent publications on the historical novel include "The Geography of Violence" in *Novel* and "*Old Mortality* and the Future of Terror" in *Triade*.

Suzanne Gilbert is lecturer in English studies at the University of Stirling, Scotland. The author of numerous articles on Scottish literature, ballads, chapbooks, and oral traditions in such journals as *Scottish Studies Review* and *Studies in Hogg and His World*, she is the editor of James Hogg's *The Mountain Bard* and editor (with Douglas Mack) of Hogg's *Queen Hynde*. She is writing a monograph on the ballad as a genre and editing an edition of Hogg's early poetry.

Evan Gottlieb teaches English at Oregon State University. He is the author of *Feeling British: Sympathy and National Identity in Scottish and English Writing, 1707–1832*, as well as articles in such journals as *Studies in Romanticism* and *Eighteenth-Century Fiction*. He is at work on a book project on Romanticism and globalization.

Antony J. Hasler is associate professor of English at Saint Louis University. He is the author of the forthcoming *Court Poetry in Late Medieval England and Scotland: Allegories of Authority*, translator of Georg Heym's *Poems*, and coeditor of James Hogg's *The*

Three Perils of Woman. His current project is an edition of Hogg's *The Poetic Mirror*. He is the American editor of the Renaissance section of Blackwell's online journal *Literature Compass* and an advisory member of the International Committee of the Association of Scottish Literary Studies.

David Hewitt was, until his recent retirement, Regius Chalmers Professor of English at the University of Aberdeen. He has published widely on Scottish and Romantic literature and is editor-in-chief of the Edinburgh edition of the Waverley novels, the first scholarly edition of Scott's fiction.

Diane Long Hoeveler is professor of English at Marquette University. The author *of Romantic Androgyny: The Women Within* and *Gothic Feminism: The Professionalization of Gender from Charlotte Smith to the Brontës*, as well as essays and book reviews on a variety of literary topics, she has coauthored a critical study of Charlotte Brontë and coedited the MLA volumes *Approaches to Teaching* Jane Eyre and *Approaches to Teaching Gothic Fiction*. She has published three recent coedited collections of essays, *Romanticism and the Law*, *Orientalism*, and *Women's Literary Creativity and the Female Body*.

Celeste Langan is associate professor in the English department at the University of California, Berkeley. She is the author of *Romantic Vagrancy* and other essays on Romantic poetry. An essay on Scott's *Lay of the Last Minstrel* led to her ongoing interest in media theory and media archaeology. Her current book project, *Post-Napoleonism: Imagining Sovereignty after 1799*, interrogates Napoléon as, among other things, a figure of mass mediation.

Douglas Mack is professor emeritus in the University of Stirling's Department of English Studies. A frequent contributor to periodicals such as *Scottish Literary Journal* and *Studies in Hogg and His World*, he is a general editor of the Stirling–South Carolina research edition of James Hogg (his work for which includes editions of *The Shepherd's Calendar* and *The Queen's Wake*), as well as a member of the advisory board of the Edinburgh edition of the Waverley novels (for which he has edited *The Tale of Old Mortality*). He has published *Scottish Fiction and the British Empire*.

Caroline McCracken-Flesher is professor of English at the University of Wyoming. She publishes widely on Scottish literature and culture, most recently *Possible Scotlands: Walter Scott and the Story of Tomorrow* and the edited volume *Culture, Nation, and the New Scottish Parliament*.

Kenneth McNeil is associate professor of English at Eastern Connecticut State University. The author of *Scotland, Britain, Empire: Writing the Highlands, 1760–1860*, he has published several articles on Scottish literature of the Romantic era. His current projects include a study of Anne Grant's transatlantic writing and border identity in Scott's *Minstrelsy of the Scottish Border*.

Clare A. Simmons is professor of English at Ohio State University and the author of *Reversing the Conquest: History and Myth in Nineteenth-Century British Literature*; *Eyes across the Channel: French Revolutions, Party History, and British Writing, 1830–1882*; and papers and articles on nineteenth-century English and Scottish literature and medievalism. She is the editor of the Broadview edition of *The Clever Woman of the Family*, by Charlotte Mary Yonge; an essay collection, *Medievalism and the Quest for the "Real"*

Middle Ages; and the coeditor of *Prose Studies*. She is completing a study of Romantic-era medievalism and the common-law tradition of rights.

Janet Sorensen teaches in the English department at the University of California, Berkeley. She is the author of *The Grammar of Empire in Eighteenth-Century British Writing* and of several articles on eighteenth- and nineteenth-century British texts, including the writings of Walter Scott.

Graham Tulloch is professor of English at Flinders University, Australia. He is the author of *The Language of Walter Scott* and *A History of the Scots Bible* and has published articles and chapters on the Scots language, Scottish literature, and Scottish writers in Australia. He has edited Walter Scott's *Ivanhoe* for the Edinburgh edition of the Waverley novels and Marcus Clarke's *His Natural Life* and Catherine Martin's *An Australian Girl*.

Tara Ghoshal Wallace is associate professor of English and associate dean of graduate studies in arts and sciences at George Washington University. She is the author of *Jane Austen and Narrative Authority*, editor of Frances Burney's *A Busy Day*, and coeditor of *Women Critics, 1660–1820*. Her most recent articles include "Reading the Metropole: Elizabeth Hamilton's *Letters of a Hindoo Rajah*," in *Enlightening Romanticism, Romancing the Enlightenment: British Novels from 1750 to 1832*; "Frances Burney as Dramatist," in *The Cambridge Companion to Frances Burney*, and "'. . . About Savages and the Awfulness of America': Colonial Corruptions in *Humphry Clinker*," in *Eighteenth-Century Fiction*. Her monograph entitled "Imperial Characters: Home and Periphery in Eighteenth-Century Literature" is forthcoming.

SURVEY PARTICIPANTS

Sharon Alker, *Whitman College*
Samuel Baker, *University of Texas, Austin*
Alyson Bardsley, *State University of New York, College of Staten Island*
Oliver S. Buckton, *Florida Atlantic University*
James P. Carson, *Kenyon College*
Katherine R. Chandler, *Saint Mary's College*
Julian Meldon D'Arcy, *University of Iceland*
Ian Duncan, *University of California, Berkeley*
Simon Edwards, *Roehampton University*
Mary A. Favret, *Indiana University*
Penny Fielding, *University of Edinburgh*
Douglas Gifford, *University of Glasgow*
Evan Gottlieb, *Oregon State University*
Jonathan H. Grossman, *University of California, Los Angeles*
Antony J. Hasler, *Saint Louis University*
David Hewitt, *University of Aberdeen*
Diane Long Hoeveler, *Marquette University*
C. M. Jackson-Houlston, *Oxford Brookes University*
Claire Lamont, *Newcastle University*
Yoon Sun Lee, *Wellesley College*
Alison Lumsden, *University of Aberdeen*
Deidre Lynch, *University of Toronto*
Caroline McCracken-Flesher, *University of Wyoming*
Randall McGowen, *University of Oregon*
Kenneth McNeil, *Eastern Connecticut State University*
Murray G. H. Pittock, *University of Manchester*
Ann Wierda Rowland, *University of Kansas*
Clare A. Simmons, *Ohio State University*
Charles Snodgrass, *Grambling State University*
Janet Sorensen, *University of California, Berkeley*
Anne McKee Stapleton, *University of Iowa*
Graham Tulloch, *Flinders University*
Tara Ghoshal Wallace, *George Washington University*
James Watt, *University of York*
Fiona Wilson, *Fordham University*

WORKS CITED

Abbotsford. 2001. Web. 25 Feb. 2006.

Abraham, Nicolas, and Maria Torok. *The Shell and the Kernel*. Trans. Nicholas T. Rand. Chicago: U of Chicago P, 1994. Print.

The Adventures of Robin Hood. Dir. Michael Curtiz. Warner Bros., 1938. Film.

Agamben, Giorgio. *State of Exception*. Trans. Kevin Attell. Chicago: U of Chicago P, 2005. Print.

Aiton, William. *A History of the Rencounter at Drumclog*. Hamilton, 1821. Print.

Alexander, J. H. Introduction. Scott, *Kenilworth* xiii–xxxi.

———. "The Major Images in *Kenilworth*." *Scottish Literary Journal* 17.2 (1990): 27–35. Print.

Alexander, J. H., and David Hewitt, eds. *Scott and His Influence: The Papers of the Aberdeen Scott Conference, 1982*. Aberdeen: Assn. for Scottish Lit. Studies, 1983. Print.

———, eds. *Scott in Carnival: Selected Papers from the Fourth International Scott Conference, Edinburgh, 1991*. Aberdeen: Assn. for Scottish Lit. Studies, 1993. Print.

Alford, Henry. *The Queen's English: Stray Notes on Speaking and Spelling*. London: Strahan, 1864. Print.

Allingham, Philip V. "Sir Walter Scott and Illustration." *The Victorian Web*. 28 Jan. 2002. Web. 23 Aug. 2005.

Altick, Richard. *The English Common Reader*. 1957. Columbus: Ohio State UP, 1998. Print.

Arac, Jonathan. *Huckleberry Finn as Idol and Target: The Functions of Criticism in Our Time*. Madison: U of Wisconsin P, 1997. Print.

Arata, Stephen. "Scott's Pageants: The Example of *Kenilworth*." *Studies in Romanticism* 40.1 (2001): 99–107. Print.

Armstrong, Nancy. *Desire and Domestic Fiction: A Political History of the Novel*. Oxford: Oxford UP, 1987. Print.

———. *How Novels Think: The Limits of Individualism from 1719–1900*. New York: Columbia UP, 2006. Print.

Auerbach, Emily. *Searching for Jane Austen*. Madison: U of Wisconsin P, 2004. Print.

Austen, Jane. *Northanger Abbey*. 1818. Ed. Claire Grogan. 2nd ed. Peterborough: Broadview, 2002. Print.

———. *Persuasion*. 1818. Ed. James Kinsley. Oxford: Oxford UP, 2004. Print.

———. *Sense and Sensibility*. 1811. Ed. Tony Tanner. Harmondsworth: Penguin, 1969. Print.

Balzac, Honoré de. *Les Chouans*. 1829. Trans. M. A. Crawford. London: Penguin, 1972. Print.

———. *Père Goriot*. 1834. Trans. A. J. Krailsheimer. Oxford: Oxford UP, 1991. Print.

Baudrillard, Jean. *The Gulf War Did Not Take Place*. Trans. Paul Patton. Bloomington: Indiana UP, 1995. Print.

———. *The Spirit of Terrorism*. Trans. Chris Turner. Rev. ed. New York: Verso, 2003. Print.

Beiderwell, Bruce. *Power and Punishment in Scott's Novels*. Athens: U of Georgia P, 1992. Print.

———, ed. *Romantic Enlightenment: Sir Walter Scott and the Politics of History*. Spec. issue of *European Romantic Review* 13.3 (2002): 223–324. Print.

Bentham, Jeremy. *Rationale of Judicial Evidence*. Ed. J. S. Mill. 4 vols. London: Hunt, 1827. Print.

Bhabha, Homi. "Of Mimicry and Man: The Ambivalence of Colonial Discourse." *Discipleship: A Special Issue on Psychoanalysis*. Spec. issue of *October* 28 (1984): 125–33. Print.

The Bible. Introd. and notes by Robert Carroll and Stephen Prickett. New York: Oxford UP, 1998. Print. Oxford World's Classic. Authorized King James Vers.

Blackstone, William. *Commentaries on the Laws of England*. 4 vols. London, 1765–68. Print.

Bloch, Ernst. *The Principle of Hope*. Trans. Neville Plaice, Stephen Plaice, and Paul Knight. 3 vols. Cambridge: MIT P, 1986. Print.

Bolton, Philip. *Scott Dramatised*. London: Mansell, 1992. Print.

Braveheart. Dir. Mel Gibson. Icon, 1995. Film.

British Fiction, 1800–1829: A Database of Production, Circulation, and Reception. Centre for Editorial and Intertextual Research, Cardiff University. 2004. Web. 30 May 2008.

Brown, Charles Brockden. *Wieland; or, The Transformation*. 1798. Ed. Jay Fliegelman. Harmondsworth: Penguin, 1991. Print.

Brown, David. *Walter Scott and the Historical Imagination*. London: Routledge, 1979. Print.

Brown, Homer O. *Institutions of the English Novel: From Defoe to Scott*. Philadelphia: U of Pennsylvania P, 1997. Print.

Bruzelius, Margaret. "'The King of England . . . Loved to Look upon a Man': Melancholy and Masculinity in Scott's *Talisman*." *Modern Language Quarterly* 62.1 (2001): 19–42. Print.

———. *Romancing the Novel: Adventure from Scott to Sebald*. Lewisburg: Bucknell UP, 2007. Print.

Buchan, John. *Sir Walter Scott*. London: Cassell, 1932. Print.

Bunyan, John. *The Pilgrim's Progress*. 1678. Ed. W. R. Owens. New York: Oxford UP, 2003. Print.

Burgess, Miranda. *British Fiction and the Production of Social Order, 1740–1830*. Cambridge: Cambridge UP, 2000. Print.

Burke, Edmund. *The Portable Edmund Burke*. Ed. Isaac Kramnick. London: Penguin, 1999. Print.

Burns, Robert. *Selected Poems*. Ed. Carol McGuirk. New York: Penguin, 1994. Print.

Butler, Judith. *Bodies That Matter: On the Discursive Limits of "Sex."* New York: Routledge, 1993. Print.

———. "Performative Acts and Gender Constitution: An Essay in Phenomenology and Feminist Theory." *Performing Feminisms: Feminist Critical Theory and Theatre*. Ed. Sue-Ellen Case. Baltimore: Johns Hopkins UP, 1990. 270–82. Print.

Butler, Marilyn. *Romantics, Rebels, and Reactionaries: English Literature and Its Background, 1760–1830*. New York: Oxford UP, 1981. Print.

Buzard, James. *Disorienting Fiction: The Autoethnographic Work of Nineteenth-Century British Novels*. Princeton: Princeton UP, 2005. Print.

———. "Translation and Tourism: Scott's *Waverley* and the Rendering of Culture." *Yale Journal of Criticism* 8.2 (1995): 31–59. Print.

Byron, George Gordon. *Don Juan*. 1819–24. Ed. Susan J. Wolfson and Peter J. Manning. New York: Penguin, 2005. Print.

Calder, Angus. Introduction. *Old Mortality*. By Walter Scott. London: Penguin, 1975. 9–43. Print.

Chandler, James. *England in 1819: The Politics of Literary Culture and the Case of Romantic Historicism*. Chicago: U of Chicago P, 1998. Print.

Chatterjee, Ranita, and Patrick M. Horan. "Teaching the Homosocial in Godwin, Hogg, and Wilde." *Approaches to Teaching Gothic Fiction: The British and American Traditions*. Ed. Diane Long Hoeveler and Tamar Heller. New York: MLA, 2003. 126–32. Print.

Chisholm, John. *Sir Walter Scott as a Judge*. Edinburgh: Green, 1918. Print.

Christensen, Jerome. *Romanticism at the End of History*. Baltimore: Johns Hopkins UP, 2000. Print.

Cockshut, A. O. J. *The Achievement of Sir Walter Scott*. New York: New York UP, 1969. Print.

Coleridge, Samuel Taylor. *Biographia Literaria*. Ed. James Engell and W. Jackson Bate. 2 vols. in 1. Princeton: Princeton UP, 1983. Print. Collected Works of Samuel Taylor Coleridge 7.

Colley, Linda. *Britons: Forging the Nation, 1707–1837*. New Haven: Yale UP, 1992. Print.

Cooney, Seamus. "Scott's Anonymity—Its Motives and Consequences." *Studies in Scottish Literature* 10 (1973): 207–19. Print.

Cooper, James Fenimore. *The Deerslayer*. 1841. Ed. Donald E. Pease. London: Penguin, 1987. Print.

———. *The Last of the Mohicans*. 1826. Ed. Richard Slotkin. London: Penguin, 1987. Print.

———. *The Prairie*. 1827. Ed. Blake Nevius. London: Penguin, 1987. Print.

Corson, James C. *Notes and Index to Sir Herbert Grierson's Edition of the Letters of Sir Walter Scott*. Oxford: Clarendon, 1979. Print.

Cottom, Daniel. *The Civilized Imagination: A Study of Ann Radcliffe, Jane Austen, and Sir Walter Scott*. Cambridge: Cambridge UP, 1985. Print.

Craig, Cairns. *Out of History: Narrative Paradigms in Scottish and English Culture*. Edinburgh: Polygon, 1996. Print.

Crawford, Robert. *Devolving English Literature*. 2nd ed. Edinburgh: Edinburgh UP, 2000. Print.

———, ed. *The Scottish Invention of English Literature*. Cambridge: Cambridge UP, 1998. Print.

Crawford, Thomas. *Scott*. Edinburgh: Scottish Academic, 1982. Print.

The Crown of Christ. May 2008. Web. 30 May 2008.

Culloden. Dir. Peter Watkins. BBC, 1968. Videocassette.

Daiches, David. Introduction. *Kenilworth*. By Walter Scott. New York: Limited, 1966. v–xiii. Print.

———. "Scott's Achievement as a Novelist (Part One)." *Nineteenth-Century Fiction* 6.2 (1951): 81–95. Print.

———. "Scott's Achievement as a Novelist (Part Two)." *Nineteenth-Century Fiction* 6.3 (1951): 153–73. Print.

Dances with Wolves. Dir. Kevin Costner. Tig, 1990. Film.

D'Arcy, Julian Meldon. *Subversive Scott: The Waverley Novels and Scottish Nationalism*. Reykjavik: Vigdís Finnbogadóttir Inst. of Foreign Langs. and the U of Iceland P, 2005. Print.

Davis, Leith. *Acts of Union: Scotland and the Literary Negotiation of the British Nation, 1707–1830*. Stanford: Stanford UP, 1998. Print.

Davis, Leith, Ian Duncan, and Janet Sorensen, eds. *Scotland and the Borders of Romanticism*. Cambridge: Cambridge UP, 2004. Print.

Dekker, George. *The American Historical Romance*. Cambridge: Cambridge UP, 1987. Print.

———. *The Fictions of Romantic Tourism: Radcliffe, Scott, and Mary Shelley*. Stanford: Stanford UP, 2004. Print.

Devine, T. M. *The Scottish Nation, 1700–2000*. London: Lane, 1999. Print.

Dickens, Charles. *Barnaby Rudge*. 1841. Ed. John Bowen. London: Penguin, 2003.Print.

———. *A Tale of Two Cities*. 1859. Ed. Andrew Sanders. New York: Oxford UP, 1998. Print.

Duncan, Ian. "Authenticity Effects: The Work of Fiction in Romantic Scotland." *South Atlantic Quarterly* 102.1 (2003): 93–116. Print.

———. Introduction. Scott, *Ivanhoe* [ed. Duncan] vii–xxvi.

———. Introduction. Scott, *Rob Roy* vii–xxviii.

———. *Modern Romance and Transformations of the Novel: The Gothic, Scott, Dickens*. Cambridge: Cambridge UP, 1992. Print.

———. "Primitive Inventions: *Rob Roy*, Nation, and World System." *Eighteenth-Century Fiction* 15.1 (2002): 81–102. Print.

———. "Scott's Romance of Empire: The *Tales of the Crusaders*." Alexander and Hewitt, *Scott in Carnival* 370–79.

———. *Scott's Shadow: The Novel in Romantic Edinburgh*. Princeton: Princeton UP, 2007. Print.

———. "Shadows of the Potentate: Scott in Hogg's Fiction." *Studies in Hogg and His World* 4 (1993): 12–25. Print.

———. "The Upright Corpse: Hogg, National Literature and the Uncanny." *Studies in Hogg and His World* 5 (1994): 29–54. Print.

Duncan, Ian, Ann Wierda Rowland, and Charles Snodgrass, eds. *Scott, Scotland, and Romantic Nationalism*. Spec. issue of *Studies in Romanticism* 40.1 (2001): 3–168. Print.

Dunn, Douglas, ed. *The Oxford Book of Scottish Short Stories*. 2nd ed. Oxford: Oxford UP, 1995. Print.

Dyer, Gary. "Ivanhoe, Chivalry, and the Murder of Mary Ashford." *Criticism* 39.3 (1997): 388–408. Print.

Edelman, Lee. *No Future: Queer Theory and the Death Drive*. Durham: Duke UP, 2004. Print.

Edgeworth, Maria. Castle Rackrent *and* Ennui. 1800; 1809. Ed. Marilyn Butler. London: Penguin, 1993. Print.

Elias, Norbert. *The Civilizing Process*. Trans. Edmund Jephcott. Cambridge: Blackwell, 1994. Print.

Eliot, George. *Adam Bede*. 1859. Ed. Stephen Gill. Harmondsworth: Penguin, 1980. Print.

———. *Daniel Deronda*. 1874–76. Ed. Terence Cave. Harmondsworth: Penguin, 1996. Print.

———. *Middlemarch*. 1871–72. Ed. Rosemary Ashton. New York: Penguin, 2003. Print.

———. *Romola*. 1862–63. Ed. Dorothea Barrett. Harmondsworth: Penguin, 1997. Print.

Felluga, Dino. "Modules on Butler: On Performativity." *Introductory Guide to Critical Theory*. Purdue U. 28 Nov. 2003. Web. 30 May 2008.

Ferris, Ina. *The Achievement of Literary Authority: Gender, History, and the Waverley Novels*. Ithaca: Cornell UP, 1991. Print.

———. "Translation from the Borders: Encounter and Recalcitrance in *Waverley* and *Clan-Albin*." *Eighteenth-Century Fiction* 9.2 (1997): 203–22. Print.

Fielding, Penny. "Burns' Topographies." Davis, Duncan, and Sorenson 153–69.

———. *Scotland and the Fictions of Geography: North Britain, 1760–1830*. Cambridge: Cambridge UP, 2009. Print.

———. *Writing and Orality: Nationality, Culture, and Nineteenth-Century Scottish Fiction*. Oxford: Clarendon, 1996. Print.

Forbes, Duncan. "The Rationalism of Sir Walter Scott." *Cambridge Journal* 7 (1953): 20–35. Print.

Forster, E. M. *Aspects of the Novel*. 1927. New York: Harcourt, 1955. Print.

Fraiman, Susan. "Jane Austen and Edward Said: Gender, Culture, and Imperialism." *Janeites: Austen's Disciples and Devotees*. Ed. Deidre Lynch. Princeton: Princeton UP, 2000. 206–23. Print.

Freeman, Michael and Andrew D. E. Lewis, eds. *Law and Literature*. Oxford: Oxford UP, 1999. Print. Current Legal Issues 2.

Freud, Sigmund. *Totem and Taboo*. 1913. New York: Norton, 1962. Print.

Frye, Northrop. *The Secular Scripture: A Study of the Structure of Romance*. Cambridge: Harvard UP, 1976. Print.

Gallagher, Catherine. *Nobody's Story: The Vanishing Acts of Women Writers in the Marketplace, 1670–1820*. Berkeley: U of California P, 1994. Print.

Galperin, William. "Austen's Earliest Readers and the Rise of the Janeites." *Janeites: Austen's Disciples and Devotees*. Ed. Deidre Shauna Lynch. Princeton: Princeton UP, 2000. 87–114. Print.

Galt, John. *The Entail*. 1823. Ed. Ian A. Gordon. Oxford: Oxford UP, 1970. Print.

———. *The Provost*. 1822. Ed. Ian A. Gordon. New York: Oxford UP, 1982. Print.

———. *Ringan Gilhaize*. 1823. Ed. Patricia J. Wilson. Edinburgh: Canongate, 1995. Print.

Gamer, Michael. *Romanticism and the Gothic: Genre, Reception, and Canon Formation*. Cambridge: Cambridge UP, 2000. Print.

Garside, Peter. "Scott and the 'Philosophical' Historians." *Journal of the History of Ideas* 36 (1975): 497–512. Print.

Garside, Peter, and Rainer Schöwerling. *1800–1829*. Vol. 2 of *The English Novel 1770–1829: A Bibliographical Survey of Prose Fiction Published in the British Isles*. Oxford: Oxford UP, 2000. Print.

Gaskell, Elizabeth. *Ruth*. 1853. Ed. Alan Shelston. New York: Oxford UP, 1985. Print.

Godwin, William. *Caleb Williams*. 1794. Ed. Maurice Hindle. London: Penguin, 1988. Print.

Goethe, Johann Wolfgang. *The Sorrows of Young Werther*. 1774. Trans. M. Hulse. London: Penguin, 1989. Print.

Gogol, Nikolai. "Taras Bulba." 1835. Village Evenings Near Dikanka *and* Mirgorod. Trans. C. English. Oxford: Oxford UP, 1994. 241–366. Print.

Goldsmith, Oliver. *The Vicar of Wakefield*. 1766. Ed. Arthur Friedman. Oxford: Oxford UP, 1999. Print.

Goslee, Nancy. "Witch or Pawn: Women in Scott's Narrative Poetry." *Romanticism and Feminism*. Ed. Anne K. Mellor. Bloomington: Indiana UP, 1988. 115–36. Print.

Gosse, Edmund. Introduction. Vasov i–xiv.

Gottlieb, Evan. *Feeling British: Sympathy and National Identity in Scottish and English Writing, 1707–1832*. Lewisburg: Bucknell UP, 2007. Print.

———. "'To Be at Once Another and the Same': Walter Scott and the End(s) of Sympathetic Britishness." *Studies in Romanticism* 43.2 (2004): 187–207. Print.

Guillory, John. *Cultural Capital: The Problem of Literary Canon Formation*. Chicago: U of Chicago P, 1993. Print.

Hamilton, Paul. *Metaromanticism: Aesthetics, Literature, Theory*. Chicago: U of Chicago P, 2003. Print.

Hardy, Thomas. *Tess of the D'Urbervilles*. 1891. Ed. Juliet Grindle and Simon Gatrell. New York: Oxford UP, 1983. Print.

Hart, Francis R. *Scott's Novels: The Plotting of Historical Survival*. Charlottesville: UP of Virginia, 1966. Print.

Harvie, Christopher. "Scott and the Image of Scotland." *Sir Walter Scott: The Long Forgotten Melody*. Ed. Allan Bold. London: Vision, 1983. 17–42. Print.

———. *A Short History of Scotland*. New York: Oxford UP, 2002. Print.

Hayden, John O., ed. *Scott: The Critical Heritage*. New York: Barnes, 1970. Print.

Hazlitt, William. Lectures on the English Poets *and* Spirit of the Age. London: Dent, 1910. Print.

———. "Lord Byron." 1825. Hazlitt, *Lectures* 223–44.

———. "My First Acquaintance with Poets." 1823. *Selected Writings*. Ed. Jon Cook. Oxford: Oxford UP, 1998. 211–30. Print.

———. "Sir Walter Scott."1825. Hazlitt, *Lectures* 223–44.

Hechter, Michael. *Internal Colonialism: The Celtic Fringe in British National Development, 1536–1966*. Berkeley: U of California P, 1975. Print.

Hennelly, Mark. "*Waverley* and Romanticism." *Nineteenth-Century Fiction* 28 (1973): 194–209. Print.

Hewitt, David. "The Phonocentric Scott." Alexander and Hewitt, *Scott in Carnival* 581–92.

Hewitt, David, and Alison Lumsden. "Historical Note." Scott, *Heart* [ed. Hewitt and Lumsden] 581–600.

Hill, Christopher. *Puritanism and Revolution*. London: Secker, 1958. Print.

Hockenhull-Smith, Marie. "'How Can Ye Criticise What's Plain Law, Man?': The Lawyer, the Novelist, and the Discourse of Authority." Freeman and Lewis 239–62.

Hoeveler, Diane Long. *Romantic Androgyny: The Women Within*. University Park: Penn State UP, 1990. Print.

Hoffman, E. T. A. The Golden Pot *and Other Tales*. Trans. R. Robertson. Oxford: Oxford UP, 1992. Print.

Hogg, James. *The Private Memoirs and Confessions of a Justified Sinner*. 1824. Ed. John Carey. Oxford: Oxford UP, 1999. Print.

———. *The Three Perils of Man: War, Women and Witchcraft*. 1822. Ed. Douglas Gifford. Edinburgh: Canongate, 1997. Print.

Hook, Andrew. *From Goosecreek to Gandercleugh: Studies in Scottish-American Literary and Cultural History*. East Linton: Tuckwell, 1999. Print.

Hopkins, Lisa. "Clothes and the Body of the Knight: The Making of Men in Sir Walter Scott's *The Talisman*." *Wordsworth Circle* 27.1 (1996): 21–24. Print.

Horace. *Satires, Epistles, and Ars Poetica*. Trans. H. Rushton Fairclough. Cambridge: Harvard UP, 1929. Print.

Hugo, Victor. *Les Misérables*. 1862. Trans. Norman Denny. New York: Penguin, 1982. Print.

Hume, David. *Commentaries on the Law of Scotland, respecting Crimes*. 2 vols. Edinburgh: Bell, 1844. Print.

Hume, David. *Dialogues concerning Natural Religion*. Ed. Richard H. Popkin. 2nd ed. New York: Hackett, 1988. Print.

———. *A Treatise of Human Nature*. Ed. Ernest C. Mossner. New York: Penguin, 1984. Print.

Irvine, Robert P. *Enlightenment and Romance: Gender and Agency in Smollett and Scott*. Oxford: Lang, 2000. Print.

Ivanhoe. Dir. Richard Thorpe. MGM, 1952. Film.

Ivanhoe. Dir. Stuart Orme. BBC, 1997. Film.

Jameson, Fredric R. *The Political Unconscious: Narrative as a Socially Symbolic Act*. Ithaca: Cornell UP, 1981. Print.

Jeffrey, Francis. Rev. of *Waverley*, by Walter Scott. *Edinburgh Review* 24 (1814): 208–43. Print.

Johnson, Claudia. *Jane Austen: Women, Politics, and the Novel*. Chicago: U of Chicago P, 1988. Print.

Johnson, Edgar. *Sir Walter Scott: The Great Unknown*. 2 vols. New York: Macmillan, 1970. Print.

Johnson, Samuel. *A Dictionary of the English Language*. 1755. 2nd ed. London, 1774. Print.

Jondot, Jacqueline. "Saladin: Le même et l'autre dans *The Talisman* de Sir Walter Scott." *Études écossaises: La poésie écossaises anciennes et contemporaine* 4 (1997): 181–95. Print.

Jones, Catherine. *Literary Memory: Scott's Waverley Novels and the Psychology of Narrative*. Lewisburg: Bucknell UP, 2003. Print.

Jones, Darryl. *Jane Austen*. New York: Palgrave, 2004. Print.

Jordan, Frank. "Scott, Chatterton, Byron, and the Wearing of Masks." Alexander and Hewitt, *Scott and His Influence* 279–89.

Julius, Anthony. Introduction. Freeman and Lewis i–xxv.

Kaufmann, David. *The Business of Common Life: Novels and Classical Economics between Revolution and Reform*. Baltimore: Johns Hopkins UP, 1995. Print.

Keats, John. "Ode to a Nightingale." *The Major Works*. Ed. Elizabeth Cook. New York: Oxford, 2001. 285–88. Print.

———. *Selected Letters*. Ed. Robert Gittings. Rev. Jon Mee. 2nd ed. Oxford: Oxford UP, 2002. Print.

Kelly, Gary. *English Fiction of the Romantic Period, 1789–1830*. New York: Longman, 1989. Print.

Kerr, James. *Fiction against History: Scott as Storyteller*. Cambridge: Cambridge UP, 1989. Print.

Kidd, Colin. *Subverting Scotland's Past: Scottish Whig Historians and the Creation of an Anglo-British Identity, 1689–1830*. Cambridge: Cambridge UP, 1993. Print.

Kleist, Heinrich von. *Michael Kohlhaas*. The Marquise of O *and Other Stories*. Trans. Nigel Reeves and David Luke. London: Penguin, 1978. Print.

Knox-Shaw, Peter. *Jane Austen and the Enlightenment*. Cambridge: Cambridge UP, 2004. Print.

Lacoue-Labarthe, Philippe, and Jean-Luc Nancy. *The Literary Absolute: The Theory of Literature in German Romanticism*. Trans. Philip Barnard and Cheryl Lester. Albany: State U of New York P, 1981. Print.

Lamont, Claire. "Note on the Text." Scott, *Chronicles* xliii–xlvi.

———. "Walter Scott: Anonymity and the Unmasking of Harlequin." *Authorship, Commerce and the Public: Scenes of Writing, 1750–1850*. Ed. E. J. Clery, Caroline Franklin, and Peter Garside. Basingstoke: Palgrave, 2002. 54–66. Print.

Lampedusa, Giuseppe Tomasi di. *The Leopard*. 1958. Trans. Archibald Colquhoun. New York: Pantheon, 1991. Print.

Landscape Illustrations of the Waverley Novels, with Descriptions of the Views. 2 vols. London, 1834. Print.

Langan, Celeste, and Maureen N. McLane. "The Medium of Romantic Poetry." *The Cambridge Companion to British Romantic Poetry*. Ed. James K. Chandler and Maureen N. McLane. New York: Cambridge UP, 2008. 239–62. Print.

The Last Samurai. Dir. Edward Zwick. Warner Bros., 2003. Film.

Leavis, F. R. *The Great Tradition*. 1948. Harmondsworth: Penguin, 1980. Print.

Lee, Yoon Sun. *Nationalism and Irony: Burke, Scott, Carlyle*. Oxford: Oxford UP, 2004. Print.

Liebermann, F., ed. *Die Gestetze der Angelsachsen*. 3 vols. Tübingen: Scientia Aalen, 1960. Print.

Lincoln, Andrew. *Walter Scott and Modernity*. Edinburgh: Edinburgh UP, 2007. Print.

Lockhart, J. G. *Memoirs of the Life of Sir Walter Scott*. 1837–38. 10 vols. New York: AMS, 1983. Print.

Lowth, Robert. *A Short Introduction to English Grammar*. London, 1762. Print.

Lucia di Lammermoor. Dir. Pier'Alli. Opus Arte, 1994. DVD.

Lukács, Georg. *The Historical Novel*. Trans. Hannah Mitchell and Stanley Mitchell. London: Merlin, 1962. Print.

Lynch, Deidre Shauna. Introduction. Austen, *Persuasion* vii-xxxiii.

Lynch, Michael, ed. *The Oxford Companion to Scottish History*. Oxford: Oxford UP, 2001. Print.

——— *Scotland: A New History*. London: Pimlico, 1992. Print.

Macherey, Pierre. *A Theory of Literary Production*. Trans. Geoffrey Wall. New York: Routledge, 2006. Print.

Mack, Douglas. "Revisiting *The Private Memoirs and Confessions of a Justified Sinner*." *Studies in Hogg and His World* 10 (1999): 1–26. Print.

———. *Scottish Fiction and the British Empire*. Edinburgh: Edinburgh UP, 2006. Print.

Mackie, J. D. *A History of Scotland*. Rev. and ed. Bruce Lenman and Geoffrey Parker. 2nd ed. Harmondsworth: Penguin, 1978. Print.

Macpherson, James. *Fragments of Ancient Poetry Collected in the Highlands of Scotland*. London, 1762. Print.

Makdisi, Saree. *Romantic Imperialism: Universal Empire and the Culture of Modernity*. Cambridge: Cambridge UP, 1998. Print.

Manning, Susan. "Did Mark Twain Bring Down the Temple on Scott's Shoulders?" *Special Relationships: Anglo-American Affinities and Antagonisms, 1854–1936*. Ed. Janet Beer and Bridget Bennet. Manchester: Manchester UP, 2002. Print.

———. *Fragments of Union: Making Connections in Scottish and American Writing*. New York: Palgrave, 2002. Print.

———. *The Puritan-Provincial Vision: Scottish and American Literature in the Nineteenth Century*. Cambridge: Cambridge UP, 1989. Print.

Manzoni, Alessandro. *The Betrothed*. 1840. Trans. B. Penman. London: Penguin, 1972. Print.

Marx, Karl, and Friedrich Engels. *The Communist Manifesto*. 1848. Trans. Samuel Moore. London: Penguin, 1967. Print.

Master and Commander: The Far Side of the World. Dir. Peter Weir. Twentieth-Century Fox, 2003. Film.

Maxwell, Richard. "Inundations of Time: A Definition of Scott's Originality." *ELH* 68.2 (2001): 419–68. Print.

———. "Pretenders in Sanctuary." *Modern Language Quarterly* 61.2 (2000): 287–358. Print.

McCracken-Flesher, Caroline. "Narrating the (Gendered) Nation in Walter Scott's *The Heart of Midlothian*." *Nineteenth-Century Contexts* 24.3 (2002): 291–316. Print.

———. *Possible Scotlands: Walter Scott and the Story of Tomorrow*. Oxford: Oxford UP, 2005. Print.

———. "*Pro Matria Mori*: Gendered Nationalism and Cultural Death in Scott's 'The Highland Widow.'" *Scottish Literary Journal* 21.2 (1994): 69–78. Print.

———. "The Recuperation of Canon Fodder: Walter Scott's *The Talisman*." Shaw, *Critical Essays* 202–17.

McCrie, Thomas. Rev. of *Old Mortality*. By Walter Scott. *Edinburgh Christian Instructor* 14 (1817): 41–73, 100–40, 170–20. Print.

McGann, Jerome J. "Walter Scott's Romantic Postmodernity." Davis, Duncan, and Sorensen 113–29.

McLynn, Frank. *Crime and Punishment in Eighteenth-Century England*. Oxford: Oxford UP, 1991. Print.

McMaster, Graham. *Scott and Society*. Cambridge: Cambridge UP, 1981. Print.

McNeil, Kenneth. *Scotland, Britain, Empire: Writing in the Highlands, 1760–1860*. Columbus: Ohio State UP, 2007. Print.

Mergenthal, Sylvia. "The Shadow of Shylock: Scott's *Ivanhoe* and Edgeworth's *Harrington*." Alexander and Hewitt, *Scott in Carnival* 320–31.

Merivale, J. Rev. of *Waverley*, by Walter Scott. *Monthly Review* 75 (1814): 275–89. Print.

Michaels, Walter Benn. *The Trouble with Diversity: How We Learned to Love Identity and Ignore Inequality*. New York: Metropolitan, 2006. Print.

Mill, John Stuart. Introduction. Bentham, *Rationale* 1: i–xvi.

Millgate, Jane. "*Persuasion* and the Presence of Scott." *Persuasions: Journal of the Jane Austen Society of North America* 15 (1993): 184–95. Print.

———. *Walter Scott: The Making of the Novelist*. Toronto: U of Toronto P, 1984. Print.

Milton, John. *Paradise Lost*. 1667. Ed. Alistair Fowler. 2nd ed. London: Longman, 1998. Print.

Mitchell, Margaret. *Gone with the Wind*. New York: Macmillan, 1936. Print.

Moretti, Franco. *Atlas of the European Novel, 1800–1900*. New York: Verso, 1998. Print.

———. *The Way of the World: The Bildungsroman in European Culture*. London: Verso, 1987. Print.

Morgan, Susan. "Old Heroes and a New Heroine in the Waverley Novels." *ELH* 50.3 (1983): 559–85. Print.

Muir, Edwin. *Scott and Scotland: The Predicament of the Scottish Writer*. London: Routledge, 1936. Print.

Murray, W. H. *Rob Roy MacGregor: His Life and Times*. Edinburgh: Canongate, 1998. Print.

Nairn, Tom. *After Britain: New Labour and the Return of Scotland*. London: Granta, 2000. Print.

———. *The Break-up of Britain: Crisis and Neo-nationalism*. 3rd ed. Altona: Common Ground, 2003. Print.

Owenson, Sydney (Lady Morgan). *The Wild Irish Girl*. 1806. Ed. Kathryn Kirkpatrick. New York: Oxford UP, 1999. Print.

Packard, Elizabeth A. Introduction. *The Lady of the Lake*. By Walter Scott. New York: Macmillan, 1900. ix–xlii. Print.

Paine, Thomas. *Rights of Man*. 1791–92. Rights of Man, Common Sense *and Other Political Writings*. Ed. Mark Philip. New York: Oxford, 1995. 83–331. Print.

Parker, W. M. Introduction. *Kenilworth*. By Walter Scott. London: Dent, 1959. v–xiii. Print.

Pelckmans, Paul. "Walter Scott's Orient: *The Talisman*." *Oriental Prospects: Western Literature and the Lure of the East*. Ed. C. C. Barfoot and Theo D'haen. Amsterdam: Rodopi, 1998. 97–110. Print.

Peters, Julie Stone. "Law, Literature, and the Vanishing Real: On the Future of an Interdisciplinary Illusion." *PMLA* 120.2 (2005): 442–53. Print.

Petrie, David. "The Sinner versus the Scholar: Two Exemplary Models of Mis-re-membering and Mis-taking Signs in Relation to Hogg's *Justified Sinner*." *Studies in Hogg and His World* 3 (1992): 57–67. Print.

Pittock, Murray G. H. *The Invention of Scotland: The Stuart Myth and Scottish Identity, 1638 to the Present*. London: Routledge, 1991. Print.

———. *Irish and Scottish Romanticism*. Oxford: Oxford UP, 2008. Print.

———, ed. *The Reception of Sir Walter Scott in Europe*. London: Continuum, 2006. Print.

The Poems and Songs of Robert Burns. Narr. John Cairney. Trafalgar Square, 1999. Web. 3 June 2008.

Portraits of the Principal Female Characters of the Waverley Novels. London, 1833. Print.

Posner, Richard A. *Law and Literature: A Misunderstood Relation*. Cambridge: Harvard UP, 1988. Print.

Pratt, Mary Louise. *Imperial Eyes: Travel Writing and Transculturation*. New York: Routledge, 1992. Print.

Prebble, John. *The King's Jaunt*. London: Collins, 1988. Print.

Price, Leah. *The Anthology and the Rise of the Novel: From Richardson to George Eliot*. New York: Cambridge UP, 2000. Print.

Punter, David. "Scottish and Irish Gothic." *The Cambridge Companion to Gothic Fiction*. Ed. Jerrold E. Hogle. Cambridge: Cambridge UP, 2002. 105–24. Print.

Pushkin, Aleksander. *The Captain's Daughter*. 1836. Trans. R. Edmonds. London: Penguin, 1962. Print.

———. *Eugene Onegin*. 1831. Trans. C. Johnston. London: Penguin, 1979. Print.

Radcliffe, Ann. *A Sicilian Romance*. 1790. Ed. Alison Milbank. Oxford: Oxford UP, 1999. Print.

Ragussis, Michael. *Figures of Conversion: "The Jewish Question" and English National Identity*. Durham: Duke UP, 1995. Print.

———. "Writing Nationalist History: England, the Conversion of the Jews, and *Ivanhoe*." *ELH* 60.1 (1993): 181–250. Print.

Rigney, Ann. *Imperfect Histories: The Elusive Past and the Legacy of Romantic Historicism*. Ithaca: Cornell UP, 2001. Print.

Ritson, Joseph. *Robin Hood: A Collection of All the Ancient Poems, Songs, and Ballads*. 2 vols. London: Egerton, 1795. Print.

Robertson, Fiona. *Legitimate Histories: Scott, Gothic, and the Authorities of Fiction*. Oxford: Clarendon, 1994. Print.

Rob Roy. Dir. Michael Caton-Jones. United Artists, 1995. Film.

Rosenberg, Edgar. *From Shylock to Svengali: Jewish Stereotypes in English Fiction*. Stanford: Stanford UP, 1960. Print.

Rushdie, Salman. *Midnight's Children*. 1981. New York: Random, 2006. Print.

Russett, Margaret. *Fictions and Fakes: Forging Romantic Authenticity, 1760–1845*. Cambridge: Cambridge UP, 2006. Print.

Sacher-Masoch, Leopold von. *Venus in Furs*. 1870. Trans. U. Mueller and L. Lindgren. New York: Blast, 1987. Print.

Sade, Marquis de. *The Misfortunes of Virtue*. 1794. Trans. D. Coward. Oxford: Oxford UP, 1992. Print.

———. "Reflections on the Novel." 1800. The One Hundred Twenty Days of Sodom *and Other Writings*. Trans. A. Wainhouse and R. Souver. New York: Grove, 1966. 97–116. Print.

Said, Edward W. *Culture and Imperialism*. New York: Vintage, 1993. Print.

———. *Orientalism*. New York: Vintage, 1978. Print.

Saintsbury, George. *A Short History of the English Novel*. 1898. London: Macmillan, 1966. Print.

Schoenfield, Mark. "Waging Battle: Ashford v. Thornton, Ivanhoe, and Legal Violence." *Medievalism and the Quest for the "Real" Middle Ages*. Ed. Clare A. Simmons. London: Cass, 2001. 60–86. Print.

Scott, David. *Conscripts of Modernity: The Tragedy of Colonial Enlightenment*. Durham: Duke UP, 2004. Print.

Scott, Walter. "Ancient History of Scotland." 1829. *Critical and Miscellaneous Essays*. Vol. 3. Philadelphia: Carey, 1841. 108–56. Print.

———. *The Antiquary*. 1816. Ed. David Hewitt. New York: Penguin, 1998. Print.

———. *The Antiquary*. Ed. Nicola J. Watson. New York: Oxford UP, 2002. Print.

———. *The Betrothed*. 1825. New York: Harper, 1901. Print.

———. *The Bride of Lammermoor*. 1819. Ed. Fiona Robertson. New York: Oxford UP, 1991. Print.

———. *The Bride of Lammermoor*. Ed. J. H. Alexander. New York: Penguin, 2000. Print.

———. *Chronicles of the Canongate*. 1827. Ed. Claire Lamont. New York: Penguin, 2003. Print.

———. Rev. of *The Culloden Papers*. *Quarterly Review* 14 (1816): 283–333. Print.

———. Rev. of *Emma*, by Jane Austen. *Quarterly Review* 14 (1816): 188–201. Rpt. in *Jane Austen: The Critical Heritage*. Ed. B. C. Southam. London: Routledge, 1964. 58–69. Print.

———. *The Fortunes of Nigel*. Ed. Frank Jordan. Edinburgh: Edinburgh UP, 2004.

———. "General Preface." Scott, *Waverley* 349–85.

———. *Guy Mannering*. 1815. Ed. P. D. Garside. New York: Penguin, 2003. Print.

———. *The Heart of Midlothian*. 1818. Ed. Claire Lamont. New York: Oxford UP, 1982. Print.

———. *The Heart of Midlothian*. Ed. Tony Inglis. New York: Penguin, 1994. Print.

———. *The Heart of Mid-Lothian*. Ed. David Hewitt and Alison Lumsden. Edinburgh: Edinburgh UP, 2004. Print.

———. Introduction. Scott, *Rob Roy* 5–53.

———. *Ivanhoe*. 1820. Ed. Graham Tulloch. Edinburgh: Edinburgh UP, 1995. Print.

———. *Ivanhoe*. Ed. Ian Duncan. Oxford: Oxford UP, 1996. Print.

———. *Journal*. Ed. W. E. K. Anderson. Oxford: Clarendon, 1972. Print.

———. *Kenilworth*. 1821. Ed. J. H. Alexander. New York: Penguin, 1999. Print.

———. *Lady of the Lake*. Ed. William J. Rolfe. Boston: N.p., 1883. *Project Gutenberg*. 9 Feb. 2009. Web. 17 Apr. 2009.

———. "The Lay of the Last Minstrel." 1805. *The Poetical Works of Sir Walter Scott*. Ed. J. Logie Robertson. London: Oxford UP, 1904. 1–88. Print.

———. *Letters*. Ed. H. J. C. Grierson et al. 1932–37. 12 vols. New York: AMS, 1971. Print.

———. *Letters on Demonology and Witchcraft*. 1830. Ed. Raymond Lamont Brown. New York: Citadel, 1968. Print.

———. *Minstrelsy of the Scottish Border*. 1802. 4 vols. Edinburgh: Blackwood, 1902. Print.

———. *The Monastery*. 1820. Ed. Penny Fielding. Edinburgh: Edinburgh UP, 2000. Print.

———. *The Pirate*. 1822. Ed. Mark Weinstein, with Alison Lumsden. Edinburgh: Edinburgh UP, 2001. Print.

———. *The Prefaces to the Waverley Novels*. Ed. Mark A. Weinstein. Lincoln: U of Nebraska P, 1978. Print.

———. *Quentin Durward*. 1823. Ed. Susan Manning. Oxford: Oxford UP, 1992. Print.

———. *Redgauntlet*. 1824. Ed. Kathryn Sutherland. New York: Oxford UP, 1985. Print.

———. *Redgauntlet*. 1824. Ed. G. A. M. Wood, with David Hewitt. New York: Penguin, 2000. Print.

———. *Rob Roy*. 1818. Ed. Ian Duncan. New York: Oxford UP, 1998. Print. Oxford World's Classics.

———. *Saint Ronan's Well*. 1823. London: Dent, 1906. Print.

———. *The Surgeon's Daughter*. Scott, *Chronicles* 158–288.

———. *The Tale of Old Mortality*. 1816. Ed. Douglas S. Mack. New York: Penguin, 1999. Print.

———. *Tales of a Grandfather*. 3rd ser. Edinburgh: Cadell, 1829. Print.

———. *The Talisman*. 1825. London: Dent, 1948. Print.

———. "The Two Drovers." Scott, *Chronicles* 124–46.

———. "The Two Drovers." *Norton Anthology of English Literature: Norton Topics Online*. 18 Apr. 2006. Web. 14 May 2008.

———. *Waverley*. 1814. Ed. Claire Lamont. Oxford: Oxford UP, 1986. Print.

Scott's Novels, a Brief Guide. Ed. Michael Peverett. 2000. Web. 25 Feb. 2006.

Sedgwick, Eve Kosofsky. *Between Men: English Literature and Male Homosocial Desire*. New York: Columbia UP, 1985. Print.

Shakespeare, William. *Measure for Measure*. 1603. *Riverside Shakespeare*. Ed. G. Blakemore Evans et al. Boston: Houghton, 1974. 545–86. Print.

Shane. Dir. George Stevens. Paramount, 1953. Film.

Shaw, Harry E., ed. *Critical Essays on Sir Walter Scott*. New York: Hall, 1996. Print.

———. *The Forms of Historical Fiction: Sir Walter Scott and His Successors*. Ithaca: Cornell UP, 1983. Print.

———. *Narrating Reality: Austen, Scott, Eliot*. Ithaca: Cornell UP, 1999. Print.

———. "Scott, Women, and History." Beiderwell, *Romantic Enlightenment* 285–97.

Shelley, Mary. *Frankenstein*. 1819. Ed. Maurice Hindle. New York: Penguin, 2003. Print.

Shelley, Percy. *Defense of Poetry*. Shelley, *Major Works* 674–701.

———. *The Major Works*. Ed. Zachary Leader and Michael O'Neill. New York: Oxford UP, 2003. Print.

———. *Prometheus Unbound*. Shelley, *Major Works* 229–313.

Simmons, Clare A. "A Man of Few Words: The Romantic Orang-Outang and Scott's *Count Robert of Paris*." *Scottish Literary Journal* 17.1 (1990): 21–34. Print.

The Sir Walter Scott Way. Mar. 2005. Web. 25 Feb. 2006.

Smith, G. Gregory. *Scottish Literature: Character and Influence*. 1919. London: Macmillan, 1972. Print.

Smollett, Tobias. *The Expedition of Humphry Clinker*. 1771. Ed. Louis M. Knapp and Paul-Gabriel Boucé. New York: Oxford UP, 1984. Print.

Sorensen, Janet. *The Grammar of Empire in Eighteenth-Century British Writing*. Cambridge: Cambridge UP, 2000. Print.

———. "*Rob Roy*: The Other Eighteenth Century?" *Eighteenth-Century Fiction on Screen*. Ed. Robert Mayer. Cambridge: Cambridge UP, 2002. 192–210. Print.

St. Clair, William. *The Reading Nation in the Romantic Period*. Cambridge: Cambridge UP, 2004. Print.

Stephen, Leslie. *Hours in a Library*. New York: Putnam, 1894. Print.

Stevenson, David. *The Covenanters: The National Covenant and Scotland*. Edinburgh: Saltire, 1988. Print.

Stewart, Garrett. *Reading Voices: Literature and the Phonotext*. Berkeley: U of California P, 1990. Print.

The Story of English. PBS. 1986. Television.

Sutherland, John. *The Life of Walter Scott: A Critical Biography*. Oxford: Blackwell, 1995. Print.

Sutherland, Kathryn. Introduction. Scott, *Redgauntlet* [ed. Sutherland] vii–xxxiii.

Thompson, E. P. *The Romantics: England in a Revolutionary Age*. New York: New, 1997. Print.

Thompson, Jon. "Sir Walter Scott and Madge Wildfire: Strategies of Containment in *The Heart of Midlothian*." *Literature and History* 13.2 (1987): 188–99. Print.

Thomson, Derick S., ed. and trans. *Gaelic Poetry in the Eighteenth Century: A Bilingual Anthology*. Aberdeen: Assn. for Scottish Lit. Studies, 1993. Print.

Todd, William B., and Anne Bowden, ed. *Sir Walter Scott: A Bibliographical History, 1796–1832*. New Castle: Oak Knoll, 1998. Print.

Tolstoy, Leo. *War and Peace*. 1865–69. Trans. Louise Maude and Aylmer Maude. New York: Oxford UP, 1998. Print.

Toomey, Sheila. "Trouble in Perryville: Village Banished Their Problem Resident, but State Officials Say They Had No Right." *Anchorage Daily News* 2 Nov. 2003. Web. 28 Feb 2006.

Trumpener, Katie. *Bardic Nationalism: The Romantic Novel and the British Empire*. Princeton: Princeton UP, 1997. Print.

———. "National Character, Nationalist Plots: National Tale and Historical Novel in the Age of *Waverley*, 1806–1830." *ELH* 60.3 (1993): 685–731. Print.

Tulloch, Graham. "Historical Note." Scott, *Ivanhoe* [ed. Tulloch] 495–501.

———. *The Language of Sir Walter Scott*. London: Deutsch, 1980. Print.

Twain, Mark. *The Adventures of Huckleberry Finn*. Berkeley: U of California P, 1988. Print.

"Unsigned Review of *Rob Roy*, *Heart of Midlothian*, *Bride of Lammermoor*, *Legend of Montrose*, *Ivanhoe*, *The Monastery*, *The Abbot*, and *Kenilworth*." Hayden 215–55.

Vasov, Ivan. *Under the Yoke*. Introd. Edmund Gosse. 1893. London: Dent, 1994. Print.

Walker, John. *General Idea of a Pronouncing Dictionary*. London, 1774. Print.

Wallace, Tara Ghoshal. "The Elephant's Foot and the British Mouth: Walter Scott on Imperial Rhetoric." *European Romantic Review* 13.3 (2002): 311–24. Print.

The Walter Scott Digital Archive. Dept. of Special Collections, Edinburgh U Lib. 7 Feb. 2006. Web. 25 Feb. 2006.

Walter Scott Research Centre. U of Aberdeen. Web. 25 Feb. 2006.

Ward, Ian. *Law and Literature, Possibilities and Perspectives*. Cambridge: Cambridge UP, 1995. Print.

Watson, Nicola. *Revolution and the Form of the British Novel, 1790–1825: Intercepted Letters, Interrupted Seductions*. Oxford: Clarendon, 1994. Print.

Watt, Ian. *The Rise of the Novel: Studies in Defoe, Richardson, and Fielding*. Berkeley: U of California P, 1957. Print.

Watt, James. *Contesting the Gothic: Fiction, Genre, and Cultural Conflict, 1764–1832*. Cambridge: Cambridge UP, 1999. Print.

———. "Scott, the Scottish Enlightenment, and Romantic Orientalism." Davis, Duncan, and Sorensen 94–112.

The Waverley Album: Containing Fifty-One Line Engravings to Illustrate the Novels and Tales of Sir Walter Scott. London, n.d. Print.

Waverley Hypertext. Ed. Andrew Monnickendam. 1997. Web. 25 Feb. 2006.

Rev. of *Waverley*, by Walter Scott. *Critical Review* 1.3 (1815): 288–97. Print.

Rev. of *Waverley*, by Walter Scott. *Port Folio* 5.4 (1815): 326–33. Print.

Welsh, Alexander. *The Hero of the Waverley Novels*. New Haven: Yale UP, 1963. Print.

———. *The Hero of the Waverley Novels: With New Essays on Scott*. Princeton: Princeton UP, 1992. Print.

———. *Strong Representations: Narrative and Circumstantial Evidence in England*. Baltimore: Johns Hopkins UP, 1992. Print.

Wickman, Matthew. *The Ruins of Experience: Scotland's "Romantick" Highlands and the Birth of the Modern Witness*. Philadelphia: U of Pennsylvania P, 2007. Print.

Williams, Ioan, ed. *Sir Walter Scott on Novelists and Fiction*. London: Routledge, 1968. Print.

Wilt, Judith. *Secret Leaves: The Novels of Sir Walter Scott*. Chicago: U of Chicago P, 1985. Print.

———. "Steamboat Surfacing: Scott and the English Novelists." *Nineteenth-Century Fiction* 35 (1981): 459–86. Print.

Wodrow, Robert. *The History of the Sufferings of the Church of Scotland*. 2 vols. Edinburgh, 1721–22. Print.

Wollstonecraft, Mary. *A Vindication of the Rights of Woman*. 1792. *Political Writings*. Ed. Janet Todd. Toronto: U of Toronto P, 1993. 67–296. Print.

Womack, Peter. *Improvement and Romance: Constructing the Myth of the Highlands*. Houndmills: Macmillan, 1989. Print.

Wordsworth, William. "Preface to *Poems* (1815)." *Wordsworth: Poetical Works*. Ed. Thomas Hutchinson and Ernest de Selincourt. New York: Oxford UP, 1961. 752–56. Print.

———. *The Prelude: 1799, 1805, 1850*. Ed. Jonathan Wordsworth, M. H. Abrams, and Stephen Gill. New York: Norton, 1978. Print.

Wordsworth, William, and Samuel Taylor Coleridge. Lyrical Ballads *and Related Writings*. Ed. William Richey and Daniel Robinson. Boston: Houghton, 2002. Print.

Zimmerman, Everett. *The Boundaries of Fiction: History and the Eighteenth-Century British Novel*. Ithaca: Cornell UP, 1996. Print.

Žižek, Slavoj. *Iraq: The Borrowed Kettle*. New York: Verso, 2004. Print.

———. *The Sublime Object of Ideology*. New York: Verso, 1989. Print.

INDEX OF NAMES